A
Starnader
Fool

———◦∙◦———

Sylvia Waldon

Published in the United States by
Arvin and May Street Publications, Cincinnati, Ohio.
www.amspublications.com

Library of Congress Control Number: 2011908877

Cover and interior design: Jonathan Gullery

Author bio photo:
Kim Rice, Keepsake Photography Studio, Cincinnati, OH.

ISBN 978-0-9836762-1-8

*This book is dedicated to my entire family
and closest friends, with a special dedication
to my mother, Annie M. Benton*

Part I

Aldania

———❦———

I hate funerals. I hate that my grandmother has died and now my family has to sit here on the front pew of the church near her rose- colored casket, greeting the parade of friends and other people who have come to pay their last respects. I hate the stares of nosey folk, watching and waiting for one of us to break down and cry and scream and ask the Lord why He had to take her from us. Well, if they're waiting to see me perform, they're in for a long wait.

A great number of people have come to pay their respects and see my grandmother off to glory, which would make a person think she was well loved. Everyone who has come up to speak has talked about the kind, good deeds Grandmother did in her life. One lady spoke highly of her work at the soup kitchen where she helped feed the hungry. Another lady praised her for her work as a tutor in the Help Thy Neighbor Learn to Read program sponsored by the local library.

Even Mr. Herschel, our longtime, next-door neighbor went up to speak and labeled Grandmother a fine, decent woman. Mr. Herschel was lying through his teeth, because for as long as I've known him, he and Grandmother never had a kind word to speak about the other. They didn't even like each other. They were constantly bickering from their back porches about any and everything, but mostly about the continual barking of the old hound dog Mr. Herschel kept tied to the tree in his back yard. And Grandmother always started the confrontations with Mr. Herschel because she never minded her own business. Oftentimes, the arguments between Mr. Herschel and my grandmother went to name-calling. He called her a meddling, hateful, witch and she retorted that he was a 'no count, drunken sot'.

When I was a little girl and Mr. Herschel and my grandmother argued, it sometimes frightened me, but by the time they were deep into it, I would silently cheer Mr. Herschel on as he shot insults back at Grandmother just as fast as she spat them at him. I think he knew I was on his side because whenever he saw me present during their heated encounters, he would go after her even harder, like he was doing it for me. Without me ever telling him, I knew Mr. Herschel knew how I felt about my grandmother.

I couldn't understand why Grandmother didn't like Mr. Herschel. I liked him just fine, but she could always find something wrong with him. That's the kind of person she was. She always had her nose in somebody else's business, telling them what they should and shouldn't do. But for some reason she concerned herself with Mr. Herschel's business more than necessary. She disapproved of the women he kept company with. Their clothes were too tight and they wore too much makeup and they were much too young for his old butt. And no decent woman would go over to a man's house to sit up and smoke and drink. If he didn't cut his grass according to Grandmother's timing, she complained about it being too long. She had something to say about the way he hung his wash on the line to dry. The pole wasn't propped in the ground the right way, and she was tired of seeing his clean clothes drag onto the ground. And he never straightened his clothes out on the line. He just threw them up there all wadded up. She wanted to know why he didn't just go on and buy himself a dryer so she wouldn't have to see it.

And that wasn't all she complained about. He hacked and coughed too loud. She shouldn't have to hear him over there in his house making all those noises. He shouldn't have his windows open anyway, which led to another one of her complaints. She didn't like the fact that she could look out of her side living room window and see into his house, especially when he had his clothes off. Now I did agree with her on that one. I didn't like catching glimpses of Mr. Herschel staggering around his house in his underwear when he had had too much to drink.

My mind wanders from one thing to another so that I don't have to focus on where I am. I wish the service would hurry and be over. I'm tired of hearing the sniffling and nose blowing around me. I know everyone's probably wondering why I don't have my handkerchief out, dabbing my eyes.

I turn my attention towards several of the wood engravings of The Passion that are hung along the church walls within my eyesight. There are several vases with red roses placed in the windowsills between the scenes of our Lord's journey with the cross up to Calvary. The alter is nicely decorated with a plethora of floral arrangements of red and white roses, and pink carnations and amethyst, calla lilies, orange tiger lilies, even a few African violets. The rays of the sun shine brightly through the stained glass windows, lighting the sanctuary with an array of vibrant, pristine color. The church scene is so beautiful and is deserving of a kinder person.

I look down at the picture of Grandmother on the cover of the funeral program I'm holding in my hand. Her face is as serious as usual. She never smiled. Even when she had her picture taken she couldn't pretend to be happy.

I open the booklet and begin to read the first paragraph of Grandmother's obituary. Aldania R. Cressford (nee Gray) was born May 1, 1910 here in Westfield, Illinois and died peacefully in her sleep on May 20, 1993.

My grandmother had four children, one of whom preceded her in death, which was my mother. My grandfather died when my mother was twelve. All five of Aldania's grandchildren are listed from oldest to youngest with my name being first. My daughter, Lisa, is listed as the oldest of Grandmother's nine great-grandchildren.

Mary Dean is mentioned as the aunt who raised Aldania from a small child. None of us had ever met Aunt Mary Dean because she passed on when Grandmother was a young woman, but I sure did hear a lot about her growing up. Aunt Mary Dean was a strong woman who made sure things were taken care of properly. And if it had not been for the kindness of Aunt Mary Dean, Grandmother wouldn't have been the woman she was. 'People, especially grandchildren, need to be thankful when someone takes them in because no one owes any of us anything. It costs plenty of money to keep a roof over a child's head, especially when there isn't extra money coming in'. Of course she was directing her statements towards me. Lord knows it wasn't my fault my parents died when I was a baby and Grandmother was the one who took me in because if it had been up to me, I surely would have asked someone else to be my guardian.

I read from the section of the program that lists the clubs and societies Grandmother belonged to. Of them all, she prided herself most on being a member of the Violets. The Violets were a group of twenty or so older, Black, Christian women whose purpose was to give back to their fellow brothers and sisters in the community. They were the wives of Westfield's two handfuls of prominent Black men, which consisted of several business owners, a couple of doctors, a few ministers, a lawyer and an insurance salesman, who happened to be my grandfather, Tillman Cressford. I had heard many good things about him and not just from my family. I remember as a teenager, many elders from our neighborhood would tell me how Tillman was a self-made man who was well respected. I was told plenty of times to follow in my grandfather's footsteps; to be successful and well liked at the same time.

Grandfather was the first Black man to be hired by Compton and Wells Casualty and Life Insurance Company, and he worked very hard to convince most of Westfield's Black population that they needed insurance and to purchase it from him. This made him one of Compton and Wells' best salesmen. With the earnings from his job and his frugal nature, Grandfather was able to obtain the house in which he and Grandmother made their home and nine properties that he leased out.

My grandfather had intended to one day found Westfield's first Black-owned insurance company and run the business with his two sons, but his dream never came to fruition. After Grandfather's death, both of his sons openly expressed how they felt about insurance companies. They would never toil and sweat for none of them, especially Compton and Wells. The way they treated Grandmother when she went to cash in Grandfather's life insurance policy, infuriated the whole family.

It only made sense that Grandfather took out his life and property insurance policies with the company for which he worked. Grandfather had come home many evenings and told Grandmother about the white men he worked with in the office, so when Grandmother went down there about a month after Grandfather died to cash in his life insurance policy, she said as soon as she entered the office and saw the man sitting at one of the desks who asked her, 'What can I do fer ya'? in that southern drawl, she knew right away he was Sam Houston. The other two white salesmen didn't bother Grandfather much, but Sam was a dumb hillbilly with two teeth missing from the bottom of his mouth, who didn't like 'nigras' and always had some snide remark to make about Black people.

Sam was real nice to Grandmother at first because he must have thought she was a new customer, but when she explained who she was and why she was there, his whole attitude changed. He frowned up his face and looked her up and down. He spoke not one kind word of condolence. When Grandmother gave Sam the life insurance policy, he flipped through the pages and after a few minutes, he looked at Grandmother and told her to have a seat. As she sat down in one of the chairs along the wall of the office close to the inner hallway, Sam picked up the telephone. Grandmother thought he was calling someone to start the process for her payout, but as she overheard his conversation she realized he was calling one of his customers to see if they were still interested in buying a policy from him. Grandmother wasn't going to say anything at first, but when he made the second phone call to a different person, she got up from her seat, walked to his desk and looked him dead in his eyes, interrupting his call. She told him she had other business to attend to and she would appreciate it if he would go ahead and get the papers in order for her check. For a brief moment Sam looked at Grandmother like she was crazy, making him hurry up with his calls, but for some reason he didn't give her any flack. He huffed a little bit and asked the customer on the phone if he could call them back. Grandmother stood there with her eyes still fixed on Sam as he snatched the policy up off the desk and told her to wait while he talked to Mr. Compton, one of the owners. Sam walked a few steps down the hallway and went into an office. Grandmother hadn't quite gotten settled back into her seat when she overheard Sam and Mr. Compton's conversation. Grandmother knew Sam intentionally left the door open so she could hear them.

"That's a lot of money to be giving a nigger," she heard Sam say.

"Now I know you didn't like Tillman," Mr. Compton said, "but to tell the truth Sam, he was a good salesman. He was the only salesman who could get that many colored people to buy as many policies as he did. That boy worked hard for me. I was impressed with him the first time I saw him and I knew he would do a good job. He spoke well and kept himself clean. People take to salesmen with good appearances."

Grandmother said she felt proud hearing Tillman's boss speak highly of him. She saw how sloppy and greasy Sam was and hoped he was insulted by Mr. Compton's comments praising her husband. But as the conversation went on, she changed her mind.

"If there were more coloreds like Tillman, I might hire more than one of 'em," Mr. Compton said.

"Well if you hire more of 'em 'round here, I ain't gonna be workin' for ya' by God. 'Specially if they's anything like that damned Tillman. I never did like that uppity nigger. One time he even had the nerve to look at me like he was better 'en me. I told him if he ever gave me a look like that again, I'd beat his ass."

"So why didn't you? Were you scared of him?"

Mr. Compton started laughing and Grandmother could hear from the tone in Sam's voice that he was furious that Mr. Compton insinuated he was afraid of a Negro.

"Now you wait a goddamn minute, Fred! Don't you be thinkin' I'm afraid of no nigras! And I reckon I'd better be watchin' out for you, up here actin' like you got some kind of affection for 'em. You talkin' about how you would hire more of 'em if they was like that Tillman. Sounds like to me like they got a friend in you, huh Fred?"

All of a sudden Mr. Compton became a bit more serious.

"Cut the crap, Sam," Mr. Compton told him. "Don't go twisting things around. I'm not about to hire a bunch of coloreds to come in here to work. And

I ain't got no kind of soft spot in my heart for 'em, either. This is about business and making money. You just don't know how things work. See, coloreds buy from other coloreds, so I need at least one colored man in here to sell insurance to his own people. Tillman used to be our man. His people looked up to him. Some of 'em wanted to be like him. He made his people think he was somebody and he made them feel like they was somebody too, and when a nigger thinks he's special, feels like he's worth something, he protects that worth. That's why he buys insurance. Now I don't care what colored boy comes in that door thinking in his mind that he's as proper as any white man in the world. I don't care one bit and you know why, Sam? 'Cause I know better. See, that's your problem, Sam. You look at a uppity nigger and it makes you mad, 'cause in your mind you believe he is better than you."

"Now you looka here, Fred. Don't you go tellin' me what I believe. There ain't a nigger in this world that's better than any white man ever born."

"Then stop acting like it! You need to change the way you think, Sam. Look at me. I don't get mad when I see a fine example of a colored citizen. I don't get myself upset at all. You know why, Sam? 'Cause I know the truth. I ain't got to tell him what I think. I ain't got to call him names. All I got to do is sign him up and let him feel he's worth every penny he can afford to pay this company. The bigger the policy a colored man has, the bigger our profits. And that's the main reason I hired Tillman Cressford. Hell, he was friends with all the colored money makers over on his side of town. To tell you the truth, they help keep us ahead of the competition. Ain't none of the other companies got a colored boy workin' for 'em. So if I have to pay one of 'em that much money then let it be the one that brought the money in."

"I don't care how much money he brought in. I can't see givin' none of 'em no more than a dime and ain't none of 'em worth that. If this was my company, nare one of 'em would see no money."

"Well, this ain't your company and if it was, you'd be broke in a week. Hell, the premiums we get from them poor crackers you been sellin' to don't amount to much of nothin'! You better take note and start to think with your head. Money ain't got no color, and you better learn to take it from whoever is willing to give it to you. You see Sam, in business sometimes you got to put out money to make some money. Now you call that woman and you let her know her check is coming in the mail. Hell, tell her she can come back and pick it up when it's ready if she wants to. Don't worry yourself, Sam. We'll make that money back soon enough. The same colored people who bought their policies from Tillman will stay with us once we hire another upstanding colored boy. We'll up their premiums just a little and make that money back before you know it. You just wait and see."

Sam came back out into the outer office with a smug look on his face, as if he was happy in the fact of knowing Grandmother heard their whole conversation and just how important Tillman really was to the company he had worked so hard for. Sam told her to sign the paper and that they would be sending her the money in the mail. Then he sat back down at his desk and picked up the phone.

Grandmother told the Violets about her experience at Compton and Wells and they told their husbands. Word got around quick, and most all of my grandfather's former clients switched companies. Of course, Grandmother cashed her check before she told everyone what happened.

With the money and property that my grandfather left Grandmother, she was well able to take care of her children without having to get a job. This allowed her the time to volunteer a few days a week at places like the Buford House. The Buford House was a home for aged Black men and doubled as a soup kitchen for the homeless. Although she despised the dirty souls who dropped in to fill their appetites, she felt it was her duty as a good, Christian woman to serve them. I once overheard her complain to one of her friends how after eating for free, not one of those lazy, good-for-nothing beggars asked if they could help clean up or wash their dirty dishes.

She hated Negroes who looked for handouts. They were just ungrateful and lazy, nothing but eyesores and bad examples of Negro men and women. I never understood why she committed to giving her time to help others, because she complained so much after doing it. She didn't do things out of the goodness of her heart, so what was her point? Did she think that her good doings would add up to enough of a care to get her into heaven?

My grandmother was a devout Catholic and proud of it. She was arrogant about being Catholic, like she was better than other Black people who were Baptist or Methodist or Holiness. She would turn up her nose when she heard other people talk about their involvement at a Methodist church function or when she heard about a Holiness Revival coming to town. She must have thought being Catholic put her in an elite group.

I grew up with the constant reminder that I was a Cressford and Cressfords were proper Black people. We didn't put on the shine for anybody. Grandmother would tell me as she had told her children, 'You will not go through life being a smiling, lazy, uneducated Negro'. And none of us were smiling, lazy, uneducated Negroes. We were proud Black people. We all had jobs that we dedicated ourselves to and we all owned our own homes. We went to mass on Sundays. We dressed nice and treated people respectfully, for the most part.

From the time we learned to talk, Grandmother constantly reminded us that we needed to speak properly when addressing people, especially White people. She didn't want them to think we were ignorant. She wanted White folk to be able to say, 'Now that's a Negro family that I wouldn't mind being around'. Grandmother claimed to be a proud Black woman, but in my opinion, everything she did or didn't do was to impress White folk.

Expectations of happiness and kindness were not important to my grandmother, and she let us know they shouldn't be important to any of us either. Those were things we could do without. Appearances were what mattered most. It was stressed to me early on as a child that I was a young lady and young ladies acted and dressed respectfully. I was never to be seen in wrinkled or too-little clothing. My shoes had to be polished and laced properly. I better not be seen with ashy arms and legs and there should never be any strands of hair sticking up on my head. How else would I ever grow up to find a decent husband?

It was expected that all of us Cressfords married, but when we did get married it should be out of what Grandmother felt was necessity, not for a stupid reason like love. Marrying for love is a foolish reason to marry, as Grandmother put it. People don't stay in love. I had to marry somebody who was going to build a future with me. My husband had to come from good stock. I couldn't marry an uneducated, poor, lazy, trifling man. And I had to try to find me somebody with good hair, so my children could have good hair. And one last thing, 'Make sure he ain't too black and ugly'. That one I didn't quite get, because from the pictures I saw of my grandfather, he did have a nice grade of hair and he was a fairly handsome man but he was dark. Maybe Grandmother overlooked that part because he had a little money.

As a child I tried to live up to my grandmother's expectations, but I never felt like I could because I felt that my grandmother didn't like me. As a matter of fact, I felt like she hated me, like I was a bad person. She made me feel worthless and ashamed. There were times I would catch her looking at me over the dinner table or while we were watching television, and I would see a condescending smirk on her face. I'm sure it was hard for Grandmother to look at me and not think about her daughter, but I often felt that deep down inside, she blamed me for the loss of my mother. I felt I was an unwanted, necessary obligation to my grandmother. For as long as I've been conscious of my own being, she let me know that taking care of me was a chore, not a pleasure. I wanted to be a welcomed blessing. I wanted a lovable grandmother. She was never like the sweet, hugging grandmothers that I would see in the movies or at the department stores in the toy sections, picking out new playthings for their darling little grandsons or granddaughters. Indulging me in such niceties was beyond her practice let alone giving me something that wasn't material. I wanted her to take care of me the way my friend Eva's grandmother did. Miss Margaret didn't have much money but Eva knew she was loved. I envied the way nine year old Eva was allowed to sit on her grandmother's lap as they sat out on the front porch at dusk, rocking back and forth in their favorite chair. Miss Margaret's arms would cradle her grandbaby as Eva laid her head on her grandmother's bosom with a soft, secure look on her face. Eva wouldn't cry to get the attention because she was sick or hurt. It was just because. I longed for that same comfort from my grandmother, but she was so standoffish and I learned at an early age that seeking solace from her was not allowed. Grandmother had her way of raising me and it was with discipline and orderliness and no affection.

I look at the obituary again and read the names of Aldania's children. Tillman Wendell, Jr. is listed first. He's the oldest of Grandmother's children and I can't stand him. He thinks he's so much better than everybody else because, as he put it, 'White folks like me'. After he was discharged from the army, he came back home to Westfield and got a job at the Westfield News where he started on the delivery dock and moved up to his current position as a foreman. He's been there long enough to retire, but he won't. He boasts that he was the first and only Black man who was employed there back in the '70s with an important job, because all the other Black folk worked in the cafeteria or cleaned the offices. His wife, Aunt Lydia, is a receptionist for a white doctor in town and he brags about that too. She was offered a job with Dr. Kerry, one of the Black doctors in town, but Uncle Wendell didn't want her to take the position because 'nigger doctors don't know what they're doing'.

Grandmother bragged about Uncle Wendell as much as he did himself and although she never said it out loud, he was her favorite child.

I thought Uncle Wendell would be the main one sobbing, but he hasn't cried once since we've been here at the funeral. I really didn't expect him to, because Grandmother would have frowned upon that. She didn't think grown men should show that kind of emotion.

Uncle Stanley is listed next as Grandmother's second child. He's my favorite uncle. Aunt Myrtle is Uncle Stanley's wife, and I think my grandmother hated her more than anybody I know. Aunt Myrtle is a short, brown-skinned woman with a round face whose cheeks get real big when she flashes that wide, cheery, gap-tooth smile. She was Uncle Stanley's longtime girlfriend before he went into the service. After he was discharged from the air force, he snuck off and married Aunt Myrtle, and when Grandmother found out she was furious with him. She said Uncle Stanley shouldn't have married that 'common girl'. She wasn't Cressford material. She didn't have a high school diploma like Aunt Lydia, and she didn't know who her father was. Grandmother wanted him to marry 'someone with substance, someone whose parents were established'.

Regardless of what Grandmother said Aunt Myrtle didn't have, she's a good woman and out of everyone in my family, she and Uncle Stanley have always been in my corner. I tell them all the time how grateful and blessed I am to have had their support and love all these years. Growing up in my grandmother's house was tough in itself, but I managed with their help.

They have a daughter and a son, Geneva and Derrick. When we were little, Geneva, who is two years younger than me, was my best friends. I often went to stay with Aunt Myrtle and Uncle Stanley on the weekends and Geneva and I would have a ball. I never had fun at home, but my aunt and uncle let me be a kid when I was with them. Geneva and I played dress up and had tea parties with our dolls. We ran through the lawn sprinkler in the summertime and made snowmen in the wintertime. We told each other all our secrets including which boy at school we were going to marry when we grew up. And we grew up fast. Geneva had intended to attend college, but she got pregnant in her senior year of high school and dropped out. And to make matters worse, the boy she was pregnant by didn't want anything to do with it. Grandmother was so mad that she stopped speaking to Geneva. Grandmother blamed Aunt Myrtle for letting Geneva get pregnant, and Uncle Stanley got mad at Grandmother for blaming Aunt Myrtle so they all stopped speaking to Grandmother for a long time. Uncle Stanley eventually made amends with his mother. Aunt Myrtle told me she wished they all would have stayed mad so she didn't have to keep making up excuses why she didn't want to go see the 'ole crow'!

My mother, Marietta, was the third child. Both of my parents died when I was a baby, and I was their only child. My family never really told me much about my parents, and my grandmother never spoke either of their names from her mouth. Aunt Myrtle and Uncle Stanley would tell me how nice and cute and sweet my mother was, and Aunt Myrtle would tell me my father was a handsome fellow, but that was it. Aunt Myrtle said nobody talked about my parents because it upset my grandmother when she heard their names.

Aunt Josette is Grandmother's youngest child. She's never left home and has never had children. She's never even had a boyfriend as far as I know. I don't remember any men coming by the house to see her. Maybe she had a secret lover at work or at church that she didn't tell anyone about because she was afraid Grandmother would have run him away. I suspect that when she was younger, she wanted to get married and leave home, but I think she just didn't have the backbone to be independent of Grandmother.

I turn my head to look at my daughter who is sitting right next to me. She gives me a smile that's half an expression of sympathy. I smile back at her with the same look. I started not to bring Lisa. Here she was fourteen years old at the funeral of her great-grandmother whom she didn't even know. Grandmother never called to see how Lisa was or invited her to spend the summer with her in Westfield. We didn't even get Christmas cards from Grandmother. I'm raising my daughter to be a respectful person, to treat people with civility no matter the circumstances, but as I sit here in the presence of my dead grandmother, I think differently. That woman didn't deserve Lisa's respect.

I take in a deep breath and exhale hard, not realizing how loud it sounds until my friend Mona, who's sitting next to Lisa, leans forward and looks at me. She mouths the words 'Are you okay'? I nod yes to let her know I'm fine. Mona and I were roommates in college and have been best friends ever since. I was so glad she volunteered to come with me and Lisa. She's the kind of friend who's there when you need her and other times when you don't realize you do.

I had lived with my grandmother and Aunt Josette until I went off to Chicago to attend college. Knowing that I would be leaving her for good, I thought Grandmother would finally soften up and even pretend she would miss me. But she didn't.

I remember vividly coming home on my last day of working my summer job to find her and one of her friends boxing up my things. I was leaving in two weeks to start school and hadn't packed yet. When I asked her why she was getting my things together, she told me that I had been procrastinating for too long and she wanted to make sure everything was done before the last minute so that I would be ready when it was time for me to leave. She pretended to be helping, but to me it was her way of letting me know she couldn't wait to get me out of her house.

On the day I left, I told her thanks for allowing me to live in her house for as long as she did, and I hoped that she would be happier now that I was leaving. She didn't say a word. I hugged Aunt Josette and told her good-bye as she wiped her eyes with her handkerchief. She told me to be sure to call her when I got settled, and I promised her I would. I got into the taxi hoping Grandmother would feel something inside of her that might make her realize this could be the last time she would see me or even how proud she was that I had made it this far in life, to attend college and try to prepare a way for myself. I wanted her to acknowledge that she had taught me to be a decent, young woman. I wanted her to celebrate my passage into adulthood, that she was free of being responsible for me and that she and I had done something right to get me to this point. Instead, she just stood there with her arms crossed, and after a while she walked back into the house, leaving Aunt Josette at the curb waving me on.

Money became a problem while I was in school so I had to quit after a year and a half. There was no way I was going back to Westfield to hear my grandmother bad mouth me about not finishing school. Plus the idea of me even asking her if I could come back was out of the question. Mona was in the same boat as me and she invited me to stay with her and her mother in Indianapolis until I could get a job and my own place. I was there only ten days before I started working with Indianapolis Bell and before long I had my own apartment not too far from where Mona lived. It took me a while, but I enrolled in a junior college and during my internship at an accounting firm I met Lisa's father, Gerald.

When I graduated from junior college, I just knew my grandmother would be proud of me and finally give me the respect and caring I felt I deserved, but instead she didn't even show up for the ceremony. She sent ten dollars in a card by Aunt Josette who made up the excuse that Grandmother wasn't feeling well and couldn't make the trip. Grandmother attended my cousins' graduations, but not mine.

I was surprised she showed up when Gerald and I got married. I actually felt good that she came. I thought that day would be the day she would tell me how proud she was of me in my choice of a husband, but during the reception as I made my rounds to greet my guests, she told me he wasn't the right man for me. She had never met Gerald or had a conversation with him, but she told me that she could tell his family was from the wrong side of the tracks. At first my feelings were hurt by her remark. After I considered where the comment came from, I let it go. I wasn't going to let her ruin my wedding day.

I seldom went back home to Westfield except for the times I went to spend the holidays and have brief visits with Aunt Myrtle and Uncle Stanley. There were a few times when Grandmother and Aunt Josette were there. After not seeing me for long periods of time, I had hoped that Grandmother would have changed. I thought she might be excited to see me and smile and hug me or even wonder what good things I had been up to, but she didn't. She would greet me with some snide remark like, 'Why are you wearing all that fancy jewelry'? or 'Those heels on your shoes are too high. They make you look like a Jezebel.' She was the one who drilled it into my head to always dress nice and here I was looking my best and she had to bring some negative comment to the table. There was no pleasing her. Ever!

Grandmother didn't make the drive to Indianapolis with the rest of the family when I had my baby. She did call me on the telephone right after my delivery. I had hoped she was going to tell me how proud she was to be a great-grandmother for the first time or that she was coming to see us after I got home from the hospital, but that didn't happen. During the whole conversation she lectured me on how to care for my newborn baby.

The first time Grandmother ever saw Lisa was when she was three months old. Gerald and I drove up to stay with Uncle Stanley for a weekend and Grandmother came over to visit while we were there. She barely said a word to me or Gerald except when she instructed me on what to do when I changed Lisa's diaper or how Gerald needed to make sure he had his arm positioned up under Lisa's head while he was holding her. She never smiled at Lisa or asked to hold her. Over the years I had learned to live with the lack of affection my grandmother showed me, but for her to act so uncaring towards my baby was uncalled for and that made me mad as hell! After that, I stopped caring about having any kind of a relationship with her and I made every effort to make sure I didn't see her again. I didn't want to come to her funeral today. Thinking about it all makes me angry.

I'm the only one in our family who is divorced though it wasn't by my choosing. I once had what I thought was the perfect marriage. Gerald and I dated a little over a year before we got married and by the time I was twenty-eight, we both had good jobs, a nice home in an upper class neighborhood of Indianapolis and a beautiful baby girl. Lisa was the apple of her daddy's eye.

I bragged to my friends about my wonderful husband who bought me expensive gifts and took me out to dinner and made love to me ferociously. And we were happy. Or so I thought.

One day, out of the blue, Gerald came home and told me he was leaving me for someone else. The first thing I thought was how I would ever face my grandmother with a failed marriage. I cried as I begged and pleaded with him to stay. I tried to convince him I could be a better wife and lover and our marriage was worth saving. All we needed was to go to marriage counseling. He told me counseling was a waste of time, because they couldn't counsel him on how to love me as his woman again. I tried to fight him and he pushed me down onto the floor, telling me to stop groveling, to be a woman and handle my business better than this.

We hadn't even been divorced a whole year before I allowed Gerald to come crawling back into my bed. He hadn't left his girlfriend, but I was determined to get him back.

I was out with a few of my friends one night, and I was bragging about my sexual escapades with my ex-husband. I had been telling them how there were no good men out here who met my standards. One of my friends informed me that I had lowered my standards a long time ago when I let Gerald take advantage of me. I told her he came when I wanted him to, not just because he could. I was in control of that. She told me nobody was looking at Gerald as being stupid. He was just being a man. I was so mad at her that night for saying that to me, but a few days later, when I really thought about it, she was right. I was so wrapped up in getting him back to save face with my grandmother that I stooped to being his outside woman.

One afternoon after we had finished having sex, I told Gerald I wasn't going to do this anymore. He needed to leave his girlfriend and came back home to me. He asked me why. He told me he still loved me, but he couldn't be married to me or anyone else. He said what we had was fine, and that we shouldn't mess things up by talking about marriage and commitments. Besides, his other woman understood that, and she didn't hassle him about getting married and their relationship was fine. That was why he loved her so much, because she took his feelings into consideration over her own. I got mad and told him I was going to tell his girlfriend about what we had been doing if he didn't leave her. He ranted and raved and said if anything ever happened to them because of my meddling, I would regret it. He told me he was only sleeping with me because he knew I couldn't find anybody and he felt sorry for me.

I didn't even bother to cuss him out because I felt so ashamed by his remark. He didn't respect me. He didn't love me. He felt sorry for me. I told him to get the hell out of my house and don't ever come by or call me again. I thought about calling his girlfriend and telling her what had gone on, but what good would it do? The bottom line was he wasn't mine anymore. This time I finally got the message and I made up my mind to stop the charade. I had worked hard at being a good wife for Gerald and for what? Where had it gotten me? All those years of putting my all into my husband and my marriage, and I ended up with nothing. Gerald was getting what he wanted from me, his live-in girlfriend and several other girls, that I found out about later, with whom he had been cheating on me. I had the house and money for my daughter, but that wasn't what I wanted. I could get those things on my own. I wanted a man who was committed to me.

For a while I became dismayed about ever finding a good man and being in a relationship. I felt that men didn't commit to marriage. They didn't have to. Men knew women were desperate for love and men used that premise to their advantage. So after my marriage was destroyed, I decided not to care about any other woman's marriage. None of the tramps Gerald had messed with cared about my feelings so why should I care about anyone else's?

I slept with a few married guys and had them buying me gifts and taking me on weekend vacations, and just when I thought they were becoming too attached, I would break the relationship off. I soon grew tired of playing the 'date them, hate them' game, because deep in my heart, I still longed for a man to love me and be all mine. Maybe one day it can still happen.

I bring my focus back to the service as a woman at the podium begins to read the acknowledgement from our family that is written on the back of the obituary. The church recites The Lord's Prayer and then the organ starts up for the final hymn. Father Beasley gives the benediction. I'm so glad this is over. I don't want to look at her up there in that casket anymore.

As the congregation heads outside to affix the processional funeral flags to their cars, Mona asks if it's okay that she and Lisa skip the burial and head back to Grandmother's house for the repast. I tell her that's a good idea. I can tell Lisa's bored and ready to go somewhere other than a graveyard.

The immediate family piles into the two limousines waiting in the parking lot. I ride with Uncle Stanley, Aunt Myrtle, Geneva and Derrick and their spouses. Uncle Wendell, Aunt Lydia and their two sons and spouses ride in the other car with Aunt Josette.

During the drive to the gravesite, everyone is quiet except for Uncle Stanley, who tries to force light conversation by talking about who was there at the funeral that he hadn't seen in years. We pull into the graveyard and drive up the path to the burial plot. Uncle Wendell and the others get out of their car first and we follow. Other cars have pulled up and people trail behind us as we make our way over to the gravesite where the priest and some other people are waiting for the rest of us to get in place. My aunts, uncles, cousins and I are seated in the chairs that have been placed alongside the burial plot. Everyone else finds a place to stand behind us or along the other side of the grave opposite us.

Father Beasley looks to us all for our attention. He asks us to bow our heads before he starts to pray. The crying and sniffling has started around me again and I pray to God that the priest will hurry with the proceedings. A gentle breeze blows faintly as I focus my attention on the green hillside in the background of the people standing on the other side of me. The finals words are said as Father Beasley makes the sign of the cross. People start to pull stems of flowers from the many arrangements and baskets that adorn the site. One by one they place flowers on the hood of the casket as they pay their last respects and leave the gravesite to go back to their cars. I get up from my seat and stand next to my chair, watching as everyone makes their way toward their cars. I'm left standing there alone, staring at my grandmother's casket, thinking about how I had disliked her all my life and I finally feel a twinge of sadness hit my heart. My eyes fill with tears that spill over my lashes and trickle down onto my cheeks. As I let out a whimper, I feel a hand slip into mine and pull me away from the gravesite. I'm led back to the car as I sob, blinded by my tears. Several hands pat my back, shoulders and arms, offering comfort as we go. They've finally seen me cry.

Our limousine pulls up to Grandmother's house and I see all the cars that are lined up and down the street. I watch through the car window as people stand in the yard, talking before they go inside. I look at the old, brick house with its huge porch and large, wood-framed front door and window, and I feel the same dread I felt two days ago when I arrived back in town. When I left this house twenty years ago, I vowed I would never, ever return. And I hadn't come back except for this sorrowful occasion.

I enter the front door of the house, and as I make my way through the living room, I pause to speak to a couple of people who came for the wake but didn't stay for the funeral. Maybe they don't like funerals either.

I look up at the far wall of the living room and see the same photos of the family that have been hanging in the same spot for years. There is a large portrait of Grandmother and Grandfather in their younger days which is placed directly above a row of eight-by-ten photos of each one of their children as teenagers. My mother's picture is missing and has been since I was a child.

I glance into the dining room and see a few of the neighbors arranging food at the dining room table. As I make my way to the kitchen through the dining room, I stop and talk with a few of Grandmother's friends who offer their condolences. They tell me how lucky I was to have had such a good woman for a grandmother. I thank them without further conversation and go into the kitchen where I'm offered a plate of food. I'm passed a glass of iced tea and told to sit at the kitchen table from which I excuse myself and head out the back door to the patio. Lisa is sitting at a table with some of her younger cousins, eating and talking. I see Geneva and Mona sitting at another table and I go over to where they are and sit next to Geneva. The three of us talk about days gone by and how we need to keep in touch with one another. We are deep into our conversation when all of a sudden Uncle Stanley calls to me from the kitchen screen door, asking me to come inside for a minute.

I go inside to see Uncle Stanley standing by the door with a puzzled look on his face.

"What's wrong?" I ask.

"I want you to see this white woman in here in the living room," he says, "and tell me if you remember ever meeting her. Ain't none of us ever met her before, but she just told us Mother was her maid at one time."

"Her maid?"

"Yeah, that's what she says."

We walk into the living room, where Uncle Wendell and Aunt Josette are standing with the woman who is accompanied by two middle-aged, white men.

"Mrs. Snyder, this is my niece, Francine," Uncle Stanley says.

"Nice to meet you, Mrs. Snyder," I say, offering her my hand to shake.

"It's so nice to meet you all," she says, cupping my hand with both of hers. "I'm so glad to finally meet you all. I wish it could have been under better circumstances."

She looks at us with the excitement of a long-lost relative finally finding her kin.

"I was sorry to read that one of Aldania's children passed before her," Mrs. Snyder says. "That has to be a heart-wrenching experience for a mother. I'm still fortunate to have my two boys with me. This is Raymond and this is David."

"Nice to meet you," I say as I shake their hands.

"My sister, Marietta, died a long time ago," Uncle Stanley says, placing his hand on my shoulder. "Francine is her daughter."

"Would you all like something to eat or drink?" I ask the three of them.

They all decline.

"Uncle Stanley says Grandmother used to work for you," I say.

"Indeed she did," Mrs. Snyder says.

"How long ago was that?"

"Oh dear, that was well over fifty-five or some odd years ago. My boys were little then."

"So what kind of work did my grandmother do for you?" I inquire, already knowing the answer.

"Aldania was my maid."

"Oh."

The four of us look at one another, certain that this woman is talking about the wrong person. Grandmother would never have stood for any of us to have been a maid or nanny, let alone herself.

"When my husband and I moved here from Ohio, Aldania came with us," Mrs. Snyder tells us.

"From Ohio?" Uncle Wendell says.

"Yes. My husband's brother needed help with his business, so we moved here in 1929 to this lovely little town."

Mrs. Snyder must be getting senile. My grandmother was born and raised here in Westfield. Now I know she's mistaken Grandmother for someone else.

"Mrs. Snyder, our mother never lived in Ohio," Uncle Wendell says politely.

"Of course she did," Mrs. Snyder tells him.

He raises his eyebrows and stares at her.

"You look just like your mother," she says, turning her attention to Aunt Josette, taking her hand. "I thought she was the prettiest colored girl I had ever seen. She had the prettiest hair. It was long and black and wavy. You could touch it without it being rough on your hand."

Her sons look embarrassed by her remarks.

"I suspect that Amelia and Ambrose's health must be failing, since they didn't attend the funeral," Mrs. Snyder says.

We all look from one to the other again.

"Who are Amelia and Ambrose?" Uncle Wendell asks.

Mrs. Snyder looks confused for a moment, as if we had some sort of problem.

"Why, Aldania's brother and sister, of course," she says.

We look one to the other again without speaking.

"Mrs. Snyder, my mother was an only child," Aunt Josette finally says.

"Oh no, honey," Mrs. Snyder says. "Your mother had several brothers and sisters. I remember when she first came to me looking for work she said she had a brother and sister older than her, and a brother and sister who were younger. I remember she was smack dab in the middle, and Amelia and Ambrose were up under her because she was taking care of them before she left to come with me to Westfield."

"No ma'am," Aunt Josette says. "Mother never lived in Ohio. She was born and raised here in Westfield. Her parents died when she was a child and her father's sister, Mary Dean, raised her. I'm sorry, but I think you have Mother confused with someone else."

"I may be old but my mind is still very, very sharp," Mrs. Snyder insists. "Just as sure as I'm standing here living and breathing this very moment, I know who Aldania was. Yes, her parents did die when she was young, but she didn't live with any aunt like it said in her obituary. All of her relatives were in some small town in Georgia and she didn't know how to get in touch with them when her parents died, so she and Amelia had to live in that dreadful orphanage until she came to me and I hired her as my maid. Ambrose lived with one of the neighbor ladies, but she couldn't take on the two girls. Their older brother went to live with his father up in Detroit, I believe, and their older sister left to get married before the girls went to the orphanage. I can't believe you all don't already know this."

Mrs. Snyder looks at us peculiarly, waiting for one of us to say, 'Oh yes, I remember now'. She continues on.

"Amelia and Ambrose used to come to my house sometimes on Saturdays to have lunch with Aldania. My husband took a few pictures of the three of them in our yard back when we lived in Hamilton."

Again we look from one to the other, not understanding what's going on.

"I really don't think our mother is the same person you're talking about," Uncle Wendell tells her. "We've never heard any of this."

I can tell from his tone of voice he's becoming irritated with Mrs. Snyder's story.

"I know who I'm talking about," Mrs. Snyder says adamantly. "Aldania was with me almost three years. She was my first maid and Sally was my second, up until fifteen years ago. My husband and I only stayed here in Westfield for a few years then we moved to Wisconsin in 1931. Aldania wouldn't come with us that time, even though I begged her to. Before we left she found another job. I wrote to her several times, but I never heard from her, so I figured she must have got homesick and moved back home to Ohio to be with her family. She told me she kept in touch with them while we were living up here in Westfield, but they never did come up to visit. One of my dear friends still lives here in town and she called me and said she saw Aldania's obituary in the paper. I had to come and pay my last respects. She was such a lovely girl." Mrs. Snyder's eyes start to water. She pulls out her handkerchief and dabs at her eyes.

"I'm so disappointed that Amelia and Ambrose didn't come," she continues. "I was looking forward to seeing them after all these years. Like I said, they were the cutest colored people. Your whole family has nice features. You know, some colored people aren't pretty, especially the ones that have the really dry hair."

"Uh, Mother," Raymond interrupts. "We should be going now."

"No, I want to stay and get to know Aldania's children. I don't understand why they don't know Amelia and Ambrose. Something must have happened. Aldania lost touch with them like she did with me, but I'm going to help you all find them again. "

"It's getting late, Mother, and we need to be getting back to the hotel," David says.

"Well, if we must," Mrs. Snyder says reluctantly.

She turns her attention back to us.

"I'm going to have Raymond write down my telephone number for you to call me," she says to us, "and let me know when you would like to come up to see me. I'll show you the pictures I have of your mother and her family. They were the nicest colored people."

David looks at us with an apologetic face for his mother's comments. He carefully takes her arm and leads her towards to door.

"I'm sorry for your loss," Raymond says, shaking each of our hands before he turns to leave.

"Thank you for coming," Uncle Stanley says.

"Good-bye," says Mrs. Snyder.

The three of us stand there and watch as Uncle Stanley escorts Mrs. Snyder and her sons through the living room to the front door. When he returns, we try to figure out who those people were and why they had mistaken Grandmother for their maid.

"That was strange," Uncle Stanley says as he comes back to us.

"Yes it was," Uncle Wendell says.

Aunt Josette is standing facing the three of us and as she speaks, Raymond has returned and is standing in back of her before we can warn her.

"That woman must be getting senile in her old age," Aunt Josette tells us.

"No, she's not," Raymond says.

Aunt Josette is startled and embarrassed at the same time as she turns to face him.

"I was coming back to give you my mother's phone number," he says, handing one piece of paper to Uncle Stanley and another to me. "My mother wants you to call her so that she can mail you the pictures she's talking about. I could tell by the looks on your faces that you might think my mother's memory has failed, but that's not the case. I'm not sure why your mother never told you about her family, but she did have brothers and sisters. At least I can vouch for the two I met. You may want to try and find them to let them know their sister has passed on. I would start in Hamilton, Ohio if I were you. It's been a pleasure meeting you, and I'm sorry about the loss of your mother."

We all thank him as he turns to leave a second time. We make sure he's gone before we get back to our conversation.

"I still say they got the wrong person," Uncle Wendell says. "Mother wasn't ever no maid. They don't know what they're talking about."

"What kind of work did Grandmother do before she married Grandfather?" I ask.

"She and Father both worked at Westfield General Hospital," Aunt Josette says. "That's where they met and after they got married, Mother stopped working and became a housewife. Father worked there until he went to work at the insurance company."

"Where did she work before that?"

"I don't know," Aunt Josette answers with wide eyes as she shrugs.

I look to Uncle Wendell and Uncle Stanley for an answer as well.

"Maybe she worked for Mrs. Snyder before she worked at the hospital," I tell them.

They still don't know.

"It don't make no never mind where she worked before she married Father," Uncle Wendell says in his usual sarcastic manner. "I just know she wasn't nobody's maid."

Uncle Wendell walks away from us towards the dining room.

"They definitely have the wrong person," Aunt Josette says assuredly as she follows Uncle Wendell in the same direction.

"I'm going over here and talk to Mr. Herschel for a little bit," Uncle Stanley says, leaving me standing in the middle of the living room.

I cross my arms over my chest as I stand there alone, thinking about what Mrs. Snyder just revealed, knowing deep down in my soul she's talking about the right person indeed.

By eight-thirty that evening, the house is cleared of friends and family and the place is back to normal. Aunt Josette and I are putting away the last of the dishes and platters in the kitchen pantry. I grab the dish towel from the sink and start to wipe the droplets of water standing on the kitchen counter surface. Aunt Josette is standing at the kitchen table, straightening the tablecloth.

"Thank you for coming home, Francine," I hear her say.

I look over at her. She looks so sad. She's been having a rough time being here alone in the house since Grandmother died, so she asked me to stay with her for a few days. I give her a slight, sympathetic smile and put the towel down on the counter. I walk over to where she is and embrace her.

"I had to come and support my family," I say.

She pulls away and holds both of my hands.

"I'm sure it was hard for you to come back after all these years, but I want you to know I appreciate you being here, and I thank you."

"You are welcome, Aunt Josette."

She lets go of my hands and I go back over to the counter to finish wiping it.

"Did Lisa get back home with your friend?"

"Yes, I called Mona a little while ago and she said she dropped Lisa off at Gerald's house. She's staying with him until I get back home."

"You're lucky to have a good friend like her."

"I know."

"I've never had a good friend to be there for me. Mother was so protective of me when I was young. She didn't let me do much of anything."

"She was like that with all of us, Aunt Josette."

"I don't know what I'm going to do," she says all of a sudden. I look over and Aunt Josette has her hands cupped to her face. I can hear her muffled cries.

I go back over to her and hold her again.

"It'll be okay, Aunt Josette," I say. "Don't worry. It's going to be okay."

She moves her hands and wipes her eyes with the bottom of her apron. I help her sit down in one of the side chairs at the kitchen table, and I sit down in a chair at the head of the table near her.

"I just don't know if I should stay here or if I should sell this house. I just don't know. I've never lived anywhere else. I'm too old to learn my way around a new neighborhood. I hear it's real bad in some of these neighborhoods. I don't want to go buying an apartment and having somebody living over my head, making a lot of noise. But this house might be too much for me. Mother paid people to come in and fix things. She paid someone to come over and cut the grass and shovel the driveway when it snowed. And now that she's gone, I don't know who to call."

Aunt Josette cries harder. I reach over and pat her shoulder until she stops crying.

"Mother left the house to the three of us," she continues. "I know Wendell is going to want his part in cash. He told me that years ago. He asked me if I had saved up enough money to buy him out of his part when the time came. Stanley never talked about it, so I don't know what he wants."

"I'm not surprised that Uncle Wendell said that to you," I tell her. "He's always been a money-grubbing bastard."

"Francine!" she says, slapping her hand on the table.

"I'm sorry, Aunt Josette. But that's what he is."

"You shouldn't say bad things about your uncle. You know better."

"I'm sorry for saying that."

She goes back to mourning and continues from where she left off.

"We're all supposed to split the money in the bank. You know Mother sold all of her other properties a few years ago. This is just as much their house as it is mine. I'm not worried about paying either of them, if I do decide to stay."

"Why do you think you have to leave? If you're able to pay them off, then you don't have to leave and try to start over somewhere else. You can just stay here."

She looks at me with relief on her face, like I've just given her the answer she needs to her dilemma.

"Aunt Josette, you can use the same people Grandmother used to keep up your yard and do all the other repairs around here."

She thinks about it for a minute longer.

"You're right," she says. "I can just tell the same men that instead of them working for Mother, they work for me now."

"Right," I say encouragingly.

"You're right, Francine. It'll be okay. I can stay right here. I won't be afraid to stay in the house by myself. This is my home. I'll be able to take care of it and keep it up."

"Yes, you can."

"I know, I know."

"You look tired, Aunt Josette. You go on up to bed and I'll make sure everything is locked up."

"I am very tired," she says, standing up from the table. "I'm not thinking straight."

"It's okay under the circumstances."

"I'm going to go on up to bed. I want to take a sleeping pill, but I'm scared to."

"Why?"

"Because I might not wake up! What if the house catches on fire?"

"Oh, Aunt Josette. I'm here. You can take a pill if you need to. I'll check in on you during the night. You'll be okay. I promise."

"Thank you, honey. I'm so glad you're here."

Aunt Josette looks relieved again. She kisses my forehead and walks out of the kitchen. I hear her footsteps as she climbs the stairs and walks across the floor into her room.

Poor thing. I'm worried about Aunt Josette. She's never made many decisions on her own, but the conversation we just had proved to me something wasn't right with my aunt. I'm sure she's grief-stricken right now, so she's not thinking clearly. I'm hoping she will be able to make it on her own living here alone. She's always been so dependent on Grandmother.

I finish up in the kitchen, checking to make sure the back door is locked. I go upstairs to my old room and put on my nightgown and robe. I'm tired, but I'm not ready to go to sleep so I head back downstairs to the living room to watch the television for a while. I make myself comfortable on the sofa and use the remote to skim through the six channels, which is all that is available on this television. Cable TV was not something my grandmother would consider necessary, so she never got it. When I first saw the remote, I was taken aback until Aunt Josette informed me Uncle Stanley had bought the new television as a present for Grandmother.

I settle for a re-run of I Love Lucy and as I begin to watch the show, my mind drifts back to Mrs. Snyder and again I find myself mulling over what she said earlier this evening. I try to think back to when I was a child and remember if I had ever heard Grandmother mention the names Amelia or Ambrose, but I don't recall hearing them. If Grandmother did have family, why would she not tell us about them? Maybe Mrs. Snyder and her sons were delusional. Grandmother couldn't have had brothers and sisters, because we most definitely would have known. Family was very important to her. And if she did have family we didn't know about, what would be the reason for keeping them a secret? Were they retarded? Was she ashamed of them for some other reason? The more I think about it, the more curious I become. But why should I be concerned with Grandmother's supposed family? I never wondered about her life growing up with Aunt Mary Dean. I never asked her anything about her past when she was alive. Why was I so concerned now? Why did I now have such a great desire to find out? There was no way I would ever find an answer. If her own children didn't know, I'm sure none of her close associates or friends would know either. Our family is small. There's my aunt and uncles and their children, and my grandfather's sister, Aunt Katherine, who never married or had children, and me and Lisa. My grandfather did have a few distant relatives, but none of them were ever close enough to my grandmother that she would have told them her family history. There's no one I can ask who would be able to tell me, one way or the other. I need to forget about it.

I try to watch television but a few minutes later, I'm wondering about Amelia and Ambrose again. I know they're real. There has to be something somewhere in this house to prove what Mrs. Snyder told us. And I bet it's somewhere in Grandmother's room! That's the one place that was off limits to everybody.

I get up, leaving the lights and television on, and go upstairs to my grandmother's bedroom door. It has been closed since the day Grandmother died. I look across the hall and make sure Aunt Josette's door is completely closed. I put my hand on the doorknob, but I hesitate before opening it, feeling anxious. It's amazing how restrictions from your childhood stay with you. Here I am, standing at my dead grandmother's bedroom door, feeling like any minute she's going to reprimand me for going in there. I think back to the pinches and slaps I got as punishments for running into her room without permission when I was a child.

I remind myself that Grandmother is dead and this isn't her room any more before I slowly open the door. I slip inside and flip on the light switch next to the door. I close the door behind me, being careful not to let it click loudly, afraid I might wake Aunt Josette, but then I remember she took a sleeping pill. When I walk into the closet and turn on the light, I see all of Grandmother's clothes, hanging there so neat, in order, with her blouses together and then skirts and dresses. Above her clothes are many shoe boxes lined up on the shelf, and next to them are several neatly folded sheets and a bedspread. In the far corner at the back of the closet is another shoebox. I wonder why she put this one alone by itself. I take the box down from the shelf, being mindful not to make any loud sounds, and sit on the floor inside the closet, readying myself for whatever secrets the box is holding. I remove the lid and find a stack of old photographs on top. I thumb through a few of the pictures, hoping to see unfamiliar faces of the brothers and sisters that Mrs. Snyder says are out there, but I only find pictures of Grandfather, my aunt and uncles and my mother when they were children. Under the pictures I find several envelops. One is marked 'insurance papers'. Another is labeled 'Violets'. I look in that envelope and see a few newspaper clippings of functions sponsored by the Violets, with mentions of Grandmother's name. There's another envelope marked 'car'. I also find an envelope labeled 'bank'. I look inside and find a single key. It looks like the key to a safety deposit box. I know she had one at her bank because I've waited for her many a time while she was in the vault. I look at the key again and wonder what is in the box that it will unlock...

I get to Central Savings and Loan a little after it opens the next morning, trying to beat the payday Friday customers. When I get inside, I see Mr. Thomas, the bank manager, sitting in his office. He's still here after all these years! I sit in one of the chairs and wait for him to finish with the customer at his desk. He looks out into the lobby and acknowledges my presence, waving his hand and flashing me that same unwanted, dirty-old-man grin he always smiled whenever he had seen me in the past. He's so disgusting!

Mr. Thomas had said many inappropriate things to me when I was younger. Aunt Myrtle and his wife have been good friends for many years, and the Thomases still come to some of our family gatherings.

One time, when I was still living with Grandmother, Uncle Stanley had invited everyone over for a get-together at his house. I was in the kitchen by myself when Mr. Thomas walked in. He told me it was amazing that my breasts had popped out so quickly when they were flat as pancakes a few weeks ago. I gasped at his comment and left him standing there by himself.

Another time, when I was fifteen, Uncle Stanley and Aunt Myrtle took me and my cousins fishing at a lake on the outskirts of Westfield. Aunt Myrtle asked Mr. Thomas, his wife and their son to come with us. While everyone was sitting around the lake fishing, I went over to the picnic table where we had our lunch set up. I was reaching into the picnic basket to get a sandwich when Mr. Thomas came up behind me quietly. All of a sudden I felt the palm of his hand on my butt! It startled me and I screamed loud enough for everyone to look in my direction. Mr. Thomas apologized loud enough for everyone to hear him say he hadn't meant to bump into me like that and scare me. I never told my family what he had done for fear that one of them might kill him.

For the life of me, I couldn't understand why Mr. Thomas acted the way he did with me. He should have known there was no way I could be interested in his bald, fat, pot-bellied self! He should have known I didn't like old men. He should have guessed by the way my face lit up, whenever I was around his nephew, Randall, that I was crazy about him, not some tired, old relic such as himself.

Randall was my first love. I would see him every so often when we were kids and I had the biggest crush on him, but when we started going to the same high school, I thought he was the most handsome dude I knew. He was one of our high school's star football players and he sure did look like one! That big, hard chest and strong arms made me melt every time I saw him. And his eyes were beautiful, just dreamy. I used to stare at him on the sly in the lunchroom, and he even caught me a couple of times. He would just smile at me, like he was letting me know he saw me, and my heart would skip a beat.

By the time Randall was a senior, I was a lovesick junior who longed to be his girl, but couldn't because he was already dating Betty Lawry.

One day, we had an afternoon talent show at school in the gym, and a group of guys were singing Baby I Need Your Loving by The Four Tops. The whole audience was listening in amazement because no one even knew they could sing. I had a feeling that someone was staring at me and when I turned and looked over my shoulder, I found Randall sitting a few seats in back of me with some of the other football players, staring dead in my face with a look that made me feel like he had requested that song to be sung for the two us. He wasn't smiling, just staring with those seductive, beautiful eyes. I didn't want anyone to catch me looking at him, so I quickly turned away. I couldn't help but look back at him again and when I did, he was still staring at me. He smiled at me and turned back to watch the talent show. I had to restrain myself from jumping up out of my seat and climbing over the bleacher seats to go sit next to him. But I knew one day he was going to be mine.

A couple of days later, I was on my way to the bathroom during class. I looked down the hallway and saw Randall coming my way.

"Hey, pretty lady!" he said, right before he passed me.

"Hi, Randall," I said coolly keeping my pace and walking past him. I didn't want to smile and cheese at him like I was an easy catch.

Just as I got to the corner to walk into the bathroom door, he called my name. I turned around and saw him making his way to me.

He stopped a couple of inches from my face and didn't say anything. He just looked into my eyes. He was so close I could smell the scent of the Juicy Fruit gum he was chewing coming from his luscious mouth.

"I know you be watching me in class sometimes," he said in his baritone voice. "So when you gonna let me call you so we can go out?"

I was so nervous I couldn't make my mouth move to give him an answer.

"Do you like me?" he asked, tilting his head like he was readying himself to move in closer to put his lips onto mine. He tilted his head to the other side, waiting for my answer.

"Yes," I told him, pretending to be shy.

"Yes what?"

"Yes, I like you."

"Well, I'm glad to know it. I've been likin' you for a long time."

My heart raced with delight and I smiled at him.

"So can I call you?" he asked. "Maybe take you out?"

My smile quickly faded. There was no way I could let him call me or take me out. My grandmother would never go for that. I wished he would have just said, 'Can we eat lunch together or talk after school'?

"I can't," I told him. He could tell by the look on my face that there was a serious reason I couldn't accept his offer.

"You worried about me being with Betty?" he asked me.

"I don't care about Betty," I said sarcastically. "I just can't accept phone calls from boys."

"Oh. Your grandmomma don't let you have male friends?"

I shifted my stare towards the wall next to him without answering.

"I forgot you got one of them old-fashion grandmommas," he said. "She got you under lock and key."

I looked back at him, hoping his interest wasn't swayed by that fact.

"So no boyfriends, huh?"

I tried not to show my feelings of embarrassment and shook my head no.

"But it's alright," he said. "We'll play it Grandma's way. We just won't let her know I'm your new boyfriend."

My face lit up again and I looked back into his eyes.

"When can you come see me?" he asked.

"Come see you where?" I said naively.

"Over my house. My people don't get home 'til late, so we got plenty of time to get to know each other better."

I felt nervous thinking about being alone with him at his house.

"You think about it and let me know tomorrow," he said. "I want to be your first."

"I've had a boyfriend before," I told him boldly, not wanting him to think I was so afraid of my grandmother that I wouldn't chance anything. "My grandmother isn't around me every minute of the day."

"I wasn't talking about being your first boyfriend."

"I've kissed a boy before," I said, thinking that was what he was referring to.

"I ain't talking about that either."

He stepped backwards a couple of feet, smiling at me before he slowly turned and walked back around the corner, leaving me dazed with my mouth hanging slightly open.

For the rest of the day, up until I went to bed, all I thought about was Randall. I daydreamed about what it would be like to be alone with him, just to sit and talk and really get to know him. I wanted to know everything about him. I knew he would try to get me to let him be my first, but I wasn't ready for that. I just wanted to use the time to be around him and kiss him.

The next day, the teacher sent me to the office to pick up some papers for her. As I walked back to my classroom, I saw Randall coming around the corner at the end of the hall. I hadn't given him my answer yet so us meeting in the hallway was right on time. When he realized it was me, he stopped where he was and watched as I made my way to him.

"Hey, pretty lady," he said as I got within a few feet of him. I loved to hear him call me that.

"Hi, Randall," I said sweetly.

"Did you think about what I asked you?"

"Yes."

"Well, what's it gonna be?"

"You tell me what day."

He blinked and widened his eyes, not expecting my answer. His surprised look changed to a delighted grin.

"Tomorrow after school," he said. "Be at my house at three-thirty."

"I'll be there," I told him.

I went back to my desk, not able to concentrate on my schoolwork for thinking about Randall and what might happen.

I snuck to his house that next day. At first we talked, but it didn't take long for him to kiss me with his warm, luscious lips, and before I knew it, I let Randall be my first. And afterwards, when he said he loved me, I felt an unexpected ease come over me. I was seventeen and I had finally felt the closeness I had been looking for so long. I had received love from someone and I mattered.

I went to be with Randall at his house several more times, and before long everybody knew he and Betty had broken up and I was his new girl. Geneva was the only one who knew about my lovemaking with Randall. I'm sure he told his friends, and I didn't care because I wanted it known I wasn't a little girl anymore. I was a woman now, Randall's woman. When I saw Betty at school or out in the neighborhood, she would look me up and down and roll her eyes, but she never said anything because she wasn't sure how I would react.

Randall and I hadn't been together long when he asked me if I could go to the prom with him. When I asked Grandmother, she told me no, that I was only allowed to go to one prom and that was in my senior year and it was only going to be with one of the Violets' grandsons. She didn't trust me with any of those other uncouth boys at my school.

Randall was so upset when I told him I couldn't go. He told me he was still going and I would just have to deal with it. We argued about it for weeks. I didn't find out until the day after the prom that he had taken Betty. Going to the prom was one thing, but taking the girl he broke up with to be with me was a definite no-no!

When I saw him that next Monday morning, standing out in front of the school with his friends, I walked right up to him and slapped him in the face. He was embarrassed and asked me if I was crazy. His friends laughed as I fussed at him and told him we were through. A few weeks later, he caught me after school, and being the smooth talker that he was, he made it seem like it was my fault that he had to take Betty to the prom because I couldn't go, so technically I was to blame. He said he was sorry and he still wanted us to be together. Of course he won me over and I was his girlfriend again.

His graduation had come and gone, and a month or so later it was time for Randall to leave for football camp at the college he was going to attend. Before he left, we got together one last time. I cried, telling him I didn't want him to leave me. He wiped my tears and promised me he wouldn't be gone long.

That was the last time I saw or heard from Randall. I couldn't get phone calls from him, so I had asked him to call Geneva to send me messages and let me know when he was coming home, but he never did.

It was a big shock to me when Aunt Myrtle told us at one of our family picnics that Randall and Betty had gotten married a few weeks back and Betty was pregnant. My poor heart was crushed. I sat there emotionless, listening as Aunt Myrtle told us how Randall was still going to finish school and Betty was living with her parents until she had the baby. Betty was going to move down there to be with Randall as soon as he finished his freshman year. Geneva waited a few minutes until her mother was onto another topic before she excused us, telling everyone we were going to walk down by the lake. She knew I needed to be away from everyone so that I could let loose the shame and humiliation that I was feeling. I cried as Geneva and I trotted down one of the paths in the woods, until we came across a fallen tree, where we sat as she hugged me. I was so hurt, so in love. I never felt that same way about any other man and tried to protect my heart so I wouldn't ever hurt like that again. And although I loved Gerald when he was my husband, it was nothing like the way I loved Randall.

I come back from reminiscing and tend to the business at hand.

"Well, hello there, Miss Cressford," Mr. Thomas says as he comes out of his office, extending his hand to me.

I truly want to avoid shaking his hand because I know he's going to keep holding it all the while he's talking to me, rubbing and squeezing it. But today I need to be polite.

"Hello Mr. Thomas," I say dryly, returning his handshake. His grip gives me the creeps and I immediately pull my hand back before he, accidently-on-purpose puts it down the front of his pants!

"I'm not Miss Cressford anymore. I'm Ms. Martin."

"I did hear you had gotten married," he says, "but I never knew what your married name was. Where's your husband?"

"I'm not married anymore," I tell him. "I'm divorced."

"Oh yes, that's right. My wife did mention you got divorced. She still keeps in touch with your Aunt Myrtle. I saw your daughter at the funeral. Is she still here?"

"No, I sent her back home and she's with her father."

"Well, it's good to see you back in town. I'm so sorry about your grandmother."

"Thank you for your sympathy."

"She was a fine woman, a real fine woman. What can I do for you?"

"I came to get the contents out of my grandmother's safety deposit box. Can you come in and unlock it with me?"

"Well, I have to pull her signature card to see who she had signed as her beneficiary. It'll take me a few minutes because I have to go downstairs to find it. Normally we ask for the family to give us a day or two to get these things prepared."

I know my name is nowhere on that card!

"Mr. Thomas, I'm really in a hurry and don't have time for this," I say sternly.

"I'm sorry, Francine, but checking the signature card is bank policy."

Damn him! Why is he making this difficult?

"Can I talk to you in the vault?" I ask in a lower tone, so no one else can hear me. I walk into the vault and he follows behind me.

"Mr. Thomas, you've known my family for many years," I tell him. "You know good and well that my grandmother put all of us on her signature card to conduct business in a situation such as this. Now you know my aunt and uncles sent me down here to pick up my grandmother's things from her safety deposit box. They're all still grieving and don't have time to deal with all this business stuff."

"I don't know," he says, unconvinced.

"Do you think they would have given me the key if I wasn't supposed to get her things out of the box?"

He looks at me suspiciously.

"Look," I tell Mr. Thomas, "you can let me into my grandmother's safety deposit box or I can call my family and let them know you're giving me a hard time. You know they'll be insulted about it. I'm sure Aunt Josette would talk her brothers into closing their accounts with this bank and going over to another savings and loan."

"No, that won't be necessary, Miss Cressford," he says, smiling and pulling his keys from his pocket. I don't correct him about my name.

He walks over to the boxes and puts his key in the lock and waits for me to come over and insert the one I have. We unlock the box and he excuses himself. I remove the box from the niche and sit at one of the tables inside the room. I get nervous as I wonder what I'll find inside. Will I find a copy of the picture that Mrs. Snyder was talking about?

I lift the lid of the box and see a stack of dollar bills with three twenties, two fifties and two hundreds in a giant paper clip. There are also two stacks of envelopes with a rubber band around each stack. The top envelope in the first stack is unsealed and blank. I pull the folded piece of paper from inside the envelope and read the heading 'Morton Asylum, Spaulding, Missouri,' dated 'June 18, 1956'. I skim over a few lines and look down to the part that says 'patient'. The line next to it is filled in with the name 'Marietta Cressford'. At the bottom of the paper are two signatures listing 'Dr. Walter Leathers' as 'Psychiatrist' and 'Aldania Cressford' as 'person committing patient'.

I feel a hard thud in my heart and I feel the heat rise in my face as I realize what I'm reading. My family told me my mother died in a car accident around this very same time, but this paper says my mother was committed to a mental hospital! I don't understand. Why hadn't anyone told me about this? I need to go talk to my aunt and uncles to see what this is about.

I put the money and both stacks of envelopes into my purse. As I leave the vault, I can see Mr. Thomas back in his office with another customer. I stop at one of the counters and give the key to the teller, asking her to explain to Mr. Thomas that we will no longer need the box.

Mr. Thomas sees me leaving and he excuses himself from his customer and walks up to me.

"Did you get everything you needed?" he asks.

"Yes, I did. I left the key with the teller. Thanks, Mr. Thomas."

"Are you alright, Miss Cressford? You look a bit flushed."

"I'm okay. I just got overcome thinking about my grandmother while I was in the vault."

He puts his hand on my shoulder and immediately I want to slap it off.

"I understand," he says. "It happens all the time when people come to pick up their loved ones' belongings out of their boxes."

"Thanks for your sympathy, Mr. Thomas. I have to get going. I'll be alright as soon as I get home."

"Okay, then. You drive carefully."

He grabs my hand one last time.

"You let me know if there is anything you need," he says, "anything at all."

I look at him and see that seedy grin of his.

"Goodbye, Mr. Thomas," I say as I pull my hand away from his.

Once I get into my car, I sit inside for a minute, trying to make sense of what I just found out. I wonder if my aunt and uncles knew about this. Maybe they all knew about it, but were too embarrassed to talk about it.

I put both stacks of envelopes into my glove compartment and keep the one with the paper from the mental hospital in my purse. I drive until I find a telephone at a convenience store and call Uncle Wendell and Uncle Stanley, telling them to meet me at Grandmother's house as soon as they can. I explain to them that I can't tell them what it's about over the phone.

When I get back to the house, I see Uncle Wendell's car on the street. I park my car and go up to the front door. The screen door is locked, so I ring the bell and wait anxiously as I see Aunt Josette walking down the hall from the kitchen to let me in.

"Hi," she says, unlatching the door.

"Hi," I reply.

I walk past her into the house and go into the dining room, where Uncle Wendell is sitting at the table in one of the side chairs.

"So what's this big meeting about?" he asks, smiling.

I should probably wait for Uncle Stanley, but I'm in too big of a hurry to find out the truth.

"I have something for you all to see," I say as I take the envelope from my purse and hand it to Uncle Wendell.

Aunt Josette walks into the dining room and while she and I take our seats at the table, Uncle Wendell pulls the paper from the envelope and reads it. After a few minutes, he looks at me.

"Where did you get this?" he says. His voice sounds agitated.

"What is it?" Aunt Josette asks.

Uncle Wendell passes her the paper, still looking at me, waiting for my reply.

"I got it out of grandmother's safety deposit box at the bank," I say.

"You got it from what?!" he snaps.

"Oh no!" Aunt Josette says skimming the paper. She looks as pale as a ghost. She lays the paper down in front of her on the table.

"Did you all know my mother was in a mental hospital before she died?" I ask them both.

"How did you get into Mother's safety deposit box?" Uncle Wendell asks, evading my question.

"I was looking for something Grandmother might have left behind that would help us find her brother and sister. I looked through her closet and I found the key in an envelope and took it down to the bank and then I came across this."

"Mother isn't even cold in the ground and you go snooping through her things?!" Aunt Josette yells. "Why Francine? Because some old, senile, white woman claims she had a brother and sister? I don't believe you. You don't know that woman. And I don't believe she knew Mother as well as she claims. Mother never told us she worked as a maid for some white people."

"But what reason would Mrs. Snyder have to lie?" I ask her.

"Who knows?"

"Her sons said it too. They said they met the brother and sister. Why would they lie? But I'm not concerned with that right now. What about this paper?"

"That's a lie, too," Uncle Wendell says. "Marietta wasn't never in a mental hospital."

"Somebody is mistaken about that too," Aunt Josette says.

"Then why would Grandmother have this paper if it wasn't true?" I ask them.

Neither of them says a word. Maybe they really didn't know about it. But how could they not? How can someone commit a person and hide it from the rest of the family? What reason would she have not to tell them anyway?

"Did my mother die in the car accident after she left this place?" I ask.

They avoid looking me in the eye. They look at one another for a moment and then Uncle Wendell gets up from the table and walks into the hallway. Aunt Josette sits there, looking away from me.

"What happened back then?" I ask, loud enough for Uncle Wendell to hear. From the way they're avoiding my questions, I can tell that they know something about this.

"This isn't right," I say. "You all are hiding something from me. You all need to be honest and tell me the truth."

Aunt Josette sits there sighing and clasping her hands.

Uncle Wendell walks back in and sits back down at the table. He lets out a long breath and looks at me.

"We don't know anything about that paper," Uncle Wendell tells me. "Nor do we know anything about Marietta being in an asylum. But your mother and your father did die when you were a little girl. Your daddy used to own a store up on Simpson, sold men and women's clothes and shoes. Had a good business and made a lot of money. One night, he was leaving out his store and somebody came up in back of him and shot him in the head. They took all his money."

"Oh my God!" I gasp, putting my hands to my mouth. "Someone killed my father?!"

"Yes," Uncle Wendell sighs.

"Did they find out who did it?"

"No. They never did find out."

"Well maybe that's why Grandmother had to take my mother to Morton. She might have had a nervous breakdown when she found out my father was killed."

"I keep telling you Mother didn't take Marietta to that place!" Uncle Wendell snaps. "That didn't even happen at the same time! Your daddy died in '64."

"What do you mean he died in '64? I was nine years old in '64. Why didn't I ever see him?"

Uncle Wendell readies himself to continue, but he stops when Aunt Josette looks at him as if to say, 'You better not open your mouth'.

"She needs to know, Josette," Uncle Wendell says, looking at her.

"There's nothing to tell, Wendell," she says to him.

"Oh, there's plenty to tell and she needs to know. She can't keep accusing Mother of putting Marietta away when we know what really happened."

"What?!" I demand. "What happened?!"

"Nothing!" Aunt Josette says.

"Aw damn it!" I holler. "Stop with these lies and tell me the truth!"

Uncle Wendell sighs before he goes on. Aunt Josette looks at him stone-faced like she doesn't want him to say anything else.

"The truth is, we don't know where Marietta is," Uncle Wendell says. "Nobody does. Your daddy didn't even know before he got killed."

"Why wouldn't he know where his wife was?" I ask.

"She wasn't his wife."

"Oh Lord!" Aunt Josette says, covering her face with her hands.

"What?!" I say with confusion.

"Francine, your parents were never married," Uncle Wendell says to me. "Your father was married to somebody else when he got your mother pregnant."

My heart starts to feel heavy as I blink in disbelief over what I just heard.

"Charles Smith wasn't your father," Uncle Wendell tells me.

"What?" I say again. "Then who was Charles Smith?"

"There never was a Charles Smith."

"Oh no!"

"Your real father's name was L.C. Boone. He was married and had a wife and two boys. Nobody knew Marietta was fooling around with him until she got pregnant with you. Marietta moved in with him while he was still married. She left him a couple of times because she found out he was still seeing his wife. Mother kept telling her to leave him alone, but she wouldn't listen. She was hardheaded. She even had the nerve to go over to the woman's house and got into a fight with her. Marietta was livin' back at home with Mother when she had made up her mind to move out of town with L.C., but when he came to pick y'all up, Marietta was gone."

"Gone where?" I ask.

"Nobody knows. Mother said she took you to the baby sitter that morning and when she got back home, Marietta was gone. She didn't say good-bye. She didn't take no clothes or nothing. Just walked right out that front door and ain't never looked back. She's never called. She's never written a letter saying she was alive or nothing. Mother called the police and told them about Marietta and L.C.'s wife getting into a fight 'cause she started to wonder if that woman had done something to Marietta. They questioned L.C. and his wife, but the police never did come up with nothing. So to this day we still don't know."

I sit there in shock for a few minutes as I take in what I just heard. I look at my uncle and then at my aunt.

"Would my mother happen to have disappeared on June 18th, 1956?" I ask sarcastically.

They both look at each other and then at me.

"That's the date on this letter," I say.

Uncle Wendell picks it up again and looks for the date.

"Maybe the police couldn't come up with anything because Grandmother put her in Morton Asylum!" I tell them.

"I don't believe this!" Uncle Wendell says, flinging the letter across the table. "Mother would have told us if she took Marietta to that place. And if she did, she wouldn't have kept her there without us knowing it."

"For all I know, anything could have happened!" I scream. "You all lied. You all said both of my parents died when I was a baby. Now you tell me the man I thought was my father never even existed and my real father never married my mother and one day she just walked out the house and never came back. And then you tell me somebody killed my real father some years later. And to top it off I find this paper saying my mother was admitted to a mental hospital."

All of a sudden something else dawns on me.

"And if she was discharged," I say, "why isn't there another paper saying so? Since nobody went to a funeral, maybe she's still there."

Uncle Wendell gets up from the table and walks away again.

Aunt Josette sits nervously wringing her hands.

"We might have been wrong," Aunt Josette says, "for hiding the truth from you about your mother and father not being married, but we thought it was the best thing to do at the time. You didn't need to grow up knowing that your mother had you by somebody else's husband. Think about how you might have turned out if you knew that."

Uncle Wendell walks back in and sits down again.

"Did you think about how I would feel now, when I found out about it?" I ask. "At least now I know why Grandmother hated me so much."

"Mother didn't hate you," Aunt Josette says, offended by my accusation.

"Oh yes she did!" I holler. "And she let me know it every chance she got! I was the constant reminder of the shame my mother brought on her! I don't believe my mother just up and walked out the front door. I think Grandmother took her to this place and left her there and lied about it to everybody!"

"Now you looka here!" Uncle Wendell says, pointing his finger at me. "Mother never lied a day in her life!"

"Apparently she did!" I say, picking up the paper and shaking it in front of him. "And this paper is more than any proof I need to confirm it! Grandmother would tell you all whatever she wanted you to believe, and she knew you wouldn't question a word she ever said!"

"You better watch what you say, gal!" Uncle Wendell yells hatefully at me.

"Or what?!" I say, standing up from the dining room table.

"I'll knock the hell out of you!" Uncle Wendell says rising from his seat.

"The way I feel right now, Uncle Wendell, you better be careful about threatening me!"

He lunges toward me halfway over the table, slamming his hands down on it.

"You better watch who you talking to!" he tells me through gritted teeth. "I don't care how old you get, you will not disrespect me or Mother!"

"Your mother never respected me!"

He makes his way around the table to me.

I snatch my purse from the table, stuffing the paper in it as I stomp away quickly from the other side of the table.

Aunt Josette stands up from her seat and blocks him from me as I make my way towards the front door.

"Let her go, Wendell," Aunt Josette says, holding him back by his arm.

I walk out of the house and storm down the stairs to my car.

Just as I'm about to get into the driver's seat, Uncle Stanley pulls up and parks right behind me. I stand there and wait for him with my arms crossed and a frown on my face.

"What's wrong with you?" he asks as he gets out of his car.

"I got to go!" I say, shaking with anger.

"What happened?"

"I can't talk right now."

"You want me to drive you somewhere?"

"No!" I say reaching for the car handle.

"Hold on now! You are entirely too upset to be driving."

I look over the roof of my car towards the sidewalk, and I see Uncle Wendell and Aunt Josette standing near my car.

"That's right!" Uncle Wendell hollers. "Get on out of here, and far as I'm concerned, you ain't never gotta come back! We all was doing just fine without you! When you left home you didn't bother to never come back here and pay your respects when Mother was living, so you didn't need to come back now.

You only came back to see if she left you any money. As you can see, she didn't, and I'll be damned if I give you anything she left for me!"

"Wendell!" Aunt Josette hollers. "Get a hold of yourself! What is wrong with you?!"

"Man, you quit talking to this girl like she ain't nobody to you!" Uncle Stanley says to Uncle Wendell.

"Well she was just in there talking about Mother like she wasn't nobody to her!" Uncle Wendell retorts.

"What in the hell is going on 'round here?!" Uncle Stanley asks.

"Go head and tell Stanley all the awful shit you just said about your grandmother!" Uncle Wendell says to me.

"What I said was the truth!" I tell him. "And as far as me coming back here to get anything from Grandmother, that's a lie. I don't want a damn thing she had! She never gave me anything out of the kindness of her heart when she was living, so what would it mean to take it from her now that she's dead?"

"Well you came back here for something! That's why you went looking through Mother's stuff!"

"Something did make me come back here and it was to find out the truth about all the lies you all and Grandmother told me!"

"I'm gonna knock your teeth right out of your mouth if you don't stop calling Mother a liar!"

"All of y'all stop it!" Uncle Stanley screams, straining his voice. "What is wrong with y'all?!"

"Your niece done come in here accusing Mother of being a liar," Uncle Wendell says, "just 'cause she wants to believe what that woman said about Mother having sisters and brothers. Then to top it off, she found the key to Mother's safety deposit box and took it upon herself to go down to the bank and look through her things!"

Uncle Stanley turns to me in disbelief.

"Did you do that?" Uncle Stanley asks me.

"Yes I did," I tell him. "And I found a paper saying my mother was committed to an insane asylum."

"What?!" Uncle Stanley says, still confused.

"Yeah," Uncle Wendell continues. "I told her about Marietta and L.C. Boone and how Marietta walked out and left her, but she has it in her mind that Mother put Marietta in the nut house. She claims she found some paper in the deposit box that's got Marietta's name on it and she thinks Mother put her in an insane asylum!"

"Let me see the paper," Uncle Stanley says.

"You know what?" I say. "Right now, I don't want to talk to any of you!"

As I start to get into my car, Uncle Wendell starts up again.

"And since you want to know everything, your daddy wasn't nothing but a no good thug! Yeah he was. He was a pimp and a hustler!"

All of a sudden, I stop and step back out.

"Shut up!" I holler at him. "Shut the hell up, you hateful, dumb ass bastard!"

Uncle Wendell stomps from the sidewalk off to the curb and tries to come to where I am. Aunt Josette grabs his shirt from behind and screams for him to stop as Uncle Stanley grabs him from the front. He tries to break free, but Uncle Stanley has him tight. I wait for them to let him go because as mad as I am right now, I will fight him tooth and nail! Uncle Stanley and Aunt Josette push Uncle Wendell up the front porch steps and into the house.

I get into my car and sit there for a few minutes as the anger wails inside of me. I start my car and just as I'm ready to put the gear into drive, Uncle Stanley reaches in the window and grabs my steering wheel.

"Turn this car off!" he demands.

"Get off my steering wheel and move Uncle Stanley!" I tell him.

"Or what? You gonna run me over?"

"You better move!"

"Who you think you talkin' to?! Turn this damn car off right now!"

I sit there looking up at him. I blink a few times before my face is wet with my tears. Uncle Stanley reaches for my ignition and turns off the car. He opens the door and stoops down next to me.

"Come on now," he says, putting his hand on my shoulder.

I reach my arms out and hug his neck, crying into his shoulder. He helps me out of my car and then puts me in on the passenger side. He gets into the driver's seat and we pull away, not speaking to one another.

When we stop in front of Aunt Myrtle's sister's house, he gets out of the car and stands on the sidewalk waiting for me to get out. The side windows are down and I sit there, sulking like a child, looking out the front windshield.

Uncle Stanley walks up beside the passenger side door and stands there for a second, and then he taps his knuckle on the frame of the side window.

"Come on, Francine," I hear him say.

"I'm not coming," I say in a weak voice.

"Yes you are. We need to talk about this."

"I said I don't want to talk about it."

"Too bad. We got to figure this out."

He waits for me to say something, but I don't.

"I know you're mad," he says to me, squatting on the ground. "But you got to talk to me. I need to know what happened so we can get to the bottom of this."

I don't react at all.

Uncle Stanley stands back up, looking tired of being ignored by me.

"Let's go!" he demands.

I feel like a scolded child as I get out of the car. I follow Uncle Stanley onto the porch where Aunt Myrtle and Miss Laila are sitting in chairs. Their chatter comes to a halt as they watch the two of us come up the steps, me with my red, puffy eyes and Uncle Stanley with a worried look on his face.

"What's done happened?" Aunt Myrtle asks as she rises from her chair.

"Josette and Wendell told her about Marietta and L.C.," he tells her.

"Oh, Lord!"

"Can you get me a cold rag?" I ask Miss Laila.

"Of course I can, sugar," she says. "I'll be right back."

Miss Laila walks into the house. I sit in one of the porch chairs, sighing as I lean back. Uncle Stanley sits across from me in another chair.

"Now why did them two dumb asses go and open they mouths?" Aunt Myrtle asks in an angry tone.

"Let me see that paper you got," Uncle Stanley says to me.

"What paper?" Aunt Myrtle asks.

"She went down to the bank and went into Mother's safety deposit box and found some paper."

"What kind of paper?"

I pull the paper from my purse and hand it to Uncle Stanley. Aunt Myrtle waits her turn as Uncle Stanley skims over the paper. When he's finished reading, he hands the paper to her, then gets up and walks across the porch towards the top of the steps. Aunt Myrtle reads it.

Miss Laila comes back out onto the porch. She hands me a cool, damp face towel. I hold my head back and place it over my eyes, letting it rest on my face. Miss Laila sits back in her chair.

"I knew it!" Aunt Myrtle says, gritting her teeth. "Ooww that damned woman! I knew that girl didn't just walk out of that house like that. I just knew it!"

"What is it?" Miss Laila asks.

"Francine found this paper," Aunt Myrtle tells her sister. "It says Miss Aldania had Marietta put away in the crazy house on the exact same day she said that girl left home. All these years nobody knew where she was, and all this time she must have been locked away."

"We don't know anything for sure," Uncle Stanley says.

"We don't know anything for sure?" Aunt Myrtle says as she walks over to where he is, holding the paper and stretching her arm out towards him. "It's all here in black and white, Stanley. What else do we need?"

"We need to get in touch with that place first before we go speculating."

"Speculating? This paper ain't no speculation, Stanley. The facts is on this here paper. It says Aldania Cressford committed Marietta Cressford on the same day she disappeared into thin air. Ain't no speculating."

"Like I said, we ain't sure of nothing," he tells her.

"Aw, come on Stanley," Aunt Myrtle says as she repositions herself, planting both of her feet firmly on the ground and placing her balled fists into her hips. "What the hell else is there to know? This is your momma's signature right here on the paper."

"But we don't know if Marietta is still there," Uncle Stanly says. "Mother might have taken her there for a day and they sent her home before she walked away."

"Well whatever happened, Miss Aldania took it to her grave and wouldn't nobody never knew it if this child hadn't found this paper."

Aunt Myrtle directs her attention to me.

"Tomorrow we gonna call this place," she says.

"Call them?" I ask, confused. "Call them for what?"

"Don't you want to find out where your momma is?"

"Excuse me, miss," I say to the woman sitting at the receptionist desk. She looks up from the book she is reading. Her name badge has Teresa Hayden inscribed on it.

"Yes?" she says, greeting me with a smile.

"I'm Francine Martin and I'm looking for Miss Marietta Cressford. Can you tell me if she's a resident here?"

"I'll check." She keys in something into her computer and waits.

The day after I found the admittance paper, Aunt Myrtle tried to find the telephone number to Morton Asylum. The operator told her there was no listing. I decided I needed to go to Spaulding, Missouri to see what I could find.

I got in touch with my boss and Gerald, and told them I would be gone a few more days and explained why.

Uncle Stanley and I made the hour and a half drive from Westfield to Morton only to find it had closed. We went to the city hospital, where one of the representatives in the admitting department told us Morton had closed over fifteen years ago and that most of the older patients were placed in nursing homes. She gave me the names of eight homes in the area and told me to check with them. We went to three different nursing homes and none of them had any record of Marietta Cressford ever being a resident. Upset and angry, we drove back to Westfield that evening.

Uncle Stanley couldn't make the drive back with me today. I think he's given up already. I can tell it's been an emotional strain on him. It's been a big strain on me. I didn't leave Westfield until four o'clock this afternoon and this is the sixth home on the list that I've been to and I'm tired. Tired and weary from searching and looking and not finding. Anxiously waiting, I stand there, anticipating what the inquiry will disclose.

"Yes, we do."

I gasp at first, putting my hand over my mouth, trying to muffle the sound, and then I choke back the lump I feel building in my throat. I'm overcome by a wave of emotions and I cry.

"Are you all right?" the woman asks me as she gets up out of her seat and makes her way around the desk to where I am.

I try to control myself, but I can't stop crying. She takes my arm and leads me to an empty room with a sofa and two chairs.

"You got anybody here with you?" she asks me as she sits me down on the sofa.

I breathe in hard and try to exhale an answer, but I can't talk.

"It's okay, honey," she says in a consoling voice.

She sits with me quietly until I gain my composure and can talk again. She goes to a closet in the corner of the room and comes back to me with a box of tissues.

"Do you need me to call someone for you?" she asks, passing me the box.

I pull out a few tissues and blow my nose. I get a clean tissue to dab my eyes.

"No," I tell her, shaking my head. "I'll be okay in a minute."

"Are you related to Ms. Cressford?" she asks.

"Yes," I say. "She's my mother. I haven't seen her since I was eleven months old. I just found out a few days ago that she might still be alive."

"Oh Lord, have mercy!" she says. "What happened that you didn't know she was here?"

I tell my life story to this stranger as she listens intently, frowning and raising her eyebrows in disbelief.

"Oh my Lord! That is something else," she tells me. "I've heard some things in my life, but I ain't never heard of nobody doing something like that and not telling nobody. That's a shame!"

"I know," I say in agreement.

"Well, you ready to go back and see your momma?" she asks me.

I hesitate before responding. I wasn't sure what I wanted to do. I never knew my mother and after almost forty years, I know she won't know who I am. What was I going to say when I saw her? I sit there for a minute.

"Are you ready to see Ms. Cressford?" she asks me again.

"Miss Hayden..," I begin.

"Honey, call me Teresa," she tells me.

"Teresa, I'm nervous about this."

"Don't be nervous. You won't be by yourself. I'll go back there with you. You ready now?"

I think about it for a few seconds and then nod my head yes.

Teresa stands up and walks to the door, waiting for me to follow her. We walk down a long hallway and come to a locked door. She uses a key to open it, and once we pass through she locks it back. We pass by two rooms on the right, and she stops at the third door. She turns to look at me.

"You ready?" she asks me.

I look at the nametag on the door, 'M. Cressford'. I nod yes and take in a deep breath. Teresa knocks lightly on the door as she opens it.

"Ms. Cressford?" she says softly.

There is no answer. Teresa pushes the door open wide and I see my mother sitting on her bed with the side rails up. Her back is against the headboard with a pillow propped in between. She looks straight ahead at a small television sitting on top of a dresser against the front wall.

"I'm Teresa, the receptionist from the front desk," she says as we walk in and stand at the side of her bed.

Teresa bends in front of her, taking her hand. My mother doesn't move.

"Ms. Cressford, this lady here has come to see you," she tells her, pointing at me with her other hand. "She says she's your daughter."

Teresa steps back from the bed to allow me to move in closer. I bend over, facing her so she can see me better, but I'm the one who gets the better look. It is her. She looks just like the pictures I've seen of her, only she's older.

"Are you Marietta Cressford?" I ask.

She doesn't look at me or say anything.

"Momma, it's me, Francine," I say. "Do you remember me?" I lower the rail and sit on the bed next to her as the tears start to stream down my face. She stares into space as I continue talking to her.

"Momma, I've been looking for you for a long time," I tell her. "I'm going to talk to the doctors and see about getting you out of here."

I hear movement in the room and look up to see a woman in a white uniform standing at the door. I stand up from the bed.

"What is going on in here?" she demands.

"I brought Ms. Cressford's daughter in to see her," Teresa tries to explain.

"Ms. Cressford doesn't have a daughter," she says, "and if she did, it is way past visiting hours, so the both of you need to leave this room this very minute. Visitors are not allowed on the premises after eight o'clock. Teresa, you know this. Please show this woman to the door. I will be out to speak with you later."

"I'd like to speak with you before I leave," I say to the woman, as I wipe the tears from my eyes.

"You will have to come back in the morning, ma'am."

"No, I want to speak with you when you come out of this room!

She looks at me callously for a few seconds.

"Please wait out at the front reception area," she tells me.

"Oh, Lord!" Teresa says under her breath, but audible enough for me to hear. "Come on, Miss Francine. Let's go back to the front."

Teresa takes me back to the front reception area where she busies herself nervously while I wait for the woman to come out to talk with me. We sit in silence as I try to calm myself from the whole ordeal.

"It's gonna be all right, honey," she says to me from behind her desk. The desk phone rings and she answers it.

"Shorterville Nursing Home," she says. "Oh, I didn't realize this was an inside call. Yes. Yes. I'll be right there." She hangs up the telephone and rolls her eyes.

"That was the charge nurse," she says. "I have to go talk to her."

"I'm sorry," I say. "I did not mean to get you in trouble."

"Oh honey, it ain't your fault. I'm supposed to check with the nurses before I do anything concerning the residents. But I thought if you saw your mother and she saw you, it would help the both of you. Don't you worry about me. I'm gonna be okay. Now that you've found your momma, you concentrate on taking care of her. One of the nurses is coming out to talk to you, and if you're gone by the time I get back, you take care and I know I'll be seeing you around here from time to time."

"Thank you so much for your help, Teresa," I say.

Just then a woman comes from the corridor and approaches me.

"Hello, I'm Mrs. Harrison the evening shift manager and you are?" she says.

"I'm Francine Martin," I say, as I rise from my seat.

"I'm sorry, but visitors are not allowed in the patients' rooms without prior notice. Besides, our visiting hours are over."

"I understand, but my situation is different. I recently found out that one of your residents, Marietta Cressford, is my mother."

"I've known Ms. Cressford for five years now. Our records show she has no family."

"I'm sure that's what her records say, but she does have family. As I said, I'm her daughter."

Mrs. Harrison looks at me with doubt in her eyes.

"I'm sorry, ma'am, this will have to wait until tomorrow morning," she tells me. "You'll have to call our social worker and make arrangements with her to show proof of your relationship to Ms. Cressford."

"I just told you I was her daughter. What kind of proof do you need?"

"Ma'am, we can't just accept the word of a stranger who walks in here and claims to be a relative. I'm sorry, but you'll have to leave for the night and work on this matter with the appropriate staff tomorrow."

I feel the anxiety overcoming me again, only this time it's accompanied by anger.

"Oh no! I'm not waiting until tomorrow! I want to talk to someone tonight!"

"I'm sorry, ma'am, but there's no one here for you to talk to. You will have to speak with one of our social workers tomorrow."

"No!" I say shaking my head. "You get somebody in charge on the phone. I want to talk to someone now! I've been looking for my mother for a long time and I just found her. Now you get me somebody that's over you! Call the damned psychiatrist and tell him I said I want to see him right now!"

Mrs. Harrison's face starts to turn red. She turns away from me and heads back down the hall from where she came.

I go sit back down and wait for her to return. I am so angry right now. This is just too much to handle. I start to cry again.

How did all this happen? Why did Grandmother do this?

When Mrs. Harrison comes back from down the hall, she's accompanied by a security guard.

"Ma'am, you need to leave the premises and come back tomorrow," he tells me. "I'm sorry, but there's nothing we can do for you tonight."

I decide I should leave so that I won't cause any trouble and be banned from the nursing home. I get up and roll my eyes at the both of them as I leave.

"I found her," I say to Uncle Stanley after he answers the telephone.

He doesn't respond to me.

"Uncle Stanley? Are you still there?"

Still there's no answer. I hear him lay the telephone down.

"Hello? Who is this?" Aunt Myrtle says a few seconds later when she picks up the phone.

"It's me, Aunt Myrtle."

"What's wrong, baby? Stanley just walked out the room crying and ain't said a word. What happened?"

"I found my mother," I say, and I start to cry as well.

"Oh, Lord Jesus!" she hollers into the phone. "Oh Lord, have mercy! Praise God, she's alive!"

I hear Aunt Myrtle start to cry and it takes us both a few minutes to get it together.

"Wait a minute, baby," she tells me. "Stanley just came back in here and he wants to talk to you."

Uncle Stanley returns to the telephone.

"Did you get to see her?" he says in a very low, cracking voice.

"I did for a minute," I tell him. "The lady at the front desk let me sneak back, but one of the nurses caught me and had the security guard make me leave. They said I have to make an appointment to talk with the social worker, so I'm going back over there in the morning."

"Did Marietta say much?"

"Not a word. She just sits there staring."

"Where are you now?"

"I found a hotel and I'm staying here for the night. I just couldn't drive back to Westfield now that I know where she is."

"I'm on my way up there," he says.

"No, Uncle Stanley. Wait until tomorrow. It's too late to be driving here tonight, and they won't let anybody visit this late anyway."

"I don't care. I'm coming up there tonight. What's the name of the hotel where you staying?"

"Are you coming by yourself?"

"Naw. I'm getting Wendell and Josette and we all coming tonight. That way all of us can be there at that place when they open the doors first thing in the morning. And now that I know, I won't be able to sleep tonight no how. Give me the name and number of where you are so I can call you if I get lost."

"I really wish you would wait until tomorrow."

"What's the name of the place?" he insists.

I give him the name and number of my hotel.

"I'll call you if I have to," he says. "It's almost nine o'clock right now. It won't take us long to get there. I have to get me an overnight bag together and pick up Josette and Wendell, so I'll see you around ten-thirty or so. Bye."

I hang up the phone and sit there feeling a mix of emotions. I want to go back to the nursing home and beat the hell out of that woman for throwing me out. I feel happiness in finding out my mother is alive. I feel the sorrow for all the years lost, not knowing her. But mostly, I hate my grandmother for not telling me about it all. I'm so tired. All this emotional stress is wearing on me. I need to go somewhere and get a drink.

As I drive around looking for a grocery store, I think about how I'm going to break the news to Lisa that my mother is alive. She knows nothing about the admission papers I found. I didn't want to tell her about it and have her wondering and worrying like me. Now I have to figure out a way to tell my daughter what's really going on.

I find a store and buy a bottle of Merlot and a bottle of Coca- Cola and go back to my room. I settle in my bed with a glass of wine and drink it while I flip through the channels of the television set. I find an old episode of Good Times and try to watch it while I drink another glass of wine.

The banging on the door startles me from my sleep. I jolt up from the bed and look around to see where I am.

"Who is it?" I ask in a hoarse, sleepy voice as I approach the door. I open it and find Aunt Myrtle and Uncle Stanley standing on the other side.

"Hey, sugar," Aunt Myrtle says, hugging me tightly before she walks in.

Uncle Stanley walks in behind her and hugs me.

"Everything alright?" he asks me as he closes the door.

"I'm fine. I just went to sleep for a minute," I say, rubbing my eye.

"It took you long enough to answer that door," Aunt Myrtle says. "We heard the TV so we knew you was in the room."

Aunt Myrtle walks over to my nightstand.

"You sure you didn't pass out from this?" she says, picking up the bottle and shaking it.

"I only had a little bit of that," I say as I walk back to my bed and sit down. "Where's Aunt Josette and Uncle Wendell?"

"They said they ain't coming 'cause they don't believe it," Uncle Stanley says.

"I'm not surprised. I figured Uncle Wendell wouldn't come. He probably told Aunt Josette she better not come either."

"I'm sure he did," Aunt Myrtle says. "I told your Uncle Stanley they momma is dead and gone and them two sorry asses still got they noses stuck up her ass."

"Hey woman, watch your mouth," Uncle Stanley says scornfully. "That's still my mother you're talking about."

"Well, it's true," she tells him. "They've always been scared of that woman. Damn shame they ain't never grew up from her."

"We was raised to be respectful of other people. We don't talk bad about the dead, especially our mother."

"Aw shit, Stanley. Your brother and sister ain't no saints and neither was your mean ass mammy!"

"Damnit, I done told you, you better watch your mouth!" he yells at Aunt Myrtle. "You keep it up and see if I don't knock you down!"

Aunt Myrtle gives him the 'I dare you' look, but she doesn't say another word.

"Did you all get a room yet?" I interrupt, trying to ease the tension.

"Naw," he says, turning his attention away from Aunt Myrtle. "We came straight up here. I guess I better go do that."

He walks towards the door and opens it.

"You keep up with them smart remarks and you'll be sleeping out in the car," he says to Aunt Myrtle before he walks out.

"He's full of shit," Aunt Myrtle says to me.

She sits down in the chair at the small table in my room and takes off her shoes.

"So, how does Marietta look?" Aunt Myrtle asks.

"She looks old and tired."

"That's a damn shame. I knew all along Marietta didn't walk out and leave. Ain't no way she would leave you or L.C. I knew it."

Aunt Myrtle pulls a cigarette from her purse and lights it.

"Where's your ashtray?" she asks.

"Here it is," I say, picking it up from the nightstand and extending it to her.

She walks over and takes the ashtray from me and returns to her seat. She takes a puff from her cigarette, and then taps it over the ashtray, letting the ashes fall into it.

"I got something to give you," she tells me.

Aunt Myrtle rests her cigarette in the ashtray and then reaches into her purse and pulls out an envelope. She comes back over to where I am, bringing the ashtray with her and sits next to me on the side of the bed closest to the nightstand.

"These are some pictures of your momma and daddy," Aunt Myrtle says passing the envelope to me. "Your daddy used to keep them pictures in his desk drawer at his store. When L.C. died, I made his friend Russell go get 'em out of there before his wife got a hold to 'em and threw 'em away. I would have let you have 'em sooner, but I didn't want to cause no problems. I didn't want you showing those pictures to people and they see who your daddy was and they go running they mouth about what happened back then."

I pull the photos out and we look at them together.

"You know your mother was a beautiful girl," she says smiling. "You remember that picture?"

"I do," I tell her looking at the wallet sized shot of my mother's high school picture. Someone had written 'eleventh grade' on the back of it. There is another postcard-sized picture of my mother and her brothers and sister posing in front of Grandmother's house. My mother looked younger in this photo than she did in the high school picture.

I had seen both of these photos before, many years ago in Aunt Myrtle's photo album. But there were a few more pictures in the envelope that I had never seen before.

There's a picture of my mother looking glamorous in a beautiful, black dress. She really was a beautiful woman when she was younger. She looked so classy, so elegant.

"And that's your daddy, L.C. Boone," Aunt Myrtle says as I pull out the next picture.

I look over the black and white full shot of my father wearing a dark suit and hat, standing in front of a faint, backdrop painting of a forest. He was a very handsome, well-dressed man.

The next picture I see is of my mother and father, facing the camera as they sat on a couch, with my mother holding me on her lap. There's another picture of them on the same couch with my father's arm around my mother's shoulder.

I'm still sitting on my mother's lap but this one shows them both looking lovingly at one another.

"At least my parents looked happy together," I say.

"They were. That was the happiest I had ever seen L.C."

"Did you know my father before he met my mother?"

"Yeah, I knew your daddy before him and Marietta ever got together. I wasn't too particular about L.C. I didn't like men who were into the streets. He used to go with a friend of one of my cousins, way before he was with your mother. Nobody even knew your momma was with him. Both of your uncles was away in the service when all that happened, but if they would have heard she was tipping around with him, they would have kept her away from him."

"Wasn't he married at that time?" I say.

"He was. Him and his wife had a house over in Sterling, but L.C. had a three family over in Mont Reid where he rented out two of the apartments and the third one was his place. That's where he took Marietta to stay with him. I was so mad at her for getting pregnant by him. But she called me and we talked about it. She told me she loved him so much and she couldn't help it. I told her it wasn't my place to judge her. I used to go see her and your daddy. The cats that L.C. ran with would be there with they girlfriends or they wives. We would play cards and party and sit up and laugh at Russell while he cut the fool. Honey, Russell would have you in tears with his silly self. We had too much fun back in them days."

Uncle Stanley knocks at the door before he opens it and walks in. I can tell he's still sour from his riff with Aunt Myrtle.

"I got us a room right next door to this one," he says. "Come on so we can all get us some rest and be ready to meet with these people in the morning."

"I'll be there in a few minutes," she tells him. "Me and Francine are still talking."

Uncle Stanley goes over to the door in the wall and unlocks it.

"I'm gonna unlock this door from the other side so you can just come on through," he tells Aunt Myrtle.

He walks to the door leading to the hallway and opens it.

"I'll see you in the morning," he says, looking at me.

"You ain't gonna say goodnight to me?" Aunt Myrtle asks taking a puff from her cigarette.

Uncle Stanley walks out the door and closes it. I get up from my bed and lock the door behind him.

"He gets on my damn nerves," Aunt Myrtle says, pursing her lips.

I sit back on my bed and ready myself to listen to Aunt Myrtle as she continues on with her story about my parents.

"L.C. was known for being a ladies' man. You couldn't blame him with all them heifas coming in his shop, grinning and flirting with him. But when he met your mother, all of that stopped. He used to hold after hours parties in the basement of his store and people would go and play cards for money and buy reefers and that other stuff he was selling, but he stopped that too. People couldn't believe it. Word on the street was L.C. was quitting the business 'cause he was hooked up on some young girl. Far as I know, his wife didn't know why he had quit, but I heard she was mad that he wasn't bringing in the same money as he used to. I heard they had always had problems and argued all the time. She told him to get out even 'fore she found out about Marietta. L.C.'s wife loved his money, but your momma loved L.C., and her love made that man want to change his ways. But then Marietta found out L.C. had been seeing his wife on the sly and she caught him a couple of times. I was with her that first time. Marietta was pregnant and we saw him with his wife and they lil' boys at the store. He told Marietta he was buying some toys for the kids but she didn't believe that was the only reason he was with them. That was the first time she left him and went back home. It was a few weeks before you were born. She went back to him when you was about four or five months old. I was too mad at her for going back with L.C. that first time. 'Specially when she saw he was still with his wife. I stopped going to see her 'cause I couldn't stand him! The next time Marietta caught him sneaking off to see his wife was when she went over to the woman's house. She caught L.C. over there having a party with her and some of her people. Your momma left him again and went back home. But your daddy had a way with Marietta 'cause she changed her mind again and this time she was gonna leave town with him. On the day y'all was supposed to go, she came up missing."

We both sit silently for a few minutes.

"Yeah, child. I was mad as hell at your daddy," Aunt Myrtle says taking one last draw from her cigarette before smashing it in the ashtray. "At first I thought his wife had done something to Marietta and he knew about it and he wasn't telling. About a week after Marietta was gone, I went over to your daddy's store to give him a piece of my mind. Miss Ella was at the counter and she let me go on back to his office. He had the door closed and I knocked, but he didn't answer so I went on in, and he was sitting at his desk smoking a cigarette, just staring at nothing all frowned up like he was thinking real hard. He didn't even look to see who I was. I just started talking and I told him 'Listen here, you lowlife dog! Something done happened to Marietta and it's all your fault'! And I just went on and on 'til I couldn't talk no more, and when I finally shut my mouth it hit me that L.C. hadn't said a word. Now that wasn't like him, 'cause everybody who knew L.C. Boone knew he was a bad cat, and if you came at him wrong you better be ready for a fight. But honey, I was ready for him that day. He got up from that chair and walked over to where I was and stood right in front of me, and that's when I got scared 'cause at first I thought he was gonna do something to me, but when I saw that sad face and them empty eyes, I went from feeling scared to feeling sorry for that poor man. He looked sick, like a person that hadn't eaten or slept in days. He talked real low like he was 'shamed. He told me 'Myrt, you right. I messed things up. I messed them up real bad'.

"Child, I looked into them sad eyes and I could see his soul was hurting. He said 'You know Myrt, I've done a lot of wrong in my time. I never thought about doing right. I never had it in me. But then she came along and she made me feel things I never did before. She made me want to be right. Not just for myself, but for her. My own momma, as much as she tried, she couldn't even make me do right. But Marietta was the only somebody that ever made me feel that way. I was gonna take her and move away and leave this madness all behind. I was gonna marry her, Myrt. I had finally found a woman that I loved and I mean loved for real. I wanted her to be my wife and make a life with her and my little girl. And I was all set to go. Now she's gone and I don't know where she is. Mrs. Cressford won't even let me see my baby. But I know why all this happened to me, Myrt. I know why all this happened. I never told God I was sorry about all the bad shit I've done. That's why God did this to me. He brought it all back on me. He knew just how to get to me, and He used Marietta to do it. Folks say it's never too late for God to forgive you, but they're wrong. A man can wait until it is too late. I know. I know it's too late, because I've been telling God I'm sorry and He's not listening. If He was, He would forgive me, and He would let her come back to me. He's not listening to me, Myrt. I said I was sorry but He won't send her back to me. Why won't God send her back'?

"L.C. tried to choke back his tears, but he couldn't fight it no more. He put his arms around me and laid his head on my shoulder and that man cried! This was the same man I had heard about whooping on prostitutes and beating up people who owed him money, but the man standing in front of me was somebody different. I felt so sorry for him. All I could do was hold him and let him get it out. I ain't never seen a nigga from the streets love nobody like your daddy loved your momma. Gangsters don't fall in love. Hell, most men go through life and don't never really love a woman. But L.C. loved Marietta. I never told nobody about L.C. breaking down like that, not even your Uncle Stanley. Didn't nobody else need to know. The only other person needed to know was your momma and she already did."

Aunt Myrtle and I both wipe away the wetness from our eyes. She gets up from the bed and goes over to the counter to pour herself a glass of Coca-Cola. She brings her drink with her and sits back down.

"'Bout a week after that," she continues, "I picked you up to take you to my house for a while to babysit, so Miss Aldania could go run her errands and do her volunteer work, and I stopped by the store so your daddy could see you for a little while. I told him I didn't think it was right for nobody to stand in the way of a father seeing his child. That helped him feel a little bit better. He was happy sitting up there, holding and kissing on you.

"That's when he told me what happened when your momma disappeared. He said when he went to the house to get you and Marietta to take y'all to St. Louis, Miss Aldania told him Marietta was gone, and she didn't know where she was. He said he knew your grandmamma was hiding something. Said he could just feel it 'cause she had this look on her face that wasn't right. L.C. told me he didn't believe in hitting no old lady, but that was one woman he wanted to hurt real bad, and I know what he meant! He left from there and went to his store to wait for Marietta to come by, and he waited all night long. He didn't even go to sleep. He called to the house the next morning and Miss Aldania told him Marietta still wasn't there and for him not to call never no more. He told Miss Aldania he would be coming for his baby soon, and she told him he wasn't your daddy. He said he was gonna take her to court. She said he didn't have a leg to stand on 'cause he wasn't married to Marietta.

"I took you to see him a few more times until your grandmother found out. I don't know who told it. She didn't come right out and say nothing when she first found out. She waited 'til I came over her house and she had me caught up in the corner. She told me as long as I live, I better not ever interfere with her family business again or she would cut my throat. I told her she better get to her knife before I could get to my gun, 'cause I would surely shoot her! I never did tell your Uncle Stanley about that, either.

"She stopped letting you go with me unless Stanley was with me. I told your daddy what happened, and he told me not to worry about it. Then I found out later he was stopping at your babysitter's house to see you when you went over there! You only went once a week when Miss Aldania had to work at the soup kitchen. The lady that watched you would call your daddy and tell him you was there. He would come over and spend his time with you at her house. He gave her a little money for letting him come over to see you. Then for some reason Miss Aldania changed your babysitter. She had the nerve to ask me if I knew about L.C. coming over to your babysitter's house to see you. I told her if I did, I wouldn't have told her! Miss Aldania found you a couple of different babysitters. She called herself keeping L.C. away from you but it didn't work. Your daddy always knew where you was and every one of them babysitters let him come see you when he wanted to.

"L.C. never did move to St. Louis. He had his brother sell the house and the store he had set up there. I suspect he wanted to stay here in town in case Marietta ever showed back up and he had to watch over you.

"After a while, L.C. went back to his old ways. He started pimping and running numbers again and eventually he went back to his wife. I'm sure he just did that 'cause of his lil' boys. He didn't come around as much to see you when you started getting old enough to talk. I think he was scared you might mention his name to your grandmother, and she would find out you had been around him. Then he might not ever get to see you at all.

I look into Aunt Myrtle's face as she smiles at me sympathetically.

"When your Uncle Wendell came home from the service, he did all this big talk about how when he saw L.C., he was gonna whoop his ass for doing your momma wrong. Wendell never did run into him and to tell the truth, I don't think Wendell ever did go looking for him 'cause if he wanted to, he could have found L.C. right at his store.

"Now, Stanley did run into L.C. when he came home. He never told me nothing about it, but L.C. did. L.C. and his boys was in the High Top Lounge one night and Stanley walked right up to him and punched him in the face! L.C.'s boys grabbed Stanley and dragged him outside. They was holding him and L.C. pulled out his gun and put it up to Stanley's head. L.C. asked him who he was and when Stanley told him, L.C. made his boys turn him loose and let him go on his way. L.C. told me if he had a sister like Marietta, he would have done the same thing."

"My father was a violent man," I say with a sigh.

"In some folks' eyes, he was. In other folks' eyes, your daddy did what he had to do. I saw him as a man with a troubled soul."

We pause for a moment and look at the television.

"L.C. used to buy toys for me to give to you," Aunt Myrtle continues. "He always gave you a baby doll for your birthday. He bought you stuff for Christmas and Easter and all your uniforms for school and coats. And all your things were expensive. He didn't give you no cheap made stuff. He would call me to come pick your clothes up from the store and I would tell everybody I bought 'em for you. I think Stanley knew better. He never said nothing, but I think he knew.

"One time your daddy came to see you when we was all at Miss Aldania's house one Sunday evening. He brought Russell and Wilson and some other boy I hadn't never seen with him. Now that time, I thought him and your Uncle Wendell was sure enough gonna fight. L.C. went on and left, but if he would have got a hold to Wendell he would have beat the hell out of him. I think that would have been a whooping that was meant for Miss Aldania, but Wendell would have been the one to get it!"

We both laugh at her remark.

I vaguely remembered the incident, but I never knew who the man was. I must have been about five or six years old when it happened. We all were sitting on the front porch, enjoying the nice summer breeze the way we usually did after we had dinner at Grandmother's house. My cousins and I were playing in the front yard when a big, shiny, white car pulled up in front of our house. I could see four men inside the car. My grandmother must have known right away who they were because before the men got out of the car, Grandmother told everyone except Uncle Wendell to go into the house. I remember Uncle Stanley wasn't there. Aunt Myrtle and Aunt Josette and my cousins went inside, but I wanted to know what was going on with this handsome man in the dark suit and tie, with the dark hat and shiny shoes, standing at the fence, trying to open the gate. I saw Uncle Wendell step off the porch and walk to the gate with Grandmother right behind him. She made her way in front of Uncle Wendell and put her hand on the gate and held it closed. With all of the commotion going on, no one noticed I had stayed outside and was stooping down beside a bush inside the yard, close enough to hear and see everything.

"What are you doing at my house?" Grandmother asked L.C. "I done told you don't come around here anymore!"

Seeing that neither of them was going to let him in, L.C. moved his hand from the gate.

"I came to see my daughter," L.C. said.

"You don't have a daughter over here," Grandmother insisted.

L.C. stood there looking at Grandmother like he wanted to wring her neck. Then I saw the expression change on his face, as if he thought he could use a different approach and appease Grandmother.

"Look, Mrs. Cressford," he said, "I don't understand why we keep going through this. I'm not trying to cause any trouble. I just want to see my baby girl."

"I told you she ain't yours," Grandmother said. "I told you Marietta had another fellow she was seeing and he's that child's father. That ain't your baby!"

"Marietta was my woman and I know she was never with anybody else. That baby is mine. Besides, she looks just like me. I know who my children are."

"Well, you wrong about this one! You might have babies all over town, but this one ain't yours!"

"I don't have babies all over town!" he said, getting mad.

"Oh, I know you have two children outside your marriage."

"Mrs. Cressford, whatever my business is outside of my marriage, it's mine, not yours. That little girl is my daughter, not yours. I'm her father. I take care of my children."

"Don't stand here trying to act all noble with me. If you had any decency about you, you wouldn't be in the business you in. I know all about you selling liquor and letting folks gamble in your basement at all hours of the night. And I know you pay off the police to keep them from shutting you down. But your day is coming."

L.C. paused again and looked at Grandmother intensely.

"You need to stop putting your nose where it doesn't belong," he told her. "If you weren't my child's grandmother..."

"What?" she said, cutting him off, putting her hands on her hips.

He stepped closer to the fence.

"I might have you put out of your misery!" L.C. said to her.

"You better watch your mouth, man!" Uncle Wendell said angrily.

"No, your momma better watch her mouth!" one of the men who was with L.C. told Uncle Wendell.

"Step back, man," L.C. told him. "It's alright."

"Yeah, you better step back," Uncle Wendell said.

"Look Mrs. Cressford," L.C. said as he turned his attention back to Grandmother, "you know as well as I do that I'm that child's father and I have a right to see her, regardless of what you think of me."

"You don't have a right to nothing! You've already caused enough confusion in my house, making my daughter run off with you twice. You made her lose what decency she had. You had her doing all kinds of sinful things with you and you messed up her mind! Then you sat up there and let her get stabbed by your wife. That's why she ran away. She wanted to get away from you! You ain't nothing but trouble!"

"You're a damned liar!" he told Grandmother.

"Look nigga," Uncle Wendell said, bristling up. "You don't call my mother no liar."

"She is a liar," he said to Uncle Wendell, giving him a daring look, waiting for him to do something. L.C. looked back at Grandmother. "You don't even know your own daughter. If you did, you would know she's a sweet, respectable woman. Her only fault is she loves me. You need to stay out of our way and let us make things right."

Grandmother became outraged.

"How you gonna make things right?!" she hollered. "You can't leave one wife and make things right by taking on another while the first one is still alive! The both of you are going straight to hell for going against God, committing adultery! So boy, you tell me how you gonna make things right?! I'm telling you for the last time get away from my property and don't come around here no more! You ain't seeing my grandchild!"

"Oh, I'm going to see my little girl," he told her with fierce eyes. "You won't be around forever."

"She ain't yours!" Grandmother shouted. "I don't care who you think you are. You don't scare me!"

L.C. looked at Grandmother with disgust, but didn't say anything else. He turned to walk to his car, then stopped all of a sudden and turned back and walked up to Grandmother, pulling out a fold of money from his pants pocket. I saw him peel off several bills. He held them out for Grandmother to take.

"That's for my daughter," he told her. "And I will be back to give you some more to take care of her expenses. Like I said, I take care of my children."

That really hit a nerve with Grandmother. She was so mad that she snatched the money from him, balled it up and threw it at him, hitting him in the face.

"You keep your money!" she hissed at him. "We don't take dirty money from niggas like you! That money got the devil's blood on it, and I ain't never gonna have nothing to do with you or your money! Now you get on from around here, and don't you ever come back 'cause if you do I'm calling the police!"

Before L.C. turned to walk away, he smiled, grimacing at Grandmother and said, "If you hear from Marietta tell her I love her, and I'm still waiting for her."

He chuckled as he walked away. As I watched him and his companions get into the white car and drive away with Uncle Wendell and Grandmother standing at the gate fuming, I wondered who he was talking about. Now I know.

"I remember that," I tell Aunt Myrtle as I come back from thinking of the incident.

"You do?" she says with surprise in her voice.

"Yes, I remember."

I go through the photos again and as I study the one of my father, standing there looking dapper and confident, seeing the resemblance of myself in him, I'm hit with a revelation. I did know him!

"Aunt Myrtle," I gasp, "I know him! I used to see him in a lot of different places!"

"I know," she says smiling. "I figured it would come to you once you saw those pictures."

I had seen my father around our neighborhood many times after the incident at Grandmother's house. His handsome features and style of dress weren't the only things that brought my attention to him when I was a child. He had an aura about him that I didn't forget. When I used to see him around town, I felt like there was something familiar about him, like there was a reason for him to be around me, but I never knew what it was.

He had come to my elementary school a few times and I saw him on the playground talking with one of the nuns and in the hallway talking with Father Munson. I remember seeing him standing against the back wall of the gym when I was in the third grade and me and the other kids from my class sang carols at our Christmas program. He didn't sit in the seats like the other guests. He came in late and left right after the performance was over. I assumed he was one of my class mates father or some other relative. And those weren't the only times I remember seeing him.

There were a few times, when Grandmother was out of town on her excursions with the Violets or with her church, that Aunt Josette let me walk to the store with my friend, Virginia and her older sister. One particular time, we were waiting our turn in line at Joe's Groceries and I saw my father standing near the counter talking with the store owner. I thought nothing of it that day when he offered to pay for me and my friend's candy and told us to get a few more pieces. We were so excited about getting extra candy and thanked him. Before I left the store, I turned around to wave good-bye to him and I gave him the biggest, most grateful smile I could muster. At that moment I had a feeling like the two of us had some sort of bond, some connection. And now, remembering the smile he gave me back, knowing who he was makes my heart ache. If only I would have known who he was back then.

"He never told me who he was," I say sadly. "He was always somewhere nearby and he never let me know who he was."

"I'm sure he wanted to tell you but at that time he knew he couldn't."

I sigh as I think again about the lie I was told about my parents.

"I kind of figured my mother and Charles Smith weren't married when I was born," I say. "It lists father 'unknown' on my birth certificate, but I thought they must have gotten married shortly after I was born and they were going to change my last name to Smith but didn't get the chance to before they died. All these years I thought my father was somebody named Charles. I even asked about his side of the family and was told no one knew anything about them except that they lived somewhere in California. And now I find out it was all a lie. Aunt Myrtle, why didn't you all tell me about this from the beginning? Why did I have to find out like this?"

"I told all of them before L.C. died that they needed to let you know," she says looking sympathetically. "I told them you would find out eventually. But your grandmother said you had no need to know. She said she wanted to bring you up like you was the child of decent, married folks and we better not ever tell you nothing otherwise. I told her she was wrong, but she didn't care what I had to say. I kept my mouth shut 'cause I felt it wasn't my place to tell you."

"I wish Grandmother would have just let my father take me to live with him," I say bitterly. "I would have been better off with my father. He tried to come and get me, and she wouldn't even let my own father have me."

"Baby, as much as your daddy wanted you to be with him he couldn't take you and he knew it. For one, your daddy worked all day and night and he was out there in the streets. And two, his wife wouldn't have let him bring you to live with them. He couldn't let you know who he was. You was his lil' girl, and he didn't want you caught up in no grown folks mess. He ain't want you wondering about where your momma was or that he was married to somebody else and him having to tell you why you couldn't go stay with him. I'm sure he was gonna tell you about it one day when you was a grown woman. Your daddy was a smart man. He knew that you being with your grandmomma was the best place for you to be. You know he thought the world of your momma, and he wanted you to turn out to be just as sweet and smart as she was. And look at who had the hand in raising your momma."

I love the way my aunt has of explaining and justifying things to me. She can find a good outcome, a reason for anything, whether it was right or wrong, and it always made it a little easier for me to handle.

"I guess you're right," I say as I rethink the situation.

Aunt Myrtle repositions herself on the bed and looks at me with concern. I can tell she has something else to tell me, and she's wondering how I will take it.

"You was nine years old when your daddy died," Aunt Myrtle says. "L.C. was closing up his basement at the store after one of his card parties, and he was by himself. Russell and Wilson was usually with him but not this particular night. Somebody came up behind him and shot him in the back of the head. They took all of his money and left him on them basement steps to die. You know, the talk around town was that Miss Aldania had somebody do it."

I look at Aunt Myrtle with surprise.

"Do you think she would do that?" I ask.

"Naw, I don't think she would," Aunt Myrtle says. "She wouldn't wanna go to hell for having somebody killed."

I take in a deep breath and let it out slowly.

"You know, Aunt Myrtle, finding out all of this has just been too much for me."

"Aw, sugar. You have been hit with a lot of things all at one time. But we feeling it too, baby. We all feeling it with you."

"But not like me. All my life, I thought I came from respectable parents. And now I find my father was married to somebody else when I was conceived. My mother should have known better than to have an affair with somebody else's husband."

"Alright, girl," Aunt Myrtle says sternly. "You ought not to be throwing no stones 'cause seems like I remember somebody else being with a married man once or twice."

"Yeah, but I didn't have a baby with him," I tell Aunt Myrtle, trying to justify my actions. "Having an affair is one thing, but having a baby is something else. People can ride out affairs. But having a baby is a constant reminder of somebody cheating on you. That's why Grandmother hated me so much. She hated my father for getting my mother pregnant."

"Aw, come on Francine."

"But that's the truth. I was the shameful reminder of what my mother did, and she took it out on me."

"I agree she didn't like your daddy and she was mad at your mother, but she didn't take nothing out on you. Miss Dania was just a hard woman."

"She wasn't mean and hard to her friends."

"Yeah, I know. But honey, regardless of how she acted, you have to know that in her heart, she loved you. She didn't show love like most folk do, but I'm sure she loved you. She did raise you and made sure you had everything you needed. I know some folks that have put they children and they grandchildren out in the street."

"There's a difference between caring about people and responsibility. Grandmother was very responsible, so taking care of me was something she felt like she had to do. And knowing what I do about my parents, I think Grandmother had my mother committed to keep her away from my father. The more I think about her, the more I hate her!"

"You stop talking like that, Francine."

"Well, she hated me!"

"I don't think she hated you. You were her grandchild."

"Me being her grandchild didn't make a bit of difference to her. My mother was her child. She was her flesh and blood more than I was, and look what she did to her."

"Listen child, you stop feeling like that. Miss Aldania did love you, and one day you'll realize it."

She gives me a kiss on my cheek before she stands up from my bed.

"I'm gonna go on to my room and take myself to bed," she says.

She walks over to the door leading to her room. "You try to get you some sleep, and I'll see you in the morning."

"I'll try," I tell her as I let out a heavy sigh.

"Good night, baby."

"Good night. And thank you for being here for me."

She looks back at me without saying a word and gives me that reassuring smile she's given me since I was a child, letting me know its all okay, and then she disappears through the door.

I lay in the bed, tossing and turning, wondering about my mother and father. How could they have done something like that? How could my mother have a baby with another woman's husband? They both were irresponsible. They should have thought about what they were doing. They should have thought about how this would have affected my life. They should have known that people would talk about me. Everybody in Westfield probably knew about it. I bet when I was growing up, people knew my secret and made fun of me behind my back. My mother and father were wrong. They were so wrong.

My thoughts shift gears as I picture my mother and father sitting somewhere on a blanket by a lake on a bright, sunny day, cuddled up, smiling at one another lovingly, not caring what the rest of the world thought of them.

Uncle Stanley, Aunt Myrtle and I get to the nursing home as soon as it opens the next morning. We go to the same desk as I did the night before to tell my story to the day shift receptionist. She refers me to the nursing home social worker, Mrs. Hill, and I explain my situation once again. We try to convince her that we are in fact relatives of Marietta Cressford. She assures us she will try to do all she can to help us with whatever legalities we need, and then she directs us to wait in a large room off one of the hallways while she goes to get the staff psychiatrist.

We sit silently, anxiously waiting until Mrs. Hill reappears with a short, stocky white man. He doesn't look like the typical psychiatrist with the beard and glasses. He looks more like the guy who used to play Cannon on the TV series. They come over to where we are.

Mrs. Hill introduces the three of us to Dr. Albertson and before she leaves, she gives us her card so we can call her if we have questions.

"We can talk over here," Dr. Albertson tells us, pointing to an area in an alcove off of the waiting room. We follow him over to a group of chairs and we each take a seat.

"The reason we're here," I say, "is because I just found out my mother, Marietta Cressford, is still alive and has been here for some years."

"Really?" he says as he raises his brow. "How did you come to this conclusion?"

"My grandmother died recently and I found this paper in her safety deposit box at the bank," I say, pulling the paper from my purse and handing it to him to read. "I have reason to believe my grandmother put my mother away and she wasn't ill."

Dr. Albertson stops reading and looks at me.

"And why do you think that?" he says shifting in his seat.

"Because that's my mother sitting back there in that room," I say adamantly. "My grandmother lied and said that my mother just left home without me and never returned, which is something that she wouldn't do. That letter says my grandmother committed Marietta Cressford to Morton mental institution back in the fifties on the same day my mother supposedly disappeared. I know that lady is my mother."

"And furthermore," Aunt Myrtle chimes in, "Marietta wasn't crazy, so Miss Aldania had her committed for nothing."

"Well it's highly unlikely that Ms. Cressford would have been committed without a full psychological evaluation and even less likely that she wouldn't have stayed if her condition did not warrant it."

"Excuse me doctor," Aunt Myrtle says. "Marietta is my sister-in-law and we were very close before all of this happened. She never acted like she had no mental illness the last time I talked to her. I can tell you she wasn't crazy."

"I'm Marietta's brother," Uncle Stanley says. "I was away in the service when all of this happened, but I kept in contact with my family pretty regularly. When I called home, nobody ever said Marietta was acting peculiar. That's why we find it hard to believe she was in an insane asylum, 'cause she didn't have a legitimate reason to be in one."

Dr. Albertson looks at the three of us for a moment. He's probably wondering what our mental conditions are.

"This is very interesting," he says.

"Do you still have her records from when she was first at Morton?" I ask.

"No, we wouldn't have those records here at the nursing home. Ms. Cressford was institutionalized many years ago. Her records from Morton are in storage. When residents are transferred to us, we get a summary of their recent stay and their current conditions. We typically don't read over all of the records of a patient who has been institutionalized for decades."

"What did her summary say?" I ask.

"I can't tell you much about her until we can confirm your relationship to her. As soon as we can establish kinship, I can go into further detail about her medical and mental condition."

"Well tell me this, doctor," Uncle Stanley asks. "How did she end up here in the nursing home? Did Morton send her here because she was cured? I mean, if she's not there anymore, then she must not be crazy."

"When Morton closed, they sent some of their patients to other mental health facilities and then there were some patients whose conditions were mild and controllable with medication, and they went to group homes where they're being taught to care for themselves with supervision. Some of the elderly patients, such as Marietta, were stable enough mentally to be cared for in nursing homes like this one."

"So she doesn't have a mental illness anymore?" I ask.

"Again, I'm not at liberty to discuss Marietta's condition," he says.

"Well, what do we need to do now that we know Marietta is alive?" Aunt Myrtle asks.

"It depends," Dr. Albertson says. "What do you want to do?"

Uncle Stanley and Aunt Myrtle turn their attention to me. I hadn't thought any more about my plans after I left the nursing home last night. What was I going to do? I look helplessly at Uncle Stanley for guidance. He puts his hand onto mine.

"Whatever you decide to do me and your Aunt Myrtle will be there to help you," Uncle Stanley tells me.

"Do you want to move Marietta back home with you?" Aunt Myrtle asks.

"I'm not sure," I say. "I don't know if I should take her home to live with me or if I should take her to Westfield."

"You don't have to decide right this very minute," Dr. Albertson says.

He continues talking with us as he explains the process of how I can petition the court to establish next of kinship and what I need to do to have my mother transferred to a nursing home near me. He tells us that none of this will be easy, and he suggests we all might need to speak to a counselor as a family. Dr. Albertson tells us to discuss things amongst ourselves, and he gives us his card with his contact information in case we need his help. We thank him for his time and as we are about to leave, Uncle Stanley has a question.

"Excuse me sir," Uncle Stanley says. "Is there any way I can go back and see my sister just for a few minutes? I know Francine knows it's her mother, but I want to see her for myself."

Dr. Albertson pauses for a minute, as he looks into our solemn faces.

"Yes," he says sympathetically. "I'll take you back, but only for a few minutes. I'm not sure how Ms. Cressford will react. She's been on medication for almost forty years and she no longer speaks or interacts with anyone. You can only stay back there for a few minutes. Is that understood?"

"We understand," Aunt Myrtle tells him.

Dr. Albertson directs us down the same hallway that I traveled the previous night. He opens the door and we step into my mother's s room. This time she is sitting in her chair, facing the door. She doesn't move or look in our direction.

"Stanley," my mother says, barely audible.

We're all shocked as we look from one to the other, including Dr. Albertson.

Uncle Stanley is speechless. I can see from the expression on his face that he can't believe it's her. Aunt Myrtle lets out a whimper and starts to cry.

Uncle Stanley walks over to his sister and kneels down in front of her, taking her into his arms. She doesn't say another word and she doesn't return his hold. Uncle Stanley sobs, as he rocks his sister back and forth. Aunt Myrtle and I wipe the tears that are streaming down our faces. And as I stand there watching my mother and her brother, I wonder what thoughts, if it were at all possible for her to have any, are going through her mind.

Part II

Marietta

———◦○◦———

I can't stay in this room anymore. How long have I been here? I don't know and it doesn't matter. I have to leave. If I don't get out of this room, I'm going to suffocate. I don't care if I have to go back into that other room with all those crazy people. I can't stay in here alone. I can't take this.

I go over to the door and try to open it, but it's locked. I knock on it and say 'hello', waiting for someone walking by to say something, but I don't hear any footsteps. I bang on the door, hoping someone nearby will hear me. I say 'hello', louder. Again, no one answers. Am I the only one on this floor? I start to panic.

"Open this door!" I scream over and over again.

Still no one comes.

"Let me out of here," I try to cry, but my voice is strained from all the yelling. I stand with my forehead against the door, crying, trying to muster the strength to bang on the door again.

I go over to the bed and lay down on my side, pulling my knees into my chest.

"Mother, why have you put me here?" I say aloud. "What have you done to me? Somebody, get me out of here!"

I get up off my bed and stand in the middle of the room. Somehow, I find the strength to scream uncontrollably. I'm hollering at the top of my lungs, but I can hear the lock click. The door opens and two men dressed in white walk in.

"Alright lady!" one of them says. "You have to stop that screaming."

I try to but I can't. They both step towards me and one of them grabs my arm. I yank away and back up against the wall.

"We don't want to hurt you," he tells me. "We just want you to stop screaming like that. You're scaring the other patients."

I press my back against the wall, hoping it will open and swallow me so these men can't get me. They both grab me and I try my best to break away, but they're too strong. One manages to get up under my arms and hold me as the other scoops up my legs. I still scream as they rush me out of that room and run me down the hall into another room. They take me over to an examination table and slam me down onto it. I scratch their arms and kick at them with my feet. One of them hits me in the face with his fist. I stop screaming. My face aches and I wince. I lay there, moaning, as a leather strap is tightened across my chest and my arms and legs are bond to the table. I hear a new voice in the room and I look up to see who it is. The doctor leans over me.

"What seems to be the trouble, Marietta?" he asks me. "Why are you screaming?"

"Because I want to go home!" I cry. "I don't need to be here! There's nothing wrong with me. I keep telling you I'm not crazy. You've made a big mistake. Why don't you listen to me?"

"Your mother brought you here because there is something wrong with your mind," the doctor says.

"There is nothing wrong with my mind! My mother is lying. She gave me some medicine and it made me sleepy. She did this to me!"

I get madder and madder as I try to break free and get up off the table.

"Get these damn straps off of me!" I scream.

A nurse has come into the room and is standing next to the doctor with a very long needle.

"Don't you stick me with that!" I say to her.

I wrestle with my restraints and start to scream again.

"Dr. Leathers, please don't stick me with that," I say, trying to sound calm. "I promise I'll stop screaming."

He ignores my pleas and I feel the sting of the needle in my arm and soon I feel the blackness creep into my head.

"Hello Marietta," Dr. Leathers says as he walks into his office and sits at his desk.

I don't reply. I just sit there on the opposite side of him watching as he opens a dark brown folder and takes out a piece of paper. He starts to write on it, not looking at me while he talks.

"How are you feeling today?"

"When am I going home?" I ask instead of answering his question.

"As soon as you are well enough."

"There's nothing wrong with me," I tell him contemptuously, irritated by his response.

Dr. Leathers stops writing and looks at me over the top of his glasses.

"There is something wrong with you and the sooner you accept it the sooner we can get you well." He looks back at his paper and starts to write again.

"Does your shoulder still hurt?" he asks.

"No it doesn't hurt. It's fine. I told you the cut wasn't that deep."

"Do you know what day it is?

"Why do you keep asking me that same question? No I don't know what day it is. You keep giving me that medicine that knocks me out. How am I supposed to keep up with what day it is? What day is it?"

"Today is the 27th day of July, 1956."

"July 27th?" I say blinking several times. "My baby's birthday was the 17th. She just turned a year old. You made me miss my baby's birthday! Call my fiancé and tell him where I am so he can come and get me!"

"You don't have a fiancé," Dr. Leathers says looking at me over his glasses again. "Your mother told me the man you've been having an affair with is married. Therefore he can't be your fiancé."

"He is my fiancé! And we are going to get married as soon as I get out of here. My mother put me in here to keep me away from him. But she can't stop us from being together. Why don't you just sign the papers and let me go home?"

"Your mother brought you here because you have an illness. She explained to me that your behavior has changed drastically since you've been with this man you call your fiancé. She told me everything, how you've been behaving out of character, the violent temper, the social misconduct. I would agree with her that it's all due to your relationship with this man."

"She's lying."

"I don't think she is. You were under the influence of an unknown substance when you were admitted."

"She gave it to me! She drugged me and brought me here to make you think something was wrong with me!"

Dr. Leathers looks at me with doubt. I look back at him with resentment and anger.

"You know there's nothing wrong with me," I say leaning forward in my chair. "I'm just as sane as you and you know it. You're keeping me her because my mother is paying you to do so."

Dr. Leather's face starts to turn red. I ready myself for him to holler at me about my remarks.

"Young lady, I'm a medical professional," he says in a controlled voice. "I don't accept money to keep patients in my institution against their will. This is a hospital, not a jail!"

"Then you're a dumb doctor because I'm not sick!" I yell at him.

"You are," he says calmly.

I get up from my chair.

"Send me home right now!" I scream banging my fist on his desk.

"Orderly!" Dr. Leathers yells, standing up from his desk.

One of the orderlies who restrained me before comes into the office and grabs me from behind. I don't try to fight him.

"Take her back to her room," Dr. Leathers instructs him.

When he sees that I'm not going to resist, the orderly takes my arm and leads me back to my room. He takes one last look at me, as if to make sure I'm not going to do anything rash before he leaves me there alone and locks the door behind him.

I lay on my bed, with my knees curled up to my chest, thinking about my baby and her father. I just know he's sick with worry, wondering where I am. Mother must not have told him where I am. That's the only reason he hasn't come for me.

But he'll find me. I just have to wait. He will find me. He won't let me rot in here. He loves me.

I start to feel sick to my stomach when I think that he won't come. He can't come because he doesn't know where to find me. What's going to happen to my little girl? I jump up from my bed and start to pace around my small room.

God, please let him find me! I've got to get back home. He can't leave town without me! Help me please!

I drop to my knees and scream as loudly as I can for someone to let me out of here. I get up from the floor and run to the door, pounding on it as hard as I can.

"Mother I hate you!" I scream "I hate you!"

The same man that brought me to my room from Dr. Leather's office unlocks my door and comes in.

"Shut up!" he hollers at me.

I try to be quiet but I can't. I can't stop screaming. He grabs me from behind again and wrestles me onto the bed until I'm on my stomach. He holds my hands together behind my back for a long time. I don't hear or see anyone else in the room with us, but I feel something sharp sink into my arm and after a few minutes I see blackness.

I open my eyes to the annoyance of bright sunlight shining in my face. I look around and find I'm still in my room. What did they do to me? I don't feel right. My mouth is as dry as cotton and I start to feel queasy in my stomach as I take in deep breaths.

I hear movement in my room and look up to see a woman with her back to me, bent over the dresser in the corner, looking through the drawers.

"Who are you?" I whisper groggily.

She doesn't answer.

"Do you hear me?" I say louder. "Who are you?"

She rises up from the dresser and turns to face me.

"Good morning, Miss Cressford. My name is Susie and I'm gonna be your nurse aide."

Susie is a tall, thick Black woman with big arms and legs.

I slowly struggle to sit myself up on the side of the bed.

"You ready to go eat your breakfast?" she says cheerfully.

"Do I have to go out there and eat with those other patients?"

"Yes, you do."

"Then I won't be eating breakfast."

She turns back to the dresser and rummages through the drawer again.

"Well then I'm going to take you down to the bathroom so you can get yourself washed up," she tells me. "You've been asleep for a couple of days and…"

"A couple of days?!" I interrupt. "I've been knocked out for some days?"

"You was havin' a rough time."

"You would too if you were locked up in here for no reason."

"Miss Cressford, people don't get put in the hospital if there ain't no reason for it."

"Well I am. My mother lied to the doctor."

"Well, when the doctor looked you over, he must've found out somethin' wasn't right, or else he wouldn't have kept you here. He wouldn't be givin' you medicine for nothin'."

"He would if my mother was paying him to keep me in here."

Susie turns back to me.

"Now don't you say things like that. People don't get put in the hospital for nothin' and hospitals don't keep nobody that ain't sick."

"Do I sound like I'm crazy to you?"

Susie stares at me for a moment.

"Not really, but I ain't no doctor, so I can't say for sure."

"A crazy person wouldn't be able to have a normal conversation with you, would they?"

"Some people's mind is worse than others. You might be at the beginnin' stages of bein' crazy."

I look at her in disbelief. What sense does that make? I'm in the beginning stages of being crazy. She's irritating me.

"You sound stupid as hell," I say to her.

Susie's expression changes.

"Who you callin' stupid?" she asks looking at me with insulted eyes.

"You and I are the only ones in here talking, so I must be talking to you."

Susie walks over to where I'm sitting. She stands right in front of me, placing her fists into her hips. She narrows her eyes and tightens her lips.

"Looka here, gal!" she says gritting her teeth. "I don't know who you think you are, but don't you ever call me stupid! You don't talk down to me. You ain't no better than me or nobody else."

She looks me up and down.

"I know your type of nigga, gal. I saw your expensive clothes and shoes when your momma brought you in here. I can tell you come from one of them families where y'all ain't got to want for nothin'. You think you're special. But I heard what happened to you. You got just what you deserved. And naw, I don't think you crazy. I think you a damn fool! You ended up in here while that man you was chasin' done gone on about his business! You in here locked up and you might not even be crazy. But your momma knew what she was doin'. She put your hot tail on ice until you get that man outta your system and cut out all this foolishness. You better be glad you got a momma like that. And when you do get outta here, you need to thank her for savin' your soul. Now you might be heartbroken or grief stricken or guilty hearted or whatever, but I'ma tell you this. Don't you ever talk to me like I'm beneath you. I don't care how special you think you are, 'cause honey, I will kick your ass and think nothin' of it! So you better go wash your nasty face and brush your stinkin' mouth and get ready to eat your breakfast."

How dare she talk to me like that!

I sit there shocked, not knowing how to respond. I don't want to say anything more out of fear that she might beat me up. She wouldn't get in trouble for it if she did. She could lie and say I tried to attack her and they would believe her.

"I didn't say I was better than you or anybody else," I say solemnly.

"You don't have to. It's that 'Miss Prissy' attitude you got."

"There is nothing wrong with my attitude. You don't know me, so don't go judging me by what I wore in here or how much money you think I have. Just because I have nice things and I was raised to speak well doesn't mean I think I'm better than other people."

"Well you need to stop talkin' down to folks! You got a smart-aleck answer for everything anybody says to you. You been actin' like you from high society since you got here. The other nurse got her feelins hurt, but I'm here to tell you, you ain't gonna hurt mine. I could care less. The only reason I come in here is 'cause I'm doin' my job. Now the sooner you know you got a bad mind, the sooner you can take the help these doctors is givin' you and get better so you can go home."

Big tears spill from my eyes.

"You can stop that damn cryin'," Susie says as she looks at me unsympathetically, "'cause I don't feel sorry for you, either. Now let's go get you clean."

I've lost track of time, but I think I'm well into my second month of being in this place. This room is cold. I'm sad. I'm scared. No one has come to visit. They won't let me write any letters and I haven't gotten any. I know my baby wants me. I know her daddy has been trying to find me. Mother is keeping them from me. But he will find me. She can't keep me here forever. She wouldn't keep me here forever. Would she?

Panic seizes my mind and I start to feel scared and sick. I can't breathe. Why can't I breathe? I stand up and try to get to the door to bang on it for someone to help me. I hold my hand to my chest. I cry and try to scream, but I can't. I keep gasping for air.

God, give me some air so I can breathe!

"Help me," I whisper, before I fall onto the floor and black out.

Again I wake up to sunlight in my eyes. Why do they keep opening those damn curtains and let all that light hit me in the face?

I don't know what day it is and I don't know how long I've been here. The medicine they're giving me is making me weak.

"Time to rise and shine lady," Susie says, pulling underclothes from a drawer.

I don't respond. I lay there, closing my eyes again.

"Can you come back later?" I ask her. "I need to sleep some more. And please, close those curtains."

"You can go back to sleep after you eat your breakfast and wash up, so come on and pull yourself out of that bed and let's get goin'."

I pull the covers over my head and roll over. Susie snatches them off. I pull them back on again.

"Come on, lady. You ain't the only one I got to get clean this mornin' and I'm on a schedule, so get up."

I don't move.

"Do you hear me talkin' to you?" she hollers at me.

Still, I don't respond. I hear her walk across the floor and go out of the door. A few minutes later, I feel strong hands snatch the covers off of me and pull me out of my bed.

I immediately start to kick and scratch. The same two men who restrained me the last time wrestle with me again.

"Get your damn hands off of me!" I scream as I'm being carried down the hall to the bathroom. "Put me down! Put me down!"

With clothes and all I'm dropped into a bathtub filled with water. I stop screaming and fighting and sit there.

"Now let's get you washed up," Susie says, pulling the gown over my head.

I'm mad as hell and I want to pull all her hair out of her head, but I resist my impulses. Fighting is doing me no good in this place. I sit in the tub, listless, as Susie finishes my bath.

When I get my clothes on, Susie takes me to the dining hall with the rest of the patients. I don't like eating with them. Some of them spit their food out onto the table. Some of them smear it on themselves. Some try to take other people's food. I sit at the table, but I don't eat.

After breakfast, they take us all to the Great Room to sit and listen to the radio and watch the television. Some of them go out through the solarium into the yard. I don't want to go outside because most of them are out there. I sit at a table by myself, not doing anything. I don't want to read. I don't want to talk. I want to go home.

Maggie Mae comes over to my table and sits down.

"Hi, Marietta," she says smiling.

"Hi, Maggie," I say. I speak to her because she's the only patient who seems to be a little sane.

I can tell Maggie used to be a pretty girl. She's a small boned, almost tiny woman, with long, sandy-colored hair she keeps braided in one thick plait that hangs down her back. The nurses take turns keeping her hair groomed and always talk about how beautiful her hair is. Her light skin, once smooth and clear, is now blotchy and uneven. The circles under her eyes look like they've been made from worry and fright. Her teeth are slightly bucked and she has a gap in the front.

Maggie's old man, Jack, is the reason she is in here. He beat her one time too many and damaged her brain. The right side of her mouth twitches and when she's sitting, her right leg is constantly rocking from side to side while her foot is firmly planted on the floor.

At times, I'm not sure if Maggie is crazy or just pretending to be. One minute she talks with as much sense as the doctors and nurses, and the next she's wailing like a mad woman about her head hurting. Then all of a sudden she stops like nothing ever happened, finishing the conversation she was having with you as if she never missed a beat.

"You thinkin' about your little girl's daddy again?" Maggie asks me.

"No," I say.

"What's his name?"

"I'm not telling you again."

"Does he ever come to see you?"

"He doesn't know where I am."

"Why ain't you told him to come see you?"

"I can't use the telephone Maggie."

"Why he run out on you?"

"Maggie, stop asking me questions."

"Why? You get sad when you think about him? I get sad when I think about Jack. He ain't treat me right. He made me do some awful bad things. Did your man make you do bad things?"

I don't answer her.

"Was he good to you?" she asks me.

"Yes, he was."

"Why you leave him? Was he messing around on you?"

I close my eyes, hoping she will disappear. I don't want to listen to her anymore. I don't want her to ask me any more questions about my life with the man that I had grown to have unconditional love. I don't want to feel the pain of not being with him. I don't want to think about that day, the day that sealed my fate, when he first looked at me and made up his mind that one day I would be his. I don't want to think about any of it. But I can't help but think about it. I'll always think back about us...

I get off the bus at the stop several blocks up the street from Boone's Clothing Store. I usually wait until the weekend to shop, but all the stockings I have at home have runs in them and I need a pair for work tomorrow. I'll have to hurry to get there before they close within the next twenty minutes.

Boone's was one of the many Negro-owned stores that sprang up in the business district of our neighborhood. All the Negroes from our side of town used to go downtown to shop for clothes and shoes, but when Boone's opened everyone took their business there.

Mr. L.C. Boone is the sole proprietor. He's a very handsome, sharp fellow who dresses in good taste and style. His face is clean shaven and his skin is nice and smooth and has a beautiful color, sort of a creamy, reddish brown. He has black, wavy hair and he keeps it cut perfectly. Mr. Boone always wears a suit and tie and any shoes he wears are so shiny that you can see yourself in their reflection. And if you happen to catch a whiff of his cologne as he breezes by you, you know it's not cheap.

I'm not the type of girl who is attracted to older men, but I think a lot of Mr. Boone. He's such a nice guy. He's a respectable businessman, and what I like most about him is he's so suave, so debonair.

I rarely see Mr. Boone out in the neighborhood. I mostly see him when I go with Mother to shop at Boone's. He walks through the store, putting boxes on shelves or hanging clothes on the racks, greeting his shoppers with nods and 'how you doin'', but he never waits on the customers. He has a few sales clerks who work for him. Miss Ella works on the ladies' side of the store the majority of the time, and Mr. Woods works on the men's side.

I notice how beautiful the spring evening is as I hurry along. I love spring. April is my favorite month because it's the time of year when the trees and flowers start to bloom and the air is filled with their smells. The sky looks so vibrant in its blue and the clouds so young and fresh.

I also love spring because it's a time for lovers. I'm a romantic at heart. I love reading about the chemistry of romance between a man and a woman. I like fantasizing about the tenderness of romantic kisses and caresses and how love makes you feel. And although I haven't yet experienced this wonder, I know from all the romantic movies I've seen and books I've read, it is something I want to happen to me. I just know my day will come soon. I'm going to fall in love with a man who will cherish me and care for me and sweep me off my feet. I want a man who comes to realize he can't live without me. I want him to love me and only me. And one day I'll find a man like that and we'll get married and I'll have his babies and we'll live happily ever after and oh, how I anticipate that day.

When I get inside Boone's, I walk towards the back counter on the ladies' side where the personal items are kept. As I approach the back counter, I hear Mr. Boone counting back change to the customer standing near the cash register. Miss Ella and Mr. Woods must have left early for the day, because one of them always closed the store. I wait my turn at the glass jewelry counter, bending over to look at the new necklaces and earrings that have been added since the last time I was here. I can hear Mr. Boone bag his customer's items and thank him for his business. As the customer walks down the aisle and out the door, I hear Mr. Boone's footsteps on the hardwood floor as he walks around to the clerk side of the counter in front of me.

"Hello. What can I help you with?" he says with his velvety, smooth deep voice.

"Hi, Mr. Boone," I say, looking up from the counter. "I need a pair of stockings."

And when his eyes meet mine, an indescribable feeling comes over me. He has a stunned look on his face, like this was the first time he's ever seen me and I don't know what to make of his expression. He doesn't move for a very long time. He just stands there, looking at me.

I start to feel nervous, so I look away.

"I don't mean to stare, but you are simply gorgeous," he says.

"Thank you, sir," I say shyly, still looking elsewhere.

"Are you from around here? You look familiar."

I become annoyed that he doesn't recognize me as a loyal customer. As many times as I've been in here, he should remember me. He says hello to me every time I've come in here with Mother.

"Yes, sir," I say, looking back at him. "My family shops here all the time."

"What's your name?" he asks me.

"Marietta Cressford."

"Cressford?"

He mumbles the name a few times until it comes to him.

"Are you Mrs. Cressford's daughter?" he says with surprise.

"Yes, sir."

"Yeah, I remember you. You were a young, little lady last time I remember seeing you."

I feel better now that he remembers who I am.

"Yes, sir. I was sixteen when you opened your store."

"Sixteen, huh? And how old are you now?"

"I just turned nineteen back in February."

"Nineteen!" he says with a slight grin, leaning over the counter towards me. "Time sure does fly. You sure have grown to be a beautiful lady."

"Thank you," I tell him as I blush.

"What brings you in here so close to closing time?"

"I usually come here on Saturdays, but I have to have stockings for work tomorrow."

"Where do you work?"

"Across town at the Berkdale Company. I work in the accounting department, posting payments."

"Oh, yeah. I know where that company is. So what size stockings do you need?"

"I need a size eight."

"What color you want?"

"Something in a light brown, please."

He turns to the shelves behind him, looking through the small thin boxes in the slots on the wall. When he finds the box he's looking for, he places it on the counter and pulls out one of the pair, gently laying it across his open palm.

"Is this the right color?" he asks.

"Yes, I'll take those."

He puts the stocking back in the box and puts the box in a bag.

"Here you go," he says, holding out the bag for me to take.

"How much do I owe you?" I ask.

"Don't worry about it," he tells me, flashing those beautiful, white teeth of his.

"I can't take these without paying you," I say adamantly.

"Why not?"

"I just can't."

"Listen, I own this store, so I can give what I want to whoever I choose."

I stand there, not knowing what to say.

"Consider it a belated birthday present," he tells me.

I smile politely and decide to take the present. As I take the bag from him, my hand lightly brushes against his and it makes my insides tingle. He stares at me with an alluring softness in his eyes and for a moment, I'm captivated.

"Thank you, Mr. Boone," I say as I look down onto the counter, pretending to be interested in the merchandise.

"Call me L.C. I'm not that much older than you. Besides, you're not a little girl anymore. You're a grown woman now."

I look back at him.

"Thank you, L.C.," I say as I force a tight-lipped smile.

He smiles back.

I turn and walk down the aisle leading to the front door. I can feel him watching me. I look back to find him standing with his arms crossed with that same alluring softness, smiling at me.

"Have a good evening, Marietta," he says in his smooth, deep voice.

"You too," I say as I turn the doorknob and walk out.

I walk away from the store feeling strange, but excited. I hadn't noticed up until this very moment how strikingly handsome Mr. Boone is. Remembering how his hand rubbed against mine makes me all tingly again.

What's wrong with me? I can't act like this. That man is married and has a family.

I begin to feel ashamed.

But why should I feel shamed? I haven't done anything wrong. He was the one being overly friendly and flirting with me! But I shouldn't have been so nice and polite. I should have been more formal with him. When he told me to call him L.C., I should have told him I don't call my elders by their first name. But he said he wasn't that much older than me. I'm making too much out of a smile and a nice gesture. He wasn't flirting with me. He was just admiring how nice and pretty I've become since I've grown up. That has to be it. I need to stop imagining such a thing. But no, I didn't imagine it. He was flirting with me! There was something there. It was more than just admiration. I felt it. Oh, shoot! I need to stop preoccupying myself about him. I don't know what he's feeling. He's probably not even thinking about me. Not at all!

But something in my heart tells me he is.

I have to go over to Waylene's house to tell her what just happened with Mr. Boone. Waylene has been my best friend since we met at school the beginning of the seventh grade. Actually, she's like a sister to me. She was the only one I could confide in. We told each other everything. She told me about the time she let Harold Palmer sneak into her house late one night and she let him kiss her breast. We both cried when she told me about the time she was at church alone in the basement washing off the tables, and Reverend Little walked up behind her and tried to force himself on her. She vowed she would never go to church again. I was there for her after she gave herself to her boyfriend, Doug, and he told everyone about it in a note he passed around at school. We both were so mad at him. We swore we would get him back somehow.

My mother didn't approve of me being friends with Waylene at first. She told me Waylene was too common for me to be hanging out with and that Waylene's mother, Miss Lucille, lacked supervision in her home. Actually, Mother just doesn't like Miss Lucille.

Miss Lucille is outgoing. She's loud and talks to any and everybody she runs into, even strangers. I think of Miss Lucille as a woman with a free spirit. That's what she calls herself, a free spirit. Miss Lucille does what she wants to and dares someone to say something about it. She goes out on a lot of dates. She comes home late at night and other times she might not come home until the next day.

Mother calls Miss Lucille a 'Jezebel' because she wears tight dresses that showed off her big bosom and curvy hips and she wears high heels and puts on a lot of red lipstick. Mother said most loose woman dressed that way in the evening, but Miss Lucille dressed like that day and night.

My mother has big bosoms too, but you would never know it. She's a tall woman with an hourglass figure and if she would dress in softer fabrics with brighter colors like pink or sunflower instead of the heavy, plain garments with dark colors like grey or black or forest green that she's accustomed to, you could see how pretty she really is. Mother has a beautiful face with smooth, caramel-colored skin and pretty brown eyes with thick, long lashes. She has just the right amount of pout to her lips, not too much and not too little. Her hair is more wavy than curly, and it's a pretty shade of black that isn't too harsh for her skin tone.

Mother doesn't believe in women bringing attention to themselves in glamorous ways and she expects me and my sister, Josette, to be like her. But

I don't think there's anything wrong with a woman being pretty as long as she keeps it decent.

I often wondered what attracted my mother to my father. I miss my father so much. He died seven years ago, but it seems like only yesterday he was here with us. I think my parents married one another because they saw each other as stable partners, not love mates. They were alike when it came to taking care of business and caring for their home, but they were so different in other ways.

Mother is snobbish and prudish and very old-fashioned. She's very strict and disciplined and no fun at all. My mother is a very responsible woman but she's not a loving person, and I don't think she genuinely likes people. I think Mother has a hard time showing affection because she grew up without her parents, and that makes me feel sad for her.

Mother concerns herself too much with what people think of us. I got so tired of hearing 'stand up straight, fix your clothes, use proper English,' when I was growing up. My mother was quick to correct us when we were children if we mispronounced anything. Mother speaks well all the time except when she's mad, and then she doesn't care how the words come out.

Father, on the other hand, was a friendly man. He was a very encouraging, down to earth man who made people feel like they mattered in the world. I seldom heard my father talk bad about anyone. When he did talk about people it was with concern, not gossip. Father didn't stand for any foolishness and he had high expectations of people. 'I can't' was not accepted by my father. He felt anybody could do what they wanted to if they put forth the effort.

My father understood the importance of making his children feel wanted. He was encouraging to all of us, and he made sure we knew how important we were to him. He didn't raise us to think we were better than others, but he wanted us to be examples for people to follow.

Mother thought Waylene would grow up to be a 'Jezebel' like her mother, and she thought they both might be a bad influence on me. I told Mother that she and Father had raised me to carry myself like a lady, and I would never do anything to embarrass myself or my family. I reminded Mother that we don't always take on the unlikable qualities of other people. Most times it's the other way around. They pick up on our good qualities. I told my mother that it was because of Waylene being around me that she had learned to be more proper and lady like. I must have convinced her because she eventually lightened up about me hanging with Waylene.

Now that my father has passed on, my brothers are very protective of me and my sister. Before my oldest brother, Wendell, left for the service, he tried to be more of a bully about it than my brother Stanley. Mother didn't do much about it when we complained about Wendell bossing us, because she felt we needed a man somewhere around to keep us in line. Stanley would come to mine and Josette's rescue whenever Wendell was being over bearing, and the three of us would gang up on Wendell until he ran to Mother.

I'll be glad when Stanley comes home. He's gone to the service too. I really miss him. He's my favorite brother. We had a lot of fun together growing up. I never ran around with him when he played baseball or played with the fellows. We had different interests. He was all boy and I was all girl, but we hung around together at home or when we went walking in the neighborhood. We joked around and laughed and talked seriously about relationships and life. He was the one who told me to always be a lady and to be careful about what I did when it came to boys.

I'm almost to Waylene's house when I see her brother, Donald, walking my way.

"Hi Marietta," he says with a cheesy smile.

"Hi Donald," I say. "Is Waylene in the house?"

"Yeah, she's in there."

"Where are you off to?"

"I'm goin' over Scooter's house, but I can go back to my house with you if you want me to," he says. He raises his eyebrows up and down in a flirting gesture.

"Boy, get out of here."

He laughs and goes on his way.

I walk onto the porch and ring the bell. Miss Lucille answers the door with that same, 'Hey sugar, how you doin' greeting she's given me since I've been coming to her house. She directs me up the stairs to Waylene's room where I find her sitting on her bed looking through a Sophisticated Lady magazine.

I close the door behind me so that no one else will hear me as I tell Waylene about my experience with Mr. Boone.

"Aw girl, I don't think he meant no harm," she tells me. "Mr. Boone does nice things for a lot of people."

"Well I think he was just a bit too forward with all that grinning he was doing," I say.

"You don't know Mr. Boone very well, do you?"

"I don't want to know him either," I lie.

"If he was flirting with you, you would surely know it. He ain't the kind of man that beats around the bush."

"If he would have been any fresher, he would have just told me to take off my clothes!"

Waylene laughs.

"Hush your mouth, Marietta!" she tells me. "Mr. Boone ain't after you. You too sweet of a girl. He's after them rough women that he can make work for him out on the street."

"What do you mean, work for him on the street?"

"You know he's a pimp."

"What?!"

"Yeah. You didn't know that?"

"No! He won't be getting my business anymore."

"Why? 'Cause he's a pimp? That ain't no reason not to shop at his store. Plenty of businessmen got part-time gigs. That old, white man that owns Hock's does the same thing and you used to buy clothes from him."

"Mr. Hock is a pimp?"

"No, not a pimp! He runs moonshine. Have you been under a rock or something? All these business people do things on the side. Mr. Boone is just gettin' his piece of the pie like everybody else."

"Waylene, that man makes good money selling clothes. Every Negro in town shops there. He doesn't have to put women on the street to make money for him."

"And you know he sells liquor in the basement on the weekend after he closes."

"What?!"

"And he runs numbers and all kinds of stuff."

"Hush your mouth!"

Waylene laughs again.

"That man would do anything to make a dollar and he does," she says.

"How do you know all of this?"

"You know momma talks to a lot of people so she knows it all. I heard her talking about it on the phone with my auntie."

I sit there in disbelief as Waylene informs me of how Mr. Boone operates his fine, fashion shop during the day, and at night he uses the basement of his building as an after-hours joint where the poor and not-so-poor folk in our community go to gamble and dance. Some buy liquor and even women for a moment's pleasure. He's the man to go to if you want reefer or something stronger to alter your mind when troubles wouldn't let go. If you want to play the numbers, you talk to one of Mr. Boone's boys. You could borrow money from him too, but you better make sure you pay it back on time. All these years, I thought Mr. Boone was an upstanding businessman. Now I find out he's really nothing but a common gangster in disguise.

"Do you think he might be trying to get me to be one of his girls and put me out on the street?" I ask naïvely.

"Girl, cut it out," Waylene tells me, smirking. "If the man would have given you a diamond ring, then I would say he was after something, but he gave you a pair of stockings. That ain't hardly nothin' to be worried about. Hell, as much as we all shop there, he should be givin' everybody somethin' free every once in a while."

I tell her she's probably right, but something inside of me doesn't believe he was just being nice. Something tells me he does have another motive. And now I'm afraid to find out.

Waylene and I had been planning for a whole month to go out to this new nightclub called Mitchell's. Mitchell's is a few miles down the road over in Seton, two towns north of Westfield. We didn't get a chance to celebrate my birthday the way we wanted so we were doing it this one Saturday night. Everybody we knew had been there at least once or twice and we were dying to get there. We heard Mitchell's was the hottest joint around our way and that all kinds of stars and agents popped in from time to time to listen to the different bands, looking to spot new talent. We were hoping we would get to see a famous singer. We couldn't wait to get there and see all the handsome fellows we heard about. One of the girls from work met her new boyfriend there, and all she talked about was the men who hung out there and how handsome they were, so we had to get there and find us a boyfriend. My mother would never allow me to go to places where they sold liquor, so on the weekend she just happened to be out of town on one of her church tours, I decide to go.

I don't have any fancy evening clothes, so I put on one of the suits I wear to work. It really isn't fancy enough to wear to a club, but it's the best I have. I always wear my long, black hair pulled up in a ponytail with my bangs curled but tonight I want to be daring and let it hang down my back.

I put on my final touches of the makeup I keep hidden in my drawer and take one more look in the mirror.

I check in to make sure Josette is asleep before I sneak downstairs to wait for Waylene. It's only eight-thirty and normally she doesn't go to bed this early on a Saturday night, but she had done a lot of work today and she's tired. I pray nothing will happen to wake my sister during the night to find that I'm not home. If she ever told Mother, she would kill me for sure. For some reason I don't care. I'm willing to face Mother and whatever else I have to, just to go out to this club tonight.

Neither Waylene nor I have cars, so she asked her cousin, Harold, to drop us off and pick us up from Mitchell's. I continually peek out of the front room window until I see them pull up in front of the house. I tip toe down the porch steps and as I approach the car, I can see Waylene checking out my clothes. She takes one look at my outfit and frowns.

"I thought you said you were buying something special for tonight," Waylene says as I get into the back seat.

"Well hello to you too," I say sarcastically.

"Hi girl," she says.

"Don't listen to her," Harold says. "It don't matter what you wear. You fine all the time! She just mad 'cause she have to dress herself up and she still don't look as good as you!"

"Shut up, ugly!" Waylene tells Harold, elbowing him.

"You sure are fine Marietta," Harold says to me.

"Thank you Harold," I say, grinning.

I've always considered myself a pretty girl, but I'm also modest. People tell me all the time how pretty I am. I'm often told I look like my mother, but I don't think I do.

Waylene looks okay and I would never say it directly to her, but she's not as cute as I am. Her skin is beautiful and brown like cocoa. Her eyes are narrowly shaped and she has very long eyelashes. Waylene's nose is wide but it's got a nice shape. Her lips are bigger than mine. Her hair is regular Negro hair, but she keeps it straightened and greased. I'm a different color brown than Waylene. I'm more Indian brown. I once heard someone say we had Blackfoot Indian in our bloodline, but I don't know if it's true. Waylene is tall and lanky and doesn't have much of a shape. I'm not as tall as Waylene, but I'm much more curvier than she is. No one can mistake my femininity, especially with my big breasts and my long, wavy, black hair. I've straightened my hair with a hot comb a few times, but it doesn't need it. Waylene never says anything but I can tell she gets a little jealous when the fellows flirt with me instead of her. But what can I say?

When we get to Mitchell's, we tell Harold he doesn't have to stick up under us all night but he better not leave without us. Waylene and I walk inside the back entrance and head down the stairs where we hear a band already playing. There are so many people dancing and laughing and talking. People are drinking and smoking and off in the corner kissing. Women are dressed in sophisticated, after-five gowns and dresses. Men have on suits and ties. Everyone is enjoying themselves, talking over each other while the loud music of the band plays on. I have never seen this kind of action going on all at once. I'm amazed and excited at the same time. We walk deeper into the club and halfway towards the front of the place, there is a man and woman sitting at a table along one of the walls who let us take the seats they had been saving for friends who didn't show up. We sit down and listen to the band play, talking into each other's ear over the music every so often. As I look around the night club to see who is in the audience, I actually happen to see someone I know sitting along the wall at a table with two other gentlemen. It's L.C. Boone! He sees me looking and he smiles at me. I turn away, pretending not to notice who he is. I lean over to tell Waylene that he is there. She looks over and he catches her looking for him in the crowd. He waves to her and she waves back.

"Why did you wave to him?" I ask her.

"Well he waved at me," she says. "What was I supposed to do?"

I look back in his direction and he has started to make his way over to us.

"Oh no, now he's coming over here," I tell her.

"Good evening ladies," he says as he stoops down between our chairs.

"How you doin' Mr. Boone?" Waylene says.

I don't say anything and continue to pretend to give all of my attention to the band.

"And how are you tonight Miss Cressford?" he asks, directing his attention to me.

I still don't respond.

"What's wrong with your friend?" I hear him ask Waylene.

Out of the corner of my eye, I can see Waylene shrug.

"Maybe you didn't hear me," he says, leaning into my ear.

I lean back slightly, away from him and continue to look at the band. His raised eyebrows lead me to believe he's annoyed by my silence.

"Tell Miss Cressford it's not very becoming of a lady to act so rude," he says to Waylene, loud enough to make sure I hear him. He gets up and walks back to the table where he was sitting before.

"Girl, why didn't you say something to Mr. Boone?" she asks me.

"I'm not talking to that hoodlum," I say adamantly. "I'm scared of him!"

"Why you scared of him? You owe him some money?"

"No I don't owe him any money. He's a pimp Waylene!"

"Oh my goodness. Are you still mulling over that?"

"Yes I am! I don't converse with his type."

"Girl, get down off your high horse! I told you that man ain't thinkin' about you. And stop judgin' what other folks do. You never know. One day you might be out on the street sellin' your twat."

"Waylene!" I say frowning, hitting at her. "Watch your mouth! I'll never be out there walking the streets."

Waylene laughs at my chastising.

"Okay," she says. "What do you want to drink?"

"Get me a cola," I tell her.

"Girl, we didn't come to a night club to drink no cola. We are grown women now. I'm gettin' me some bourbon. What do you want?"

"I don't know. You get yours first and let me taste it."

Waylene goes to the bar and comes back with her drink. She tastes it and closes her eyes afterwards, making a horrible face.

"Ooww that hurts going down!" she says. "Here, taste it."

"I don't want that!" I tell her. "Get me something that doesn't hurt going down."

"All of it hurts at first, but once you get used to it, it gets better. Go on and taste this."

I pick up her glass and sip a tiny bit. It burns my tongue and I give her back her glass.

"You got to take a drink," she tells me.

Reluctantly I pick up the glass again and take a bigger sip. I hold the alcohol in my mouth for a minute and swallow with one gulp.

"Whoa!" I say. "Take this stuff back."

She laughs at me as she reaches for her glass.

We talk and listen to the band for an hour or so until I decide it's time to go. I need to get back home.

We go outside to find Harold. I can tell Waylene is a little tipsy. She leans her back against the building as we glance up the street looking for Harold. I look down the street and see Mr. Boone standing next to a car, talking with another man. He looks my way and I turn my head, pretending not to see him, but it's too late. I watch him as he comes over to us.

"So you feel like speaking now?" he asks me as he gets closer.

I tense up inside but I try to act natural, not wanting him to notice.

"Good evening Mr. Boone," I say dryly, looking down the street past him.

He stops and stands directly in front of me with his hands in his pockets.

"Last month when I saw you at the store, you were calling me L.C.," he says. "Now you're calling me Mr. Boone. Why so formal?"

"I prefer to call you Mr. Boone," I tell him. I step out of his path and look up the street again. He tries a different approach.

"Your hair looks nice tonight," he tells me softly. "I like the way you look with it down on your shoulders."

"Thank you," I say, still looking everywhere but at him.

I can tell I'm starting to irritate him.

"What's with the cold shoulder?" he finally asks. "The last time I saw you, you were just as nice and polite. Now you act like I got leprosy or something."

I turn my attention directly to him.

"I'm not giving you the cold shoulder," I say. I look up the street again, pretending to ignore him.

"Who are you looking for?" he asks all of a sudden.

"We're waiting for Harold," Waylene says.

"I just saw Harold around the corner with some young lady," he says to Waylene, while looking at me. "You run around there and go get him. I'll stay here with Miss Cressford until you get back."

I watch as Waylene pushes herself off the wall and I give her that 'you better not leave me with him' look, but she snickers and goes on her merry way to find Harold. Mr. Boone and I stand there silently for a few minutes. He steps closer to me. I can feel him looking me over.

"Now you gonna tell me what I've done wrong?" he asks.

"Mr. Boone, I don't hold long conversations with married men," I say.

"Oh, so that's it," he says, shifting his weight onto one leg. "Is it against the law for a married man to talk to somebody other than his wife?"

"No. I just don't feel it's appropriate for me to be standing outside a nightclub talking to someone's husband. That's how gossip gets started."

"I don't pay no never mind to what people say about me."

"Well, you should," I tell him.

"Why?" he asks curiously.

"Because you just should. I care about what people think about me. I don't want any bad talk going around about what I do."

"I don't think you would do anything bad," he says in that low, deep tone. "An angel like you doesn't have that kind of a heart."

I look him in the eye and when I do, I feel that same feeling I had at the store when his hand touched mine. Waylene walks up to us.

"Harold is on his way around here," she tells me. Just then Harold's car pulls up to the curb in front of us.

"Well, I best be getting on home myself," Mr. Boone says. "I got a wife and children to get home to."

He grins and winks at me.

"You ladies have a good night," he says as he tips his hat and walks down the street.

I watch him walk away.

"What did he say?" Waylene asks me.

I don't answer her at first. I'm still watching Mr. Boone walk away.

"What's gotten into you?" she says, giving me a nudge with her elbow.

She breaks my concentration and I look at her.

"What?" I say.

She looks at me peculiarly for a moment.

"Ooo!" Waylene squeals all of a sudden. "You all dreamy-eyed about Mr. Boone!"

"No I am not!"

"Yes you are! What did he say to you?"

"Not a doggone thing worth repeating."

She smirks and crosses her arms, waiting for me to tell her something.

"He must have said something," she says, "'cause before I left, you was talkin' about how much of a hoodlum he is and now you standing here lusting over him."

"I am not!"

"Who do you think you talkin' too? I know you about as well as you know yourself."

And indeed she does.

"He was just saying how nice I was and he made me feel bad about not speaking to him," I tell her. "Didn't you hear him say he had to go home to his family?"

"What else did he say?"

"He said I had a heart like an angel."

"Uh oh," she says seriously. "Now I'm like you. I believe he is after somethin'."

"No he's not."

"You better watch out. This is the second time that man has been in your face talkin' real nice to you. The third time is when he's gonna make his move." She bursts out laughing.

"Girl, stop laughing at me," I tell her. "You were right the first time. He's just being nice. That's all."

As we step to Harold's car, I see a woman sitting in the front seat and Harold's friend, Al, sitting in the back.

"This is my friend Minnie," Harold says as Waylene and I climb into the back seat. "I'm givin' her and Al a ride home, too."

On the way home, the four of them talk as I sit looking out the rear side window, thinking about Mr. Boone.

I keep trying to run into Mr. Boone. I stop by the store twice to buy whatever I can pretend I need just to get the chance to see him, but he isn't there either time. I yearn to run into him again, to hear him say something nice about me. I know I shouldn't think about him, but I do.

I talk Waylene into going back to Mitchell's again in hopes that I will see him there like I did the last time. I lie to Mother the night before, telling her Waylene is having a hard time with her 'lady days' and her mother is going out of town, so I'll be spending the night at her house to help care for her. Mother tells me Waylene is too old to be baby sat and this is the last time that I need to be spending the night at her house.

When I get to Waylene's house, Miss Lucille is heading out the door. She doesn't know I told my mother I was spending the night and she has no idea the two of us are going out, but when she comes home later that night and sees me sleeping in Waylene's room, I'm sure she won't mind.

I still don't have any after-five clothes to wear to a place like Mitchell's, so Waylene lets me go through Miss Lucille's closet to find a dress to wear. This time I want to look like I belong at the club and not like some office worker out on the town. I don't want anything too revealing or sexy so as not to send out the wrong signal to some man. I pick a red dress with a boat neck and three-quarter length sleeves. It would be busting at the seams if Miss Lucille were in it, but it's a bit too big on me. Miss Lucille wears shoes a half size smaller than me, so I have to pick a pair of slings to wear. I put on a little lipstick and eye brow pencil and I'm ready to go.

We sneak back over to the club again, hitching a ride with Harold. It's just as crowded as the last time, but this time we're able to get a table by ourselves. A gentleman stops at our table and asks me if I'd like to dance. I tell him no thank you and he sits down in one of the empty seats and carries on a conversation with Waylene. As they talk, Waylene giggles and acts foolish.

After an hour or so, I start to get bored. I tell Waylene I'm ready to go. She tells me she's not ready yet. I don't bother her about it again. After all, it was my idea to come and just because I'm not having a good time doesn't mean I should mess up hers. I decide to just sit it out and listen to the band while Waylene enjoys her time with her newfound fellow. The lights are dimmed and I turn my chair away from under the table to position myself better to see the next band that has come onto the stage and started to play. I listen to the band for a minute and then turn around to the table to take a sip of my cola. Waylene's friend has it in his hand and is trying to hurry and put it back from where he got it. They both giggle as I look at them from one to the other. I pick up my drink and look into the glass.

"What did you do to my drink?" I say loudly, leaning over far enough for him to hear me over the music.

"Taste it," the gentleman says.

I frown while I look back into my glass.

"What's in it?" I ask looking at him and Waylene.

"Aw girl, just go 'head and taste it," Waylene says.

I swallow some of my drink. I can taste the liquor and it's smoother than the bourbon Waylene had me try the first time we came to the club.

"You like it?" he asks me.

"It's not bad," I tell him. I take another sip and sit the glass back down on the table.

I turn back around and continue to watch the band, looking around the club, checking out the people as I take sips of my drink every so often. After a few minutes I start to feel mellow, relaxed. I watch the band until the lights are turned back up. As I check out the crowd again, I look towards the entrance of the club and I see two men come through, followed by Mr. Boone. That man has a presence about himself, and each time I see him I get excited. His clothes fit him perfectly. A silk tie compliments his dark, blue suit and of course the polished shoes and a glimmering wristwatch finish his look. He hasn't even taken off his hat yet and several people have walked up to him. Men shake his hand and women bat their eyes and flirt with him. He moves closer inside the club and stops to talk with two women. I feel a little twinge of jealousy. He continues to talk to the women until he catches my stare. He smiles as soon as he sees me and then excuses himself from his present company. I try not to be too obvious as I watch him walk towards our table. His stride is slow and even and controlled.

He stops right in front of me and looks down at me seductively without speaking. Then he directs his attention to Waylene and her friend and tells them hello before he bends over to speak to me.

"Is it okay for me to talk to you this time?" he asks, putting his hand on my arm.

His touch makes me feel giddy and I hold my breath so that he can't see the excitement rise and fall in my chest.

I don't answer him. I pretend to look for familiar faces in the crowd to hide my giddiness.

He pulls an empty chair from the table right next to ours, places it next to me and sits down. I see several women in different sections of the club whispering to each other as they watch to see what Mr. Boone and I do.

"I hope you don't mind me sitting here next to you," he tells me. "I don't want you to feel uncomfortable by being seen with me. You know people might take the wrong notion and I know how you feel about gossip, with me being married and all. I don't want to ruin either one of our reputations."

"Too late," I tell him faking a little smile. "Everyone's looking over here to see who you're sitting with."

As he looks around the club, most of the women quickly look elsewhere while the men smile and tip their heads in approval.

"To tell the truth, I really don't care what they have to say," he says. "These women in here know not to come up to me asking me who you are."

"I already know you don't care what they have to say Mr. Boone," I say sarcastically as I turn to him, looking him square in the eye.

For a minute he stares back at me as if I've challenged him in some sort of way and he's ready to go toe to toe with me. But then his look slowly changes to one that's softer, more relaxed.

"How you doing tonight Marietta?" he says in that deep, soothing voice of his.

"I'm fine, and yourself?" I ask coyly.

"I'm well." He leans closer into my face. "You're a lot friendlier than the last time I saw you."

"Forgive me for being so rude before."

"It's alright. We all have bad days every now and then. What are you doing up here in Seton again?"

"We came to see the show."

"You sure that's all you came to see?"

"What do you mean?"

"I mean you sure you didn't come here looking for me?"

I blush as he waits for me to answer.

"No," I say shyly. "I didn't even know you would be here."

"I was hoping you were gonna tell me you went to one of them ladies that read your palm, and she told you the man of your dreams was gonna be at Mitchell's and you better hurry up and get there to see him before some other woman steals him away."

He grins.

"Mr. Boone!" I say. "I assure you, nobody is trying to steal you away."

"You'd be surprised," he says. "What are you drinking tonight?"

"I had a plain cola until Waylene's friend put some kind of liquor in it."

"What are you doing drinking liquor?"

At first I get defensive.

"I'm old enough to drink what I want," I tell him.

"A lady such as yourself shouldn't be drinking in a place like this."

"I know how to handle myself. Besides, I don't see the harm in having a little sip every now and then."

"You know how to handle yourself?"

"Yes, I do," I say indignantly.

"Well you better keep an eye on your girlfriend over there, 'cause she's had more than a sip or two. And I bet that fellow getting friendly with her has something in mind when you two get ready to leave here."

"What?!"

"Oh, yeah. I bet his plan was to get the both of you drunk and take you home with him."

I drop my jaw in disbelief. How dare Mr. Boone tell me something like that, let alone think that the gentleman sitting at our table would approach us that way. He was just being nice by sharing his liquor with us so we didn't have to buy any.

"You shouldn't talk about people like that!" I tell him. "That is an awful thing to say!"

"You don't believe me? You and Waylene go to the ladies room and ask her what they're over there talking about."

I glare at him for a minute.

"Go ahead," he tells me.

I stand up from the table.

"Would you excuse us, please," I say. "We ladies need to go the ladies room. Come on Waylene."

"I don't need to go to the ladies room," Waylene says.

"Well I don't want to go by myself," I tell her.

She smirks and gets up from her seat.

We get inside the ladies room and I turn to Waylene.

"What are you doing getting so liquored up?" I ask her.

"Girl, I'm out to have a good time," she says. I can tell she's a little high but not really drunk.

"We can do that without you getting drunk," I tell her.

"Aw, it ain't hurtin' nothin'. I used to have a drink every now and then with Michael."

"You did?" I say, surprised.

"Yeah. It helped make me relax before we would do it."

"Well I hope you're not thinking about doing it to anyone tonight."

"Hey," she says. "You never know! He asked me if we wanted to go to his place after we left here. I told him we might."

"Waylene!" I snap. "What is wrong with you? You don't know that man!"
She laughs.

"Aw, stop being so self-righteous!" she tells me.

I roll my eyes at her. I didn't want Mr. Boone to be right, but he was.

"Anyway, you over there talkin' to Mr. Boone. I bet you thinkin' about doin' somethin' with him ain't you!"

I smack Waylene's hand.

"Stop that!" I tell her, frowning.

"Uh oh!" she says. "It must be true. You like Mr. Boone."

"No I don't."

"Yes you do."

"No, I don't!"

"Well let me tell you, you may not be interested in him like that, but he damn sure is interested in you."

"No he's not."

"Well then, you stupid or naive or both!"

"Hush your mouth Waylene."

"You have to be if you can't see that that man wants you!"

"Well, I don't want him."

"And you keep right on not wantin' him. That man wouldn't be right for you. He comes from a whole different background."

"And that's the reason I don't want him. I don't want to be with a gangster, let alone a married man. Mr. Boone is the business owner of the store where I used to shop. That's all. You remember that."

"No, you remember that while he's touchin' on you all nice and soft," she teases.

I shoot Waylene a 'stop it' look.

"It's time for us to go home," I tell her.

"I ain't ready to go home. We still got a little while. And I might go home with Thatch, to be honest with you."

"No you're not," I say.

She laughs as we walk out of the restroom.

Mr. Boone is standing right next to the ladies' restroom door as we walk out.

"Okay ladies," he says to us. "It's time to go."

"I don't want to go yet," Waylene says. She looks at our table and sees that it is empty.

"Where's Thatch?" she asks Mr. Boone.

"He said to tell you he would see you next time. He had to leave."

"Aw damn," Waylene says. She covers her mouth immediately after she speaks, remembering she's in the presence of an older gentleman.

I lead the way outside and once we get there, I look up and down the street for Harold's car.

"He's around back again," Mr. Boone says. "Waylene, you sober enough to walk around to the back and get Harold?"

"I'm not drunk," she tells him as she slowly starts to make her way down the street.

"Did you talk to her about Thatch?" he asks.

"Yes," I answer without looking at him and not saying anything else.

"You don't have to say I was right. I talked to him when you got up. I told him to find some other broads to hang out with."

I cross my arms and look down at the sidewalk, avoiding his stare.

"Marietta, look at me," he says to me in a chastising tone.

I look into his face.

"You have to be careful out here. Everybody's not honest and a lot of people don't mean you any good."

All of a sudden I become angry. I want to tell him about himself. How he should be ashamed. Here he is doing his dirt selling reefer and gambling and he's talking about the harm someone else might do me. But instead, I don't say a word. I don't know what kind of temperament he has, and I'm not about to make him mad. This man has people beaten up and I'm not about to get myself hurt.

Harold pulls up to the curb in front of where we are standing with a woman in the front seat and Waylene in the back.

"Here's your ride," Mr. Boone says. "Listen, before you go, I wanted to let you know a friend of mine is opening a real classy joint. It's called The Elegance Lounge and it opens next month on the eleventh. You bring Waylene with you. I'm sure you two will like it much better than this hole in the wall."

"Thank you for telling me about it."

"I have to ask you something and I don't want you to be offended, but whose dress are you wearing?"

I can't believe he just asked me that! I look at him, insulted by his remark, not knowing how to answer him.

"You don't have to answer my question," he says, smiling. "And don't get mad at me for asking. Keep in mind I'm a professional. It's my business to ask when it comes to clothing."

Here I am thinking I look good in Miss Lucille's sophisticated dress. I actually become embarrassed and don't know what to say.

"I know it's not yours," L.C. tells me. "That dress doesn't fit you right. I also know it's not your style."

I look down at the dress. I didn't realize it was so big on me that someone would notice.

"Don't get me wrong," he continues. "You're still a fine, beautiful lady no matter what you have on. You're very classy and I just think you should dress that way. You should be wearing something that shows off the real you, something tasteful, sophisticated. I got in some new dresses from New York and there's one in particular that I'll set aside just for you. I have a good eye for matching people up to clothes, so take my word for it when I say this dress was made for you. Stop by when you can and try it on."

"You don't have to hold it for me," I say indignantly, crossing my arms. "I'm sure some other lady would look just as nice in it."

"Aw, see there!" he says. "I'm up here trying to give you constructive criticism and you're getting mad."

"I'm not mad. I'm just not interested in your dress."

"But it's beautiful, just like you."

"Then sell it to some other beautiful woman."

"No, this dress is special. It won't look good on nobody but you and I mean it."

I raise my eyebrows, wondering what he is up to. I don't know what to make of this man. What does he have up his sleeve? Is he really just a nice guy or is he a true slickster?

He studies my expression until I respond.

"I'll try to make it this Saturday when Miss Ella is there," I tell him. I hope it's clear to him that I won't be stopping by when I know he will be in the store.

"I'll let her know you'll be coming," he says with a sly grin.

"Good-bye Mr. Boone."

"Good night Marietta."

I walk to the car and get into the back seat.

On the way home, the three of them talk about who was at the club and again I find myself staring out the window, thinking about Mr. Boone.

I can't stop thinking about Mr. Boone. It's been two weeks since I last saw him at Mitchell's and I can't shake this desire I have to see him again. I know I think of him as being a bad guy and all, but for some reason I like him. He's not like the typical gangsters I've seen in the movies, and he's not brash or mean. Actually I think if I really got to know him, I would find some goodness in him.

I know he'll be at the opening of his friend's club. I'll make sure to be there too, and when he sees me I want to be stunning. I'm going to stop by the store tomorrow to ask Miss Ella to show me that dress he told me about. I'll let Mother know I'll be late getting home so she won't have a fit.

When I get to the store, I'm surprised to see Mr. Boone putting the closed sign in the window near the front door. He sees me and holds the door open with his arm stretched out.

"Well, hello there," he says with a wide grin. "Long time no see."

"Hello Mr. Boone," I say trying not to sound shocked to see him.

"Do you need more hose?" he asks me.

"No, I was over this way so I decided to come and take a look at the dress you were telling me about, but if you're closed I can come back on Saturday."

"I'm always open for you. Come on in."

I walk in past him and I hear him lock the door behind me.

"How have you been?" he asks me.

"I'm fine. And how are you?"

"I'm doing well today. It's beautiful outside and business is good."

"It is a beautiful day."

He looks into my face for a long time without saying anything.

"Follow me," he finally says. "The dress is back here in the stock room."

He turns and starts to walk towards the back of the store.

My mind starts to race as I hesitate.

I can't go back there alone with him. He wasn't even supposed to be here this late. What if he does something to me?

"You coming?" he asks as he stops and turns back to me.

"I was just going to wait here for you to bring the dress to me," I say, trying not to sound nervous.

"But you can't try it on up here by the front door."

"Maybe I should come back and try it on when Miss Ella is here."

Mr. Boone stares at me as if he can tell why I'm hesitant to go to the back of the store with him. He puts his hands in his pockets and slowly walks towards me.

"I promise you, you are safe in here alone with me," he tells me. "I'm not going to do anything to you."

"I'm not worried about you doing anything to me," I say.

He studies my face for a few minutes.

"Listen Marietta," he says seriously. "I got senses like a dog and I can tell I make you nervous. I know you've heard things about me, and I know that's why you're apprehensive about being around me."

"I haven't heard anything," I lie.

"Yeah you have. Everybody in town knows me and what I do. I know someone has already told you. But like I said before I don't care what people have to say about me. I am who I am, and you can take it or leave it. Now I'm going to tell you this and I'm only going to say this one time. And you have my word when I say this. I swear to you, you never, ever have to fear me. I would never do anything to cause you any harm. Not ever. Alright?"

I turn my head, looking away from him.

He steps in closer, stopping inches away from me, and gently places his warm fingers on the side of my face, turning it back towards him, making my eyes meet his.

"Alright?" he asks me again.

I feel a wave of sincerity flow from him into me, and I believe what he just said. I lower my guard and start to feel more comfortable as I nod yes in agreement.

His senses must have kicked in and he can tell I'm not as afraid of him as I was before.

"Okay then," he says, smiling. "Follow me."

He leads me to the back and we go through the curtains that separate the stock room from the store. I walk into the huge room and look around to see several different racks of clothes. Many shipping boxes and crates are stacked up against the far wall.

Mr. Boone walks over to a rack of special occasion dresses and looks through them. He pulls out a beautiful mid-calf, silk, black dress with capped chiffon sleeves. He walks back to where I am standing and lays the top of the dress across his forearm, allowing me to see the detail of the bodice. The fabric is gathered with a rhinestone pin to create a low, v-cut neckline that will show off the cleavage.

"It's lovely," I say, admiring the detail. "But I can't wear that."

"Why?"

"It's too low cut. My mother would never let me out of the house with this on."

"This would be beautiful on you. This is the kind of dress that accentuates what you have."

"I wouldn't feel comfortable wearing that."

"Before you go making up your mind that you don't like it, try it on to see how it looks."

"No, I couldn't."

"Just try it on and if you don't like it, you don't have to take it."

He's very persistent about seeing me in it and I can see he's going to keep trying until I put it on.

"Alright," I say reluctantly. "I'll try it on. I need to go to the dressing room."

"You don't need a dressing room. Just take off your clothes right here and try it on. I'll turn my head."

I look at him in shock.

"I'm just joshing you." He laughs. "You know where the dressing room is."

I smile nervously and go to change my clothes.

I'm not so sure about taking off my clothes with him so close by, but I can hear him rummaging through boxes and walking in and out of the storage room. He sounds far enough away so I figure its okay.

I hurry and put the dress on. I can't reach the zipper to pull it all the way to the top. I need Mr. Boone to help me with it. The dress is cut very low in the front, so I put my hands on my chest to keep my cleavage from showing and to prevent the sleeves from falling off of my shoulders. I walk out to where he is and stand in front of the mirror standing in one of the corners. He stops what he's doing and I can see him behind me through the mirror, looking at the back of me.

I ask him to zip the dress the rest of the way up for me while I still cover my cleavage. He comes up in back of me and I feel his fingers at the back of my neck, holding the top of the dress together as he slowly pulls the zipper up.

"Move your hands," he tells me.

I put my hands down to my side. The dress is tight across my breasts and is pressing them flat.

"You're going to have to adjust yourself up top," he says and turns his back to mine.

I'm not about to stand in the same room with him and adjust the top of this dress. I go back into the dressing room and hurry as I push each of my breasts up so that they sit into the top of the dress correctly. Then I go back out to where he is.

"Okay," I say whizzing by him, going back to the mirror with my hand back up to cover my cleavage.

I thought he would have a comment to make about me going into the dressing room, but he doesn't.

"Here, try these on," he says handing me a pair of black, high-heeled slings.

I bend down and put the shoes on one by one, while keeping one hand over my cleavage at all times. The shoes fit perfectly.

When I stand back up and look into the mirror, I can see his reflection as he looks me up and down from behind. He steps up closer in back of me.

"Can I take these pins out of your hair?" he asks me.

"I guess so."

I feel his fingers on my scalp as they gently search through my hair for the pins. He finishes taking them all out and arranges my hair so that it hangs down over my shoulders.

His eyes rest on my frontal view in the mirror.

"Move your hands, Marietta," he says softly into my ear.

I can't make myself move my hands fast enough, so he moves them for me.

His eyes focus upon my cleavage and watching him in the mirror arouses me, making my heart beat profusely. His lustful eyes meet mine.

"I've never seen a woman more beautiful than you," he says.

"This dress is beautiful," I say, trying to divert the attention from myself.

Still standing behind me, he places his hands on my hips, resting his thumbs at the top of my buttocks. I feel the goose bumps rise on my skin and I breathe in hard.

"Don't ever be ashamed of how you look," he tells me. "You have a beautiful figure and there's nothing wrong with wearing clothes that accentuate what you have."

I feel the heat rushing to my face as I blush.

"You look like royalty," he tells me, moving his hands from my hips and gently placing them on my shoulders.

As I look at him through the mirror, I wonder what his six foot, well-built frame looks like underneath his clothes. I hold my breath as I anticipate that he will turn me around and kiss my mouth. But he doesn't. He removes his hands and takes a few steps back. I look away from the mirror.

"So do you like the dress?" he asks in a more business-like tone.

"I do, but I can't wear it," I say, pretending to busy myself by looking down at the intricacies of the dress.

"Why not?"

"My mother would never let me wear this. I still live under her roof, so I have to abide by her rules and wearing revealing clothes is not acceptable to her."

"I understand."

"You do?" I say, surprised as I turn around to face him. I was expecting him to convince me I was old enough to defy my mother.

"Of course. If one of my children went against what I had to say, they would be in serious trouble."

"Yes, but your children are young and they have to listen to you. How old are your boys?"

"My boys are three and five."

"Mr. Boone, if you don't mind my asking how old are you?"

"I'm thirty. I'll be thirty-one September the twenty-sixth."

"You look very well for your age."

"Well I hope so. I'm practically still a baby." He laughs and then looks at me pleasantly for a moment.

"You go ahead and change," he says. He goes back to rummaging through the boxes.

I stand there dumbfounded for a minute. I just knew he was trying to get me in the back of the store to make a move on me and except for a few friendly caresses, nothing happens. I've never gotten past a few kisses with my former boyfriends, but from what I've heard through many of my girlfriends, the kind of caressing and sweet talk he just did leads to something other than 'go ahead and change'.

I put my clothes back on and come out of the changing room with the dress and shoes.

"It's a beautiful dress," I say, handing everything to him.

"So you really like it?"

"Yes."

"Then you can have it. It's yours."

"Mr. Boone, I can't accept this dress and besides, I told you I can't wear it even if I did take it."

"I want you to have it. You're the only lady I know who looks good in this dress and believe me when I say it, it looks good on you."

I can't figure this man out. He pretends he doesn't want anything, but he's too friendly, too interested.

"Why are you being so generous to me?" I ask him.

"I like you my lady," he says. "I like your character and the way you carry yourself. It's nice to see a young woman who is sweet and respectable looking glamorous."

"I can't keep accepting gifts from you, and I'm not sure about what you're looking for in return."

"Sweetheart, I'm not looking for anything from you."

I start to frown.

"Then why are you doing this?" I ask.

"Because I want to. Look Marietta, just because I tell you you're a beautiful, intelligent woman doesn't mean I'm trying to get in your panties."

"Mr. Boone!" I exclaim.

"What?" he answers with a sly grin.

"It's improper to say things like that."

"What? Panties?" he says seductively.

"Stop saying that in front of me!"

"What's wrong with saying panties?"

"You're not supposed to talk about what's under folks' clothes."

He laughs at me as I stand there embarrassed.

"See, that's what I like about you," he tells me. "You're so dainty and delicate. But you also have to learn that just because a man gives you a compliment doesn't mean he's after you. Women have a problem thinking that a man is always after them because he says something nice to them. I'm here to tell you that isn't what I'm trying to do. I'm not looking for you to give me anything other than your friendship. I promise."

I start to feel foolish for jumping to conclusions.

"I didn't mean to insult you," I tell him. "I'd be happy to accept your gift."

"Thank you," he says. "Let me box that dress for you and I'll send you on your way."

We go from the stock room to one of the counters inside the store where the box for the shoes he had me try on is sitting on top. I stand on the customer side of the counter and wait while he puts the dress in a fancy box that has a red satin, ribbon handle on the side. He also puts the shoes back in their box and puts them in a shopping bag.

"I want you to have these shoes too," he says as he walks around to where I am, carrying both packages in one hand.

I follow him to the front door and before he passes me the bag and the dress box, he takes my hand.

"Until we meet again," he says. Then he kisses the back of my hand and I feel the goose bumps rise on my skin.

"And stop calling me Mr. Boone."

"Thank you very much L.C.," I say with a sincere smile.

"You take care of yourself my lady."

"You too," I say and walk out the door.

I stop over Waylene's house before I go home to hide my dress and shoes so that Mother doesn't see them and make me take them back. The front door is open and I can see Miss Lucille in the kitchen through the screen door.

I knock on the door and wait for her to come down the hall.

"Hey, cutie," Miss Lucille says to me, unlatching the screen door and opening it.

"Hi Miss Lucille," I say, stepping inside.

"How you doing today?"

"I'm fine," I say grinning from ear to ear. "Real fine."

"Who put that big ole smile on your face?" she asks me. "You got a new boyfriend?"

"No," I say trying to change my look as not to give up my secret. "Is Waylene home?"

"Yeah, you know where she is. What you got in that box?"

"It's a new dress. I want to show it to Waylene."

I walk up the stairs to Waylene's room. She has her door closed. I knock and go in before she answers. She's propped up against the headboard of her bed, reading another magazine. She looks over the top of it as I enter, feeling around for something on her bed.

"Girl, I thought you was Bobby," she says. "You almost got a shoe threw upside your head."

"And why are you throwing shoes at Bobby?" I ask her.

"He keeps coming into my room without knocking."

"Waylene, that's no reason to throw a shoe at your little brother."

"It is when I tell him to stay the hell out my room and he don't."

I laugh at her. I put down the dress box, leaning it against the wall and set the bag next to it.

"Guess where I went today?" I say to her as I sit on the end of her bed.

"Where?" she asks.

"Over to Boone's. I was there alone in the store with L.C."

"Hush up!" she tells me, widening her eyes as she sits up on the side of her bed. "So what happened?"

"Nothing. Just like I told you before, he's a perfect gentleman. I tried on the dress he was holding for me."

"You changed your clothes in front of him?"

"No! I went into the dressing room and changed."

"Did he try to peek behind the curtain?"

"You have a wicked mind. Anyway he let me have the dress and a pair of shoes to go with it."

"What? Let me see that dress!"

I pull the dress and the shoes out of their boxes and she looks them over.

"He let you have this dress and these shoes? For free?"

"Yes, for free."

"And he didn't try to do it to you?"

"Waylene! You ought to be ashamed of yourself thinking that he would look at me like some common girl off the street. He wouldn't even approach me like that."

"Well it's something you ain't telling me. I can't believe L.C. got you alone and gave you all of that and he didn't even try to do nothing. Girl, he was all over you up at Mitchell's."

"I keep telling you he's not like that."

She sits silently looking as if she's analyzing the situation.

"He's taking his time with you," she finally says. "That's what it is. He knows that if he tries too hard, he'll run you away. He wants you to come to him."

"You're wrong. He's nothing like that. That man has class."

"Class? Marietta you slow. L.C. Boone ain't nothing but an upscale street nigga. You don't know nothin' about men."

"I do too know about men. I also know that all men are not alike."

"I don't know about other men, but I know L.C., and that man gets what he wants."

"Well he must not want me like you said before, because according to you he had his chance and he didn't make a move."

"We gonna ask momma about it," she tells, me getting up from her bed and opening her bedroom door.

"What do you mean you're going to ask your mother?" I say following her. "Are you crazy?"

"Momma!" Waylene hollers down the stairs.

"What?" Miss Lucille answers.

"I got something to ask you," she says, hurrying to the kitchen with me fast on the trail behind her.

"Waylene, you better not tell your mother!" I say, gritting my teeth.

She pays me no mind. As we step into the kitchen, Miss Lucille turns to us. "What is it?" Miss Lucille says.

"Momma, I think that Mr. Boone is after Marietta."

"You talking about that handsome, young man that owns the store over on Simpson?"

"Yeah," she answers. "He keeps givin' Marietta things for free when she goes over there."

"Oh yeah?" Miss Lucille says looking at me.

"Yeah," Waylene says. "And he just gave her that dress and them shoes she brought in the door."

"Yeah," Miss Lucille says. "Sounds to me like he trying to get up under somebody's dress!"

I gasp at Miss Lucille's comment. Waylene gives me an 'I told you so' look.

"You take them things right back to L.C. and tell him you can't accept 'em," she says, pointing her finger in my face.

"But Miss Lucille, he's been nothing but polite," I assure her. "He hasn't said anything disrespectful. He's just given me a pair of stockings and that dress and shoes for being a good customer for all these years."

"Good customer, huh?" Miss Lucille says. "Girl, don't you fall for that mess! When a man gives you somethin' it's 'cause he wants somethin' in return. And I would say he is after you. But you listen to me. That boy is married and he got two children. He ain't your type of man no way. That's a street man. He opened that store to cover up what he's really doin'. He got four or five girls workin' the street for him. He does good business in that store from what I see, so he needs to leave them streets alone and just worry about that store 'fore somebody start takin' from him. He's a cute lil' ole boy but he sure ain't nobody for you to get involved with. Naw, Marietta you stay as far away from him as you can. He'll be done got you by yourself and done somethin' to you."

"But I was just alone in the store with him before I came over here and he didn't do anything. He gave me my things and let me try them on to make sure they fit and I left."

"Y'all was all alone and he didn't try nothin'?" Miss Lucille asks.

"No ma'am. Not a thing. He was quite the gentleman."

"Huhm," Miss Lucille says rethinking the matter. "Maybe he ain't after you."

"I would know for sure if a man was getting fresh with me."

"Oh," Miss Lucille says all of a sudden. "Then he must have gave you that dress so you can get some business for him. He's using you in a different way. See, you a pretty girl and when women see you all dolled up in that expensive dress and them shoes, they gonna wanna look as cute as you and they gonna ask you where you got it from. He's using you to move his merchandise."

"Waylene thinks he's waiting patiently for me to throw myself at him," I say.

"Naw, that ain't it," Miss Lucille tells me. "He knows you ain't that kind of girl. He knows he would have to make a move on you. If he wanted you, you would know it. He don't bite his tongue. He'll let you know how he feels. I know a woman that was a little older than him that he tried to mess around with. She wasn't havin' it and he sure didn't wait for her to change her mind. He went right on and found him another fool woman. He gets 'em. Gets what he wants and moves on. And once he's done with 'em, he's done. He don't fall in love with no woman. Naw, he ain't tryin' to get with you."

"I told you," I say to Waylene. She still doesn't look convinced.

Miss Lucille turns back around to attend to her cooking.

"You find you a nice unmarried young man to be with," Miss Lucille says, turning back to us. "Don't you go out there and get yourself in a situation like some of these young girls."

Waylene and I both look inquisitively at Miss Lucille like we didn't know what she means.

"Miss Lucille, you don't have to worry about me doing anything foolish," I tell her. "I don't bother myself with married man. And I keep telling Waylene that he doesn't like me."

"I know he don't," Miss Lucille says. "Married men like loose women. They already got a decent woman at home, so they go out in the street and look for a whore. Somebody they can make do all them nasty things they wife ain't gonna do."

"Oh my Lord!" Waylene exclaims. "Momma, I can't believe you saying this in front of us!"

"Aw hell, Waylene, y'all ain't no little girls no more. Y'all grown ass women. I know y'all talk about this kind of stuff with one another. And I ain't gonna ask if either one of you still got your virginity, but I'm just gonna tell you be careful out here with these men."

"I'm still a virgin," I say.

"Me too," Waylene says, lying through her teeth.

"Well, y'all better keep it that way," Miss Lucille says. "Y'all right at the age where you get real hot in the tail and can't wait to fall in love. Just make sure you ready to get married before you go pulling up your dress for one of these fools. They'll be done knocked you up and left you."

"Come on, Marietta," Waylene says, leading me by my arm out of the kitchen.

"Y'all better take heed to what I'm telling you!" Miss Lucille calls after us.

"I can't believe she was saying that to us," Waylene says.

"Well at least your mother talks to you about men," I say.

We walk back up to Waylene's room.

"I don't care what you or Momma say," Waylene says to me. "I saw how he's been lookin' at you and he wants you. He knows you ain't like the other women he's used to chasin', but maybe that's why he wants you. He don't really know how to handle you 'cause you a good girl. But all I have to say is you better be careful 'cause he wants you and he's gonna to do his damnedest to get you."

She gets on my nerves, thinking she knows everything. I know what her problem is. It's her old boyfriend. I wish she would get over him and find her a man that she can trust. As for myself, I know me and I know that I would never get involved with a married man. And I mean never.

I convince myself that L.C. doesn't like me in that way. I was just alone with him and he had his chance to say something to let me know that he was interested in me. But he didn't. In a way, I'm relieved. In another way, I'm sad, because deep down inside I was hoping he did want me.

Waylene and I talk our friend Doris into driving us to the opening of The Elegance Lounge. I hadn't let Waylene know that L.C. told me about the new club. I told her that one of my friends at work told me about it. Mother just happened to be out of town again and this time she took Josette with her. I couldn't believe it. Fate could not have planned this any better. I desperately wanted to go to this opening because I knew L.C. would be there. I get my dress and shoes from Waylene's house the day before we go out so I can take my time getting ready at home. I want to make sure I look stunning when he sees me.

When we pull up to the place, we can see it is packed. Doris parks on one of the side streets and we walk a block to the club. They both comment on how beautiful I look, telling me they had no idea I could look so good. As we get closer to the entrance, there are several people standing around outside. I spot L.C. leaning against a street light post, smoking a cigarette.

"Ain't that Mr. Boone?" Waylene asks me.

"Where?" I say, pretending I hadn't seen him.

"Right there in that black tuxedo," she says, pointing at him.

"That is him," I say.

Waylene gives me a suspicious look. She grabs my arm and pulls me back, letting Doris walk a bit ahead of us.

"You two seem to be showin' up in the same places a lot these days," she says.

"What can I do?" I tell her. "I don't have any control over where he goes."

"No, but you can tell him where you're gonna be and have him meet you there. And that's why you have on this dress he gave you."

"Oh stop Waylene," I say.

Doris has noticed us lagging behind her and stops to wait for us.

"No, you better stop," she says seriously. "You better watch yourself with him Marietta."

I smirk and roll my eyes at her. I walk on and she follows.

L.C. watches us as we come his way and when he realizes who we are he stands up off the pole and flicks his cigarette into the street. The closer we get, the more amazed the expression on his face becomes. His eyes stay fixed on me as I sway smoothly towards him.

"Good evening, ladies," he says as we stop a few feet in front of him. He's still looking only at me.

"Hello Mr. Boone," we all say.

"This is our friend, Doris," I tell him.

"I already know Mr. Boone," Doris says, sticking her hand out for him to shake.

"Yes, I remember you also," he says. "You ladies look very lovely tonight."

We all say thank you.

"Have you been inside yet?" I ask him.

"Yes," he says. "It's very nice. You ladies should go in and take a look."

"We will," I tell him. "Hope to see you inside."

Just as we're ready to head to the door, L.C. asks me if he can talk to me for a minute. Waylene flashes me a dirty look, but I whisper to her I'll be in shortly and she and Doris go inside.

As I walk towards L.C., he slowly looks me up and down.

"You got a minute to take a walk with me?" he says, holding out his arm, waiting for mine to hook onto his. I place my arm into his and we head up the street.

There are a few people standing against buildings, smoking cigarettes and talking amongst themselves. He leads me around the corner and we slowly walk down the vacant street.

L.C. stops suddenly letting go of my arm. He steps in closer to me and I look up at him.

"Marietta, I'm sorry to keep staring at you, but you are simply gorgeous. You're the most beautiful woman I've ever seen in my life. I told you that dress would be beautiful on you."

"Thank you," I say, blushing.

"So when are you gonna let me see you where we can spend some time alone?"

"I don't think that would be a good idea," I say, surprised at his question.

"Why, you got a man?"

"No. You have a wife!" I remind him.

"I told you I can have friends," he snaps. "My wife can't tell me who I can and can't be friends with. Damn, you keep trying to make this into more than what it is!"

I feel intimidated by his tone of voice and take a few steps back from him. I think he realizes he scared me a little bit.

"Hey come here," he says, looking as if that wasn't his intention. He steps in closer to me and takes my hand.

"We are just good friends and that's all," he continues. "I'm a businessman and I come in contact with a lot of people and my wife knows this, so she doesn't listen to what nosey folks have to tell her about me, 'cause she knows the nature of my business. She knows I'm going to be seen talking to beautiful women, but that doesn't mean my intentions are disrespectful. You understand that, don't you?"

"Yes, I understand," I say.

"Now I don't want to have this conversation about my wife ever again, alright?"

I stand there for a minute, not wanting to say anything else about the subject for fear of irritating him again.

"Alright," I finally say.

"So how have you been?" he asks in a sweeter voice.

"I'm doing very well, and yourself?"

"Earlier today I was pissed off, but seeing you has made my evening pleasant."

I feel a little more relieved and I smile.

"You are so pretty," he says, shaking his head back and forth.

"Thank you," I say.

He puts his hand to my face and gently rubs my cheek with his thumb.

Here comes that electrifying feeling again. I wonder if he is going to try to kiss me this time. And if he does, will I let him?

"Listen," he says, looking into my eyes, "I had planned on staying at the opening all night but I can't. I have to leave. "

"Do you have to go now?" I ask him.

"Yes, I do. Something has come up and I can't come back tonight, but I hope I see you again real soon."

"Okay," I tell him, trying not to sound disappointed.

"Let me walk you back around to the club," he says as he takes his hand off my face and sticks out his arm again for me to take. We walk silently back around the corner to the front door of the club. I let go of his arm and he stands in front of me. He reaches for my hand.

"I hope you and your friends have a nice time tonight," he says.

"I'm sure we will."

He looks at me like he really doesn't want to leave me, then he kisses my hand and we tell one another good night.

While I watch him walk away, he looks back at me a few times and I want so badly to go with him.

When I get inside, I find Waylene and Doris sitting at a table in the middle of the club. I join them and try to pretend I'm excited about being there.

"Where's lover boy?" Waylene asks me.

"Don't start," I tell her, rolling my eyes.

"Where's Mr. Boone?" Doris asks.

"He said to tell you both good night and he hopes we all have a good time," I say.

"He's gone?" Waylene asks.

"Yes. Now do you believe me?"

She raises her eyebrows and flashes me the 'I guess you were right' look.

I sit for the rest of the night trying to enjoy the party, but I keep wondering about L.C. Here I was all dressed up, looking lovely in the gown he gave me, hoping to be with him for part of the night, and he's not here.

I don't know what to feel about this man. One minute he treats me like a young friend that he needs to keep an eye on and the next he looks at me with the lust of a man in love. I'm so confused.

There is a photographer taking pictures of the guests who have come for the grand opening of the club. He asks me if he can take my picture, explaining that he is going to put the photos in our local Negro magazine. I tell him no, because if Mother ever saw the magazine with me in it, she would kill me. But then I get an idea. I ask the photographer if he would take a picture of me that I can buy from him. I plan on giving it to L.C.

I try but I can't stop thinking about L.C. I haven't been around him much, but those brief encounters between us make me yearn to be with him, to talk to him.

I'm sitting at my bus stop after work one beautiful afternoon, looking up at the sky, daydreaming about L.C. when I'm interrupted by the sound of a car horn. A car pulls up to the curb in front of me. The windows are down and I can easily see who is in the white Cadillac with the red interior.

"Hey Miss Cressford," L.C. says.

I look at him in amazement as I wonder what he is doing here.

There are two women, who work at my company, standing not too far away from the bench I'm sitting on. They turn to see who I'm talking to.

"How you doing?" he asks with a big grin on his face.

"Hello L.C.," I answer.

"Your mother just sent me to pick you up. She said you all have an important event coming up and Miss Ella doesn't have the dresses that you and your sister need, so she's going to special order them right away. They're at the store right now and they need you to come so Miss Ella can measure you and order both of the dresses at the same time. They made me come get you. You know Miss Ella is the boss, I just own the store."

"Oh, I see," I say, looking at my fellow workers to see if they believed what I knew was a lie.

They turn back to each other and continue on with their conversation.

I get up and get into the car with L.C. and we pull off.

"What are you doing, coming to my job, letting everybody see you?" I ask him.

"So what if they see me," he says. "I can pick up my friend if I want to."

"Then why did you just tell that lie?" I ask him.

"That was for your sake," he replies. "I know how you are about people seeing you around me."

I roll my eyes at him and he laughs.

"What are you doing over here anyway?" I ask.

"I thought you might like a ride home in a car for a change instead of riding that bus."

"I don't mind riding the bus. And you're going to have to let me out somewhere near my house. I don't want people thinking anything improper if they catch me riding with you."

He doesn't say anything. Instead he drives down Hopple Street and turns onto Central Parkway.

"This isn't the way home," I tell him.

"I know. I need to talk to you about something and since you're so worried about being seen with me, I know a little spot where we can go that's secluded and quiet."

"Where?" I say uneasily.

"You'll see when we get there."

"This isn't a good I idea. I need to get home. My mother is going to ask me why I'm late getting home and where have I been."

"Just tell her the truth. You had a friend who needed some advice and you lost track of time talking with your friend."

"She won't believe that."

"Make her believe it. You got to learn how to bend the truth a little bit by adding to it and not getting caught."

"Are you sitting here trying to teach me to be a good liar?"

"I didn't say lie, I said bend the truth. You do have a friend who needs some advice. And I just don't know what to do." He pretends to cry.

He looks over at me and smiles. I roll my eyes at him again.

"Okay, friend. What do you need me to advise you about?" I say.

"I'll tell you when we get to where we going."

I begin to wonder what he is up to as we travel on the road away from Westfield into Gallatin, which is another town ten minutes away.

L.C. turns down a street lined with tall trees and grass and drives until we come to a dirt road that he turns onto. We drive for another minute or so until we come to the end of the road, where there's a large pond. He stops the car and turns off the motor. After L.C. gets out, he comes to my side of the car and opens the door. He extends his hand to help me out, leading me to the front of the car.

"You need me to help you get up there?" he asks.

"I can make it," I tell him as I put my foot onto the bumper and pull myself up.

L.C. hops up onto the hood next to me.

We sit silently looking across the pond to the other side. The reflection of the sun is shining onto the water. There's a nice, warm wind blowing around us.

"I come up here sometime when I want to be by myself and think," he finally says.

"I like the peace and quiet," I say, looking around, taking in the view.

He digs into his top shirt pocket and pulls out a cigarette. He lights it and takes a puff, letting the smoke out slowly.

"What was it you wanted my advice on?" I ask.

"I wouldn't say I needed your advice. To be honest with you, I just wanted to come out here and sit and talk to you. Get to know you. Every time I run into you, it's always the wrong time or a whole bunch of folks are around."

"L.C., are you a pimp?" I ask all of a sudden.

He stares at me with a blank expression and I can sense he doesn't like my question. He slides down off the hood of the car and flicks his cigarette into the lake. He stands in front of me with his hands in his pockets. I start to feel a bit nervous.

"Who told you that?" he asks me with narrowed eyes.

"I just heard it. You were right when you said you knew I had heard about your reputation."

"People run their mouths too much," he says, turning away from me to face the pond.

I slip down off the car and walk in front of him.

"L.C. I didn't mean to pry into your business," I say. "I just wanted to know the truth."

He ignores me for a few seconds staring out at the water.

"Do you think I'm a pimp?" he finally asks, looking down at me.

"I don't know," I tell him.

"Why don't you know?"

"I'm sorry I asked you."

He stares at me a few minutes longer with a stone-faced expression.

"Let's take a walk down that way," he says, nodding his head in the direction of a patch of tall trees huddled together, making a cove.

I feel reluctant to go.

"Don't worry. I'm not gonna get you in there and beat you up," he tells me as he starts to walk towards the greenery.

I follow him.

"Would you stop treating me like I'm some scared kid?" I say snappishly.

He stops and looks back at me.

"Don't get so indignant," he says. "I'm just letting you know I can tell you're still uneasy around me."

"Are you going to answer my question?" I ask.

"You sure you want to know?"

"Yes."

He turns back around and continues on through the pathway without saying anything as I follow.

We walk into the shade and he stops next to a large trees and leans his shoulder against it, putting his hand into his pockets. I stand in front of him with my arms crossed.

"Well?" I say.

He studies my face for a long time, like he's thinking about how he wants to answer my question.

"Well first off," he says, "I'm not a pimp. That is, I'm not a pimp any more. My mother's brother up in Chicago is a pimp and has been for a long time. He runs numbers, sells a little bit of this and that. I started out working with him when I was thirteen. That was right after my daddy got killed in a card game.

— 135 —

Two years later, my momma died from a stroke. My momma tried to raise me and my brother by herself but we were too much for her to handle so she had Wes, her brother, get us together. At first he didn't want us to turn out like him, but me and Elias wanted to be slick like Wes real bad, so he let us hang up under him and he showed us what we needed to know to make it in the streets. I was out there for a while, but I left that life alone. I got tired of looking over my shoulder all the time and having the police chasing after me and women can be trouble, especially when they go falling in love with you or when they get hooked on dope. And second, no, I don't sell dope. That is, I used to but not anymore. I sell a little reefer every now and then, but I mainly run my store. Used to sell liquor and had card parties down in the basement of my place up until recently, but I stopped that 'cause niggas wanna fight when they lose and snitch on you when you doing good. I don't like living in the spotlight and I don't like people in my personal business."

"I thought you said you don't care what people say."

"What they say behind my back is one thing. Messing things up for me is another."

"Excuse me for getting in your business," I say thinking his comment was directed at me. "I was just concerned about you."

"Why would you be concerned about me?" he says looking slightly confused.

"I just wouldn't want to see anything bad happened to you, that's all."

His mood seems to be more relaxed while he studies my face as if he needs to confirm my sincerity.

"You're excused," he finally says. "So do I pass the test?"

"What test?"

"The Marietta friendship test? The one you use to score whether or not you'll be friends with somebody like me."

"That's not nice," I tell him. "You make me sound like a prude."

"I been wondering something."

"What?"

"I know you all into what is and what isn't proper and things. And you know how I feel about me having lady friends and I'm married and all. But feeling the way you do about the sanctity of marriage and what people have to say, why did you come with me today?"

I wasn't expecting that at all.

"Aren't you the same one that keeps telling me there isn't anything wrong with a man and woman being friends?" I say, throwing it back at him.

"I know how I feel about it, but I'm asking you what you feel about it. I wasn't trying to sway you to think like me. I want to know how you feel."

He stares at me, waiting for an answer, but I don't know what to say. I can't bring myself to tell him the truth, although I wish I could.

"You're a nice man," I say.

He stands up from the tree.

"Is that it?" he says shrugging. "I'm a nice man?"

"Yes."

He looks at the pathway as I stand there, pretending to be interested in something on the ground.

"You ever been in love before?" he says, looking at me, waiting for a reply.

"I beg your pardon?" I say, taken by surprise.

"Have you ever been in love with a man?" he says seriously.

"No, not yet. I had strong feelings for this one guy when I was in high school."

"Who?"

"Why do you want to know his name? You wouldn't know him."

"I might."

"Otis Turner."

"Is that a real person?"

"Yes, he's a real person," I say staring at him peculiarly.

"What happened to him? Why ain't the two of you together now?"

"I didn't like him as much as he liked me."

"Why? He didn't pass the Marietta test?"

"Stop that!" I tell him as I hit him on the shoulder.

"Ouwww," he says pretending to be hurt. "I bet he was one of those book smart cats. That's the kind of fellows you like, right?"

"No I don't necessarily like only book smart guys."

"Was he a good guy?"

"I guess. Yes he was a decent man."

"If he would have asked you to marry him, would you?"

"No. I told you I didn't like him. I would never marry someone I didn't love."

"So love is the only reason you would marry a man?"

"No, not the only reason. I want a man who would be able to build a life with me. I wouldn't just marry a man so he could take care of me or that I would have to take care of him. We would have to do it together."

He looks at me with a longing that makes me feel like he wants to kiss me. Instead he starts to walk further along the path. I walk next to him. All of a sudden he stops and looks at me again.

"You're the only woman I've ever heard say that," he says.

"Say what?"

"You wouldn't want anything bad to happen to me. I've been with plenty of women in my time and not one of them has told me they were worried about me. My wife has never even told me that she was afraid that something bad might happen to me while I was out there in the streets. She just takes whatever I buy for her, no questions asked."

"I'm not like that. I wouldn't want you to put yourself in harm's way just to be able to buy me nice things. I would get out and work and we both would make a decent living together."

"And I'm sure you would," he says, staring at me with sincere eyes. "That's why I like you. You're not like any other woman I know. Niggas is out here fightin' for dollars and you worryin' about souls doing good and being decent. I've got a lot of respect for you lady."

L.C. takes my hand into his and I'm frozen by his touch. He brings my hand to his mouth and kisses it. My heart beats hard.

I hope he tries to kiss me. I want him to so badly. Nothing further needs to happen. Just a kiss and I'll be satisfied.

"You ready to get going?" he asks me, releasing my hand.

Damn! What is up with this man? Can't he sense how I truly feel about him?

"Yes," I tell him. "You know my mother will be wondering where I've been."

"Yes, Lord. We don't want her to send the dogs out looking for you. Or better yet, we don't want her to start sniffing the ground and barking and things!" He laughs at his comment.

"Hey, you." I giggle hitting him on the arm. "Don't you talk about my mother."

We walk back to the car and he opens my door to let me get in. He gets into the car and starts the engine.

"You want me to let you off on Wilson Street?"

"That's fine. That's far enough away."

On the way home, we don't say much to each other. I wonder if he's still sore about my asking him about his former life as a pimp.

"Can we do this again next Tuesday?" he asks me before I get out of the car.

"I don't know," I say.

"Aw, come on, girl. You like hanging around me and you know it."

"I do but...."

"But what?"

I don't respond.

"Oh, here we go again," he says, halfway throwing his hands up in the air.

"I can't help it. I keep thinking about it."

"Well from now on pretend I'm single."

"Yeah, I'll try, but I can't make any promises."

I get out of the car and close the door. I bend over to talk with L.C. through the open window.

"Thanks for letting me spend this time with you," I say, smiling.

"No, thank you for the time you gave to me. I'm going to be by to pick you up again on Tuesday."

"I didn't say I was going with you."

"You will."

"And what makes you so sure?"

"I just know. Bye-bye, gorgeous."

"Bye."

I stand up from the car and step back. He pulls away and I watch him leave. As I walk home, my soul quietly swims in joy.

Going back out to the lake with L.C. isn't in my plans, but each time he comes and asks me to go with him, I can't resist. I tell him which days Mother will be home late and I choose those evenings for us to be together.

I decide not to tell Waylene about my spending time alone with L.C. I know she won't like it and I don't want to argue with her about me going there alone with him, so I just keep it to myself.

I no longer consider the fact that he's married a problem and I don't mention it anymore. As a matter of fact, I don't care. I believe what he says about him not trying to get every woman he meets in the bed. I believe that he can just be friends with a woman and that people need to stop jumping to the wrong conclusion about him. I don't think he feels anything more than a friendship for me even though I've come to like him more than that. Sometimes, I think he wants to tell me he does feel like we're more than friends, but for some reason he's holding back. Maybe he'll change his feelings after we spend more time together.

One day after work when he picks me up and we get to our spot, I hand him the picture I had taken at The Elegance Lounge.

"This is for you," I tell him. "You can keep it."

"Whooe!" he says when he first looks at it.

He studies the picture for a long time.

"You need to be on the cover of a magazine," he tells me. "Can I put this up in my store for my customers to see?"

"No!" I say immediately. "My mother might come in and see it."

"Oh yeah," he says, rethinking his request. "Well then, what should I do with it?"

"I don't know," I say shyly, shrugging.

"I know," he smiles. "I'll keep it here in my pocket, right next to my heart."

I stare at him for a few seconds, feeling all lovey dovey.

"A person has to have at least one good friend near his heart," he says.

Is he serious? I'm still only a good friend to him?

I don't get him. It's like, one minute he's purposely teasing me, taunting me and then pushing me away the next. And if he is, what's the point? Whatever it is, it's beside me, but I still continue to want to be with him.

I learn more about L.C. each time we go out to the lake. He was born in South Carolina and he has one brother who is older than he is. His father moved their family to Chicago when L.C. was a year old. I tease him when I find out that his initials stand for Louis Clark. He was named after the explorers, only his first name is spelled differently. He tells me his mother named him that because she knew he would go places. I tell him I'm glad he was turning his life around and that we needed more good Negro men like him in our neighborhood. We laugh and joke and he tells me he wishes we would have grown up together. He says we would have had a lot of fun hanging out as kids.

I tell him about how I miss my father and how he was a good man. L.C. tells me he wishes he could have met my father. He says he would be honored to tell my father that he raised a beautiful, humble young woman. We give each other our personal views on God, good and evil. We talk about children, church and education. We talk about money, clothes and cars. I catch L.C. from time to time looking lovingly at me, smiling softly, hearing me but not listening. And yet with all the talking we do, I never tell him my true feelings, nor does he tell me what I want to hear, so after a while I truly believe what he says, that he likes to be around me because I'm a smart, respectful lady, who isn't all over him expecting anything. I try to be just that for him, but I can't shake the way I feel.

"So when can I see you again?" he asks me during one of our evenings at the lake.

"When do you want to?" I say coyly.

"You think you can get away on Saturday for the evening?"

"I might be able to. Why?"

"I need to talk to you about something. It's getting colder and colder out here and pretty soon we won't be able to come out here like we've been doing. Anyway, I want to talk with you about something that's going on, and since you're a right smart woman and I value your opinion as a dear friend, I want to know what you think. Sometime it's best to take the advice of a neutral person. You know what I mean?"

"Yes, but it depends on what the problem is. Depending on what it is, I may not have a neutral solution. Can't you tell me what it's about right now?"

"Naw," he says. "It's too complicated. I need more time to be able to explain it. We're always rushing when we come out here, and I want to take my time and talk."

"You're right, because we need to get going now," I tell him, making my way to the passenger side of the car.

We get into the car and drive along silently.

"Are you going to make me wait four whole days to wonder what you want to talk to me about?" I finally say, trying to pry the smallest tidbit of information from him.

"Sure am."

"You know that's not right," I say sarcastically.

"Yeah, I know." He grins.

When we get to my drop off point, L.C. stops the car. He takes my hand and squeezes it a little.

"Well lady," he says, "here is your stop. I wish I could spend some more of this evening with you, but we must part and until I see you again, you be good."

I smile at him. He's such a gentleman.

"You too," I say, getting out of the car.

"Can I pick you up here at about seven o'clock on Saturday? We can go over to the store to talk. Everybody will be gone by then."

"That's fine," I say. "Bye L.C."

"Bye gorgeous," he says, grinning.

Hearing him call me gorgeous makes my heart throb uncontrollably.

I watch him pull away and wonder all the way home what it would be like to lay in his arms all night long.

All week I try to figure out a good lie to tell Mother so I can get away. Mother had spent the past three weekends sitting with one of her elderly, widowed, Violet friends, who had been sick for a while. This weekend of all weekends she didn't go. I thought about what I could tell her, but something tells me this isn't a good time to try to see L.C. I have no way of getting in touch with him to let him know I can't go, so Saturday comes and goes and I hope the next time I see him he won't be too upset with me.

The following Monday evening, I'm upstairs in my bedroom, getting my clothes ready for work the next day. I hear the doorbell ring and Mother goes to answer it. My door is open and I can hear the conversation downstairs.

"Good evening Mrs. Cressford," I hear L.C. say.

I almost faint! What is he doing at my house?

"Hello Mr. Boone," I hear Mother reply.

I tip toe out of my room onto the landing to listen. I can hear that he is inside the front door.

"I have a package here for Marietta. Miss Ella had to order a couple of blouses that we didn't have in stock and they came in Thursday. She figured Marietta must have been too busy to stop by and pick them up, so she told me to drop them off since I was headed in this direction."

"I've never heard of the owner of the store making deliveries," I hear Mother say.

"Well, everybody knows Miss Ella is the boss. I just own the store."

I breathe in deeply, trying to calm my nerves and go down the stairs before Mother calls for me. She hears me coming down the steps and she turns around to look up at me.

"You got a package here," Mother says. "Ella sent it over by Mr. Boone."

"Oh, thank you Mr. Boone," I say, smiling in my normal cheerful self. "You didn't have to go through all that trouble. I had planned on stopping by this evening after work, but I had so much to do."

"Aw, it's no trouble at all," he says. "We're just glad to have your business."

"Excuse me Mr. Boone," Mother says. "I have to see about my dinner."

"You have a good evening Mrs. Cressford," he says to her as she walks into the kitchen.

"I really appreciate this," I say loud enough so that I know she can hear. "What are you doing here?" I whisper to him.

"Like I said, it ain't no trouble at all," he says loudly. "Why didn't you come Saturday?" he whispers to me.

"I couldn't get away," I tell him. "I wanted to see you but I couldn't."

"Meet me this Saturday at the store or I'm coming back again with another package until you do."

"Good evening Mr. Boone," I say loudly. "Alright," I tell him softly.

"Good evening Marietta," he says loudly, for Mother to hear. He smiles as I close the door behind him.

Now what is he up to? He acts like he has to see me. My mind starts to think of all kinds of things. Maybe he does want to be more than a friend. But no, it's been long enough that he would have told me by now. I'm excited and emotional, but I try to make myself not feel this way.

I take my package up to my room and open it. I unfold the tissue paper and find two blouses, both with long sleeves in two different colors, one cream and one light orange. I take the tissue out of the box and find more tissue wrapped around something smaller. I undo the paper and find a pair of white, silk, lace panties.

I go over to Waylene's after dinner. I don't tell her about my package, but I do tell her that I'm going to go over to L.C.'s store on Saturday after it closes.

"I'm telling you, you better not go," she says.

"But I want to. He's only a friend and he needs to confide in me about a situation he has," I tell her.

"He's lyin'. If he had any kind a problem, he damn sure wouldn't be askin' you for advice."

"And why not?" I ask indignantly.

"Aw girl, he ain't stupid. Besides he's got plenty of money and people with plenty of money don't have no problems."

"Money doesn't exempt people from problems, Waylene."

"I'm here to tell you that man ain't got no problems."

"Well, he asked me to meet him and I'm going."

Waylene looks at me suspiciously.

"You know you wrong," she says, pointing her finger at me.

"I know I'm wrong, but I'm going," I tell her.

I can tell she's getting mad.

"I have a confession," I say.

"You don't have to tell me," she says in a low tone. "I already know you like him."

"I do. You were right. The more I'm around him, the more I want to get closer to him. I can't help the way I feel."

"Aw naw, Marietta. I told you not to do it. See what's happened? And it's gonna get worse and the worst part is he ain't never gonna be yours."

"I don't care that he'll never be mine. I just want the little bit of him that I can get."

She doesn't speak.

"I'm telling Mother that I'm staying with you Saturday night," I tell her.

"Oh no you don't," she says abruptly. "I'm not bein' in on this."

"You have to, Waylene."

"I can't do it. And besides. She told you you can't spend the night over here anymore."

"I know, but if I tell her your mother is away, she'll give in."

She stares at me for a long time with disdain in her expression.

"Please?" I beg. "I have to go see him."

She sighs, closes her eyes and shakes her head.

"I'm up here actin' like a momma," she says. "I know I can't stop you from doin' this, but I'm worried. We are best friends and I don't want to see my best friend hurt."

I hug Waylene.

"If I do get hurt, then I'll have my best friend to help me get through it."

I walk in the drizzling morning rain to catch the bus to take me to work.

"Good morning, beautiful," I hear a familiar voice say loudly through the rolled down passenger side window of a car.

I peek from under my umbrella and see L.C. smiling at me. I look to if anyone is around, but the street is empty. I walk to the car and lean down to speak to him.

"What are you doing out here?" I ask him. This isn't the spot where he usually drops me off after we've met. I'm only four houses up the street from my house.

"I couldn't wait until Saturday to see you," he tells me, "so I called your job and told them you wouldn't be there today."

"What?" I gasp. I'm shocked that he would do something like that.

"I told them I was your brother and I was calling for you."

"You did what?"

"Are you gonna just stand out there getting wet, or you gonna get in and come with me?"

I close my umbrella and get in the car. We drive off.

"You might want to sit down low in the seat in case we drive by somebody you know," he tells me. "You know some folks around here are real nosey and they couldn't wait to tell your momma they saw you in some man's car."

He was right. I sink down far enough so no one would be able to see me.

"I'll tell you when we get to the highway," he tells me.

I sit uncomfortably for a minute or two until I feel the car speeding up.

"Can I sit up now?" I ask.

"Of course you can."

I straighten myself out and sit up.

"Now what do you think you are doing?" I ask.

"Like I said, I couldn't wait until Saturday," he tells me.

"You couldn't wait two more days?"

"Sure couldn't. I thought today would be a better day to spend some time with you. This way you won't have to worry about lying to your mother on Saturday and we can spend the whole day together."

"What are we going to talk about for a whole day, L.C?" I ask.

"We'll think of something", he says slyly.

"I'm going to miss a day's pay."

"I got that covered."

"Got it covered?"

"Yeah. I'm gonna make up your pay."

"That's nice of you to offer, but I can't take your money."

"You're so decent."

We get off the highway and eventually come to a big three-family house.

"This is my house I was telling you about," L.C. says.

He gets out of the car and comes to my side to open the door. He takes my umbrella, then my hand and helps me out. L.C. holds the umbrella over us as we run out of the rain into the front door and up two flights of stairs to the top floor, where he unlocks the door of his apartment. He lets me go in first. The place is nice. It's newly decorated and it smells fresh. It's cozy and inviting. After he closes the door, L.C. asks me if I want to look around. He helps me take off my coat and hangs it on the coat rack near the door. I walk from room to room. His place is clean and orderly.

"You got a maid?" I ask, standing next to a bedroom door.

"Naw, my momma taught me how to keep a place clean. Besides, I don't like living in a dirty house. This is my bedroom," he says, smiling at me.

I raise my eyebrow and turn to walk into the living room. L.C. follows behind me.

"You hungry?" he says, as I sit down on the couch.

"No, I ate already."

"Well, I'm hungry. I'm going in here and make me something to eat."

"You know how to cook?"

"Yeah I know how to cook. I got food in my refrigerator too."

I giggle at his sassy remark and go with him into the kitchen.

"Would you like for me to make you some breakfast L.C.?"

"Naw girl! I'm telling you I know how to cook. Besides, you're my guest. I don't want you thinking I just brought you over here to work for me. I want you to sit back and relax and have a nice time."

"Well then that's just what I'll do."

While he fries bacon and scrambles eggs, I sit close by and we make small talk. He takes a few slices of bread and places them in the oven.

"Hey, get me that jar of preserves out the ice box," he tells me.

I get the jar and when I open it, I can smell that it's old and no longer fit to eat.

"This has gone bad," I tell him. "You need to throw this out."

"Ain't nothing wrong with them preserves. Pass it on over."

"No! You can't eat this. You might get sick. I'm putting this in the garbage can."

"Don't you throw my preserves away!"

"Smell this." I walk over to him and put the jar under his nose.

"I don't smell nothing."

"L.C. you can't smell how strong that odor is?"

"Naw."

"I'm not letting you eat this."

I take the jar and throw it in the garbage can.

"Now what am I going to put on my toast."

I look up in his kitchen cabinets and find another jar of preserves.

"Oh," he says. "I didn't know I had some more up there."

"All you had to do was look." I smile coyly at him.

"That's why I need someone like you around," he says smiling with a very pleased look on his face. "You look out for me."

After he's finished eating, we go into the living room. I sit on the couch while he sits in the chair angled next to the couch. We laugh and talk for hours.

"I'm getting me a drink," L.C. tells me. "What do you want?"

"I don't know," I say. "Surprise me."

"You're going to let me make the decision on what you will drink?" he says, surprised. "Uh oh! Look out! I'm getting ready to get you drunk."

"That's not happening! And don't go making me a drink so strong that I'm going to choke on."

He comes back into the living room with two glasses in his hand and passes one of them to me.

"Yours is straight Coca-Cola," he says. "There's no liquor in it. You don't need to be drinking hard stuff."

"You can't go telling me what I can and can't drink." I joke. "I'm grown."

I take a sip of my soda and set it on the cocktail table. I can taste a very faint hint of liquor in my glass, but I don't say anything to L.C. about it. Actually, I need it. I can't believe I'm alone with him in his house. I sit there taking in the moment, trying not to be nervous. He takes a long swallow from his glass and sets the glass down next to mine.

"Oh yeah, guess who came in the store the other day," he says.

"Who?" I ask, not having any idea.

"Your momma. She came in to thank Miss Ella for sending your package by me. She told Miss Ella she didn't know we did deliveries."

"And what did Miss Ella say?" I ask, anxiously.

"She said we usually don't do that, but since I had to drive by that side of town she had me drop off a few packages to some other people, too. But she told your mother she didn't remember one being for you."

"Oh, no!" I gasp, almost jumping off the couch. "What did Mother say?"

"Hey, it's alright," he tells me as he pats my arm. "Don't get yourself upset about it. Miss Ella is quick to catch on. She told your mother she had forgot that she sent a box for you. She had seen me pack it, but at the time she didn't know it was for you. She saw me when I put the two blouses and the other gift in the box, but she only told your mother about the blouses. When your mother left, Miss Ella fussed me out. She told me not to be putting her in the middle of my mess."

He picks up his drink and takes a swig.

"So, how did you like the silk panties?" he asks, flashing me a devilish grin.

I don't answer him. I drink from my glass, looking at him over the edge of it.

"So does Miss Ella think something is going on between us?" I ask, evading his question.

"I don't care about what she thinks," he says in a serious tone.

"But I don't want her thinking anything. You shouldn't have put the undergarments in there anyway."

"I can do what I want to."

The troubled expression on my face lets him know I'm concerned about Miss Ella and my mother both being suspicious.

"Come on, girl," he says, trying to lighten the conversation. "Don't worry about it. Your mother didn't say anything to you about it, so she must have believed Miss Ella. You know she would have said something by now if she didn't believe it."

"That's true," I say, feeling a little relieved. "If she did think something she would have said it by now."

"I just wanted to let you know that your mother was in your business. Drink your cola and relax. Kick off your shoes if you want to."

"No thank you. I'll leave my shoes on. I'm fine for now."

"You wanna hear some music?" he asks.

"Sure," I say shrugging.

L.C. gets up from the chair and walks over to his stereo. He turns on the radio and works the dial until a song comes in on the airwaves. He walks back over and sits down on the middle of the couch close to me. He starts to talk about St. Louis, Missouri and how some Negroes are doing very well. He tells me he's thinking about starting another business.

After a while, he takes off his shoes and loosens his tie. I kick off my shoes and curl my feet up under me. I like being here with him. I feel comfortable.

It's still raining outside and the sky is growing darker.

"You know there's nothing worse than being married to somebody you don't love," he says all of a sudden. He stares at me, waiting for a reaction.

I'm stunned that he brought up marriage, since he doesn't like talking about it.

"Are you referring to your own marriage?" I ask.

"I'm not in love with my wife," he says, taking a drink from his glass.

"L.C., are you drunk?" I ask.

"Not at all," he says. "I'm just as sober as you are. I didn't love her when I married her and after seven years it still hasn't happened. I've left many times, but I go back mainly because of my boys. I want to leave again. Except for my children, I don't have a reason to stay."

"But you have all the reason in the world to stay. I'm sure she's a good wife and a good mother. And marriage isn't something that's all fun every minute of the day."

"I'm not saying that marriage can't be a good thing. It can. But the right people have to be together for it to work like it's supposed to. If you marry somebody that raises hell all the time and they complain about everything, it's gonna wear you out after so long. It doesn't matter what you got in the beginning. That's why it's important to be with somebody who has a personality that goes with yours."

I sit there thinking about what L.C. just said, wondering how I should comment when the radio starts to play a fast song I've never heard. L.C. gets up and starts to dance.

"Come on up here, girl," he tells me as he dances by himself.

I laugh at him.

"Come on, girl," he coaxes. "Show me what you can do."

I get up and stand in front of him. We dance and he makes silly faces while he gets into the grove of the music and I laugh.

Then I hear the soft sound of piano keys come in over the radio as an old song, a beautiful, slow song by Nat King Cole starts to play.

"Uh-oh," he says. "This is one of my favorite songs. You got to do a slow drag with me."

He holds out his hand, waiting for me to take it.

"I don't know how to slow dance," I say.

"Well, I'll teach you."

"No, I better not," I tell him and turn to go sit down.

Before I can get back to my seat, I feel his hand pull on my arm and I turn back to him.

"Come here," he says seriously. "Stop being afraid of getting close to me."

"I'm not afraid of being close to you," I tell him.

"Then dance with me."

He steps closer to me, but not so that his body is touching mine. He puts one of his hands on my waist and uses the other to take my hand into his and holds it out as far as we can reach.

"Now this is how you hold a woman when you dancing with her at one of them stuffy, uppity parties that she don't want to be at, but her momma makes her go 'cause they can't touch one another while they dancing."

He one steps and waltzes me around the room and I laugh.

All of a sudden he stops twirling me and stands firmly in front of me and while For Sentimental Reasons plays over the radio, L.C. finally confesses to me what I've been waiting for so long to hear him say.

"But this is how you dance with a woman when you want her to know how you really feel about her," he says, gazing into my eyes with loving softness.

He takes my arms and places them around his neck. Then he slides one of his hands over my hip and the other up my back and presses me against him. My heart starts to race. I know he feels my heart beating hard and strong because I can feel his. He puts his cheek onto mine and he feels so warm, so good. He slides his open hand up and down my back as I follow his moves slowly from side to side. I feel like I can stay there forever.

"This is how you hold the woman," he whispers into my ear, "that you've wanted to be with since the day she stood before you and it hit you all of a sudden how beautiful and sensual she's become. And you see her out at the clubs and you think destiny has to be the reason you keep running into her. And you find yourself thinking about her all day long. You even think about her when you're lying in your bed at night next to your wife, wishing you weren't there because it just don't feel right."

He presses me tighter against himself.

"And you try to convince yourself that you're just feeling lust for this fine, young woman and to leave it alone because things will end up the same way they always do when you have your way with a fine, young woman. But this is different and you can't leave it alone because your heart wants what it wants."

He pauses for a moment as he rubs his warm, smooth face softly against mine.

"You can't get her out of your mind," he goes on, "and your feelings keep getting stronger until all you can do is find ways to get closer to her. And you lie to her, telling her that you just want to be friends so you don't scare her away, but all the while you're trying to take your time to make her feel the same as you, 'cause you know the more time she spends alone with you the closer she'll become. And you know she wants you just as bad as you want her because why else would she go with you every time you ask her?"

And after the song goes off, he pulls back from me far enough to look me in the eye.

"But your biggest worry," he continues "is that you don't want to dishonor her. You want to take this tender, beautiful woman and make love to her like you never have before. But you can't. 'Cause she's not yours. And you know she won't make love to you because you're married. And that's the only thing standing in the way of what you both want to happen. But you want her to know that being married hasn't stopped what you feel for her and it never will. And you want her to know you love her."

I hold my breath, trying to keep control, hoping not to show my excitement at his confession.

He puts his lips to mine and brushes them back and forth teasingly.

And then I really become afraid. All this time I've wanted to kiss him and hold him, and now that we have this moment, I can't. I can't do this!

I take a step back, dropping my arms from around his neck, and try to turn my face from him, knowing that if he does kiss me, I won't be able to resist him. He lets go of my waist and steps closer, grasping my face with both of his hands, pulling it towards his, and I don't try to pull away from him. He closes his eyes and kisses my mouth slowly. His kiss is so warm and wet and inviting. My heart beats faster and I hear his breathing become heavier. He pulls his face back from mine, still holding it.

"I've never been in love until I fell in love with you," he tells me, caressing my cheek with his thumb. "And I know you love me too."

I part my lips to speak, but before I can say anything, he covers them with his. He puts his arms back around me and kisses me more until passion overcomes me and I find myself holding him tightly, kissing him back. He stops and looks into my eyes again.

"I want to make love to you," he says softly.

My mind tells me to grab my things and walk out right now! But my heart is making me stay. I start to feel warm, tingling sensations that I've never felt flow through my body.

He takes my hand and leads me to his bedroom. The cloudiness from the outside makes the room slightly dark but I can still see him. As we stand next to his bed, I watch him as he unbuttons his shirt and takes it off along with his undershirt. Looking at his masculine, strong, hard chest and arms arouses my femininity and I run my hand smoothly across his shoulder. He slides both of his hands onto my face.

"Do you want me?" he whispers.

"Yes," I say.

He kisses me so tenderly, so lovingly.

He slowly undresses us both, until he's down to his underwear and I in my panties. L.C. pulls back the covers on his bed. I get in and lay on my back with my head on his pillow. He lays on top of me, pulling the covers over us.

"You don't have to make love to me if you don't want to," he whispers.

"I want you," I tell him.

He gazes into my eyes.

"Marietta, I love you," he says. "I want to feel myself inside of you."

He caresses my breasts and the outside of my thighs. He kisses my neck and my shoulders and my stomach. He slowly sucks each one of my lips. His tongue glides over my nipples. Then he makes love to me ever so tenderly.

It's been seven months since L.C. noticed me in his store that day, and now I'm madly in love with him. I can't focus on anything except thinking of him and how soon it will be until I see him again and make love with him.

I call off work to spend the day with L.C. It's his birthday and it's only the second time I've been alone with him at his house. I wear the white, silk panties he gave me and when he sees them on me, he smiles seductively and makes love to me more passionately than the first time.

I haven't thought any further into the future about what I want with him. I just live in the moments we steal together. I don't know if anyone can see a difference in me since I've become L.C.'s woman, but if they do, I don't care. I like the way this feels.

"I can't keep seeing you like this," L.C. tells me while I lay in his arms after we've made love. I sit up in the bed and look at him. My heart sinks.

"You've gotten what you wanted and now you're getting rid of me." I say.

He sits up next to me.

"No baby," he says. He kisses my mouth. "That's not what I mean at all."

"Then why can't you be with me anymore?" I ask confused.

"I still want to be with you. I'm saying I just can't keep being with you for this little bit of time and then let you go on home while I lay here, wishing you were with me. Marietta, I want to be with you every day. I want to come home to you after I get off work. I want to wake up to you every morning."

"What are you saying?"

"I'm saying I'm going to get my divorce. We've been separated long enough and she knows I'm not coming back, so we don't need to waste no more time with this lie. Marietta, I want you to be my wife."

I feel the tears fill up in my eyes.

"What's wrong, baby?" he asks.

"I don't know what to say."

"Do you want to be with me?"

"Yes."

"Then tell me."

I look into my man's eyes with loving tenderness and I smile happily at him.

"I'm already yours, L.C."

It's about two weeks after Thanksgiving and I've missed my period twice and I'm worried. I tell L.C. about it and he tells me it's okay, that my body is just adjusting itself now that I've started making love. He takes me to see a doctor whose office is about an hour away from Westfield, where neither of us knows anyone. L.C. wants me to see the doctor so he can tell me the same thing.

When the doctor tells me I'm pregnant, I sit there in disbelief. How did this happen? I know where babies come from. I just never dreamed I would get pregnant.

I gain my composure and go out into the waiting room where L.C. is waiting. I don't say anything as he gets up out of his seat and follows me out of the doctor's office. We walk together silently until we get into the car.

"What did the doctor say?" he asks me.

"I'm pregnant," I say.

"Pregnant?" he says with a puzzled look on his face.

"Yes. We're going to have a baby."

"Pregnant?" he says again with a frowned face.

L.C. sits looking out the window for a few seconds.

I hadn't expected his responses, and now I don't know what to feel. I was hoping he would be happy, but why would I think that? My being pregnant isn't good news for either of us. Yes, he has plans to leave his wife for me, but this is bad timing.

After a few minutes, I sigh deeply and hang my head, feeling sad and ashamed. L.C. looks over at me.

"Hey baby," he says, scooting across the seat closer to me. He puts his arm across the back of my shoulders and pulls me into him. "Stop looking so sad. Everything is gonna be fine. It's okay."

Eventually, he drives away and we both remain silent during the drive to my house. I don't know what he's thinking. He's made a few half smiles when he's looked over at me, trying to make me think he's cool with this, but I don't think he is. I'm too afraid to ask him how he truly feels. I'm afraid to hear him blame me for our situation. I'm afraid he'll tell me he doesn't want any more children, and that I need to get rid of this one.

When we get close to my house L.C. asks me if I want him to go inside with me to tell Mother. I tell him no. I'm not ready to tell my mother about this. Not yet.

He kisses me and tells me to call him if I need anything. I get out of the car and close the door, and I swear I hear him yell 'damn' before he drives away.

L.C. has picked me up from work these last few weeks since I found out I'm pregnant. He seems to be more settled with the news of us expecting a baby. I still haven't told Mother that I'm pregnant. I'll wait until L.C. and I are married. Even though he hasn't said anything else about it, I do believe he will marry me. I hope he will. Then I'll tell Mother. I think that she will accept it better that way.

L.C. tells me he's working on his divorce and we should be married within the next few months. He needs to hurry with this. I'm afraid I'm going to start showing soon and everyone will know before we're married.

Exactly six weeks after I find out I'm pregnant, I start feeling tired and strange, but I try to act as normal as possible around Mother.

I'm in my bedroom getting my things ready for work the next day when I start to feel sick. I sit on my bed for a few minutes, hoping to feel better, when I hear a knock on my bedroom door.

"Yes?" I say.

The door opens and Mother stands in the doorway.

"How far along are you?" she asks me.

"I beg your pardon?" I say, not really knowing what she means.

"That baby you carrying. How far along are you?"

Fear strikes me and I immediately start to fumble with my bedspread.

"I'm not carrying a baby," I say without looking at her. I get up from my bed and go to my dresser, open the top drawer and look through my clothes.

"Don't lie," she tells me. "I've been with child four times. I know about being pregnant. I've heard you in that bathroom the past four days getting sick in the toilet. You were trying to cover up the sound with the water filling up the tub, but I heard what was going on in there."

I look back at Mother.

She walks into my room and stops not too far from me.

"Whose child you carrying?" she asks.

I don't answer and turn back to my drawer. I hear her walk up in back of me, and then I feel the sting of her open hand as she slaps me across the back of my head.

I grab my head at the spot where she hit me as I wince from shock more than pain. I turn to face her.

"Whose bastard is that you got growing in your stomach?!" she hollers at me.

Anger rises in me and I find the courage to face her. I've never faced up to my mother before, but at this moment I'm ready for her.

"L.C. Boone!"

"L.C. Boone?" she says in disbelief, leaving her mouth ajar. She stomps her foot and throws her arms up in the air.

"You laid down with that man and got his baby growing in you?!" she hollers. "Aw Lord, have mercy!" She screams so loud that Josette comes to see what is happening.

"What's wrong?" I hear Josette say, as she stands in the hallway in back of Mother.

"Your sister is going to hell!" Mother screams.

I looked away from her in shame.

"God is gonna strike the both of you dead! His wrath will surely be upon the both of you! You are a sinner in the worst way!"

I don't know what came over me, but at that very instant I gain the strength to tell her how I feel.

"Mother, I know what I've done is wrong," I cry. "But I love him!"

"I don't want to hear that foolish talk!" she hollers as she stomps her foot again. She leaves my room.

"I'm gonna beat that bastard out of you!" I hear her say.

I grab my shoes and my coat and run down the stairs to the front door.

"Where are you?!" she hollers through the upper part of the house.

I get to the front door and open it, putting on my shoes before she gets down the stairs. I run out of the house and down the front porch steps, carrying my coat. I hear her screaming at me as she chases me out of the gate.

"You leave my house and don't you ever come back here! Whore! God is going to strike you down!"

I'm halfway up the street before I stop running and I can no longer hear her voice. I walk and cry all the way to Waylene's house.

When I get there, I tell her everything, from beginning to end. We cry as she holds and comforts me. I calm down enough to go and pick up the phone and call L.C. on his office phone. The store is closed but I know he's still there. As I wait for him to answer, Waylene tells me not to worry, that her mother will let me stay with them until I have the baby.

"Boone's," he says when he answers the telephone.

"I'm over Waylene's house," I say trying to stifle my cries. "Would you come and pick me up?"

"What's wrong?" he asks me.

"I'll tell you when you get here. Please hurry up."

"She found out, huh?"

"Yes."

"I'll be there in a minute."

I hang up the phone and go back to sit on the living room couch.

Waylene sits next to me with her arm around my shoulders, telling me I'll be okay.

"Don't tell your mother about this," I say to Waylene.

She moves her arm from around my shoulder.

"I won't say a word," Waylene tells me. "Marietta, why did you let him do this to you?"

"He didn't do anything to me," I tell her.

"How could you let him get you pregnant?"

"All I know is I'm in love with him and I can't help it."

Waylene rolls her eyes.

"Well he doesn't love you," she says. "And he isn't leaving home for you either."

Anger rises inside of me.

"He does love me and he's going to marry me too!" I say defiantly.

"No he isn't!"

"You don't know anything!"

"You still got time to leave him alone Marietta. Don't get wrapped up in his game no more than you already are."

I sit there and don't say another word to her. I'm mad that she's not more supportive. I was there for her when she had her fling with Michael, and now she's being so judgmental towards me.

The doorbell rings. Waylene opens it and let's L.C. come in. He comes into the living room and I get up and run straight into his arms, sobbing.

"It's alright, baby," he says, holding me tightly. "I'm here. I'm here."

We stand there for a few minutes while he consoles me.

"She'll call you later," L.C. finally tells Waylene as he leads me out the door. I don't say goodbye and neither does she.

She stands on the porch with her arms crossed as she watches us get into the car and drive away.

I look out the passenger side window as we drive. Neither of us speaks during the drive to his apartment.

We get there and L.C. parks the car along the curb. He gets out and comes around to my side of the car and takes my hand, helping me to get out. As soon as we get inside, I break down and cry again.

"Come here, baby," he says, pulling me to him.

I lay my head on his shoulder.

"I'm sorry, L.C."

"You have nothing to be sorry about."

"What am I going to do? She threw me out of the house."

He pulls back from me and looks into my eyes.

"What are you going to do?" he asks. "You're going to have my baby."

"But where am I going to stay? I don't have anywhere to go!"

I drop my head onto his chest.

"Listen," he says. "Look at me."

I look up at him.

"You are my woman," he tells me. "That's my baby you're carrying. You and this baby are my responsibility. Not your momma's, not your friends, mine. I don't need anybody to take care of either one of you. I take care of my woman. You hear me? Tomorrow we'll go get your clothes and you're moving in here with me."

"But I can't move in here with you. You're still married."

"That doesn't make a difference. I'm not with her so that's just a formality. I live here and now we're going to live here. And it won't be long before we're married. Trust me. From now on it's going to be you and me."

While L.C. comforts me, I stop crying.

"Don't you worry about nothing," he says, holding me as we stand in the middle of the floor. "I got you, baby I got you."

L.C. walks me to the bedroom and pulls back the covers on his bed. He helps me take off my clothes until I'm down to my bra and panties and I lay down. He takes off his clothes and gets in with me. L.C. gently pulls me to him and I lay my head on his warm, smooth chest. His fingers massage my scalp tenderly and he kisses my forehead, telling me again he will never let anything happen to me. I cling to him, feeling secure and loved and protected, and I eventually fall asleep in his arms.

The next day, L.C. goes to talk with my mother. He wants her to know he's going to do right by me. He wants Mother to accept his apology for getting me pregnant before we are married, but he assures her he is going to restore my honor and give our baby a name. He said Mother had been listening to him through the screen door not allowing him to step foot in her house. He said right in the middle of his conversation, Mother slowly started closing the front door, telling him to take his whore's boxes with him that were stacked on the porch and to never knock at her door again.

When I open the boxes, I find some of my glass things not wrapped in paper but broken from where she had just thrown them in.

Things have moved so quickly this past year. I'm a few months pregnant and living with the father of my unborn child, who still hasn't showed me divorce papers. He's as good as gold to me, giving me everything he thinks I want to make me happy. But the one thing I want most, his hand in marriage, he hasn't given me.

I meet L.C.'s brother, Elias, and his uncle Wes. I'm nervous, actually embarrassed, about meeting them with me being pregnant and unmarried. Elias welcomes me into their family and tells me he is happy that L.C. has finally found a woman that is good for him. I'm not sure if his uncle likes me. He's a mean looking man who doesn't say much and when he does talk, it is directed only to L.C. or Elias. Before they leave, Wes says to me 'thanks for your hospitality young lady' and shakes my hand. After they have gone I tell L.C. about my uncertainty with his uncle but he assures me that I am okay with him. He says Wes only calls you a lady if he respects and likes you.

We have our first Christmas and New Year's together and I enjoy it so much. My twentieth birthday comes, and L.C. takes me out to dinner. It's the first time we've been seen in public together as a couple and I tell him I'm relieved that we don't see anyone we know. He tells me he doesn't care who sees us and if someone did he would dare them to make a comment about it. I was hoping he was going to give me an engagement ring for my birthday, but instead he gives me diamond earrings.

Being with L.C. is the happiest I've ever been, but every now and then I think about what a mess I have gotten myself into; disowned by my mother and not married to the man I love so much. I cry when I think about it. I talk to L.C. and let him know how I feel. He comforts me and assures me that Mother will come around, and it won't be much longer before he makes me his wife. He tells me he's getting everything together and that when the time is right, we're going to leave this town and start over. He's going to sell the store he has here, and he's already working on opening another one in St. Louis. He wants to get as far away from Westfield as we can so that no one will bother us or meddle in our business and we can have each other all to ourselves. I believe him and love him so much that I stop complaining and let my man handle his business affairs.

L.C. is so attentive, making sure I'm comfortable during my pregnancy. He was taking me to and from work every day up until last week when I turned eight months pregnant. He made me give my notice at work, telling them I won't be coming back.

L.C. goes away for the weekends. He tells me he's been going to St. Louis for the past month to find a good place to open a new store. I complain about it, telling him I don't like being left alone. He tells me to be patient, that it won't be much longer before everything is ready. While he's gone, I sit and wonder about my mother and my brothers and sister and Waylene.

Waylene comes to see me before she leaves town to go live with her new man in Detroit. She tells me Miss Lucille plans to move up there with them after they get settled. Waylene has a mix of emotions she lays on me. It's the first time I've seen her since Mother put me out of the house. She tells me she's happy for the both of us being with the men we love, but she's still mad at me for getting pregnant and not being married. She's sad that our friendship isn't the same, that we're two different, grown women who less than a year ago confided in one another about everything, and now we both have someone else we're intimate with. She promises to call me when she gets settled, and I promise her we will come up to visit them when the baby is old enough. We both cry as we say goodbye. And as I watch my best girlfriend walk down the stairs of my home, I know it will be the last time I will ever see her again.

I try to make peace with Mother, but she won't talk to me. I call her twice just to see how she and Josette are doing and she hangs up the telephone on me both times. I don't know if she'll ever forgive me, but I can't worry about it too much. Not right now when I have a baby to get ready for.

I still keep in touch with Stanley's girlfriend, Myrtle. She's come up to see me several times, and she wrote Stanley a letter, telling him about L.C. and me. She lets me read the letter he wrote back to her. He's very upset with me and wants to kill L.C. when he gets home. I write him back, telling him to forgive me and how this wasn't L.C.'s fault, that he's just a man and he couldn't help himself for falling in love with me and that I was the stronger one and I should have known better. I haven't heard back from Stanley yet, but when he comes home in the next couple of years, I hope that all of this will be behind us and I will be back in his good graces again and he'll be excited about having a new niece or nephew. L.C. and I are hoping it will be a boy and we'll name him Louis Clark Boone after him. If it's a girl, we'll name her Francine after his mother.

One Saturday afternoon, when I'm well into my ninth month and could deliver at anytime, I'm sitting around the house bored to death. L.C. is out of town again and I want so badly to get out of the house. I've taken all the walks to the store that I care to. I don't drive and L.C. is gone with the car, so I call Myrtle and ask her to come and get me to take me somewhere, anywhere. I just want to get out of the house.

Myrtle takes me to Woolworth's and we sit in one of the booths and order shakes and hamburgers. As we talk and laugh, I happen to look past Myrtle and I see the back of L.C. and a woman and two boys, all walking together towards the front door. I know it's him because I see his side view as he turns his head to smile at the woman. He holds the door open to let them go out before him.

Myrtle turns around to see who I'm looking at and she sees him too as they pass by the front window. Her mouth drops open as we both watch them leave.

"That no good scoundrel!" Myrtle says. "I thought he was supposed to be in St. Louis? That was his wife!"

I sit there in amazement, unable to move. My blood starts to boil and I feel sick.

"Take me home," I finally say.

We leave Woolworth's and drive back to the house. I get out of the car without saying goodbye and storm into the house. Myrtle comes in back of me, knocking on the door, making sure it's okay to come in. I don't talk. I just pace back and forth in the living room until I cry. Myrtle tries to comfort me, but I tell her to let me be. I tell her to go on home and that I'll call her later.

I sit there on the couch waiting for hours until L.C. finally comes home.

"Hey baby, how you doing?" he asks, bending down in front of me.

I look at him with hatred.

"I saw you and your wife and your little boys out at the store today," I tell him.

He stands up and puts his hands in his pockets.

"What were you doing there?" he asks me.

"No!" I shout as I stand up from the couch. "What were you doing at Woolworth's with them?"

"I just got back in town today and I stopped over to see my boys. They wanted toys, so we took them to get some."

"You didn't have to take their mother!" I scream.

"Look, I'm trying to handle my business!" he hollers. "Edie is cool with this separation thing, but I have to tell my boys what I'm doing. I got to make sure they're taken care of before I go. I can't just walk away from my children and they're not prepared for what's about to happen."

"No you don't! You don't have to walk away at all, as far as I'm concerned! You stay with your wife! You been staying with her every time you walk out of here, saying you're going to St. Louis!"

"Aw baby, that's not true! I have been going to St. Louis. Today is the first time I've seen them in three weeks."

"You're lying!"

"Baby, I'm not lying!"

"Move out of my way!" I tell him as I try to get past him.

"Wait a minute Marietta!" he says, putting both arms around me as I try to go.

"Get off of me!" I tell him.

"Just listen to me!"

"You don't have a damn thing to say to me, L.C. Turn me loose!"

"I'm not letting you go!"

"Get off of me! I'm leaving!"

"I can't let you walk away from me."

I cry in anguish and my knees buckle.

"Baby, listen to me!" he says trying to hold me up. "I haven't been staying with her. I just got back from St. Louis today. I swear! I just took them to the store to buy the kids something and after that I talked to Edie about signing the divorce papers. I told her I still don't want to be married no more and she needs to go ahead and sign the papers. She's gonna sign them."

"I don't care what you said!" I cry. "You lied to me! You told me you weren't with her anymore and here you are sneaking off to be with her, leaving me at home by myself! Get off of me! I'm leaving you! I'm moving back home!"

"Damn it, I said I wasn't with her!"

"I don't want to hear it L.C.! Get off of me!"

He lets me go. I walk into the bedroom with him following me. I pull out a suitcase.

"What are you doing?" he asks, crossing his arms, standing in the doorway.

"I'm packing my things and I'm leaving."

"Where are you going to go?"

"I'm moving back home."

"How you gonna get there?"

"You're going to take me."

"No, I'm not."

"Then I'll walk."

"Baby, you can't walk back to Westfield."

"Then give me some money for a cab."

"I'm not."

"Then drive me back to my mother's house," I say to him over my shoulder as I put my clothes into the suitcase.

"She's not going to let you come back home."

"Take me anyway. If she doesn't let me stay with her, I'll stay with somebody else."

He comes into the room and stands in back of me.

"Marietta, you're not thinking straight. Come on now. Stop being so stubborn. You're jumping to the wrong conclusion. Let's work this out."

"What are we going to work out?" I say abruptly, turning to him. "What night you get to stay with me and what night she gets to be with you? I'm not living like that. I don't want you if you're going to keep being with her."

"Quit saying that!" he snaps. "I'm not with her! All I need you to do is give me a little more time to get her to sign the papers."

"A minute ago you said she was going to sign the papers. Now you're saying you need a little more time."

He doesn't respond and stands there looking like someone who just realized they've been caught in a lie.

"I don't have any more time for you," I tell him. "I don't want you anymore. Now take me home!"

"You don't mean that."

"Yes, I do."

He stands there for a long time, looking heartbroken.

"Alright, I'll take you to your momma's house," he says and walks out of the room.

I look around to see if there's anything else I need to take with me right now. I can't think of anything and decide I will have to come back later if I need to. I close my suitcase and sit it next to the bedroom door.

I hear L.C. walk into the kitchen and make himself a drink. Then I hear him walk back into the living room. The legs of the chair make a scooting noise on the floor as he plops himself in it.

I sit on the bed as I think to myself about the mess I've made of my life. What am I going to do? I know I can't go back home. I can't hear 'I told you so' for the rest of my life.

He did this to me. He made me love him.

I feel rage come over me and I get up off of the bed and go out into the living room, where he's sitting there looking solemn as he sips his drink. I stand in front of him but he doesn't look up at me. He just sits there, staring at the glass in his hand.

"You bastard!" I holler at him. "How could you do this to me?"

He ignores me and continues to look at his glass.

"You made me think that you were going to marry me!" I scream. "You told me all those lies about how you loved me and you always wanted it to be me, knowing all the time that you weren't ever going to marry me! When did you think you were going to tell me, L.C.? What, did you think I was just going to lay up here with you for the rest of my life, just living with you?"

He doesn't say anything. He looks at me and takes a sip from his drink and sets it on the side table.

"How long ago did she put you out?" I ask him. "And when were you going back to her? Did you think you could live between the both of us from now on? How were you going to do it? Huh?"

Still he says nothing.

I turn to walk away, but I'm so enraged that I turn back around and bend over slightly in front of him. I slap him in the face as hard as I can. He doesn't move. I ball both of my fists and hit him wherever I can. He gets up from the chair and walks past me towards the bedroom. I follow behind him and use my fists to pound on his back. He walks a few feet with me following him, still pounding before he turns to me and grabs my wrists, squeezing them tightly.

"Get off of me!" I scream, trying to break free.

I struggle for a minute and he lets go of my wrists. His looks at me with disdain for the longest time, and I return the stare. Then suddenly his look turns to sadness like he's given up because he knows he can't make things right again. His eyes plead for understanding, but I have none to give. He backs up from me, saying nothing.

"I hope you rot in hell for what you've done!" I holler at him. "I hope almighty God strikes you down!"

He goes into the bedroom, and a few seconds later he comes back out, walks past me and goes out the door, leaving me there alone.

The next morning, I wake up so tired. I had cried so much last night that my eyes are still puffy. L.C. didn't come back home last night. I've made up my mind that all I can do is go back to my mother's house and beg for her forgiveness. Maybe she will find it in her heart to let me back in. I'll only stay with her for as long as I have to. I'll get another job and find a place to live when my baby gets older. It's all I can do. I can't live with him anymore.

My suitcase is still packed and sitting by the bedroom door. I only have a few dollars on me. All of my money is in my savings account. L.C. let me save all of my paychecks and he's taken care of all the expenses for everything. I look in the dresser drawer where he keeps his extra money. There's seventy-five dollars there. I take it all. I'm going to have to take the bus home and I'll have to call a cab to take me to the bus station.

I go to the door with my suitcase and look at the place one last time. I've only lived here for seven months, but those were the best seven months of my life. I felt loved, happy, cared about by the only man I've ever loved, and now I feel betrayed, empty and alone. I leave so many emotions in this place, good and bad. I go outside and sit on the porch to wait for my cab.

I get to my mother's house a little before twelve noon. The cab driver helps me to the door with my suitcase. I ring the doorbell. Mother comes to the door but she doesn't open the screen door. She doesn't say anything. The cab driver sees that I'm not left alone, so he says good-bye and leaves.

"Hello, Mother," I mumble, not making eye contact with her.

"Why are you here?" she asks.

"I need a place to stay," I say softly.

"What happened? Did he use you and throw you out?"

"No, I left."

"Oh, you did?"

This is so hard for me. A loving, forgiving mother would tell her child she understands that people make mistakes. She would take her child in and help her deal with the situation, help her ease the pain. A loving mother would make her daughter not feel like such a fool, but not my mother.

"Why did you leave?" she asks, still not offering me to come inside.

"He's still been seeing his wife."

"I'm sure he was. What made you think he was just gonna walk away from his home and take up with you?"

"Mother, I need to come back home."

"What makes you think I'm going to let you come back into my house? You have shamed this family beyond reproach. You've broken God's commandment of committing adultery."

I look my mother in the face.

"Mother, would you please be a little more compassionate? I have already been humiliated and I'm in need of your help."

"And why should I help you?"

"Because I'm your daughter! I'm your family. If you don't care about me, then think about your grandchild."

"Family? Family? That don't give you a right with me! Just because you're my daughter don't mean I got to do a damn thing for you!"

"I don't have anywhere else to go."

"Go stay with your girlfriend, Waylene."

"Waylene moved away. Listen, I have enough money to pay you for a couple of months for letting me stay."

"Where did you get some money from? Is that what he paid you for laying up with him?"

"No! I worked on my job and made my own money," I tell her. "I've always put something aside in case I need it."

"Well at least you still have that little bit of sense about you."

"Mother, out of Christian kindness, would you please allow me to stay in your house until I get back to work and find a place for me and my child to live?"

She finally opens the screen door and lets me come in.

"I'm going to let you stay until after your baby is born and you can get back out on your own," she says as she closes the door behind me. "And while you here, you better not call that man or have him coming to my house."

"I'm finished with L.C. Boone. And if I never meant anything else in my life, I mean that."

My baby, Francine Marie Cressford, is born nine days after I leave L.C., on July 17, 1955. I give her my last name, not his. I don't put him down as the father. I don't want anyone to know L.C. Boone is her father.

Francine is the most beautiful baby I've ever seen. She has a head full of curly, black hair. Her little lips are shaped like a heart. She's a fat, little old girl. I love her so much! I've been in the hospital for two days now, and the only person who has come to see me both days is Myrtle. Mother and Josette dropped me off the night I went into labor. They stayed with me until Francine was born and then they went home and haven't been back since. I could tell Josette was secretly jovial about her new niece. She just couldn't display her excitement in front of Mother. I didn't call L.C. to let him know I had her, and I'm sure my mother didn't either. I made Myrtle promise she wouldn't. Maybe one day when Francine is older I'll take her to see her father. And then maybe I won't.

I'm nursing my baby when all of a sudden I look up to see familiar fingers curled around the edge of the door, and I hear someone say, 'It's okay, I'm the father'.

L.C. steps inside and closes the door behind him. He has red roses tied with a big, white bow in his hand.

"Your nurse didn't want me to come in 'cause you were feeding the baby," he says, smiling. "I told her I already know what they look like!"

I look at him with no expression and continue to feed Francine.

"Can I be next?" he says, biting on his bottom lip, looking at me seductively.

I roll my eyes at him. He sits on the bed next to me.

"These are for you. The nurse is bringing in a vase."

I don't respond.

"How you doing, baby?" he asks me.

"Don't call me baby," I tell him.

"How you doing, Mrs. Boone?"

"Don't call me that either. I'm not your wife."

"You will be."

"No I won't."

"You will be in due time."

"L.C. don't come in here starting anything with me!"

"I didn't come here to bother you," he says. "I came to see my baby girl. Did you name her Francine?"

"Yes, I did."

"Give her to me."

"No. She's feeding right now."

"Look, I'm coming to terms with how you feel about me. But that's my baby you have. Don't try to keep her from me. Now let me hold my baby girl."

He has a way of letting me know when he means business, and on this one I can see he won't back down.

When Francine finishes nursing, I quickly cover my breast and give her to him. He takes Francine and sits in the chair next to my bed.

"Hi Francine," he says, smiling at her. "Hey daddy's baby. It's your daddy. How's my little girl?"

He places one of his baby fingers in her tiny hand and I watch her take hold of it. He sits silently looking at his daughter. He touches her hair. He strokes her little cheek. He kisses her forehead.

"She's beautiful Marietta," he tells me.

L.C. looks into his little girl's face, then smiles as he rubs his nose carefully against hers.

There's something about seeing him holding her that makes me forget how much I can't stand him. Watching him bond with Francine makes my heart melt.

"I miss you Marietta," he says without looking at me. "And I know you miss me too. I want you and Francine to come home."

My mood changes suddenly as I think about him lying to me.

"I'm not coming back L.C.," I say.

He stands up and puts Francine in the bassinette, and then he sits on the bed next to me. He tries to stroke my face with his hand, but I move. I don't want him to touch me. L.C. reaches into his pocket and pulls out a ring box and opens it. Inside is a diamond ring with a big, round stone in the center and three diamonds mounted onto the white gold band on either side of the round stone. There's a matching wedding band.

My mouth drops open. He takes my left hand in one of his and places the ring on my finger.

"I want you to marry me."

I frown at him.

"I meant what I said," he tells me. "I can't be without you Marietta. I want you to be my wife. My life ain't right without you in it."

I look into his face until I feel the love I have for him radiate in me, but I abruptly repress it back to where it's been hiding. I start to cry and my tears drop onto my cheeks. L.C. bends forward and holds my face and tries to kiss me, but I turn my head away from him.

"I'm not falling for this again L.C.," I tell him. "You need to go home to your wife and children."

"I keep telling you I'm not with her. I don't live there anymore."

"Even if you are gone from there, it still isn't right with us. You've lied to me about too many things. I don't want to be your wife or your mistress or anything else. I'll make sure you see Francine, but stop trying to make me love you again. It's not going to happen, so leave me alone."

I take the ring off my finger and give it back to him. He puts it back into the case. He gets up from the bed and leans over and kisses my face before I get the chance to move. L.C. bends over the bassinette and kisses Francine before he walks to the door.

"I'll be waiting for you at home when you're ready," he tells me before he walks out.

L.C. has come to see me a few times at my house since I've had the baby, but I turn him away. Each time I tell him no and each time he tells me to let him know when I want him to come and get me. I'm still hurting. I don't trust him, and I don't know if I'll ever be able to trust him again. Luckily, Mother isn't around when he's come over.

By September, I go back to work at my old job. Mother makes me find a sitter to watch Francine. She never watches Francine for me. Actually, she doesn't do anything with her. It angers me that she takes my mistake out on Francine. My baby had nothing to do with what happened, and it's not fair. Josette watches her for me when I have to go to the store or while I'm washing or cleaning the house. Mother barely talks to me except to see how far along I am with saving up my money and looking for my own place.

It's been so hard for me to leave Francine and go back to work. She's my heart and I just love that little girl. But I have to go to work. I have to save up enough money to get the hell out of my mother's house.

It's a cold day in November and I'm leaving work. I see L.C. in his car parked outside my job. He calls for me to come and get in the car. At first I ignore him, but I have to walk past his car to get to the bus stop and as I walk closer, I see him holding Francine. She's all bundled up in her snow suit, sitting in his lap.

"Say hi mommy," he tells Francine, waving her little arm.

"How did you get my baby?" I ask him. "How do you know who her babysitter is?"

"I know a lot of things," he says, smiling. "Get in and I'll take you home."

I get into the car and he passes her to me.

"Is it alright with you that we stop at my house before I take you home?"

"No L.C.," I tell him adamantly. "I know what you're trying to do. Stop trying to make me get back with you. It's over between us and I mean it. So stop doing this."

"Listen, I've accepted that you don't want to be with me no more. As bad as it hurts, I've accepted that. But we have a child together and we have to get along for her sake. I just want to spend some time with her and she's too little for me to handle by myself. So can you throw in the towel for a minute and be civil? I'm just asking for a few minutes of your time. That's all."

I look at his pleading face and soften up. I know I shouldn't, but I let him talk me into going to his house.

By the time we get to L.C.'s, Francine is asleep. He carries her into the house. I follow him as he goes into his bedroom. I thought he was going to put her on his bed but there's a baby crib in the room. L.C. walks over to the crib and lays Francine in it.

"Why do you have a crib in your room?" I ask him.

"Because I have a baby," he says as he takes off her hat and snowsuit. The crib is already made with baby sheets and a blanket. There are two baby dolls in one of the corners of the bed and I see several baby outfits and diapers lying on his dresser. L.C. pulls the blanket over Francine and we walk quietly out of the room.

"You want something to drink?" he asks me.

"No, I'm fine."

He walks towards the kitchen. I go to the living room and sit down in the corner of the couch.

"How was work today?" he says from the kitchen.

"It was fine," I say.

L.C. walks back into the living room with a drink in his hand.

"Want some bourbon?" he asks me.

I shake my head no. He sits down right next to me and stretches his arm onto the back of the couch behind me.

"My day was rough," he says. "Miss Ella cussed out the delivery man. Then she tried to get hainty with me and I had to tell her I'm her boss, she ain't mine. Some fat woman tried to bring back some shoes that had a split in them. Miss Ella told her she should have bought the right size and she wouldn't have had that problem. It was just one thing after another and I said to myself, I need to be in the company of somebody that can calm me down, somebody that knows how to soothe my soul. And guess who I thought of that could do it?"

I give him a fake half of a smile.

"It's working already," he says. "I feel better just sitting here talking to you."

He takes my hand and rubs it.

"I'm sorry about everything," he tells me.

I pull my hand away from him and get up from the couch. I go over to his television set and turn it on and then sit back on the couch where I was. As I watch the television, I feel him staring at me.

"Stop staring at me," I say without looking at him.

"I can't," he says as he takes my hand again. "Look Marietta, if you can't be my woman again, at least be my friend. I miss being around you."

"Being your friend is what got us into this mess," I say, still not looking at him.

I hear him sigh deeply as he looks away from me. I can tell I've hurt his feelings with the remark I just made, and I shouldn't have said it. He still holds my hand as he begins to gently rub his thumb over my knuckles.

"I wish you could find the love you once had for me again," I hear him say.

I want to pull away from him, but I don't because I like how it feels. And the more he caresses my hand, the more I let go of the resentment I have been feeling for him all these months. Being here in his house, sitting next to him again heightens my senses of desire and makes my heart ache. I yearn to move closer to him, to smell his scent, to feel his body touching mine, to receive his loving look. I try to resist, but I can't. This man has some kind of spell on me. I look him in the face and as we gaze into each other's eyes, love radiates from both of us into one another. I don't want to hold back what I feel for him anymore. I smile softly at the man I can't help but love, and he smiles back at me.

"I don't want you to think I'm making a move on you," he says. "So I'm going to ask you if it's alright with you that I lay my head on your lap."

"I guess so L.C. Go ahead."

He lays his head on me and looks up at me.

"You don't know how much I miss you lady," he says. "I want you to come back home."

He reaches his knuckles up to my check and gently caresses it.

"All day long I think about you and how your body feels up under mine," he tells me.

He slips his hand around the back of my neck and pulls my face down to his and he kisses my lips.

"I still love you," he says.

And before I know it, he's making love to me.

Afterwards, L.C. talks me into moving back in with him. He wants me to just stay the night, but I have him take me home. I want to get my and Francine's things from Mother's house. I don't want her breaking anything like she did the last time.

The next day, L.C. picks me up from work. We leave Francine at the baby sitter and we'll pick her up on the way home. I saw Mother before I left for work this morning, but I didn't tell her about my plans. I had most all of our things packed last night and had put the suitcases under my bed so that Mother wouldn't know.

When we pull up to the house, I get nervous. L.C. can see my anxiety and asks me if I want him to go tell Mother. I tell him to just wait for me to bring the suitcases to him. I take a deep breath, get out of the car and go inside.

Josette tells me Mother isn't home. I'm relieved. I go upstairs and get my suitcases and take them onto the front porch.

L.C. has gotten out of the car and is waiting for me on the porch steps until I come out.

"Everything all right?" he asks me.

"She's not here," I tell him.

I go back in and tell Josette I'm leaving and that I will call her and Mother soon.

The next day I call. I tell Mother I'm going to marry L.C. I tell her L.C. has given me a ring.

"Give him that ring back, Marietta," she tells me. "Ain't nothing good gonna come to you by being with him. That man already belongs to someone else."

"Mother, I love him. I want to be with him. I want Francine to grow up with her father. All children have that right."

"What about the children he has already? Don't they have the same right to be with their daddy?"

I hold the phone and don't respond to her.

"You just better know that what he did to his wife, he will surely do to you," she says and hangs up the phone.

I sit there thinking about what she said. She's wrong. My man loves me and I can't wait to call her back and tell her when I become Mrs. L.C. Boone.

We spend our first Christmas together with our baby. L.C. adores Francine. Every day when he comes home from work, he picks her up and kisses and hugs her. He holds her in his arms even when she's asleep. It warms my heart so much to see how he fusses over Francine. And for a while I use that to keep me patient while I wait to be his wife.

L.C. doesn't marry me the next month like he said. He promises we will be married by March. But that doesn't happen either. Each time he tells me it won't be much longer, but when the time comes there's always an excuse. My arguing doesn't move him because he knows I can't leave him. I have nowhere to go. Mother would never take me in again. I'm tired of him making me wait, humiliating me.

It's Memorial Day and I'm at home alone with Francine. I'm angry that it's the holiday and L.C. isn't here with me. He told me to be ready to go by four o'clock because we were going over to Russell's house to have a cook out with him and his family. It's almost five and L.C. isn't here. This isn't like him. He's always on time.

I don't know why but I call a cab to drive me to the house where L.C. used to live with his family. My gut feeling tells me something isn't right.

When I get there, L.C.'s car is parked in the driveway and there are people on the front porch of the house, laughing and talking. I ask the cab driver to wait as I sit there wondering what to do. He tells me he needs to collect my fare and has to get another customer. I pay him and get out of the cab. I stand there on the sidewalk in front of the house, holding my baby in my arms. My better judgment tells me not to go and confront L.C. with all these people here, but my pride doesn't care about embarrassing him. Hell, he has embarrassed me by being here.

I walk up to the porch with Francine and as I get closer, I hear someone say, 'That baby looks just like Renzo'.

"Is Edie here?" I ask one of the people on the porch.

"Yeah, she's out in the back yard," one of the ladies says. "You can go around the side or you can go on through the house."

"Who is that?" I hear someone ask.

"I don't know," I hear someone else say.

I walk around the side of the house and open the fence to the backyard.

"Where's Edie?" I ask a man at the picnic table.

"She's in the kitchen," he says.

I go up the steps into the kitchen and open the back door.

I see a woman at the sink. She turns to see me coming in the door and as I look at her, jealousy overcomes me. I'm face to face with the woman L.C. says he never loved, but he comes home to and has children with and shared this home with. She has everything he keeps telling me he's going to give me, but hasn't. I can't have him because of her. But I'm going to tell her about us.

"Edie?" I ask.

"Yes?" she answers.

"I'm Marietta."

"Marietta?" she says, like she's supposed to know who I am.

"Yes. I'm L.C.'s fiancé and this is our baby."

Edie stares at me and then looks at Francine.

"What?" she says, frowning with confusion.

"This is L.C.'s baby."

"What the hell is this?" she yells at me.

"I'm tired of this game L.C. is playing. I want you to know that he has asked me to marry him."

"You got a lot of goddamn nerve coming into my house, telling me you got a baby with my husband!"

Several people come into the kitchen to see what is going on.

"Well it's time you know!" I say.

L.C. walks in the door from the backyard and looks at me in disbelief. His friend Wilson is right behind him.

"Marietta? What are you doing here?" he says in shock.

"Get the hell out of my house!" Edie hollers at me.

Edie and I both start yelling at him and each other.

She tells me to get out of her house and tries to push me and I hit at her with the arm that isn't holding Francine. She tries to fight me while I'm holding my baby and someone takes Francine from me. L.C. keeps us apart for a minute.

"What in the hell you think you doing, Marietta?" L.C. yells in my face.

"I'm telling her what you should have told her a long time ago!" I say defiantly. "I'm tired of waiting on you L.C.!"

"Is this why you in such a hurry to divorce me Louis?" she says to L.C. "You want to marry this bitch?"

"Who are you calling a bitch?" I holler.

I try to reach around L.C. to grab at her, but he halfway picks me up and drags me through the house, out into the front yard. I try to break away from him.

With Wilson leading the way, L.C. carries me towards Wilson's car parked out on the street. All the while I'm hollering at him, telling him to let me go.

"Take her ass home," L.C. tells Wilson before we get to the sidewalk.

When we get to the sidewalk, he slings me onto the grass near the edge of the side walk.

I can't believe this! He just threw me out like I'm trash!

I get up, unhurt and try to walk past him to go back into the yard but he pushes me back.

"You get in the car!" L.C. tries to say in a controlled voice. He's shaking with anger.

Wilson is holding the car door of the back seat open, waiting for me to get in. Several people have followed us to see who I am and what is happening.

"Where's my baby?" I cry, looking around for her.

"I'll get her," some woman says, walking back towards the house.

I try to walk past L.C. again and he grabs me.

"Get your ass in that goddamned car and don't you get out!" he hollers.

"I'm going to get my baby!" I say with tears rolling down my cheeks.

I can see a woman coming towards us with Francine in her arms. As L.C. lets me go past him so I can get my baby, I see Edie coming up behind her with a knife in her hand. She rushes past the woman carrying Francine and someone screams. L.C. turns around just in time to find Edie with the knife raised and ready to strike. I don't know how it happens, but during the struggle of L.C. grabbing Edie and me trying to get at her again, I feel the sharp blade of the knife cut into my shoulder.

L.C. and another man wrestle Edie to the ground and take the knife from her. L.C. gets up and comes over to me while the other man consoles Edie. She's lying there, screaming and crying, cussing at L.C. Another man comes and helps Edie get up and walks her into the house. Blood is dripping from my shoulder. L.C. grabs my arm and leads me to Wilson's car again. The car door to the back seat is still open and L.C. pushes me in. Wilson stands next to L.C. as if guarding him from everyone standing there watching.

"What do you think you're doing?" he hollers at me, standing in the doorway. "Why did you come up here causing trouble?"

"'Cause I'm tired of this shit!" I tell him. "I'm tired of you going back and forth between her and me!"

He stands there looking at me, breathing deeply.

The woman holding Francine steps around L.C. and passes my baby to me. She steps back onto the sidewalk and continues to watch.

"Take her home," he tells Wilson without looking at him. Wilson walks to the driver's side and gets in.

"I'm not going to your house!" I tell him.

"Shut up!" he hollers at me. "Shut your ass up!"

He makes sure I'm in the car before he slams the door.

"Take her home now!" he yells at Wilson.

L.C. must have called Russell and told him what happened, because a few minutes after I walk in the door at home, he and his girlfriend Gladys come over. When Gladys sees the dried blood on my arm and sleeve, she takes me in the bathroom and cleans and bandages my wound. She makes me lay down while she sees about Francine.

When L.C. comes home a few hours later, I'm in the kitchen pouring a bottle of Coca-Cola into a glass. I've been sniffling and crying from time to time. Wilson and Russell are sitting at the kitchen table and Gladys is sitting in the living room, looking at the television.

L.C. comes straight into the kitchen and stands in front of me, mad as hell and breathing hard.

"Don't you ever do no shit like that to me again!" he hollers.

I feel the anger rise in me.

"You stop lying to me and I won't!" I yell at him.

"I haven't been lying to you!" he yells.

"You just did! I just caught you having a party with your wife and a house full of people!"

"Marietta, I just stopped by to give her some money for my children and to talk to her about our divorce! That was her party, not ours. I've told you time and time again, I'm not with her."

"And then she stabs me and you push me in the car and tell me to go home!"

"You lucky she didn't slit your goddamn throat! What did you think she was gonna do? You don't walk into a woman's house with our baby and tell her you layin' up with her ex-husband and don't expect she ain't gonna do nothin'! What if somethin' would have happened to Francine?"

"If you wouldn't have been over there, I wouldn't have gone over to her house!"

"Me being over there is beside the point! You didn't have any business goin' over there!"

"That is the point, L.C.! You were there! And I'm going to the police and tell them she stabbed me!"

"You better not step foot in no police station!"

"I'm going to turn her in!"

"Don't go causin' any more trouble, Marietta! Leave this alone!"

"She cut me and you're trying to protect her! You don't love me. You don't give a damn about me. You just want to use me when you can. You're nothing but a liar, L.C.!"

I'm taken by surprise as he uses one hand to grab me by my throat and push me up against the wall. I can see the rage on his face.

"I oughta break your fuckin' neck!" he hollers at me. "All the shit I've done to be with you and you gonna act like it don't mean nothin'!"

I hear Russell and Wilson yell at him to let me go as I claw at his hand and the two of them try to pull him off of me. Gladys tries to break between L.C. and me as she screams at him to stop. He lets me go and tells them to get off of him. They hold him while Gladys grabs me.

"You bastard!" I scream hysterically at L.C. "You damn bastard!" I try to get at him, but Gladys is holding me back, pushing me backwards into the bedroom. "I'll kill you! You better not ever put your hands on me again!"

L.C. struggles to get away from Wilson and Russell.

"Get off of me!" he hollers at them.

They continue to hold him until Gladys has me in the bedroom with the door closed. She sits me down on the bed.

"Marietta stop it!" she hollers. I'm shaking and crying uncontrollably.

She goes out of the bedroom and comes back with a cold, wet hand towel. I sniffle as she wipes my face. It takes me a while to calm down.

"Girl, why would you go to that woman's house like that?" Gladys asks me. "You could've got yourself killed!"

"Because I wanted her to know," I say. "I'm tired of sitting around here, hidden, while he's doing what he wants to."

I hear the front door slam. Russell comes to the bedroom door and steps inside.

"He just left out of here," he says. "Is she okay?"

"Yeah," Gladys says. Gladys continues the conversation with me.

"I wouldn't have went over there," she tells me. "I would've just beat the hell out of him when he went to sleep and then threw his ass out! You done made things worse than they was. But you can bet your bottom dollar she ain't gonna give him up now. She ain't never gonna take him back but she's gonna keep makin' him come see her just to spite you. Honey, I would just give him up right now 'cause from here on out, it's really gonna be some trouble. If he do decide to stay with you, then she gonna give him hell. She's gonna be callin' all the time, tellin' him the boys need this and that and he's gonna go 'cause you know he's crazy about them two lil' boys of his and he's gonna take care of them. Then she's gonna give him some, hopin' you can smell her on him when he come home to you!"

"Aw Gladys!" Russell says. "Shut your damn mouth!"

"Nigga, don't you start no shit with me!" she hollers at him. "Now you know I don't play! I'm just tellin' the girl what's gonna happen!"

"You run your damn mouth too much! Mind your own damn business."

"You don't tell me what to do!"

"I said shut up!"

"I ain't got to shut up!"

Russell rolls his eyes and doesn't respond.

Gladys turns her attention back to me.

"Honey," she begins, "if I was you, I'd tell that nigga to go right on back over there and stay where he was. He must still want her 'cause he didn't even bring you home. He gonna tell you to go home and he gonna see about her. That lets you know where his loyalty is. I wouldn't have put up with that shit. Uh-uh. You know these men will lay up with you but they always stay with they wife. Some of them don't even tell you they got a wife until way later, 'cause after so long they think you so in love with them that you ain't gonna leave when you find out. But I wouldn't even worry about him, girl. You pretty enough that you can find you another man anytime. I would tell that nigga to go right back over there."

"Don't listen to her," Russell says to me. "She ain't no authority on men."

"I know what I'm talkin' about!" she says.

"Aw, you don't know shit!" Russell tells her.

They bicker back and forth while I sit on the bed looking over at my baby in her crib, playing with her toys.

What have I gotten myself into?

As the tears well up in my eyes again, I feel ashamed for causing this grief upon myself and L.C. and his wife. What will my daughter think of me when she finds out I had her while her father was still married to another woman?

I can't marry him. And Gladys is right. Edie would give us hell after we got married. She wouldn't let us be happy. Now that I've done this, she's going to try her best to break us up. I don't want to go through all of that. It wouldn't be worth it. I know what I have to do. I have to leave again.

L.C. stayed gone all night long. Once again I decide to go running back to my mother, praying she will let me stay there again. All of this is so humiliating, so demeaning, and I know I'm going to hear it from her for the rest of my life. If I never marry it will be because I had a baby out of wedlock. If I do marry, whoever he is, he isn't going to take care of someone else's child. I'm dreading this, but what else can I do?

I pack up our things and before I leave, I take off my ring and lay it on the bed.

When we get home, I knock on the door and Mother opens it.

She stands there looking at me and Francine and the suitcase in my hand.

"You done left him again?" she asks.

I lower my eyes to the ground and shake my head yes.

I look back at Mother and see her looking at Francine. Francine is chattering away a mile a minute.

At first I don't believe it but she lets us in without any lecture. I go up to my room and find the things I had left behind are all gone. The room has been changed to a guest bedroom. I unpack my suitcase, while Francine sits on the middle of the bed playing with her toys. I put pillows around her on the bed to keep her from falling off.

I feel so tired, so drained. I think about L.C. and how much I don't like him. He's hurt me too many times now and I don't think I will ever forgive him.

Francine falls asleep not long after I finish unpacking. I go downstairs and find Mother sitting at the head of the dining room table with a stern, disgusted look. I try to go past her to the kitchen to get something to drink but she stops me.

"Sit down," Mother tells me.

I don't want to talk to her right now, but I guess I must.

I sit down at one of the side tables and look straight ahead, avoiding her stare.

"What happened?" she asks me.

Tears start to stream down my face and my lip starts to tremble.

"L.C. has been seeing his wife again," I say in a strained voice. I wipe my tears with my fingers and sniffle a few times.

"What made you think he had stopped?" Mother asks.

"He said he loved me and he wanted to marry me," I say, looking her in the face.

"And what made you believe that lie?" Mother says, as she squints at me through her glasses.

"It wasn't a lie," I tell her. "He does love me. He still wants to marry me but…"

"But what?" she screams at me, slamming her hand on the table, causing me to flinch. "But nothing! You keep running back and forth, letting that man use you up! He can never make an honest woman of you! He made you commit adultery! That man is evil, Marietta! Do you know that? The only way you can save your soul is to repent and ask God to forgive you! You better get your head together, girl. You have a child to take care of now and that baby is supposed to come first. You can't be running back and forth, thinking this man is going to be your husband! He can't! He already made a commitment to God to take care of his wife and their children. You stay away from him or both of you are going to hell!"

As mad as I am at L.C., I can't bear to hear her talk bad about him. He's my baby's father and despite the fact that he hasn't married me, I still feel like he's mine. I feel protective of him.

"Mother, I still love him," I say helplessly.

I wait for her to scream some more, but for some reason she seems to be confused by my statement. She looks at me queerly for a few moments.

"You have lost your mind," she tells me as she rises from the table.

Mother walks slowly out of the room, leaving me sitting at the table, sniffling.

L.C. comes to the house the next day, when Mother isn't home. I'm sitting on the front porch while Francine is playing on a blanket I have spread out on the floor. He comes up the walkway and slowly makes his way onto the porch. He goes over to Francine and picks her up. She smiles and coos as her daddy kisses and hugs her. He looks over at me with that soft look. I'm still mad at him and I roll my eyes.

"How is your arm?" he asks me.

"Its fine," I say dryly, looking down at the porch floor.

"You need me to take you to the doctor to have him look at it?"

"No."

"Go pack up your stuff and let's go home."

"No," I tell him firmly.

He puts Francine back down on her blanket then he comes over and sits down next to me.

"I went and talked to a lawyer a few months ago," he says looking at me. "He sent the papers to Edie. When she got them last week, she called me. She told me it was long overdue, that she knew we weren't right for one another no more. She asked me to stop over on the holiday so we could tell the boys together. She thought it would be easier with folks at the house so they wouldn't be thinking only about that the rest of the day. She wanted me to be there when she told her momma and daddy too. That's why I was over there when you came by. I talked to her again last night 'cause I thought she was gonna make it harder for me to get my divorce with everything that happened, but she's not. She said she don't want me no more than I want her. So it's finally going to happen. I suspect after a while she'll let my boys come stay with me sometimes in the summer and around the holidays."

I don't say anything and I don't look at him.

"Baby, I'm sorry for grabbing you like that," he says softly. He tries to touch me and I move out of his reach.

"Don't talk to me," I say.

We sit silently for a minute until he starts to play with Francine. I sit there, pretending to ignore him. I can feel him staring at me every so often. He stops playing with his daughter and turns his attention to me again.

"Why couldn't you just trust me?" he asks.

I look out into the yard and don't speak.

"Marietta, I told you I was working on this," he says. "I've been trying to make everything right for you and me and that's all I've been doing. You got this silly thing going on in your head about me cheating on you and you're wrong. I swear to God, I haven't been with her or anybody else since I've been with you."

He leans forward with his elbows on his knees. I can see him rubbing the palms of his hands together.

"I got the place up and running in St. Louis," he tells me. "It's been open for a month now and I'm already making good money. My brother is up there running it for me until I get there. I got us a house too. I've had it for a while but I didn't tell you about it 'cause I wanted to surprise you when we got up there."

He waits to see what I have to say.

"I found someone to buy Boone's," he says, "and I'm on my way to sign the papers for that in a few minutes. My divorce is the last thing I have to finalize."

He sighs long and hard. He stretches out his leg and reaches into his pocket. He pulls out my ring and then takes my hand. I give a weak attempt to pull it back from him, but he doesn't let go. He holds it and places the ring onto my finger. I still force myself not to look at him.

"Marietta, I've been the best with you that I ever have in my life," he says. "I've stop doing a lot of things and I've changed since I been with you. I ain't never been twisted up in no woman, but girl, you've got my heart. I love you baby, and nobody else. And I promise you I'll never love another the way I do you, no matter what happens."

He turns my face to him and I look into his eyes. He stares back at me with that loving look that makes me so weak for him. He holds my face and kisses my lips and I restrain myself from kissing him back. When he realizes I won't give in, he stops.

"I know you still mad at me," L.C. says. "And I guess you got a right to be. It shouldn't have taken me so long to make you my wife. But if you let me, I'm gonna make it up to you."

He bends down and picks up Francine. He kisses her on her cheek.

"Daddy's gotta go bye-bye," he says. He uses his nose to nuzzle her under her neck and she laughs. He puts her back onto the blanket and gets up to leave.

He walks to the top of the porch steps but before he leaves he turns back and looks at me.

"Baby, I'm leaving for St. Louis on the 18th," he tells me. "And I'm not coming back except to sign the final papers for my divorce. If you still want to be my wife and live that life we've been planning for so long, you be ready when I come for you."

He puckers a kiss at me and walks down the steps onto the walkway.

I get up and walk to the edge of the porch, wanting to walk down the steps after him, but I stop. I hold onto the handrail and watch him walk out of the yard.

I stand there feeling empty and sad. I should tell him to wait while I pack my bags. I should tell him I'm sorry for not believing him and that I knew he was making things right for us, but I don't. I want him to feel the same uncertainty I felt when I was sitting at home by myself, wondering where he was.

He looks back at me one last time and smiles at me with that loving smile of his before he gets into his car. I watch as the love of my life drives away.

For the next two weeks I go from feeling mad to feeling lonely to feeling justified. I refuse to call or go see him. But the Sunday night before he leaves, I feel differently. After a day of cussing him under my breath and thinking about how much I can't stand him, I lay awake in my bed that night next to my baby girl feeling bad that I hadn't taken her to see her daddy earlier today for Father's Day. I pull out my engagement ring from the nightstand next to my bed. I've been hiding it there from Mother. I put it on my finger and look at it in the moonlight that's shining through the window behind my bed. I think about L.C. and how I feel when he holds me and kisses me. My heart aches as I realize how much I miss him right now, and I start to cry. He told me he's leaving tomorrow and he means it. He won't be coming back except to sign those divorce papers. And all that he planned for us, all my waiting and wanting will be gone with him. I can't let him go without me.

I creep down the stairs and dial L.C.'s number. He picks up the phone. He knows it's me because he doesn't say hello.

"I've been waiting for you to call," he says, half asleep.

"Can you come over for a minute?" I beg, whispering and sniffling into the phone.

"I'm on my way."

The click of his telephone disconnects us.

I sit there in the dark living room, waiting anxiously until I think he's not far from the house. Then I go quietly outside and stand on the sidewalk in my robe and wait for him.

He pulls up to the curb and as soon as he gets out of the car and walks up to me, I grab him and lay my face onto his chest. We stand there holding each other.

"I'm sorry, L.C.," I tell him while the tears start to flow. "I am going to marry you."

"I know," he says. "I've always known."

I hold him tighter and try not to cry but I can't help it.

"Don't cry baby," he whispers to me as he rubs his hand up and down my back. "Everything's gonna be alright."

He kisses my cheeks as I sniffle.

"Stop crying" he says as he holds my face, wiping my tears away with his thumbs.

I take in a deep breath.

"I almost forgot to tell you, Happy Father's Day," I say.

"Thank you," he says smiling proudly. "You get back inside and get you some sleep. I'll be by tomorrow after two o'clock to pick up you and Francine, okay?"

"Okay."

I put my hands to his face and pull it into mine and kiss him. He hugs me tight and then let's me go.

"Kiss my baby for me," he says.

"I will."

He walks towards the driver's side of the car.

"I love you lady," he says as he puts his hand on his heart. Then puts his first two fingers to his lips, kisses them and blows the kiss to me.

"I love you too," I tell him.

I turn and walk up the walkway to go into the house, and as I look up at the unopened, second floor, hallway window, I swear I see the curtain moving.

The next morning, Mother comes to my bedroom door to remind me of the doctor's appointment she made for me. I had slept all night wearing my engagement ring. I hide my hand in my housecoat pocket so she won't see it.

"Mother, I really don't need to go to the doctor," I tell her. "My shoulder is fine."

"You need to have the doctor look at it," she says. "It's been over two weeks and that wound is not healing right. It shouldn't still be bleeding through the bandage.

"It doesn't hurt," I tell her. "Besides it only bleeds when I change the bandage and the scab comes off."

"Never you mind. I still want the doctor to look at it. You need to get some medicine to make sure that cut don't get infected," she says. "Get the baby ready so I can take her to the sitter. Then I'm coming back to get you. Hurry up, 'cause I got errands to run and I don't wanna be gone all day."

She walks out of my room and I take my ring off and put it back in my nightstand drawer. I pick up my savings account book from out of the drawer and count the money I have tucked behind the front cover. There's nine hundred and twenty-five dollars. I had closed my account at the bank in Mont Reid a week after I had left L.C. and I was going to put the money in a bank near my house but now that I'm leaving with L.C. I'm glad that I hadn't done it.

When Mother gets back from dropping Francine off, I'm ready to go. But before we leave, she gives me some medicine to take. She tells me the doctor may need to give me stitches, so I needto take the medicine before I get to the office so that it won't hurt so badly.

She pours a tablespoon of white powder in a glass of water and after she stirs it, she tells me to drink it. I don't argue with her because I want to hurry back from the doctor's office and be ready when L.C. comes for me.

As soon as we get into the car and drive along, I start to feel groggy and sleepy.

I don't know how long I have been asleep before two men dressed in all white are carrying me from the car up the front stairs of a building that I think is a hospital.

"Is this the doctor's office?" I say, slurring my words. I'm trying to wake up, but I can't.

"I don't know what she took," I hear Mother tell them as she walks with us. "She tried to kill her boyfriend's wife," I hear my mother's voice saying. "She left him and came back to my house and she was talking crazy about how much she loves him. I'm afraid she's going to try and hurt that lady again. I can't do nothing with her. She's gone out of her mind because of this married man she's been with. One of my church members told me he sells dope and I think that he gave her some and it messed up her mind. She can't control herself and I can't keep her at my house anymore. She's crazy!"

"What did you say?" I whisper. I can't wake up.

A little while later I fade in again to realize I'm strapped to a stretcher.

"Don't you worry, ma'am," I hear a man say. "We'll take good care of your daughter and I'll make sure that she doesn't contact anyone, especially Mr. Boone. We want her to get well without any interference. You go on home. We'll take over from here."

"Good-bye, Marietta," Mother says, looking down at me. "I hope you can get better."

She turns from me and I try to sit up. I can only get halfway up onto my elbows, but I can see her walking down the hallway with a nurse.

"Mother, where are you going?" I barely say.

"It's alright, Marietta," I hear a man's voice say. "I'm Dr. Leathers and I'm going to take good care of you.

"Where am I?" I whisper.

"You're in a mental hospital," he tells me.

I lay there horrified as I realize what is happening to me.

"No!" I cry. "I don't need to be here!"

I feel exhausted and my voice is strained as I talk.

"Call my mother back so she can take me home!" I beg him.

The doctor accompanies the orderly as they push me down the hall. We come to a room and they wheel me in.

"You'll be fine," the doctor says. He walks out of the room with the orderly and as I hear the lock on the door click, I lay there alone and I scream.

Part III

Amelia

—————

Going east on I-74, I pass by the mile maker sign noting Hamilton 40, Cincinnati 76. It hasn't taken me long to get from Indianapolis to what Aunt Amelia refers to as 'Little Detroit'. She told me they call Hamilton that because of the General Motors car factory which used to be there. All this time, I've been living less than a hundred miles from Grandmother's brother and sister, and didn't even know it. Why she never told us about them is still a mystery.

As I drive along, I think of what has transpired over these last three months. I'm still recovering from the funk I've been in since I found my mother alive in the nursing home. When my mother called out Uncle Stanley's name, we all had hoped that we could build relationships with her, no matter how minimal they might be. But after Dr. Albertson explained to us that her reaction was an unexplainable phenomenon that would probably never happen again, we became dismayed. But it doesn't matter what kind of relationship I have with her. She's my mother and I'm so glad I found her alive.

It didn't take long for me to get my mother transferred from the nursing home in Missouri to a nursing home of my liking in Indianapolis. It was rough, but Uncle Stanley and Aunt Myrtle supported and helped me with the move. They're both relieved to finally know what happened to my mother after all these years. It's been hardest for Uncle Stanley seeing her the way she is. He's dealing with it the best that he can.

Curiosity finally overcame Aunt Josette and she made it to Indianapolis to see my mother. When I took Aunt Josette to the nursing home, she immediately broke down crying and cursed Grandmother.

Uncle Wendell and his family still haven't come down to see my mother. When Aunt Josette told him that she saw Marietta and acknowledged the fact that it was indeed their sister, he cussed her out and told her she was crazy. He said we were all crazy. He told Aunt Josette that I had concocted this whole story, trying to fill the void of not having a mother when I was a child. He was adamant that his sister was dead and there was nothing anyone could do to make him believe otherwise.

Lisa asked so many questions when I told her part of what happened to my mother. I told her that Grandmother had my mother committed, but I didn't tell her why. I can't tell Lisa why because I really don't know for sure. No one knows for sure. Dr. Albertson explained to me that the notes in her chart said she had something like a nervous breakdown after she had taken an unknown substance. Maybe on the day she was supposed to leave with my father, she changed her mind. Maybe the pressure of telling him she wasn't going was too much for her to handle. I don't know. And now that Grandmother is gone, I'll never know.

I told Gerald everything I knew and asked him not to tell Lisa. We both agreed that she wasn't ready to deal with what we think really happened. Hell, I'm still having problems dealing with it.

In the midst of waiting for the court to acknowledge my kinship and grant me permission to oversee my mother's affairs, I went looking for L.C.'s sons. I came to find out Aunt Myrtle and my father's friend, Mr. Russell, had always stayed in touch. Aunt Myrtle knew that my half-brothers both lived in Chicago and had been there since their mother moved them back to her home town after L.C. was killed. I practically begged her to call Mr. Russell and ask him to have my brothers contact me and at first she wasn't going to do it. She said I should let sleeping dogs lie and that I needed to consider L.C.'s widow and how seeing me might bring back bad feelings for her. I understood what she meant, but I told Aunt Myrtle that I was willing to take that chance. The need for me to know my brothers, and to find out what kind of father L.C. Boone was to them, was stronger than hurting their mother's feelings. I had been an only child all my life, and now I had a chance to be a sister to someone and have them be brothers to me. At least I hoped they would.

After a lot of persuading, Aunt Myrtle agreed to pass on my telephone number to Mr. Russell, and within a few days I received a call. It was from my father's brother, Elias. He told me that he was my father's only sibling and that he and L.C. had been very close. He said after my father died, he wanted to come and see about me but because of the situation with Grandmother, Mr. Russell convinced him not to.

Uncle Elias said he had seen me a few times at my baby sitter's house and at my father's store, when he had come to visit my father. He told me he had only seen my mother a few times but he liked her very much. He said he understood why L.C. wanted to make her his wife.

Uncle Elias told me my brothers, Lorenzo and Guy, knew about me as well, and over the years they had asked him many times how they could get in touch with me. Under the circumstances, he wouldn't give them any information. He wasn't sure what I knew about my father or them and he thought it was best not to try and contact me. He said he knew one day I would find out about it all and come looking for them.

I invited my uncle to my house and asked him to bring my brothers with him. Not knowing the outcome of my first meeting with them, I sent Lisa to stay with Gerald for the weekend. I was excited about seeing them but nervous about how they might feel about me. What if they didn't like me? What if my brothers only wanted to find me to let me know how my mother and their father's relationship had ruined their childhood and they blamed me for it? I started to have second thoughts. But after I met them, I knew I had made the right decision.

My doorbell rang that Saturday afternoon and when I opened the door and saw the smiling, inviting faces of those three strong-looking men standing on the other side, with faces that resembled mine, a wave of emotions came over me. Growing up without my mother had been difficult, but I did have her people to fulfill the connection I needed from her side of my family. Not knowing anyone from my father's side, even my fictitious father's side, had left a void in me. Now, here I was standing in front of my real father's sons and his brother, my flesh and blood, and I can't describe the joy that went through my heart. I tried not to cry, but I couldn't help myself as I hugged each one of them and they hugged me back.

I felt proud looking at my tall, handsome, well-built brothers. Of course being L.C.'s sons, they were well groomed and smelled of expensive cologne. My uncle was well dressed too and despite his receding hairline, he looks very well for a man in his mid-seventies. I could tell that he was probably a very handsome man when he was younger. We sat and talked at my house for a while until Uncle Elias announced he was taking us all out to dinner.

While we ate, I came to know a little about my father's family. Uncle Elias told me about his and my father's childhood in Chicago and their adulthood out in the street as hustlers. As he talked, I tried to imagine the two of them as children and grown men and the close relationship they must have had. My uncle said he left the street life alone when my father left Chicago back in 1950 to move to Sterling. Uncle Elias left Chicago that same year and moved to St. Louis where he started a roofing business that he still runs. He's been married twice and he and his second wife have four sons who live in different parts of California.

My brothers told me a little about themselves as well. Lorenzo is a technician for a television station in Chicago. He has three girls with his wife. Two of his girls are away in college and the youngest is in her senior year of high school.

Guy works with the Illinois Department of Transportation in an administrative position. He's been married twice but he's divorced now. He and his first wife didn't have any children. He has a son with his second wife. He lives with a young woman who doesn't have any children and he's getting pressured by her to get married a third time.

Uncle Elias and my brothers had intended to visit with me for a while and make the drive back to Chicago that night, but when we got back to my house from dinner that evening, we sat and talked some more. While the three of them drank cognac, I drank wine. After a while, Uncle Elias fell asleep in the chair he was sitting in and I woke him up and put him in the guest bedroom for the night.

I asked Lorenzo and Guy if the case of our father's death was ever solved. They told me the police never found out who did it, but Uncle Elias knew. They said Uncle Elias won't talk about it. He told them it was made right, and he didn't ever want it mentioned again.

I asked my brothers to tell me what kind of father L.C. Boone had been to them. They said Lou, as they affectionately called him, was a tough father. He was raising boys and wanted to make sure they turned out to be self-sufficient men, by whatever means they needed to. He sent them to parochial schools and had always stressed the importance of getting good educations.

Lou wasn't around much when they were small because he worked a lot at the store, or so they thought. They said they didn't know about Lou's street dealings until after he died and Uncle Elias told them about it when they were grown men. Lou had moved in and out of their home several times and had even told his boys, he and their mother were getting divorced. He was gone almost two years before he finally moved back in for the last time. Guy said he thinks Lou came back home to be with them because he no longer had a reason not to be there. My brothers said they thought things would get better between their parents, but they never did.

Lorenzo and Guy spoke openly and honestly with me. They told me they had known about me since I was a baby and as children they hated me and my mother and blamed us for their parents' problems. Lou and his wife argued a lot about me and my mother, often when they thought the boys were asleep and couldn't hear them, but they heard. Lou would go off on their mother whenever she referred to Marietta as 'that bitch' or 'that tramp' and afterwards, he would walk around looking heartbroken for days.

One night when he was about eight years old, Lorenzo found Lou sitting alone at home in the living room. The lights were dimmed and Lou was drinking a small glass of liquor, listening to a stack of forty-fives he had playing on the stereo. A song called Goodnight My Love was playing when Lorenzo hopped up onto the lounge chair next to Lou and asked him what he was doing. He told Lorenzo he was just sitting there, thinking about the woman he loved with all his heart. Lorenzo giggled, and when Lou asked him what was so funny, Lorenzo told him it was funny that Lou said he loved his mommy. Lou looked down at his son, staring into his little face for a minute and told him one day when he was a grown man, he would think back on that very night and understand what his daddy had meant.

I was curious to know about their mother and asked them how she handled everything after Lou's death. They assured me their mother was fine. She never talked about me or my mother after Lou died and she never bad-mouthed him in front of her boys.

A few years after Lou died, their mother found a man that loved her very much and she married him and has been with him ever since. Lorenzo described his step-father as a 'cool dude' that they got along with real good. Guy said Uncle Elias made his presence known with their step-father and he thinks that had a lot to do with it.

I asked them if they had told their mother about their visiting me and how she felt about it. They said they did tell her and she told them that after all these years, she didn't feel one way or the other.

Lorenzo and Guy listened sympathetically as I sat on the couch and told them how I felt that I needed to apologize for what my mother and Lou had done to everyone. I don't know why I felt so responsible for it all, but I did. Maybe it was because if I hadn't come along when I did, things could have gone differently. Maybe if Lou had gotten his divorce and later married my mother and then had me, things would have been better for everyone concerned. They assured me that no one could hold me responsible for my mother's and our father's actions. All we could do was forgive the two of them for being human.

My brothers and uncle slept at my house that night and have been back many times since. I felt so grateful to them for treating me like I was their sister and niece, and not just some outside child.

I let them meet Lisa the next time they came to visit. When I explained to Lisa how they were related, I figured it was time to come clean with her and tell her about my mother and father. I also introduced them to Gerald. Gerald said he could tell by the way they all shook his hand that they wanted him to know I had brothers and an uncle who were looking out for me. I told Gerald he was overreacting, but it made me feel good when Gerald told me that.

Lorenzo invited me and Lisa to stay at his house for a weekend. He wanted us to meet his wife and daughters, and Guy's girlfriend and son. Uncle Elias and his wife, Eunice, were there. I was surprised when I saw their mother, Edie, and her husband. Lorenzo hadn't told me she would be there. She was cordial and at first she didn't say much to me. I felt so awkward being there with her.

Somehow, Miss Edie and I ended up sitting alone in the dining room. Lisa had gone upstairs to hang with her cousins. The men all went downstairs to the family room to watch television and the women were cleaning up in the kitchen. Miss Edie broke the ice and started the conversation by telling me how much I looked like my father. I told her I wished I would have known him. She told me I would have liked him. She said he was crazy about his children. She told me she heard that I had asked about her and how I wanted to know how she felt about me. Miss Edie told me she was glad that I was able to find Lorenzo and Guy. She said regardless of the circumstances, we needed to know one another and have a relationship because we were blood.

I told her I was sorry about how things turned out for her and my father. She shook her head and told me it wasn't my place to apologize for anything that had to do with L.C. She said she couldn't hold me responsible.

We talked a little while longer and right before she left for the evening, Miss Edie gave me a hug and told me I could call her "ma" if I wanted. She also told me to make sure I stopped by to see her the next time I was in Chicago. I told her how much I appreciated her kindness and that I would definitely stop by to see her.

Aunt Myrtle and Aunt Josette are fine with the relationships I have with my father's family. I didn't tell Uncle Wendell about it. I don't care what he thinks. Uncle Stanley never told me how he felt about it when he found out, but I know him well enough to know that if it makes me happy, then it's all right with him.

Guy has a friend he wants to introduce me to. Actually, his girlfriend, Jennifer, suggested that Guy set me up with him. His name is Rodney. He and

Guy used to work together up in Chicago until he moved to Indianapolis. I told them I'd have to wait to meet this person. I have too much going on right now to be trying to handle a romantic relationship.

Things are getting back in order, and now I'm on my way to meet more people from my missing family. I wasn't going to pursue this and I had changed my mind several times, but something kept gnawing at me, edging me to do this.

I had called Mrs. Snyder's house and spoke to her asking her to send me the picture she had of my grandmother and her brother and sister. She said she would, but I never did get it. Three weeks later when I called her back to find out if she had mailed the picture, she wasn't home. I left a message on her answering machine and I got a call back a few days later from her son, Raymond, who said Mrs. Snyder had had a stroke and was in the hospital. They didn't expect for her to make it. I didn't bother to ask him if he could send the picture.

I was able to find the telephone book for Hamilton, Ohio at the downtown library in Indianapolis, and looked up the telephone number for Ambrose Gray. When he answered the phone and I told him who I was, it was emotional and draining for the both of us. He told me that he and his sister, Amelia, were the only ones still living out of grandmother's immediate family. I gave him my phone number and asked him to pass it on to her. I hadn't hung up from him for more than twenty minutes when my phone rang, and it was Aunt Amelia. Her call was just as emotional. Talking on the telephone wasn't enough for her. She had to see me. She wanted to see us all.

Uncle Stanley and Aunt Josette aren't ready to meet them, but I am. I want to know why Grandmother didn't tell us about her family. I still have a longing to know the truth about my grandmother's secret past and the only way I'm going to find out is by going to see the people she hid from us.

I drive down High Street until I see the BP on my left where I'm supposed to meet Aunt Amelia and Uncle Ambrose. I told them I should be there around five this evening. As I pull onto the lot, I see a man and woman standing next to the gas station building. I'm sure it's them because they're both dressed exactly as she said they would be; her in a sleeveless yellow top with a gold belt around the waist and white 'pedal pushers', and he in a short-sleeved, white shirt with no tie, grey slacks and a dark grey hat. They both peer through my front windshield as I park.

"Aunt Amelia?" I ask politely, as I step out of my car.

She stares at me without any expression.

"You Francine?" she inquires, looking me up and down.

"Yes ma'am."

She smiles and walks towards me extending her arms. We embrace and hug one another for a few second. She steps back to look at me once again while holding my hands.

Aunt Amelia looks like my grandmother. She's a shade darker, but her skin looks just the same as her sister's, soft and smooth with a few wrinkles. She's aging well and doesn't look like a woman in her early eighties. Aunt Amelia has the same mixed gray, wavy type of hair as Grandmother, only Aunt Amelia's is cut short. She also has a few dark, fine hairs on her upper lip. She's not as tall as Grandmother and she's heavier. She does have big breasts like the rest of the women in our family.

"Hey there," the tall, thin man says, waiting his turn.

"This is your Uncle Ambrose," she tells me. "We call him Teeter. You can call him Uncle Teeter."

I decide I like his real name better than Teeter and will call him that. I give him a big hug. Uncle Ambrose has to be over six feet tall. You could tell in his younger days he was a lady-killer with that same black, wavy hair as his sisters, although his is practically all gray. His complexion is the same as Grandmother.

"Look at you," he says, stepping back after he releases me. "Youse a pretty ole gal."

"Thank you," I tell him. "It is so good to finally meet you both."

"Where are the other ones?" Aunt Amelia asks, looking around.

"They couldn't come this time, Aunt Amelia," I say.

"Why not?"

"Uncle Stanley had a doctor's appointment that he couldn't miss," I lie. "Aunt Josette wasn't feeling well and Uncle Wendell still doesn't believe Grandmother had other family. Maybe they'll all be able to come the next time."

Aunt Amelia looks me up and down suspiciously.

"She looks just like Momma, don't she?" she asks, turning to Uncle Ambrose.

"Naw, she don't look like Momma," he snaps at her. "Look more like Dania to me. Dania looked like Daddy."

"She don't look like Dania," she snaps back at him. "She looks just like Momma when Momma was a girl. Your eyesight is gettin' worse and worse."

"Ain't nothin' wrong with my eyesight. You the one that can't see straight. This child don't look nothin' like Momma."

"Aw, hush up!"

"Don't be tellin' me to hush up! I can say what I want to."

"Never mind your uncle," she says to me. "All that drinkin' he used to do done made him blind! Come on. We need to get goin'. I'm gonna ride with you around to my house."

As Aunt Amelia and I get into my car, Uncle Ambrose gets into an old Ford LTD parked next to me.

"We gonna follow you, so don't be drivin' all fast," she tells him before she gets completely in.

"Why you got to follow me?" he says. "Don't you remember where you live?"

"Damn it, I know where I live!" she shouts. "I want us all to get back to the house at the same time!"

"Aw, get on in the car and let's go."

I can't tell if they are serious or joking with one another.

Uncle Ambrose pulls off first and I follow him.

"So how long was your ride down here?" Aunt Amelia asks.

"It was less than two hours," I say.

"This is a nice car you got. What kind is it?"

"It's a Cadillac."

"This lil' car is a Cadillac? When did they start makin' lil' Cadillacs?"

"I'm not quite sure."

"This too lil' for me. I only like big Cadillacs. One of my old men friends used to drive a big Cadillac."

We drive through town and Aunt Amelia points out landmarks and old buildings.

"Pull over right here," she says to me.

"Should I blow so that Uncle Ambrose can stop too?" I ask her.

"Naw. We don't need him. I know where I'm goin'. That used to be Malone's Department Store. My momma used to work there for a long time. She used to make clothes. She worked at a place where she couldn't even afford the things they was sellin'."

Aunt Amelia tells me to drive further down the same street until we come to Cutter Avenue where I turn right. Halfway down, she orders me to pull over in front of an old bar where two men are sitting outside on metal folding chairs.

"We goin' in here for a few minutes" she says. "I got to show you off to my friends."

We get out of the car and walk to the door.

"Hey, 'Melia," one of the men says to her.

"How you doin', Chester?" she asks.

"Fine as wine baby, fine as wine."

"Who you got there with you?" the other man asks.

"None of your business," she tells him.

"Whoever she is, she looks like she got money."

"She does," Aunt Amelia tells him. "This is my great-niece. She just drove here from Indianapolis to come and stay with me for the weekend. That's her Cadillac right there."

"Well if she got money, she can't be none of your relative, 'cause you ain't seen no money since '32."

Both men burst out laughing.

"As long as I got this, I ain't never gonna be broke," she says, pointing to her crotch.

I stand there shocked, not believing what I just heard come out of this woman's mouth!

"Go on with your ole self," he tells her. "Ain't nobody gonna buy none of that dried up stuff you got!"

Both men crack up laughing again.

"Aw shut up, you ole, broke ass, snagga tooth bastard!" she says. "You couldn't afford me no how!"

I'm appalled as I listen to her talk.

"Oh, I got two dollars," he jokes. "That's about all you worth!"

"Kiss my ass Roy!" Aunt Amelia says and walks inside.

I can't believe her! If my grandmother would have heard this, she would have been sprinkling holy water on them all!

Chester and Roy are still laughing as I follow Aunt Amelia into the bar. I'm almost afraid of what is to come.

There aren't many customers inside. Two elderly women are seated at the bar on mismatched bar stools. They both turn their heads at the same time to see who has come through the door. Aunt Amelia hollers across the room to them and leads me over to where they are. She introduces me to them, telling me their names are Selma and Inez. Aunt Amelia invites them to her house tomorrow for the bar-be-que she is hosting in my honor. They promise to stop by. Before we leave, Aunt Amelia introduces me to a few other people sitting at tables inside the place.

When we get outside, Roy and Chester are still there.

"I'll see y'all later," Aunt Amelia says to them.

"I'll be over later on tonight to see you, baby," Roy says to Aunt Amelia.

"Roy, quit messin' with me!" she hollers at him.

"I love you, baby!" he tells her.

She rolls her eyes at him as he and Chester laugh.

"Nice to have met you," I say to them as I get into the car.

"Same here," Chester says in between laughs.

Aunt Amelia gets into the car and directs me as I drive to her house.

"Those ladies seem nice," I say, making small talk.

"I've been knowin' them for years," Aunt Amelia tells me. "We go way back. All three of us used to work the streets together. We looked out for one another when we was out there on the stroll. Everybody knew if you messed with one of us, the other two was gonna be somewhere nearby to kick your ass! Yeah, we've been through some things together, and we still livin' to tell it."

I hope I'm wrong, but did she just tell me she used to be on the stroll out in the streets? Did she used to have sex with men for money? I don't bother to have her clarify what she just told me. In a way, I don't want to know.

Aunt Amelia points out Milton Street and tells me to turn left.

"This is my house right here," she says, pointing out the third one on the right. "Teeter must've stopped off somewhere. He probably went home to get his wife. I'm gonna see if Bernard got here yet and he can come out and get your suitcase out the car."

"Oh, I've already been to my hotel and dropped off my bags," I tell her.

"Hotel?" she says, frowning.

"Yes ma'am. I didn't want to be any trouble and I feel more comfortable in my own room."

"If I would've thought you were gonna be any trouble, I wouldn't have invited you to stay at my house."

I get out of the car and wait on the sidewalk as she slowly makes her way out.

"I appreciate your hospitality, Aunt Amelia," I say. "And I hope I didn't insult you by staying at a hotel."

"Honey, you ain't hurtin' my feelins'," she says as she walks by me and into the yard.

I look at the front of Aunt Amelia's house. It's a two-story house shaped straight up and down like a rectangle with a front door and a stoop with two steps. Both of the houses next to Aunt Amelia's are built the same way, with a ten-foot concrete walkway between them. I look up and down her street at the other nearby homes. The neighborhood is old with several dilapidated houses with unkempt, small lawns of sparse, dried grass.

Aunt Amelia has already opened the front door by the time I catch up to her. We step inside into the living room and she leaves the front door open, securing the screen door. The living room is small. There are mixed smells of household cleaners and fried food filling the air. Her furniture is a little more updated than my grandmother's, but not by much.

"Come on and I'm gonna show you around my house," Aunt Amelia says proudly as she leads me through the doorway on the right into her dining room. We pass the dining room and go into the hallway where there's a side door that can be used to enter the house. She opens the door and latches the screen, allowing the cool breeze to come in.

"That's my kitchen back that way," she says, waving her hand in that direction. She heads left into a room that's set up as a parlor. I follow her as she leads me through a wooden frame doorway with no door that leads up to the second floor. We make our way up the stairs and once we get to the top, she points out the three bedrooms, noting the one her son, Bernard, sleeps in when his lady friend puts him out.

I follow Aunt Amelia back downstairs to the parlor. There is a hutch sitting along one of the walls with about thirty picture frames sitting on top of it. She also has several picture frames hanging on the wall over the cabinet.

"You sure do have a lot of pictures here," I say to Aunt Amelia as I stand next to the hutch, looking them over.

"Uh huh," she responds. "I got pictures of everybody in my family. I got most of them from Isabelle. Isabelle was my gran'momma's first cousin. They were two sisters chil'ren and they was raised up together. Pauline was Isabelle's momma and when she died, my great-gran'momma, Cinda, took Isabelle in and raised her. This a picture of Isabelle right here."

Aunt Amelia picks up the frame and gives it to me. I look at the woman in the black and white photo. Isabelle is a very dark-skinned, handsome woman, maybe around thirty years old. She's sitting on a prop in a studio wearing a long dress with a full shirt. Her legs are crossed and her hands are lying in her lap.

"This here is a picture of my gran'momma and her husband, Rufus Pratt," Aunt Amelia says, passing me the picture frame as I pass back the one of Isabelle.

The picture is old and the quality isn't very good, but I can see them. They're standing next to one another in no particular pose.

"Her name was Hilda Reed before she got married," Aunt Amelia says.

"And this is my momma, Kathleen Gray," she says, passing me the next photograph.

I look at the picture and see a strikingly, beautiful woman whom you could tell was half-black and half-white, with long, wavy hair. Her pose and dress are for the stage. Written on one of the corners of the photo is 'Gateway House'.

"Was she a showgirl or something?" I ask Aunt Amelia.

"Uh-huh," Aunt Amelia says. "Momma was in a few of them shows up in Cleveland back in the '20s. This is another one of her pictures."

Aunt Amelia gives me another photo of her mother. Her pose in this picture is a bit risqué, with Kathleen tooting her behind out with her hand up to her face and her lips puckered as if she's ready to kiss someone. My grandmother looked very much like her mother.

"Isabelle is the one who raised Momma," Aunt Amelia says.

"Did her parents die when she was young?" I ask.

"Naw, Isabelle just had to take her in."

"Why?"

"See, Momma weren't Mr. Rufus' child. Gran'momma was married to him when she had my momma, but he weren't her real daddy. Her daddy was a white man."

I look back and forth between the two photos to see if I see any resemblance in the women without trying to get any further information about Kathleen's white father.

"I got a picture of my auntie and all my uncles on momma's side," Aunt Amelia says. "They're all dead and gone. They had this here picture made back in the '40s. Isabelle got it after Gran'momma died. I took it from Isabelle's house when she died."

I give her the frame of Hilda and Mr. Rufus in exchange for the next picture, and I continue to hold the one of Kathleen.

"That's Uncle Matthew," she says, pointing him out. "He was the oldest child. That's Aunt Beatrice sittin' right there. She was the second child. Momma was the fourth child and Uncle Mark was the fifth one. And Uncle Sydney was the baby. That's Uncle Nathaniel, the tallest one standin' in back. He was the one right before Momma. I remember Uncle Nathaniel when he was a young man. If he hadnt've been my uncle, I would've been his woman!"

We both chuckle at her little joke.

"He was a handsome man back when he was young," she continues. "He was the best lookin' one in Momma's family. He had that pretty dark skin and them pretty white teeth. I used to love to see him smile. He had the best smile a man could have. He was the nicest one. The rest of 'em didn't wanna be bothered with us chil'ren, but Uncle Nathaniel would play with us and ride us around on his back. And he loved him some music. He had a guitar he carried around with him. He could play real good too. He came up here to see us one time before Daddy died, when I was about seven, but that was the last time I saw him 'til I went back to Georgia. He was the first one I seen when I went back down home."

I put the two photos back in their places as Aunt Amelia picks up another one.

"This is a picture of all of us when my daddy was livin'," she says as I take the picture from her. "That's my daddy right there. His name was Cuthbert. Cuthbert Gray.

"That's me and Teeter right there. And that's Dania sittin' down in front of Daddy. And that's my sister, Muriel Susan, and my brother, Lemuel Rick standing in back of Momma and Daddy."

My grandmother, with a warm smile on her face, looked like a sweet, young girl who might have had a heart of gold. As I look at the photo, I feel a bit of sorrow as I wonder how she became such an unaffectionate woman.

"You want somethin' to drink?" Aunt Amelia asks.

"No thank you," I tell her.

"Have you a seat on the sofa. I'll be back in a minute 'cause I need me somethin' to drank."

I sit down on the couch, taking the photo with me. I want to look at it some more.

Aunt Amelia comes back with a glass filled with ice and what looks like a cola.

"You sure you don't want none of this?" she asks me as she sits down on the sofa next to me.

"What is it?" I ask.

"Soda water and hooch."

"No thanks."

I look back at the photo of Aunt Amelia and her family.

"Did Kathleen keep in touch with her father?" I ask Aunt Amelia.

"Naw," she says. She takes a drink and sets it down on the side table next to her. "Momma didn't even know who her daddy was. Nobody ever told her. Isabelle knew him, but Momma didn't. Isabelle is the one who told me all about Gran'momma havin' my momma with a white man. Isabelle didn't never hide nothin'. She said if folks was shamed about somethin' they did, then they shouldn've done it so it wouldn've been able to be told. Momma never told us Mr. Rufus weren't her real daddy, but I always knew it. Hell, who's gonna call they real daddy Mr. Rufus?"

"So Kathleen's father was a white man?" I repeat.

"I told you that before," Aunt Amelia says sarcastically. "You could look at her and see that."

"I've heard how white men used to force themselves on black women back then," I say.

"That has happened to many a nigga gal, but truth be told, that ain't what happened to my gran'momma. Let me tell you what Isabelle told me about it. Back when Gran'momma and Isabelle was in they twenties, they had they own business where they used to cook up food and sell it to the peoples that worked at the mill right up from town. Most folks would pack them a lunch, but some of the young men that weren't married didn't bring nothin' to eat, so they would go to the diner or buy they food from Gran'momma and Isabelle. They would sell stew or fried chicken and greens and tomatoes, and slices of cakes and pies, too. Mr. Rufus made them a cart with two big holes where they could sit they pots down in it. Some of they customers would bring they own tin cup and plate, but Gran'momma and Isabelle put a few of they own spoons and tin pans in a box, so they could serve they food. When the peoples was finished, they put the spoons and pans in another box, and Gran'momma and Isabelle would take 'em home and wash 'em up for the next day. They had a mule to pull they cart so they could tote the food around.

"Well, one day after Isabelle and Gran'momma was finished sellin' they food and they was ready to go on home, they went a lil' ways down the road to the corner. Gran'momma told Isabelle she had to go out in the cornfield to pee. So Isabelle stood on the corner of the road waitin' for Gran'momma to come back, and she could see down both sides of the road. Well in the meantime, Isabelle saw some white man goin' into the cornfield from a different side, but he didn't see her. At first, Isabella didn't think nothin' about it but then she started thinkin' what if that white man came down to where Gran'momma was and he saw her peein' in the cornfield. So Isabelle got scared and she ran in through the rows of corn, lookin' for Gran'momma and when she finally got close enough, she could hear Gran'momma talkin' to somebody. Isabelle said she made her way a little bit closer to where she could see Gran'momma and guess what?"

"What?" I ask, intrigued by the story.

"Isabelle saw Gran'momma and the white man doin' it!"

"Oh my goodness!" I say in disbelief. "Did they know Isabelle saw them?"

"Naw. Isabelle said they was so into it they didn't even know she was nearby!" Aunt Amelia laughs loudly. "She said she couldn't believe what she was seein' and at first she thought the white man was taken it from Gran'momma, but when she heard how Gran'momma was likin' it, she said she just turned on back around and went back to wait at the corner!"

Aunt Amelia laughs and claps her hands.

"Oh my lord!" I say. "Did Isabelle ever tell Hilda that she saw them?"

"Oh, yeah. Gran'momma come on back out and they was walkin' back home and Isabelle told Gran'momma, 'I saw you with your britches down, lettin' that white man do it to you'. Isabelle said Gran'momma wasn't even surprised or nothin'. Gran'momma told her, 'So what? That's what you do with the man you love'. Isabelle told her, 'Is you stupid? You think that white man love you'? And Gran'momma said, 'That's what he say'. Isabelle told her, 'He love what's between your legs is all'! Gran'momma got mad and told Isabelle, 'You just jealous 'cause you ain't got no white man that wanna love on you'. Isabelle said, 'I got sense enough to know if I was givin' my stuff away to a white man it sure wouldn't be for no love'! Isabelle told Gran'momma she was the biggest starnader fool she had ever seen!"

"The biggest what?"

"Starnader fool," she repeats, sounding out the word.

"What is a starnader fool?"

"The biggest fool whatever walked on the earth!" Aunt Amelia laughs. "Somebody who ain't got a bit a sense!"

I raise my eyebrows and shake my head in wonderment at my great-great-grandmother's story of love.

Aunt Amelia continues on with her tale.

"Gran'momma told Isabelle she just better not tell it to nobody. But Isabelle didn't have to, 'cause when the midwife pulled that baby from out of Gran'momma and held her up, they all knew what happened! When Mr. Rufus heard the baby cryin', he busted in the room to see if he had a boy or a girl. He took one look at the baby and then looked at Gran'momma. Isabelle was already in the room, and she said she knew that was gonna happen. She knew that white man was gonna be the daddy of that baby. The midwife was quick on thinkin' and she told Mr. Rufus sometime nigga babies come out light, but they darken up when they get older. She told him to wait a while and see how dark the baby was gonna get.

"But my momma never did get no darker, and when Mr. Rufus figured out that wasn't his baby, he went on the warpath. Isabelle said they was all sittin' on the front porch one evenin' and he asked Gran'momma who the daddy of her baby was. Gran'momma told him he was. He said it was mighty curious that this lil' girl ain't got no darker, bein' that both her momma and daddy was black and how come she got curly hair when theys was nappy. Gran'momma tried to keep up her lie, but Mr. Rufus wasn't havin' it. He got up from his chair and went to Gran'momma and grabbed her by her collar and told her she better tell him what happened! He wanted to know who the white bastard was what done had they way with his wife, and then he started hollerin' at her, 'Who did this to you? Which one of them took it from you'?

"Gran'momma just cried. Mr. Rufus turned around to Isabelle and asked her, 'cause Gran'momma told her everything. Isabelle said she couldn't even answer. She just sat there in her chair. And then Mr. Rufus knew what had happened. He knew she was layin' down with some white man on purpose. Isabelle said before she knew it, Mr. Rufus was whoopin' on Gran'momma and the neighbor mens had to come over and pull him off her! They talked him into leavin' for the night and he was gone for three or four days. Isabelle said when he came back home, he looked like he had lost his mind. Said he wouldn't talk to nobody. Isabelle got scared and had to take my momma in with her 'cause she was afraid he was gonna do somethin' to her. She was scared he was gonna do somethin' to Gran'momma too, but he didn't.

"For whatever reason, he didn't never leave her, either. He stayed married to her and lived in the same house with her. He even gave her two more babies after my momma. He moved out of they bedroom and he slept in the front room. Isabelle said he had a woman that lived in town that he would go be with from time to time and told Gran'momma he dared her to say somethin' about it. He made my momma stay with Isabelle 'cause he said he wasn't takin' care of no half-white baby. Isabell ain't live but three houses away from Gran'momma. Isabelle said she would have to go knockin' at Gran'momma's door in the middle of the night when Kathleen would wake up for her momma's titty.

"When Momma got older, Mr. Rufus would walk by Isabelle's house on the way home and his other chil'ren would see him and they would run up to him and be shoutin' 'Daddy, Daddy' and climbin' on him to pick them up. Momma would call him Daddy like her brothers and sister, and he would tell her not to call him that. He made Momma call him Mr. Rufus, but she called him Daddy anyway. He wouldn't answer her until she called him Mr. Rufus. That made Gran'momma mad. Gran'momma told him he could hate her all he wanted to, but don't be mistreatin' her child."

"So did Hilda ever tell the white man about his baby?" I ask.

"Oh yeah. Isabelle said one day Gran'momma had Momma strapped to her chest when she was still a baby and she saw the white man and went up to him and told him. His first name was Ben. I don't think Gran'momma even knew his last name. Ben told Gran'momma she better not ever say nothin' else to him again about her nigga half-breed baby. Isabelle said Gran'momma was heartbroken 'cause she thought that white man really did love her. Isabelle told Gran'momma she was stupid to think a white man would take up for her. She wasn't nothin' but a nigga woman that sold food from a cart."

"Poor woman," I say.

"I ain't feel sorry for her," Aunt Amelia says. "She should've known better than that. Don't no white man love no nigga woman for real. She could've got killed over that."

The clacking of footsteps on the concrete outside the open door draws our attention. We turn to the screen door and wait for someone to appear. I can see a woman climb the side steps, and pull at the screen door while another woman and a man wait at the bottom of the steps behind her. When she realizes it's locked, she peers through the screen.

"I'll tell you about the rest of it later," Aunt Amelia tells me as she gets up from the sofa. "Here I come."

Aunt Amelia unlocks the screen door and the three of them walk into the house. The man is Bernard and the women are Rita and Simone, his two daughters. Rita is a very beautiful, tall woman with a curvy figure and shoulder length hair that she wears straight. Simone is tall and thin and has her hair pulled back into a very long ponytail. She's cute but she's not as pretty as Rita. They both are wearing sundresses with beautiful, bright patterns. Bernard is a nice looking dark-skinned fellow, probably in his late 50's or early 60's, with chemically processed curly hair. He's wearing a black, silk, short-sleeved shirt and black slacks with black leather shoes. His two gold necklaces and two gold bracelets are gleaming, as well as the diamond pinkie rings he has on both hands.

I greet them one at a time with hugs and smiles as they tell me how glad they are to finally get to meet me.

Aunt Amelia orders Rita and Simone to take me outside to the backyard and keep me company while she and Bernard go to a restaurant to buy carry-out for our dinner.

I follow my cousins through the hallway into the kitchen where Aunt Amelia offers us some homemade liquor before she leaves with Bernard. We all make sour faces at her and decide to get beers instead. She laughs at us and calls us 'sissy girls' as we head out the back door and down the steps. There's a slab of concrete at the bottom of the steps where Aunt Amelia has set up a few chaise loungers and several chairs. There are cushions on the chairs to make them more comfortable so that guests won't have to feel the basket-weave, nylon strips of material that make up the back and seat of the metal furniture.

Rita, Simone and I sit and chitchat about who's who in our families. I tell them about how I came to find out that my grandmother actually had family we knew nothing about. I show them photos of my family, pointing out the picture of my mother, father and me that Aunt Myrtle had given me.

I tell them about myself and my family and they tell me about theirs. Rita is divorced and has two sons, both in the air force, and a daughter who attends college in Pennsylvania. Rita works as a counselor at a home for abused women where they help residents to re-establish themselves in the work force and find homes of their own. Simone is married and has no children. She and her husband, Frank, are both elementary school teachers. I'm supposed to meet him along with Aunt Amelia's daughter, Ruth, who goes by the name Bay, tomorrow when the rest of the family comes over.

Rita and Simone confirm what I thought about Aunt Amelia being a former prostitute. Rita tells me how Aunt Amelia met Bay and Bernard's fathers and the up and downs of her relationships with them. Each time Aunt Amelia broke up with her children's fathers she went back to being a hooker. When she thought she was too old to keep walking the streets, Aunt Amelia finally got a job at a paper mill. She also worked as a bar maid on the weekends. The bar owner let her use one of his side rooms in the basement to service a few of her steady customers, as long as she gave him a cut of her profits.

My cousins tell me how Bay and Aunt Amelia's relationship is strained and has been for many years. Bay never agreed with her mother's lifestyle. It was embarrassing to her that the whole neighborhood knew of her mother's profession and it hurt Bay to know that her mother would rather make money the way she did, than to quit her profession and put her daughter's dignity back in tact. Aunt Amelia thought otherwise. She felt that if Bay didn't like it, she could go somewhere else and live, and that's what Bay did. One of her friend's parents let Bay stay with them until she was old enough to be out on her own. Bay eventually ended up in Buffalo, New York, where she married a minister and had two children. Aunt Amelia didn't get the chance to see her grandchildren grow up and it bothered her that Bay didn't come home to Hamilton to see her mother as often as Aunt Amelia thought she should.

After we eat and I get the chance to meet Uncle Ambrose's family, Rita, Simone and Bernard, take me out to one of the local night clubs. I find myself bonding most with Rita. I like her. She's the kind of person that makes you feel comfortable. She's easy to talk to. Simone is cool but she's rougher around the edges than Rita. I can tell Bernard is a smooth talker, a lady's man. He flirts with almost every woman in the club while we're there. We dance and drink and have a good time that night.

The next day, I go over to Aunt Amelia's house for the bar-be-que. It starts out great as I meet family members and their friends, but the big argument between Simone and her half-sister, Nellie, brings the good time to a temporary halt. Nellie is Bernard's daughter from the girlfriend he was messing around with while he was married to Rita and Simone's mother. Rita gets along with Nellie just fine, but she told me Simone and Nellie have never gotten along and every time the family gets together, the two of them get into screaming matches with Bernard taking Simone's side, and Aunt Amelia ends up cussing out the three of them. And I mean she cusses! I had never heard such words come out of an elderly woman's mouth. My nerves are frazzled and I feel uneasy standing here as I listen to the four of them holler back and forth at one another. Rita sees the look on my face and assures me I have nothing to worry about. She says they argue all the time but it never comes to blows.

The fight is over almost as quickly as it started, and after a while everyone seems to have calmed down, carrying on like nothing ever happened. This is strange to me. If this would have been one of us in the Cressford family we all would still be fuming.

The evening goes on with the men cleaning up the backyard while Aunt Amelia and some of the other women clean up the kitchen. Once the house is back to normal and everyone has gone home, Aunt Amelia and I sit in the living room. I've been anxiously waiting all day to finally get Aunt Amelia alone to talk with her about my grandmother and her childhood.

Grandmother was nothing like her sister and brother. Despite the fact that Aunt Amelia cussed like a sailor and seemed to have a quick temper, she and Uncle Ambrose were much friendlier than my grandmother. They seemed to care about how people felt. I didn't understand how coming from the same beginnings as her siblings, my grandmother became so different than her brother and sister.

I explain to Aunt Amelia again how I had begun my search to find her.

"I kept thinking back to Grandmother's funeral and what Mrs. Snyder told us that day. She kept insisting that Grandmother had brothers and sisters and I believed her. I called her on the telephone and she told me that when she and her husband were moving from Hamilton to Westfield, Grandmother had decided not to go with them at first. But a few days later, Grandmother changed her mind and told them she was going with them. Grandmother told Mrs. Snyder that Uncle Ambrose was moving down south with some relatives and you were getting married."

"Lord have mercy!" Aunt Amelia says, rolling her eyes.

"I don't understand. Why she didn't tell us the truth is just so strange."

Aunt Amelia takes a deep breath. She picks up her drink from the side table and takes a big gulp, making a sour face as she swallows. She stares at me without any expression for a long time before she speaks.

"You know," Aunt Amelia says, "me and Dania was close when we was young 'uns. She was my favorite outta all my sisters and brothers. We used to tell each other everything. We took care of each other.

"My daddy always told us family was the most important thing you can have and that it was our job to stand by one another's side no matter what happened. And we did that for the most part.

"When you called and told me who you were I thought long and hard about whether or not I should tell you everything about what happened to me and Dania and our family. At first I wasn't gonna tell it to you, 'cause I could tell over the phone you got high expectins of people. You talk proper and you been brought up with a good education. You ain't never come up on hard times."

"Oh, I've had some hard times."

"Naw you ain't. You might think they was hard, but baby, you lived a good life when you look at it from some other folks' eyes. I can tell you think highly of Dania too. But I ain't so sure you gonna feel the same way about her if you know what she went through."

"Aunt Amelia I don't judge people by their past."

"You say you don't judge folk, but you do. People don't tell you everything about 'em 'cause some things is embarrassin', even though they might not be they own fault. Some things is so painful that people wanna forget 'em and never think about 'em again.

"Is that what happened to my grandmother?"

"It is. Bad things is gonna happen to you. You can be good as gold or mean as the devil but bad things is gonna happen to you. There ain't a damn thing you can do about it but learn from it and don't make that same mistake on somebody else. The other thing you got to do is forgive folks. The reason y'all don't know about us is 'cause my sister never did forgive us. She never forgave my momma or my sister or my brothers."

"Forgive you all for what?"

As I sit and listen intently to my great-aunt tell me everything she knew, and other things that were told to her by my grandmother and other members of her immediate family, I take myself back in time to the '20's, and envision the events that led up to my grandmother disowning her family...

The early 1920's were a time when many Negro men and women were still moving from the south to the north to seek better jobs and opportunities for themselves and their children. Cuthbert Gray had that same idea in mind for his family and he was off to a good start.

Cuthbert was a simple, practical man. He was a proud, respectable man whose sole purpose in life was to support and look after his family. He and his wife both worked and for the most part, his family felt happy and safe.

The family moved from Georgia to Cleveland when Cuthbert was offered a new job. After being in Cleveland for almost a year, he found that he didn't like the fast pace of the big city. He also didn't like the lustful stares and disrespectful comments his beautiful wife received from men, Negro and white, in his presence.

Cleveland was becoming notorious for gangsters running things and he feared that as his children grew up, they might get caught up in the wayward activities of the city. He decided to pack up his family and move to a smaller town.

Cuthbert's wife, Kathleen, on the other hand, was different. She wasn't a simple woman at all. In fact, she was a high-spirited woman who loved the excitement of Cleveland. She liked that 'Negroes didn't have to kiss nobody's ass' and ran their own businesses and could hustle in the streets for money if they had to. There was money to be made in that big city and all kinds of excitement around town and Kathleen wanted some of that action.

Kathleen had dreams of becoming a showgirl. In her heart, she knew she had talent. All she needed was a chance to show it. But that wasn't what her husband wanted for her and their family. He wanted her to be a good wife to him and a good mother to their five children, two of which were hers from previous relationships.

So because she felt she had to, Kathleen put her dreams on hold and made a home for herself and her family in the white, wood framed house at the end of Hammond Street in Hamilton, Ohio where they had been living for the past three years.

"Hi Daddy," yells the cute, little girl with the long plaits hanging down her back. She's halfway up the street and is skipping towards her father who is walking home after a hard day's work.

"Hi Aldania," Cuthbert says as he meets up with her. He bends down and gives her a hug and kisses her on her cheek.

"Why ain't you playin' with your friends?" he asks as they walk hand in hand down the street.

"I was but I knew it was time for you to be on your way home and I came to get you."

"You know I'm a big man and I can make it home all by myself."

"I know. I just like walking home with you." Aldania smiles as she and her father walk along.

When they get to their house, Kathleen is sitting on the front porch. She smirks as she watches her daughter and husband come into the yard and walk up the steps onto the porch.

"Why ain't you somewhere playin'?" Kathleen asks Aldania scornfully.

"I was but I wanted to walk Daddy home," Aldania replies.

"Get out from under your daddy and go play."

Aldania stands by her father's side frowning at her mother, refusing to go.

"Don't you look at me like that!" Kathleen tells Aldania.

"Go on and do what your momma says," Cuthbert tells his daughter as he nudges her.

With a dejected looked, Aldania turns and goes down the porch steps and slowly walks back up the street to find her friends.

"You need to stop babying her," Kathleen tells her husband.

"I don't baby her," Cuthbert says. "Ain't nothin' wrong with my little girl comin' to meet me and walk with me when I come home from work."

"Well you quit makin' her think she's so special. She's gettin' to be unruly. Do you know when I whipped her the other day she told me she was gonna tell her daddy on me?"

"She said that?"

"Yeah she did! I beat her little tail even more after she said it. You done spoiled that gal. She startin' to smell herself and she's only eleven years old."

"I'll talk to her."

"You ain't got to talk to her on my behalf! I'm the momma! She keep actin' like she been doin' and I'm gonna hang her from one of them trees out yonder!"

Cuthbert snickers at his wife's remark.

"What we havin' for supper?" Cuthbert asks as he sits down on one of the porch chairs.

Kathleen gives her husband a mean look.

"You ain't even gonna ask how I'm doin' 'fore you ask me what we eatin'?" she says.

"How you doin' Kat. What's for supper?"

Kathleen rolls her eyes at him. She gets up from her seat and goes into the house. As she walks towards the kitchen, she thinks about the costume she made from the scraps of material her boss let her have from her job as a seamstress. She wants to run upstairs to her bedroom and pack it in a bag along with the rest of her things and run out that front door. She wants to get on the next train and ride it back to Cleveland and go to the club where she had auditioned to be a dancer. The owner told her she could have the job. He was the one who told her she was so pretty and fine and was made to be on the stage. He wanted to make her into the big star she longed to be. But her husband told her she couldn't. He told her no respectable wife and mother would want to be up there on a stage frolicking around with half her clothes on. The more she thinks about it the more she hates being where she is right now. She wants so badly to be away from this house and her job and her husband and her children.

Kathleen walks back outside to where her husband is sitting.

"Cuthbert, I wanna go back to Cleveland," she says standing in front of him.

"Kat, I ain't talkin' about this no more," Cuthbert says looking up at her.

"I can't stay here."

"Well you ain't got no choice. You got responsibilities. You my wife. You got children to care for."

Kathleen feels the anger rise in her as she stares her husband down.

Why can't he be on her side? Why can't he tell her how he would love to see her up on the stage being a showgirl? Why does he think all there is to life is working some boring job day in and day out?

Kathleen had told her husband many times, in a civil way, how she felt about her dreams, but today she didn't care what she said or how she said it. Today she wanted him to know she no longer gave a damn about being a mother or a wife.

"I been holdin' my tongue for a long time about how I been feelin'," she says to him. "I been a good wife and mother for as long as I could but now I'm tired. This ain't how I wanna live no more."

Cuthbert rises from his seat and returns the angry stare his wife is giving.

"What you mean this ain't how you wanna live?" he says cutting his eyes at her.

"I mean I'm leavin'. I done made up my mind and I'm goin' back to Cleveland."

"You ain't goin' nowhere!"

"Oh I'm goin' alright! I'm goin' and I'm goin' by myself!"

"Woman is you crazy? Where you gonna stay up there? Huh? Who's gonna look out for you?"

"I don't need nobody to look out for me! I'm a grown woman and I can fend for myself."

"What about the children?"

"Muriel Susan is old enough to see about them. Ain't none of 'em no little babies no more. They old enough to help out around here like they already doin'."

"What about me and you? Who's gonna take care of me while you gone?"

"I ain't gonna be gone long," Kathleen says in a more pleasant voice trying to soothe her angry husband. "Besides, soon as I get enough money I can send for all of y'all to come up there with me. Cuthbert, I know I can make it. Them show business people already said I got what it takes to be famous. And once I get famous, we ain't got to stay in Cleveland. We can move to Chicago or Detroit or even New York City."

Cuthbert looks away from his wife for a minute. He looks back into her pleading eyes and tells her, no.

Kathleen becomes enraged and starts screaming and hollering at her husband.

"Who the hell you think you is tellin' me when I can come and go? You don't own me! I do what the hell I wanna do!"

"You ain't goin' no damn where!" Cuthbert says narrowing his eyes at his wife.

"I am goin! I'm leavin' this little raggedy ass town and you in it! I ain't never had nothin' I wanted since I had them damn children and I married your sorry ass!"

Cuthbert looks towards the bottom of the steps and sees Aldania and her younger sister, Amelia, standing there holding hands as they listen to their parents argue. He looks at their young faces and sees the hurt on them, knowing they just heard what their mother said. It angers him to no end.

Cuthbert slaps Kathleen across her face. She's shocked that Cuthbert has hit her. She rubs the side of her face as she looks at him with hatred in her eyes. She turns from him and quickly goes into the house. He follows behind her with his children in tow.

"You done lost your damn mind talkin' to me like that!" Cuthbert hollers as he walks after Kathleen.

"You better get away from me!" Kathleen tells him as she turns back to him, stopping in her tracks. "I said I'm leavin' and that's that! I ain't got to ask you when I can leave! I leave when I wanna. I don't know why I married your ugly, black ass no way! You ain't got no excitement in you. You ain't the kinda man I likes no how! I ain't stayin' in this little, dumb ass town sittin' around gettin' old and ugly with you and these damn children! I'm gonna be somebody. I'm gonna be famous all over the world!"

Cuthbert looks at his wife in amazement. She's never behaved like this before and he doesn't understand what's happened to make her act this way. He's hurt and confused but he's a man with pride. He would never beg a woman to stay with him who didn't want to be there.

"You get your shit and you get outta my house!" Cuthbert tells Kathleen.

"I will!" she says defiantly and walks up the stairs to her bedroom. Cuthbert turns around and looks to see his girls standing behind him. Aldania and Amelia both grab their father around his waist on either side. Amelia buries her head in her father's side and tries to muffle her cries.

"Don't you worry about nothin' Daddy," Aldania says looking up into her father's worried face. "You still got us and we gonna take care of one another. Don't worry about her leavin'. It's gonna be alright."

Kathleen is gone for two days before she comes back home. Her children are glad to see her come through the front door and run to greet her, embracing their mother. That is, all of her children except Aldania.

"Ain't you gonna give me a hug?" Kathleen asks her daughter.

Aldania doesn't respond. She looks at her mother without expression.

Later that day, Aldania waits at the corner for her father at the spot where they usually meet up and walk home.

"Momma came back," Aldania tells her father as soon as she sees him.

"I knew she would."

"You gonna let her stay?"

"Of course I'm gonna let her stay."

"I wouldn't."

"What you mean you wouldn't?"

"I wouldn't let nobody leave my house and be comin' and goin' if they wasn't actin' right. It ain't right the way she makes you feel so bad. I wouldn't let her stay."

"Well that's not your choice. She's my wife and your momma and she gonna be with us for as long as we live."

They walk along the street holding hands.

"Your momma told me you been acting hainty here lately," Cuthbert says looking down at Aldania. "What's the matter?"

"Momma just don't like me. She's mad because I like you better than I do her."

"Don't you say things like that. You supposed to like your ma and pa the same."

"I can't help it. You like me better than Muriel Susan and 'em."

"I love all my children the same. You just happen to be my first blood born child and when I became a flesh and blood daddy it was the happiest day of my life. It ain't that I love you more, it's just that you the special one that made it happen for me."

Aldania smiles proudly as she listens to her father.

"But you still a child and you better be more respectful of your momma, you hear me."

"Yes sir."

By the time Cuthbert and Aldania reach their house, Kathleen is sitting on the porch, watching as they approach. She wants to reprimand Aldania about being stuck up under Cuthbert again, but under the circumstances she remains quiet. Aldania leaves to go play as Cuthbert walks upon to the porch and into the house, not looking at or speaking to Kathleen. Cuthbert goes into the kitchen to get a glass of water and while he is filling his glass at the spicket, Kathleen comes into the kitchen. She stands next to the wall with her arms crossed while she watches her husband drink his water.

"Where you been?" Cuthbert asks without looking at Kathleen when he finishes his drink.

"I went all the way to Cleveland on the train. I stayed with Pinkie when I got up there."

"Why you come back?"

"I thought about it for a long time and my children need they momma and my husband needs his wife."

"It ain't about what we need. It's about what you wanna be to us."

"I'm sorry I said all them bad things about you and the children," Kathleen says walking over to her husband. She looks into his eyes. "I just been tired and feeling lowly about myself. Sometime I just don't feel special."

"Ain't I always treated you right? I married you when you had two children with two different men. Neither one of them niggas even give me a dime to take care of them children but I don't never complain about it. I stay in this house with you and provide for you and our children. I go to church with my family and I'm bringing them up right. I ain't got no children with no other woman. I ain't never left you. Don't that let you know how special you is to me? Ain't that enough?"

There is a long silence between the two of them as they stand looking at one another.

"Even if I ain't one of the most important things in your life," Cuthbert says, "them children should be. You they momma. Heaven forbid that somethin' ever happened to me, but if I ain't here to see about them, then you got to do it. Don't never let nothin' split up my family. Promise me that."

Kathleen doesn't respond to her husband. She wants to tell him that he and her children mean the world to her. She wants to tell him she appreciates him for being the man he is, but she can't. As good of a man as Cuthbert is and has been, and as precious as her children should be to her, none of them can replace what she truly wants.

"I'm sorry for runnin' out on you," she tells him. "It won't happen again."

But it does happen again. And each time it happens, Cuthbert, feeling humiliated and despondent, takes his wife back. It saddens Aldania more than anyone to see the look on her father's face when Kathleen leaves out that door. It angers her even more when her mother comes back because she knows her mother is going to leave them again.

Cuthbert never comes home from work early, but one chilly day in October, he does. One of the machines at the tool company where he works broke down, and the boss man told the workers to go home for the day. It's a little after twelve o'clock and the children are still at school. Kathleen won't be home for a couple of hours.

Cuthbert turns the handle of the front door and finds it is unlocked. He walks into the house thinking about how he is going to reprimand his wife for forgetting to lock up the house, when all of a sudden he hears a rhythmic, knocking sound coming from upstairs. He quietly goes upstairs to find out what the noise is and where it is coming from. All the bedroom doors are open except his. As he approaches his bedroom, he hears the mumble of a man's voices. Then he hears the familiar voice of his woman. His heart starts to beat hard as he thinks about what might be going on behind that door. He creeps closer, pulling his switch blade from his pocket and opens it as he readies himself to confront this man and his wife. When Cuthbert opens the door and sees Kathleen in their bed in the arms of another man, his heart sinks.

Kathleen's face is frozen with fright when she looks up to see her husband standing there with fire in his eyes.

"Oh my lord!" she screams.

Her lover looks around and sees Cuthbert with his knife in his hand. He jumps up from the bed and grabs his pants from the floor next to the bed.

"Hey man!" he says nervously stepping into his pants. "Who are you?"

Cuthbert stands at the doorway shaking with anger.

Kathleen gets out of the bed and puts on her dress that is lying on the floor as well. They're both afraid as they stand on the side of the bed closest to the wall.

"Who is this man?" her lover asks her.

"My husband," Kathleen tells him with great fear in her voice.

"Your husband?!"

Kathleen starts to cry.

"Look mister," the man says turning to Cuthbert, "she ain't tell me she was married! I swear I didn't know!"

"Nigga, you a dead man!" Cuthbert hollers. He climbs onto the bed and lunges toward the man, swinging his knife at him, but he misses. Cuthbert falls halfway off the bed.

Kathleen screams and runs from where she is towards the bedroom door with her lover right behind her. They can hear Cuthbert's footsteps stomping behind them as they flee down the stairs. The man almost reaches the front door when Cuthbert jumps in front of him. He waves his knife tauntingly at the terrified man.

"Cuthbert please don't do it!" Kathleen pleads.

"First I'm gonna kill him," Cuthbert says, "and then I'm gonna kill you!"

The barefoot man turns and runs into the kitchen and tries to get to the back door but Cuthbert has grabbed him around his neck from behind. The man elbows Cuthbert in his ribs causing him to drop his knife. They tussle and fall to the floor with Cuthbert on top of the man, punching him in his face. Kathleen screams for Cuthbert to stop. Somehow, the man is able to reach the knife and with one strong stab to the chest, he stops Cuthbert.

Kathleen screams in horror as she watched her husband fall sideways off of her lover and onto the floor. The man hurries to his feet. Kathleen is on her knees crying and crawling to her dying husband. When she reaches him, she sits on the floor and holds his head in her lap and screams in anguish. Her lover looks at Cuthbert taking his last breath and then looks at Kathleen. Realizing what he has just done, the man runs out the back door.

Amelia and Aldania are almost home from school when they see the police wagon sitting in front of their house. There are several people gathered on their front porch. The girls run back up the street to where Muriel Susan and their brothers, Lemuel Rick and Ambrose are, telling them what they just saw. The children all run to the house, panicking as they get closer.

Muriel Susan tells her sisters and brothers to wait outside while she goes into the house to see what has happened. None of them pay her any mind, and they follow behind her into the kitchen. They find their mother sitting in a chair at the kitchen table with her dress falling off her shoulders. Her hands are stained with dried blood, and she has her head in her hands, crying.

Muriel Susan goes to her mother and asks her what happened, but Kathleen can't answer her. Aldania looks down at the kitchen floor and sees the blood smeared stains where something big has been dragged across it.

"Where's my daddy?" Aldania says in a frightened voice.

No one answers her. Not knowing what has happened and just from the scene in the kitchen the other children have started to cry.

"Where's my daddy?" Aldania asks again raising her voice.

One of the officers in the kitchen tells one of the neighbors to get the children out of the kitchen. Mr. Shaffen directs the children as they all leave sobbing. They all go except for Aldania.

Mr. Shaffen walks over to Aldania and bends down in front of her.

"I'm sorry to tell you Aldania," he says to her, "but your daddy is dead."

"What happened to him?"

Mr. Shaffen looks embarrassed and rises from in front of Aldania. He lowers his head and turns away from her.

Aldania looks around the room to the other adults.

"What happened to my daddy?!" she cries out loud.

Still no one responds to her.

"Get her out of here," Kathleen finally says looking up from the table.

Mr. Shaffen tries to take Aldania's hand to lead her from the kitchen, but she yanks away. He tries to grab her arm, but she takes off running to the back door. When she steps outside, she sees her father's blood drenched body lying on the back porch and she screams in agony. She tries to bend down and touch her father but before she can, Mr. Shaffen grabs her around her waist and takes her back inside. Aldania becomes hysterical and tries to break free, screaming and crying for her father.

It's been hours since the police took Kathleen down to the station to question her about what happened in her husband's death. Miss Millie from across the street offered to keep the children at her house until Kathleen was able to come home. Amelia and Aldania are sitting in the front room of Miss Millie's house while, Lemuel Rick and Ambrose are in the kitchen. Muriel Susan has gone upstairs and is lying in Miss Millie's bed.

Miss Millie is in the front yard talking with some of the other women from around the neighborhood. Word has spread fast about Cuthbert's murder and people have come to find out what happened.

"Didn't she know he might come home and catch her?" Amelia hears someone ask Miss Millie through the opened living room window. Miss Millie tries to shush the woman. She didn't want the Gray children to hear what the nosey neighbors were saying about Kathleen.

"Dania," Amelia whispers to her sister. "Come here."

Aldania walks over to where Amelia is sitting.

"Listen to them," Amelia says pointing to the women, standing in the yard outside the window.

"I don't know what that stupid heifa was thinking," another woman says. "She had a good man and she went and got him killed by her boyfriend."

"Hell, if she didn't want her husband all she had to do was let him go," another lady says. "He could have come and stayed with me! I wouldn't have ever strayed from that!"

"Yeah honey, that was a fine nigga man."

"Uh-oh, y'all be quiet," Miss Millie says. "Here she comes walkin' down street."

Miss Millie comes into the house and tells the children their mother is back. They all run out of the house and go to her, all except Aldania. Aldania goes across the street to her house and walks inside. She walks into the kitchen and finds a woman scrubbing the kitchen floor where her father's blood had been.

Tears stream down her cheeks as she stands there, looking at the spot where her father was killed.

Kathleen and her children walk into the kitchen. Her eyes are red and her lips and nose are swollen from all the crying she has done.

"Come here baby," Kathleen says extending her arms to Aldania, but Aldania doesn't come to her. "Dania come here."

Aldania looks at her mother and says nothing. She slowly walks out of the kitchen and up stairs to the bedroom she shares with her sisters. She goes inside and closes the door behind her.

Kathleen can't stand the hateful stares she gets from the women on her street. None of them have asked her what really happened to Cuthbert, but she knows they know the truth.

Her friend, Ruth, told her that a few of those nosey heifers had asked if it was Kathleen's lover who killed her husband, or was it someone who actually did break into the house. Kathleen never talked to her neighbors about it. In fact, she hasn't talked about it to anyone, not even her children. She never contacted her or Cuthbert's family in Georgia to come up for the funeral. She was afraid of what his family might do to her if they found out her lover killed him, and she was embarrassed by what her family would think of her if they found out.

Aldania and Amelia told Muriel Susan what they overheard Miss Millie and her friends saying about their mother on the day it happened. Muriel Susan told her little sisters not to pay that gossip any attention. She didn't want to believe what was said about her mother and she didn't want her sisters and brothers to believe it either.

The boss man where Kathleen works found out what actually happened in the case of her husband's death, and he fired her from her job. He told her he couldn't chance the loss of business because of her scandal and had to let her go.

Kathleen starts to think about Cleveland again. She no longer had anyone to stop her from going. She could move her children back up there and finally pursue her dream. But the more she thinks about it, she decides now is not the time. It's too soon to be uprooting her children. They've been through a lot with their father's death and she needs to give them more time to get past it.

Aldania seems to be the saddest of the children. Kathleen knows Aldania misses her father more than any of them. The other children have adjusted better than expected over these past five months since Cuthbert's death. During the day, Aldania seems to be okay but sometimes she cries at night. Kathleen doesn't know how to comfort her. She doesn't try to soothe her little girl with hugs or tell her things will be okay. She just wishes Aldania would hurry up and be done with her mourning so she doesn't have to worry about Aldania crying over her father, as well as how she's going to feed her children.

It hurts Amelia's heart to hear her big sister cry when they're in bed. She's a child but she knows what to do to help her sister get through her sadness. Amelia comforts Aldania with hugs as she pats her back until she falls asleep.

Kathleen has tried to find a job uptown but no one has hired her. She has to find a way to make money and she has to do it fast.

It's a beautiful spring evening and it's almost dark outside. Ten year old Amelia just remembered she was supposed to change the sheets on her bed. Her mother told her to do the chore earlier in the day. Her brothers and sisters are all sitting on the front porch playing and talking as they had been instructed by their mother. The other children in the neighborhood had all gone in for the evening but Kathleen allowed her children some extra time to play, restricting them to the front yard.

Amelia goes back inside to hurry and change her sheets before her mother gets back from Miss Nell's house. She quickly goes to her room and throws a sheet on her bed. She straightens it out and walks to the other side to tuck the sheet under, when she sees movement in the back yard from her bedroom window. She peeks out the window to get a better look. She can see Mr. Harold, from down the street, coming out of the shed behind their house. Mr. Harold walks towards the alley behind the shed and peers around it to see who might be looking before he goes on his way. A few seconds later, Kathleen comes out of the shed. She also looks around to see who might be watching, then makes her way to the kitchen back door. Amelia wonders for a minute why her mother and Mr. Harold had been in the shed together, but she doesn't think on it for long.

Two days later, Amelia is in the kitchen washing dishes. Her mother hadn't told her to do the dishes, but Amelia is helping out because she loves to play in the water. She has to stand on a chair because she can't reach the sink. As she plays in the water, she looks out the window over the sink and sees her mother and Mr. Jones, another neighbor, going into the shed. Amelia can't understand why Kathleen keeps going into the shed with the men. She calls to Muriel Susan who is in the pantry looking for the glass jars of green beans they will be having for tonight's dinner. Muriel Susan comes to her sister and stands next to her at the sink.

"What did you call me for?" Muriel Susan asks.

"Is momma sellin' daddy's tools," Amelia asks her older sister innocently.

"Why you say that?"

"'Cause her and Mr. Jones just went in the shed and closed the door. He must be in there lookin' at Daddy's old wheel barrow and his hammers. Momma can't use 'em so she must be tryin' to sell 'em to some of the neighbor men. It's been plenty of 'em goin' in to look."

"What do you mean plenty of 'em?"

"I saw Mr. Harold the other evenin' and I saw Mr. Wilson yesterday mornin'. And now I see Mr. Jones."

Muriel Susan thinks for a minute. Why would her mother go in and out of the shed with different men? When Muriel Susan realizes what might be going on right up under their noses, she becomes infuriated but doesn't show her anger in front of Amelia.

"They must not want none of them old tools." Amelia says. "All they do is go in and look around for a while and then they come on back out. I don't know why Momma don't leave the door open. They can't see what they looking at if it's dark in there."

"I'm sure they can see in there," Muriel Susan says hoping her sister is still naïve enough not to understand what their mother is doing. "You just don't tell anybody else about this."

"Why not?" Amelia says inquisitively.

"Because some of them men's wives might not want them to be buying Daddy's old tools. You know old tools don't work as good as new tools and they might get mad if they husbands is buying old tools from Momma. You just keep what you saw to yourself, you hear me?"

Amelia frowns at her sister's request for secrecy.

"Swear it," Muriel Susan demands of Amelia.

"I swear," Amelia says.

Just then, Muriel Susan looks out the window to see Mr. Jones casually walking out of the shed. She's appalled as she watches Mr. Jones look around the shed to see if the coast is clear as he leaves. It sickens her to think about the foul things that she speculates her mother might be doing alone in the shed with different men. But Muriel Susan knows. She knows what her mother has been doing, especially now that Kathleen has more money in her purse.

Muriel Susan is barely seventeen and hasn't finished school but she's in love with Arthur Bronson and wants to marry him. She also wants to get away from her mother. Kathleen isn't the same and she hasn't been since Cuthbert died. She's always hollering at the children and spanks them for no good reason. Muriel Susan also knows Kathleen has started drinking moonshine because she can smell it on her breath from time to time.

One day, Arthur comes to ask Kathleen for Muriel Susan's hand in marriage.

"Muriel Susan ain't marrying you," Kathleen tells Arthur as the three of them sit in the front room. "She's got responsibilities around here. She can't just up and leave."

"I understand how you feel Mrs. Gray," Arthur says nervously, "but we're ready to get married now. I got a job up in Philadelphia and I have to leave next week. Sue wants to go with me and you know I'll take good care of her. All we need is your blessing."

"She ain't goin'. Muriel Susan is too young to be gettin' married. She's got to quit school and find her a job around here and help me with these children."

"Momma, why I gotta get a job and help you take care of your children?" Muriel Susan says frowning. "They ain't my responsibility. Anyway, I'm gonna be leavin' here soon enough. I'm almost grown and it's time for me to be gettin' on. And if I leave, that's one less person you got to take care of."

"I'm not gonna take care of these chil'ren by myself! I can't do all this by myself. You know how hard it is lookin' after four chil'ren?"

"I know but I ain't the one who had 'em! It's not right that you stop me from doin' what I want to 'cause you went and had all them babies. That ain't my fault."

"You still ain't gettin' married and that's that," Kathleen says smirking her lips at Muriel Susan. "Good evening Arthur. You won't need to come by no more to see Muriel Susan since you gonna be leavin' shortly. You find you another nice young lady to settle down with."

"Momma!" Muriel Susan snaps, as she gets up from her chair.

Kathleen rises from her seat and puts her hand on her hip while she gives her daughter a disciplinary look.

"I'll walk you to the door Arthur," she says to her boyfriend, looking defeated.

Arthur picks up his hat from the table and follows Muriel Susan to the door without saying good bye to Kathleen.

Muriel Susan goes back into the front room and finds Kathleen sitting in her seat.

"That boy wants you real bad," Kathleen says.

"And I wanna marry him too Momma."

"I ain't talkin' about marriage. That boy wants to bed you."

Muriel Susan drops her jaw to say something but she's so shocked she can't find the words.

"That boy don't want no wife," Kathleen says. "All that boy wants is to get some from you."

"Momma!" Muriel Susan yells. "What's wrong with you? Why are you talkin' like this?

"'Cause that's what it is! He don't love you. That boy wants to get you away from your family so you can keep house for him. That's the only reason men take on a wife anyway. You ain't gettin' married. You don't need no husband. But what you better do is get some of that boy's money before he leave town."

"What?"

"I told you he wants you real bad. I can tell by the way he be lookin' at you. You tell him he can have you for one night as long as he pays you for it."

"Momma!" Muriel Susan says in disgust. "How can you say somethin' like that to me?!"

"'Cause I got mouths to feed and me and you the only two who can get the money to do it!"

"I'm not laying down with no men for money! How dare you even think that I could do somethin' like that! That is wrong! Momma we ain't heathens! It's decent ways to make money! We shouldn't never be that desperate to survive in this world that we would have to stoop to somethin' so low!"

"Let me tell you somethin' gal! I done found out that's one of the easiest ways to make some money and I ain't got no shame in doin' it. And I'll tell you another thing. I like havin' them men kiss on me and tell me I'm pretty. They hold me like I'm special to 'em, like for that little bit of time it ain't nobody but me and them. I like how they tell me they like me better than they do they wives and how they wives can't satisfy they needs like I can. I ain't got my own man to hold me and tell me the things a woman need to hear. So if I can give myself to 'em and feel like a woman and they pay me while they tellin' it to me then I figure I'm the one who's comin' out on top."

"But Momma if they payin' you to tell you somethin' you wanna hear, then it ain't for real. They payin' you to tell you a lie."

Muriel Susan walks out of the room leaving her mother speechless.

Muriel Susan decides she can't stay with Kathleen any longer. She can't keep pretending not to notice the men who sneak out of the back yard shed with her mother following a few minutes later. She's worried about her younger sisters finding out the truth about how their mother is keeping a roof over their heads.

One night, Muriel Susan packs up her things to leave. She wakes Lemuel Rick and Ambrose and brings them into the bedroom she shares with Aldania and Amelia. When the girls are awakened, Muriel Susan tells them all about her plans.

"I'm leavin' tonight," she tells them.

"You runnin' away to marry Arthur?" Aldania asks.

"Yes. But once I get there and I get settle, I'm gonna try and see if Momma will let y'all come stay with us."

"Why you want us to come stay with you?" Amelia. "Who's gonna stay with Momma?"

"Momma will be alright by herself. I'm gonna tell y'all a secret. I think Momma might be sick so she's gonna need some time to be by herself so she can get better."

"Then you gonna send for her later so we can all be together?" Amelia asks.

That isn't Muriel Susan's intentions. She's worried that her mother has lost her soul and is a danger to her children, and she wants to get them as far away from her as possible. But for the sake of what she needs to do, she tells them she will send for their mother later.

"I'm glad you goin' to marry Arthur," Aldania tells Muriel Susan smiling from cheek to cheek. "I like him and I can tell he loves you. I heard Momma tell him she wasn't gonna let you marry him. That ain't right of her."

"What else did you hear Momma sayin'?" Muriel Susan asks, praying her sister hadn't heard that whole conversation from a few days ago.

"That's all. I walked him down the street when he left the house. I told him not to give up on you 'cause you really did wanna be his wife."

Muriel Susan smiles with relief.

"It might take me a few months to get everything in order," Muriel Susan says, "but I promise I'm gonna come back for y'all."

She starts to cry as she thinks about leaving them.

"Quit cryin' and go get Arthur," Aldania says to her. "We can take care of ourselves 'til you come for us."

Muriel Susan hugs them all. As she goes out the bedroom door with her bag in her hand she puts her finger to her mouth, gesturing them to be quiet.

"Y'all, we got to move from this house," Kathleen tells her children one morning while they are eating their breakfast. "I got me a new job up the road in Middletown and it's too far for me to be travelin' every day. I'm gonna be workin' at another dress shop."

"You gonna write to Muriel Susan and let her know where we gonna be livin'?" Aldania asks her mother.

"Why should I let her know where we movin' to?" Kathleen says sarcastically. "She snuck outta here two weeks ago to marry that boy. She ain't care about how we was gonna get along without her so naw I ain't writin' her. Besides, I don't know where to send her a letter."

"Well, maybe we better wait until we hear from her," Lemuel Rick says. "She said she was gonna be back."

"I thought you said you ain't talk to her before she left outta here," Kathleen says looking suspiciously at Lemuel Rick.

"Huh?" he says looking like he's just let the cat out of the bag.

"What else did she say?"

"She didn't say nothin'."

"Don't you lie to me boy. What else did she say?"

The loud banging on the front door draws Kathleen's attention from her son.

"Who is it?" Kathleen yells, annoyed by the way the person is beating at her door.

She goes to answer the door and when she opens it, her neighbor, Mrs. Wilson, is standing there holding open the screen door. There are several woman and men standing in Kathleen's yard.

"You whore!" Mrs. Wilson says, "you been layin' up with my husband!" She grabs Kathleen's arm and slaps her across the face. Then she pulls Kathleen by the arm and drags her down the front porch steps into the yard. Kathleen struggles and fights to get away from Mrs. Wilson but she can't. Mrs. Wilson gets Kathleen on the ground and sits on her back. She takes her open hand and uses it to paddle Kathleen anywhere she can. Kathleen struggles desperately to get the woman off of her. People in the yard are cheering Mrs. Wilson on as she fusses at Kathleen for what she's been doing. Kathleen's children are standing on the front porch watching in horror as this woman beats their mother. Lemuel

Rick runs down the stairs and grabs Mrs. Wilson telling her to stop. A few other men have finally seen enough and pull the two women apart.

"You stinkin' bitch!" Mrs. Wilson yells at Kathleen. "You acted like you were my friend just so you could get close to my man!"

"Well you wasn't givin' him what he wanted so that's why he took to seein' me!" Kathleen screams.

"You goin' to hell, you witch!" Mrs. Wilson says as she's lead away from the yard.

Kathleen stands there humiliated when all of a sudden she realizes her children have been watching. Amelia and Ambrose look confused and hurt. Lemuel Rick and Aldania look embarrassed. They were both young but they knew what just happened and why.

"Get in the house!" Kathleen hollers at them. She walks into the house slamming the door behind her. "I'm glad to be leavin' this little piddly town anyway."

"Momma, why did she hit you like that?" Amelia asks.

"'Cause she's crazy! Y'all start packin' up you things. We movin' out of here first thing in the morning!"

"Mr. Bill is comin' for me in a little while," Kathleen tells her children excitedly one Saturday in June. "We goin' up to Cleveland for about a week. I finally got somethin' lined up for me to be on the stage!"

"For real?" Lemuel Rick says.

"Yes! I'm finally gonna be a big star! Y'all gonna be so proud of your momma! Your friends is gonna be jealous 'cause I'm gonna be makin' a whole lotta money and I'm gonna be able to buy y'all whatever you want!"

"Are we goin' with you Momma?" Amelia asks with excitement in her eyes.

"Not just yet," Kathleen says. "I got to get up there and find a place for us to live."

"But we just got in this house," Aldania says unenthused. "We ain't been here but two months. Why we gotta move again?"

"Y'all ain't movin' right this minute. Like I said I'm goin' up there today and I'm gonna send for y'all in about a week. I got to go to let these people see me first."

"Who's gonna see about us?" Aldania says crossing her arms.

"Y'all gonna see about yourselves."

"You gonna leave us all alone?!"

"Y'all old enough now to fend for yourselves. Y'all got one another to lean on. I'm gonna put Lemuel Rick in charge. He's fifteen now and he's man of the family!"

"Aw, I don't wanna stay here with him runnin' the house!" Aldania says frowning. "I wish my daddy was here!"

Kathleen narrows her eyes and tightens her lips.

"You just can't stand to see me happy, can you?" Kathleen says angrily at Aldania. "Any little tidbit of happiness I try to find, you wanna take it from me. I can't have nothin' 'cause of y'all."

Aldania is taken aback at her mother's accusation and looks confused by her remark.

"Damn it I'm goin' to Cleveland and I'm gonna be on that stage and I'm gonna be famous! I ain't lettin' nothin' else stand in my way, no man, no chil'ren, nothin', you hear me?!"

The children become afraid of the way their mother is talking and they all become very quiet.

Kathleen sits still for a minute and tries to calm herself. When she's able to speak civilly, she gives her children instructions on what to do while she's away. She tells them this month's rent is paid and she gives Lemuel Rick five dollars for whatever the children will need until she calls for them. She tells them that if any adult asks where she is, they are to say she had to leave town suddenly to visit a sick relative and will be back in two days.

When Mr. Bill comes to get Kathleen, she kisses her children good-bye and tells them not to look so sad. She assures them that she'll be back to pick them up before they know it, and she walks out the door.

"Y'alls' momma still ain't back yet?" Melvin Booker asks Aldania.

Melvin is Lemuel Rick's new best friend. He lives down the street with his aunt not too far from Aldania. She hasn't known him long, but Aldania is in love with Melvin. She thinks about him all the time and whenever she sees him, her heart skips a beat. He's the first boy to ever make her feel that way. Melvin is so handsome to Aldania. He's as dark as night and has curly hair and at age sixteen he already has muscles almost as big as a grown man. Whenever he comes to her house with Lemuel Rick, they exchange smiles behind her brother's back. She tells Amelia about how much she loves Melvin, and she tells Amelia to keep her secret. If Lemuel Rick knew Aldania liked his friend, he would find a way to keep Melvin away from her.

"No, Momma ain't back and it's goin' on seven weeks now," Aldania says standing at the kitchen table in Melvin's house. "School is gonna be startin' back directly."

"What are y'all gonna do?" he asks, walking from the kitchen sink over to where she is.

"Same thing we been doin'. Wait until she gets back."

"What if she don't come back?"

"Don't say that Melvin," Aldania says, looking worried. "She's gotta come back. She's gotta come see about us."

"Don't you worry yourself none," Melvin says stepping closer to Aldania, "If she don't come back, I'll take care of you. You know I will. You so pretty Aldania."

"Thank you Melvin." Aldania says smiling shyly at him. Melvin smiles back at her and Aldania feels her heart thump hard. She would love to stay and just be in his presence, but she left Amelia at home to watch the beans she has cooking on the stove. She needs to get back to finish preparing their supper.

"Let me have the piece of bacon you got for me," Aldania says. "Lemuel Rick is gonna be home from work shortly and I know he's gonna be hungry."

Melvin turns and walks over to the ice box to pull out the piece of meat he had promised Aldania. He grabs a piece of cloth from the counter near the sink and walks back to the kitchen table where she is still standing.

"Here," he says giving her the meat and cloth. "Wrap this around the bacon. I gotta go get something out of my room. I'll be back in a minute."

Aldania spreads the cloth on the table. She places the meat in the center and begins to cover it with the cloth.

"Hey Aldania, come here," Melvin calls to her from down the hall.

She goes over to the sink to wash the bacon grease from her hands and dries them on a towel. When she gets to Melvin's room, she finds him sitting on his bed.

"Sit down right here for a minute," he says patting the seat next to him. "I got somethin' to ask you."

Without hesitating, Aldania sits next to Melvin.

Melvin takes Aldania's hand. "You know I love you, don't you?"

"I thought you might from the way you always be lookin' at me," Aldania says, smiling softly.

"I want you to be my wife."

"Huh?" Aldania says surprised.

"I said I want you to be my wife."

"Melvin quit bein' silly!" Aldania laughs.

"I ain't playin'," Melvin tells her with a serious look on his face. "Every time I see you I have these feelins' down here." He puts his hand onto his crotch.

"Melvin!" Aldania gasps. She looks away from him.

"Aldania, listen to me," he says touching her arm.

She looks back at him as he continues.

"Sometimes it gets real bad. I can't help but think about what I wanna do to you. In the bible it says a man and a woman should take a wife or husband so they don't burn in hellfire."

"Why would you burn in hellfire, Melvin?"

"'Cause it ain't right to do to you what I wanna without being your husband. I was talkin' with a couple of fellows at work about how I felt about you and they was teasin' me about what to do with you. Pastor Smith works there with us and he heard them funnin' and talkin'. He told 'em they better stop tellin' me the wrong thing to do 'cause if I ever took a woman in my bed I had better be married to her or else I was gonna burn in hellfire. That's why I have to marry you Aldania. I don't wanna burn in hellfire. I love you and I want you so bad."

Aldania wants Melvin too. She wants him to kiss her and touch her. She even wants to marry him. She thinks back to last year when Muriel Susan had a long talk with her and Amelia about boys. Her older sister told them that they better not ever let a boy touch them until they got married.

Melvin moves his face closer to Aldania's and tries to kiss her, but she turns her head slightly and moves out of his reach.

"Melvin I can't be your wife," she smiles. "I ain't but thirteen years old."

"Well you look like you sixteen same as me," Melvin says rubbing Aldania's arm. "Your titties is big like a woman. Your hips is round. Your lips is pretty and soft. Bein' next to you right now makes me wanna kiss you and hold you in my arms and ask you to lay in my bed with me. But we can't 'cause we ain't married. I can't keep feelin' like this about you Aldania. Tell me you'll marry me and be my wife."

"My momma ain't gonna let me get married."

"Your momma ain't even here."

"The preacher man ain't gonna let us get married neither. He's gonna tell us we ain't old enough. Besides, the law says you got to be older to get married."

"The law ain't said no such thing. We are old enough. I told you, you already look like you almost grown. We ain't got to go to the law to get married no how. We ain't even got to get married by no minister."

"We don't?"

"Naw. All you got to do is say 'I do' when I ask if you promise to obey me, and all I got to do is say 'I do' when you ask me if I promise to love you and cherish you. All we got to do is promise before God. So you gonna marry me?"

"Melvin I can't. I got to finish school. I wanna be like Mr. Garner down at the drug store and make up medicines that can help people when they sick. "

"But you ain't gonna need to be a medicine woman. I'm gonna take care of you when I make you my wife."

Melvin moves his face closer to Aldania and kisses her on her neck. She giggles from the tickling sensation his kiss is causing. He stops and looks into her eyes. Melvin kisses Aldania on her mouth. He closes his eyes and waits for her to kiss him back, but she doesn't. He opens his eyes and finds her staring at him. He closes his eyes and kisses her again for a long time. This time she kisses him back. She puts her hand on his face and strokes it. When Melvin touches Aldania's breast she stands up from the bed.

"Melvin I got to get goin'," she tells him.

"No," he says standing up with her. He gently takes her hand. "Don't leave me. Come sit back down with me."

He grabs both of Aldania's hands and pulls her to him. He puts his arms around her and holds her looking into her eyes. They kiss again.

"I have to go." Aldania says as she moves herself from Melvin. She starts towards the door to go out but Melvin beats her to it and closes it. He stands in front of the door and won't let Aldania leave.

"Melvin I need to go home" she says.

"I don't want you to go," he says. "I want you to stay here with me."

Aldania sees the sincere look on Melvin's face.

"I can't," Aldania tells him. "I love you but I can't keep kissin' you like that. It's makin' me feel funny."

"I know," he says moving closer to her. "That's the same feelin' I been tellin' you about that I have. See what it does to me?" Melvin takes Aldania's hand and makes it graze across the front of his pants.

"Melvin!" she gasps.

Melvin laughs as he grabs Aldania round the waist and rushes her to his bed falling on top of her. He straddles her and uses his knees to pin down her arms. He looks down at her and smiles. He tickles her sides.

"Quit playin' Melvin," she laughs. "Get off of me!"

She squirms and tries to get from under him, but his strength over powers her.

"Stop fightin' me," Melvin says seriously as he looks down at Aldania. He lies flat on top of her, resting his weight on his elbows. He puts both of his hands onto her face and kisses her slowly on the mouth. She giggles hard as she tries to turn her face but his strong hands hold it in place. He stops kissing her and looks into her eyes. "Right here before God, do you promise to take me to be your husband, to love me and obey me?"

Aldania stops laughing and looks at him.

"Do you promise?" he asks again.

He kisses her again and Aldania's heart flutters. She can't resist him any longer but she doesn't want to burn in hellfire either. She can't think of any more reasons not to marry him. In her young heart, she really does want to be his wife.

"I do," she says as she rubs her fingers on the side of his cheek.

"Now ask me if I promise, right here before God, to love you and to cherish you and take you to be my wife."

"Do you promise to love me and cherish me and take me to be your wife?" Aldania asks him.

"I do," he says. "I love you Aldania and I'm gonna always take care of you. And now that we're married, we can do something about these feelings we got for one another."

Ambrose sees the mailman getting ready to stuff letters into the mailbox. He runs to the mailman before he can open the door to the box.

"I'll take it," Ambrose says, holding out his hand.

"I don't know," the mailman says to him. "How old are you?"

"I'm nine."

"I guess nine is an okay age to be giving letters to a little boy. Taking this mail is a big responsibility. You make sure your momma and daddy get their letters."

Ambrose takes the mail from the postman and runs into the house. His brother and sisters are sitting in the front room looking bored. He gives the mail to Lemuel Rick who thumbs through it and then lays it on the table.

"She still ain't sent nothin'?" Amelia asks.

"Nope," Lemuel Rick says.

"How long has it been since Momma's been gone?" Amelia asks.

"Can't you count?" Lemuel Rick says sarcastically.

"Yes, but I don't know how long it's been."

"She's been gone for over two months. Muriel Susan's been gone three. One of them better hurry up and get back 'cause I'm tired of lookin' after y'all!"

"We tired of you lookin' after us too!" Aldania says. "I hate you bein' in charge of me!"

"Hush up before I come over there and knock you in your mouth!"

"You hit me and I'll knock you on your tail!"

Lemuel Rick gets up from his seat and goes over to his sister. He hits the side of her face with his fists while she's sitting in her seat. Aldania lifts her foot and kicks Lemuel Rick in his stomach. He doubles over and Aldania gets up from her seat and hits him on his back with her fists. Amelia screams for them to stop while Ambrose laughs. Someone knocks at the front door. Lemuel Rick composes himself and goes to see who it is.

"Daddy!" he hollers.

The other children get up and run to the door to see who it is Lemuel Rick is calling daddy.

"Hey boy!" the man says as he hugs Lemuel Rick and walks into the house.

"I been lookin' for a letter to come from you. I didn't know you was gonna come down here."

"Well when you told me what happened I figured I better come see about my boy."

"This is my daddy, Lem Johnson." Lemuel Rick says proudly to Aldania, Amelia and Ambrose.

"How you know he's your daddy?" Aldania asks. "I ain't never seen him before and from what I heard Momma and Daddy say you ain't either."

"Well your Momma didn't tell you everything did she?" Lem says as he bends down closer to Aldania's face.

"Momma took me to see my daddy plenty of times," Lemuel Rick says to Aldania. "She took me to see him when he stopped through on the train. She told me not to tell nobody about it. Said it was mine and her secret. She even gave me some money to keep quiet."

"And I give her a few dollars every time I came through here," Lem says proudly.

"I thought Daddy was your daddy," Ambrose says.

"He was," Aldania says. "Daddy was the one who took care of him. This just the daddy he was born from."

"I see you got a smart mouth like your momma," Lem says rolling his eyes at Aldania.

"You gonna stay here with us?" Lemuel Rick asks.

"Naw, I ain't stayin' here. I got a house and a wife to get back to."

Lem looks around the front room and can see the disarray.

"How come y'all ain't been keepin' this here place clean?" Lem says looking at them all.

"Mister we been worried about what we were gonna eat," Aldania says. "We don't care about cleanin' no house."

Lem walks through the small house with the children trailing behind him. He looks disgusted as he thinks about Kathleen leaving these children alone.

"Confound that woman!" he says under his breath. "I'm gonna sleep here tonight and first thing in the mornin' we goin' back to Detroit. We gonna start packin' things up around here tonight so we'll be ready to go bright and early."

Ambrose runs out the front door without telling anyone where he is going. Aldania and Amelia go into their room, and Aldania tells Amelia to take the pillow cases off the pillows so they can fill them up with their belongings.

Lem walks into the bedroom where the two girls are busy at work. When he sees Aldania and Amelia getting their things together he tells them to stop.

"Hold on a minute," he says. "I'm not takin' all of y'all with me. I'm just takin' my son."

"What about me and my brother and sister?" Aldania asks.

"Y'all three ain't my problem."

Aldania stares at Lem tight lipped.

"We can't stay here by ourselves," Amelia cries.

"I don't know why you can't take care of us," Aldania says to Lem. "My daddy took care of your son when you wasn't nowhere around."

Lem looks at Aldania with disdain. "I said I wasn't taking y'all with me. I ain't say I was gonna just leave y'all here by yourselves. I ain't stupid."

Lem rubs his head as he thinks about what he should do with Lemuel Rick's sisters and brother.

"Y'all go to church?" he asks.

"We used to," Aldania says. "We ain't been since my daddy died."

"Is it a church close to here?"

"It's one around the corner."

"I guess y'all should go ahead and get packed up."

Lem sits in the front room and smokes a cigarette as he thinks about what to tell the pastor when he drops off the three children at the church in the morning. Ambrose comes back in the door with a woman and a boy in tow. Lemuel Rick, Aldania and Amelia come back into the parlor.

"Hi, I'm Maybell from around the corner. Is everything alright over here?"

"I'm Lem Johnson from Detroit. I'm Lemuel's pa."

"Ambrose and my son, Bruce, are best friends."

"Come on in."

"Ambrose just came to tell us he was movin' to Detroit and y'all was about to go in a few minutes."

"Me and Lemuel is leavin' tomorrow. Lemuel wrote me a letter tellin' me Kathleen had run off to Cleveland and they ain't heard from her. You know anything about Kathleen leavin' these chil'ren by they self?"

"I surely do not, but I knew somethin' wasn't right. I used to see her goin' to the catch the trolley to go to work but I hadn't seen her in a while. I asked Ambrose if everything was alright over here and he told me yes. I should have known by the way that poor boy ate when I give him supper at my house that somethin' wasn't right. These chil'ren probably ain't ate in days."

"We been eatin'" Lemuel Rick says. "I got a job and I been bringin' money in."

"Well he ain't makin' that much money," Ambrose say, "'cause we been stealin' food from the store!"

"Hush your mouth!" Aldania says angrily to Ambrose for telling their secret.

"Oh my Lord!" Miss Maybell says. "What kind of mother would leave her chil'ren to steal for food!"

"She ain't no good!" Lem says. "She ain't never been no good!"

"What are you gonna do about these chil'ren?" Miss Maybell asks.

"This one here is mine," Lem says pointing to Lemuel Rick. "I ain't able to take on them other three. I'm gonna take them around here to the church to see if somebody can take 'em in."

"Well I can take Ambrose with me but I ain't able to take on them girls."

"I'll drop 'em off at the church. If the pastor can't find nobody to take 'em, then I suspect they'll have to go to the orphanage 'til they ma get back."

"What's a orphanage?" Amelia asks.

Aldania heart becomes heavy when she hears Lem's plan to have her and Amelia placed in an orphanage. She knew what an orphanage was and there was no way she was going to one. There was a girl at Aldania's school who used to live in one before she was adopted and she had told Aldania how she was mistreated in that place.

"I gotta go next door," Aldania says. "I'll be back in a minute."

Aldania walks down the street to Melvin's house and knocks on the door. His aunt, Josephine, answers.

"Hi Miss Josephine," Aldania says red eyed. She wipes her tears from her face. "I don't mean to be no trouble, but I need to talk to Melvin."

"What's the matter child?" she says holding the door open for Aldania to enter.

"My momma has been gone for almost three months now," Aldania says entering the house. "We haven't heard a word from her. Lemuel Ricks' daddy has come to take him back to Detroit, but he's not takin' the rest of us with him. Miss Maybell says she can take in Teeter, but me and Amelia don't have anywhere to go and Lemuel Rick's daddy says he gonna take us to the orphanage. So I was hopin' since me and Melvin are married now…"

"You and Melvin is married?"

"Yes mam. We've been married now for over two weeks."

"Who married you?"

"We married ourselves. We got married in his bedroom."

"In his bedroom?"

"Yes ma'am. We got married 'cause we didn't wanna burn in hellfire. We love each other so we got married 'cause we wanted to do what husband and wives do. I been a good wife to him 'cause I come to him when he tells me to. Now it's his turn to be a good husband to me and take care of me so I don't have to go to no orphanage. I was gonna ask him to help me take care of Amelia too, at least until Momma gets back home."

Miss Josephine looks at Aldania and she becomes very angry.

"Melvin!" Miss Josephine screams at the top of her lungs.

"Yes ma'am?" Melvin says as he comes running into the front room. When he sees Aldania standing there sniffling and wiping her tears, he gets scared. "What's the matter?"

"Did you make this child think y'all was married just so you could have your way with her?"

Melvin looks away from his aunt and stares at the floor.

"Answer me boy!" she snaps.

"No ma'am," he says.

"Yes you did!" Aldania holler.

"I mean I did," Melvins says looking up. "I mean, I didn't just wanna have my way with her. I love Aldania." He looks over at Aldania as she wipes her tears. "We got married and now she's my wife."

"You had her in your bed in my house?" his aunt hollers at him. She walks over to him and hits him across his face with her open hand. "Boy what's wrong with you? Y'all ain't old enough to be married!"

"Yes we are!" Melvin says adamantly. He walks over to Aldania and stands by her side, taking her hand.

"No you're not! Can't nobody marry they own selves! You know better than that! You got to get married by a preacher."

"No we don't! The bible says all we got to do is make a promise to one another before God and that's what we did."

"Boy that ain't how people get married! You have to go in front of a minister or somebody that's able to marry you. Oooo! And I don't blame her for what happened as much as I do you, Melvin. You're older than she is so you should have more sense."

Miss Josephine looks at the two of them and shakes her head. Then something dawns on her.

"How many times have y'all been together?" she asks.

"Three times," Aldania says.

"Three times?" Miss Josephine exclaims. "Child have you started gettin' your monthly?"

"No ma'am. But my oldest sister told me about it. She said that's when you can start havin' babies."

"Ooh sweet Jesus!" Miss Josephine says as she sits on the sofa. "Thank the Lord!"

She looks at the two of them still standing next to one another as they hold hands.

"Listen," she says, "Y'all are not married. Aldania, honey I'm sorry but Melvin can't let you come and live with him. He ain't but a child hisself and I'm not able to take care of you, him and your sister."

"But Auntie, I got a job," Melvin says. "I got money."

"Boy you ain't makin' enough money to take care of yourself let alone take care of somebody else!"

"Well if we can't stay here then I'll find us our own place."

"Melvin shut up! Shut up! You ain't goin' nowhere and she can't stay here and that's that! Now y'all need to cut out this foolishness! Just 'cause y'all said 'I do' to one another don't make you married. It's probably best that she does go to that home. Y'all don't need to be around one another, not after what's done happened. Did y'all tell anybody about this?"

"No ma'am," Melvin says.

"What about you?" she asks Aldania.

"No ma'am," she answers, sniffling.

"Don't you tell nobody else about it either, you hear me? This will go away soon and y'all can forget it ever happened. Melvin you walk her to the door." Miss Josephine rises from the sofa. "It ain't nothin' else we can do to help you."

Miss Josephine walks out of the room and down the hallway.

"Why did you lie to me Melvin?" Aldania says as she turns to look at him. "I loved you and you lied to me just so you could get me in your bed."

"I didn't lie to you!" he says as he looks into Aldania's eyes and sees the hurt and uncertainty on her face. "You are my wife."

"No I ain't! Didn't you just hear your auntie? We was supposed to get married by a preacher! Now you can't take care of me 'cause you ain't my husband!"

"We made a promise before God and it was for real. You are my wife! I don't care what nobody says! I am your husband and I ain't lettin' them take you away from me! I'm gonna get us our own place and we can let your sister come stay with us until your momma comes back. I got a job. I can take care of you Aldania."

Melvin tries to hold Aldania tightly but she breaks free from him.

"I ain't your wife! You lied to me! I'd rather go to that orphanage than to stay with you now!"

"Aldania don't say that!"

"I hate you Melvin Booker for what you did to me! And I'll never forgive you for it either!"

Aldania stares at Melvin with contempt as she backs away from him. She goes to the door and opens it to leave.

"Aldania don't leave me," he whispers, looking helpless and alone.

"I see here on your paper that you're eighteen years old," Mrs. Snyder says to Aldania.

"Yes ma'am," Aldania lies. She had told the people at the Maple Hill Home for Girls that she and Amelia were two years older than they really were so they could leave the place sooner.

"How long have you been in the home?"

"It's been three years now. I was fifteen when I went in. My momma and daddy died and me and my younger sister had nowhere to go. My baby brother went to stay with his best friend and my older brother went back to Detroit with his real daddy. I have another older sister but we don't know where she is. She moved to Philadelphia to get married after my father died. We're originally from here in Hamilton, but my mother moved us up to Middletown before she died."

"Oh I see."

"All of our kinfolks are down in Georgia but we don't know how to find them. We were very little when my parents brought us to Ohio."

"Well now, tell me why I should hire you as my maid?"

"First off, I'm a hard worker. I'm a real good cook and I'm good with children too."

"Are you an honest person?"

"Yes ma'am."

"Then why have you just lied to me?"

"I beg your pardon?"

"I spoke to the head mistress at Maple Hill and she told me they have no record of a Daisy Mills ever being in their home. So why did you lie to me?"

Aldania looks embarrassed for being caught in a lie. She sighs deeply.

"I'm sorry ma'am. My real name is Aldania Gray. That's the only thing I lied about. I couldn't tell you my real name on account they might come looking for me."

"Who?"

"The people from Maple Hill. I ran away a few months ago 'cause I couldn't take livin' there anymore. I'm tryin' to get a job and a place so I can get my sister out of there too. Those people ain't right. It's only one lady there that's fair and decent to the girls livin' in that home and that's Miss Mary Dean. She's the only somebody that's right. I'm sorry I lied but I need a job real bad."

"How did you get down here to Hamilton?"

"Some kind gentleman in a wagon gave me a ride. When I first got here, I had to sleep in the park over by the school a couple of nights. They have a soup kitchen at the school so I ate there the first two days when I came to town. This lady and her husband are lettin' me stay in one of the extra rooms they got until I can find me a job and get my own place. They said I could pay them later on. The lady is the one who told me about the office that sends girls from places like Maple Hill on job assignments. I told them my name was Daisy Hill. They wasn't as smart as you 'cause they didn't call to check nothin' out. They just took my information and put it all on that paper and told me to come here to see if you were interested in hirin' me."

Aldania looks at Mrs. Snyder with sincere eyes. Mrs. Snyder stares back at her thinking whether or not she wants to hire this girl.

All of a sudden Mrs. Snyder's young son, Raymond, comes into the parlor.

"Hi brown girl!" he says, excitedly, smiling from ear to ear.

"Hi white boy," Aldania says smiling back.

"Raymond!" Mrs. Snyder says as she slaps her hand on her thigh. "Don't you see us talking?"

"What are you doing here at our house?" Raymond asks, ignoring his mother, as he goes over to Aldania and sits next to her.

"I'm here 'cause I'm hopin' your ma will let me be her maid and your new friend."

"I hope she says yes!"

"Raymond you know better than to just walk in here when adults are talking," Mrs. Snyder says. "You carry yourself out of here this instant!"

Raymond sits comfortably next to Aldania, pretending his mother hasn't said a word.

"Did you hear your ma?" Aldania says to him sternly. He shakes his head yes. "Then you get up and do like she says."

"Okay, I'll see you tomorrow brown girl," Raymond says as he gets up from his seat and walks out of the parlor.

Mrs. Snyder sits there dumbfounded by her son's actions.

"How old is he?" Aladania asks.

"That one is eight and I have another one who's seven. I can't believe he just did that."

"What, that he came in here without asking?"

"No, he did what you told him to! He never listens to anybody except his father. I have to threaten to beat him with a switch to get him to do what I tell him and he doesn't even know you and he did what you said right away."

"I told you I'm good with children."

"Can you start tomorrow?"

"This is a nice house this lady's got," Amelia says looking around at the bedroom she will be sharing with Aldania.

"Yes it is," Aldania tells her sister as she opens a few empty drawers on the dresser for Amelia to use. "Sorry, but that bed ain't big enough for both of us to sleep in. I'll get some blankets before we get ready to go to sleep so you can make you a pallet on the floor."

"That's alright by me," Amelia says. "I'll sleep anywhere as long as I ain't got to be at Maple Hill no more."

"We can take turns sleepin' on the floor."

"I'm glad Mrs. Snyder came to adopt me. I can live here with these people forever!"

"Well don't you get too used to it. She adopted you as a favor to me. That was the only way to get you out of Maple Hill. Once I get us a place we're gonna be movin' out of here. I heard Mr. Snyder complainin' the other night tellin' her he ain't runnin' no home for poor, niggas gals. He told her not to be roundin' up nobody else to bring into this house."

"Sounds like she's one of them white women that's on a mission to save us poor Negroes!" Amelia laughs and Aldania joins in.

"When you get unpacked come on out to the kitchen and we can fix us something to eat," Aldania says.

Aldania walks to the kitchen and busies herself until Amelia joins her. They talk until Mrs. Snyder comes into the kitchen followed by Ambrose.

"What are you doin' here!" Amelia says excitedly.

"I rode the train down here to visit with y'all for a spell." He hugs and kisses both of his sisters before sitting down at the kitchen table.

"I want you all to come out into the yard," Mrs. Snyder says. "My husband is out there with his camera and I'm going to have him take a picture of the three of you."

Aldania, Amelia and Ambrose follow Mrs. Snyder outside the house and down the steps to the back yard. Mr. Snyder is already outside taking pictures of the rose bushes that his wife was so proud of. He stops with his current photo session and has his new subjects strike a pose. After he takes a few pictures, Mrs. Snyder leads them back into the kitchen.

"I'm so glad the three of you are able to be together again," Mrs. Snyder says smiling gleefully. "It just warms my heart to be able to help a Negro family stay together in their time of need."

Amelia smirks at Mrs. Snyder's remark as Aldania looks at her with raised eyebrows.

"Aldania, you fix something special for dinner tonight. We are going to celebrate!"

Mrs. Snyder floats out of the room leaving the three of them to laugh and talk and catch up on how they all have been doing.

"Aldania," Ambrose says. "I saw Melvin Booker the other day. You know he left town a little while after you did. He comes down to Middletown to see Miss Josephine every once in a while. He said he lives in Columbus now. He asked about you."

Aldania stops talking. She turns her back and walks over to the ice box pretending to look for something.

"He also told me to tell you he's still in love with you," Ambrose teases. "And he hopes you still love him too!"

"Aw, that's right!" Amelia screams with delight. "I remember you and Melvin used to be in love with one another! Too bad y'all never did stay in touch. If we hadn't moved away you two probably would have kept courtin' and got married one day!"

"Don't talk to me about Melvin!" Aldania snaps. "And don't tell me nothin' he had to say."

"What's wrong with you?" Amelia asks confused.

"Ain't nothin' wrong with me," Aldania says. "I just don't want to talk about him."

Amelia and Ambrose don't understand her outburst but they don't ask her any questions about it.

"Aldania," Mrs. Snyder calls as she walks through the back yard screen door of the kitchen. "There's someone here to see you. It's someone who says they used to be your neighbor up in Middletown."

Aldania stops snapping the green bean she's working on and gets up from the table. She wipes her hand on her apron as she wonders who from Middletown could be paying her a visit.

"He's a very handsome young man whoever he is," Mrs. Snyder says as she leads Aldania out to the back yard where the visitor is waiting.

Aldania's eyes widen in disbelief as she holds onto the handrail and stands motionless when she sees Melvin standing at the bottom of the back porch steps.

"Hi Aldania," he says in a voice deeper than she had known him to have. He smiles at her tenderly.

Realizing the bewilderment on her face and not wanting Mrs. Sndyer to know her history with this man, Aldania greets Melvin civilly.

"You two can sit here on the porch and talk as long as you'd like," Mrs. Snyder says to Aldania.

"I won't be stayin' long ma'am," Melvin says. "Ambrose told me Aldania was workin' here and bein' that I was over this way I just wanted to stop by and say hello."

"Well you two catch up on how one another have been. I'm goin' back inside. Nice meeting you Melvin."

"You too ma'am."

Mrs. Snyder winks her eye at Aldania before she disappears into the house.

Melvin looks up at Aldania who hasn't moved from her spot.

"How have you been?" he asks.

"What are you doin' here?" she says.

"I came to see you."

"Why?"

"I just wanted to see you again, see how you were doin'."

"You got a lot of nerve to even come and see me after what you did to me!" she says angrily.

Melvin looks at Aldania solemnly.

"Can we go sit on that bench back there by them trees?" he asks her pointing towards the back yard. "I won't be long. I just wanted to talk with you for a minute or two."

Aldania looks at Melvin for a long time before she walks down the stairs. They walk through the grass until they reach the bench and sit down. Once they are seated Melvin continues talking.

"You been doin' okay?" he asks.

"I'm doin' fine," Adania says in a more calm tone.

"How is Amelia?"

"She's fine."

"Did she ever get out of the orphanage?"

"Yes. She got a job down in town at a store. Mrs. Snyder is lettin' her stay here with me until we get our own place."

"This is where you stayin' now?"

"Yes. I got a bedroom off the kitchen."

"That's a nice house them folks got."

"It's okay. But it ain't nothin' like havin' your own house."

"It sure is good to see you."

"Why are you here Melvin?"

"I told you I came to see you."

"Why?"

Melvin looks into Aldania's eyes for a long time.

"I felt like I needed to come and tell you I'm sorry for what happened way back when."

"Way back when? It ain't been that long ago for you to be callin' it way back when."

"To me it seems like it's been a long time ago, 'specially since I haven't seen you in so long. I still think about you every day. I still love you too."

Hearing him say that makes Aldania heart quiver. She looks away from him. She had tried to make herself stop loving Melvin when she went to Maple Hill and she thought she had. Now here he comes and makes her feel the love she had for him all over again.

"You courtin' anybody?" Melvin asks.

"That ain't none of your business," she says turning her attention back to him.

"If you ain't courtin' nobody I thought that maybe we could start over."

Aldania sighs deeply.

"I'm sorry that things happened the way they did," he tells her, "but I ain't sorry for lovin' you. And I'll never be sorry for that."

Melvin waits for Aldania to say something.

"You don't have to accept my apology if you don't want to. I done gave it to you and the rest is on you. I'm gonna be on my way. And you can sit there not sayin' nothin' and make like you never did love me but I know you did. And I know you still do."

Melvin gets up from his seat and leaves. As Aldania watches him walk away, she remembers what it was like to lay in his bed with him. He was right. She did still love him.

The next morning Aldania knocks on Miss Josephine's door hoping she won't be the one to answer it. It would be hard for her to explain to Miss Josephine what she was doing there. Mrs. Snyder said it was okay for her to have the time off to go visit a friend but Aldania didn't tell her the friend was Melvin. She waits anxiously, hoping Melvin is still there.

When Melvin opens the door he's surprised to see Aldania.

"Hi Melvin," Aldania says.

"Hi Aldania," he says. "Come in." He steps back letting Aldania into the house. They stand inside the front room in awkward silence for several seconds.

"You wanna have a seat?" he finally asks, gesturing his hand towards the sofa.

"Thank you," she tells him as she goes to sit down.

"Is Miss Josephine home?"

"No she's at work. She won't be home until later this evening."

Melvin sits down on the far end of the sofa.

"I'm surprised to see you here," he says. "Don't get me wrong. I'm happy you're here. I'm just surprised."

"I accept your apology," she says looking over at him.

"Well, I thank you."

"How long before you go back home?"

"I'm leavin' Saturday."

"Do you come down this way much?"

Melvin looks at Aldania wondering why she's questioning him.

"Not much," he says. "I could come down more often if I had a reason to."

"Maybe there might be a reason for you to."

"And what reason would that be?"

"Me," Aldania says as she smiles lovingly at Melvin.

"I knew you still loved me," Melvin says smiling as he scoots closer to Aldania.

"Amelia," Aldania says, lying on her back, looking up at the ceiling in her bedroom. A faint light from the lamp on the night stand halfway lights the room.

"What?" Amelia whispers.

"You sleep?"

"If I was would I answer you?"

"Don't you get smart with me!" she says laughing. "I got somethin' to tell you."

"What?"

"Melvin Booker asked me to marry him."

"He did?" Amelia says in amazement as she sits up on her pallet on the floor. "When?"

"Yesterday."

Amelia gets up and turns the lamp all the way up as Aldania sits up in her bed and moves over to allow Amelia to sit down next to her.

"So did you give him an answer?"

"I told him yes."

"When y'all gettin' married?"

"Next week."

"Ewww!" Amelia screams with excitement.

"He said once we get married and we get settled in our own place up in Columbus, we can send for you and Teeter to come live with us and he means it. We ain't gonna be like Muriel Susan and Lemuel Rick and Momma. We're gonna take care of you and Teeter until you're old enough to be on your own."

Amelia hugs Aldania tightly.

"I'm so happy for you Dania. I'm glad Teeter told him where you was and that he came to see you."

"I got something else to tell you. Melvin deflowered me."

"Dang Aldania! Y'all couldn't wait another week before y'all was married before you went and hopped in the bed together?

"That happened a while ago."

"Huh?"

"The first time it happened was before we left home. I've been with him a couple of times in these past few months."

"What? Why didn't you tell me about it back then?" Amelia asks scornfully. "What were you doin' givin' up your virginity to him anyway when you were thirteen?"

"I was alone with Melvin over his house one day. I knew I shouldn't have been there 'cause his auntie was at work, but I went anyway. He was in his bedroom and he told me to come in there. I sat down on the bed next to him and he started tellin' me how he loved me and he asked me to marry him. He said he didn't wanna go to hell for wantin' me so bad and not bein' able to do somethin' about it. I knew how he felt 'cause I wanted him the same way. He told me we needed to get married and that we didn't need a minister to marry us 'cause as long as we stood before God and made promises to one another it was done. So we married each other and we did what married folks do."

"Oh," Amelia says. "I guess if y'all promised to God then it was okay."

"We thought it was, but it wasn't. People can't marry themselves. Anyway, I asked his auntie to take me and you in before we went to Maple Hill but she said she couldn't. I was so mad at Melvin."

"Why?"

"'Cause he promised to take care of me and he didn't. He told me he was my husband and he was supposed to protect me. I told him I hated him. I never wanted to see him again."

Amelia cuts her sister a sympathetic smile. Aldania lies back onto her pillow and looks up at the ceiling while she continues to talk to her Amelia.

"I only told him that 'cause I was hurt about him not takin' us in with him. I still love him and I always have. You know, after the first time I was with Melvin I told him I didn't want to be with him no more. He told me I had to 'cause he was my husband and I had promised to obey him. He told me, the first time a man and woman came together it was rough on both of 'em but after that it got better and better. And it did. The second time I went to be with him, he was so sweet and gentle with me. He started out kissin' me, and then he rubbed his hands on my body real soft, and I got goose bumps. He whispered in my ear and said he loved me more than anything. The third time I went to see him, he treated me even sweeter. And each time when he finished bein' my husband, he would hold me and kiss my face and my mouth and tell me he didn't never want me to leave him.

"Melvin told me there was gonna come a time when I was gonna want him to be on top of me the same way he liked me bein' up under him. It didn't happen right away. After them three times we was together I didn't never feel nothin' like that. I just felt safe and loved laying there with him. But he was right. I used to think about him from time to time when we were up at Maple Hill. I used to wish I was in his bed lettin' him kiss on me and hold me. Then when he came to the house to see me a few months back, I had those feelings again. That next day I went to go see him and he was by hisself at Miss Josephine's house, and I let him take me into his old bedroom, and he laid me on the bed and he was so sweet to me again.

Aldania turns to her sister.

"I still got to see about you and Teeter, and I'm gonna always be here to watch over y'all, but I need to have Melvin in my life too. I love him so much Amelia."

"And we gonna see to it that you have him."

The apartment Aldania was able to find isn't too far from where the Snyders live. The place only has three rooms but it is nice and homey and just enough for Aldania and Amelia and Ambrose when he comes to stay the weekend. Aldania thought it was best that he stay with Miss Maybell so she could make sure he went to school. He obeyed Miss Maybell better than he did his sister.

As Aldania cleans the dishes she thinks about Melvin. She misses him more than she does her father. She tries not to think about what happened to him. She tries to forget how she almost fainted when Ambrose came to Mrs. Snyder's house to tell her that Melvin died at work after one of the shelves he was fixing collapsed and crushed him.

Aldania tells Amelia that she thinks she is to blame for what happened to Melvin. Aldania says that God put her in that orphanage to keep her away from Melvin the first time when they called themselves married. This time, He punished her for sinning with Melvin by taking him away for good. If only they would have waited until they got married and made things right before they made love again, he might still be here. She cries sometimes at night when she thinks about it, but her little sister lies next to her and comforts her and pats her back until she falls asleep.

They still haven't heard from their mother, Muriel Susan or Lemuel Rick and it bothers Amelia and Ambrose more than it does Aldania. They figured that Muriel Susan can't find them and their mother and Lemuel Rick just didn't care. Aldania assures her sister and brother they never had to worry about her ever leaving them by themselves.

One evening, Aldania and Amelia have invited Ambrose for supper. The three of them are almost finished with their meal when there is a knock on the door. Ambrose gets up from the table and opens it. When he sees who is there, he is frozen speechless.

"Well boy ain't you gonna invite your own momma in?" Kathleen says.

"Momma?" he says.

Amelia and Aldania get up from the table and go to the door. Amelia lets out a cheerful scream and pushes past Ambrose to embrace her mother. Ambrose joins in and hugs his mother as well. Aldania stands with her arms crossed and watches her excited siblings but does not say anything.

Kathleen releases her youngest two children and walks inside the apartment.

"I see y'all been doin' fine without me," Kathleen says smiling. "I knew y'all could fend for yourselves while I was away."

"Come on and sit down Momma," Amelia says guiding Kathleen to the sofa.

"Where you been for so long Momma?" Ambrose asks as he sits next to her.

"Well when I first got up to Cleveland," Kathleen begins, "I was workin' on the stage. I was one of them chorus line girls and they let me stay for almost a year. Then I went to another stage and I worked there for a few months. Then business got slow so I had to get a regular job. I got back on the stage some time ago and I been there ever since. They let me take some time off so I thought I better come and see about my chil'ren. Where's Lemuel Rick?"

"His daddy came for him some years ago," Amelia says. "We ain't heard from him since. Me and Aldania had to go stay at a orphanage when Mr. Lem came and took Lemuel Rick back home with him."

"Y'all was in a orphanage?"

"Yes ma'am. Miss Maybell took Teeter in, but me and Dania didn't have nowhere else to go. This lady that Dania works for adopted me and she let me come and stay with Dania."

"How come Muriel Susan didn't come see about y'all?"

"I guess Muriel Susan didn't know where we was. Remember we ain't heard from her since we went and moved to Middletown."

"Oh. Well we ain't gonna worry about all that. I'm back now and I'm gonna take all y'all up to Cleveland with me!"

"We goin' to Cleveland?" Ambrose says ecstatically.

"We sure is!" Kathleen says. "I'm gonna get in touch with that boy's people that Muriel Susan married and I'm gonna tell her to come see us up in Cleveland when we get settled. I already know how to get in touch with Lem so I'll make him send Lemuel Rick back home. Now that I'm back, we gonna be a family again!"

Kathleen looks over at Aldania who has been standing and listening all the while.

"Well hey girl," Kathleen says to Aldania. "Ain't you gonna come and say hi to your momma?"

Aldania turns and sits back down at the table to finish her meal.

"Oh, I'm sorry to interrupt your dinner," Kathleen says nervously. "Don't mind me. Y'all go on ahead and keep on eatin'."

"You want some supper?" Amelia asks Kathleen.

"She ain't eatin' at this table," Aldania says.

Amelia and Ambrose look at each other and then at Kathleen.

"But this is our momma Dania," Amelia says to her. "How you not gonna ask your own momma if she wants somethin' to eat?"

"She ain't fed me nor seen about me in over three years," Aldania says looking Kathleen in the face. "Why should I care if she eats?"

Kathleen is shocked by Aldania's remark. Amelia and Ambrose are shocked as well.

"Dania, don't talk about Momma like that!" Amelia says. "She is still our mother and no matter what has happened in the past we're still supposed to respect her."

Aldania gets up from the table and walks in front of Kathleen.

"Respect her?" she says with anger in her tone. "She don't deserve any of our respect. She can't come back here after leavin' us for all these years and expect me to act like nothin' ever happened. Far as I'm concerned I don't have a momma!"

"Baby I know you mad at me for leavin'," Kathleen says sympathetically as she rises from her seat. "But I'm back now and I'm gonna make it up to you. I'm gonna make it up to all of y'all."

"Make it up to us? How are you gonna make it up Momma? How are you supposed to make up leavin' your own children for some dream? How are you gonna make up leavin' us alone and hungry and without some place to live? How are you gonna make up for all the time we spent in that home where them people talked about us like dogs sayin' we wasn't gonna amount to nothin' and how we had a tramp for a momma? You can't make up for nothin'!"

Kathleen stares at her daughter for a few seconds.

"How dare you talk to me like that!" Kathleen finally says. "Do you know what I gave up to be with you when you was a child? I could have been some body sooner if I didn't have to stay and raise y'all chil'ren. I had to be somebody's wife and mother and I couldn't have what I wanted 'cause of y'all. But I went and I made my dream come true. Oh yeah. Despite how y'all all tried to hold me back, I did it."

"What do you mean despite us? We didn't ask you to be our momma. You're the one who chose to have a husband and children! You're the one who was supposed to take care of us, not make us feel like we pissed on your dreams! You ain't never been a mother to us and we don't see you as a mother now!"

"Listen here gal! I don't care how you feel 'bout me. You better keep it in your mouth. Don't you talk to me like that!"

"Don't you come in my house and tell me what I can and can't say! You gave up that right long time ago. You left us like somebody in the street and didn't care if we were taken care of or not. You're the one that's been whorin' around with men for money. And you're the one who got my daddy killed 'cause you was sneakin' around with that man."

Kathleen slaps Aldania in the, face and before she knows it Aldania hits her mother back. The two women fight, with Kathleen getting the upper hand on Aldania. Ambrose and Amelia try to separate the two of them. One of the neighbors and a police officer come in to help break up the fight. Both woman wind up with battle scars but Aldania has more than her mother. The officer makes Kathleen leave the house.

When Aldania calms down she looks at her brother and sister who are sitting at the kitchen table.

"How y'all gonna be all nice to Momma like everything is fine?" she says scornfully to her brother and sister.

"Dania we can't treat Momma mean," Amelia says. "She's finally come back home to get us and take us back with her to Cleveland."

"Do y'all really believe she's gonna take y'all to Cleveland? Y'all really think she done changed?"

"Yeah she's changed."

"The both of you better listen to me and listen to me good. We need to stick together and let Momma go on about her way."

"Dania I can't do that," Amelia says. "I can't turn my back on my momma. Not when she wants me to give her a chance to be with us again."

"Me neither," Ambrose says.

"Y'all better listen to me!" Aldania hollers stomping her foot on the floor. "Outta all the things that Momma done put us through, the three of us done made it together! I've been the main one to look out for y'all and make sure we stay together! Don't let her come between us. Don't go stickin' back with Momma! She's no good and she's gonna leave y'all high and dry just like she did before!"

"You stop talkin' about Momma like that!" Amelia demands.

"I can talk about her however I want!" Aldania screams. "She ain't nobody to me! I'm the one that's looked out for us. Muriel Susan ran off and left us to get married. She was supposed to come back and get us and she didn't. She knew Momma wasn't right, but she left us with her anyway! And Lemuel Rick did the same thing! He's been gone long enough to get some money together to come back and see about us, but he doesn't care nothin' about us either! I quit school so I could work and take care of this place so the both of y'all can keep goin' to school and finish your educations! Now here Momma comes struttin' back in here like nothin' ever happened and y'all gonna take to her like she's some kind of saint!"

"What are we supposed to do?" Amelia hollers as she stands up from the table.

"Y'all supposed to be on my side! Y'all supposed to tell Momma to go to hell and leave us alone!"

"I'm sorry Dania but I can't do that."

Feelings of betrayal and anguish fill Aldania's heart. She starts to cry. She can't believe that the two of them would relinquish their loyalty to her so easily. After all they had been through together, they were just going to walk away from her and take the side of the woman Aldania came to feel was her enemy.

"Y'all are fools!" Aldania says as she stomps into the bedroom.

The next morning, Amelia is awakened to the sound of drawers closing. She looks around the room and sees Aldania putting her clothes into a traveling bag.

"What are you doin'?" Amelia says sleepily.

"I'm movin' out," Aldania tells her.

"What do you mean you're movin' out?"

"Mr. Snyder is movin' his family out of town somewhere and I'm not goin' with 'em. There's another lady who needs a maid up in Dayton and I'm goin' up there to work for her. Since you and Teeter are gonna be goin' with Momma, I don't have no need to stay here."

"Aw come on Dania! We all need to stay together. Don't go to Dayton. Come go with us to Cleveland."

"I'm not puttin' my trustin' in that woman ever again! And if you had any sense you wouldn't either. Mark my words Amelia, she is no good."

Aldania picks up the two bags she has packed and walks into the living room.

"Tell the landlord I'm givin' this place up," Aldania says as she walks to the door.

Ambrose is sleeping on the couch and wakes up when he hears his sisters.

"Where you goin'?" he asks Aldania.

"She's leavin' to go work for some lady in Dayton," Amelia says.

Ambrose turns back over on the couch and pulls the covers over him.

"How are we supposed to get in touch with you?" Amelia asks.

"None of you will ever get in touch with me again," Aldania says looking at Amelia as she reaches for the door knob. "As far as I'm concerned all of y'all are dead to me!"

"My sister walked out that door and that was the last time I saw her," Aunt Amelia says as she comes back from telling her story. "I thought Dania just needed some time to cool off and she was gonna come back. But then a week went past and we didn't hear from her. I worried myself sick 'bout Dania, but Momma acted like she didn't even care, like she was glad Dania was gone.

"Momma moved in about a week or so after Dania left. She kept puttin' off movin' us to Cleveland. Then she told us she didn't think she wanted to go back up there at all. She promised she was gonna get a job and that we all could save our money and buy us a house together. She said she was gonna get in touch with Muriel Susan and Lemuel Rick to see if they wanted to move back with us so we could all be a happy family again. Me and Teeter didn't know any better. We didn't even think about Muriel Susan bein' married and havin' her own family. We just wanted everybody to be back together again, and we was hopin' we could be happy like we was 'fore daddy died.

"We never did get a house. Momma got a job and only worked for about a month before they let her go. She took to drinkin' and lettin' different men come to the house. She would go into the bedroom with 'em. I knew what she was doin' 'cause she always had money and she weren't workin'. She made me go in the bedroom with a man for the first time when I was seventeen years old. Teeter couldn't take it. He knew what me and Momma was doin' so he left and moved back in with Miss Maybell."

Aunt Amelia closes her eyes for a few minutes. The alcohol is taking effect on her, and I can tell she's feeling woozy.

"I don't know how she did it, but my momma got in touch with Muriel Susan and Lemuel Rick and they came to see us a few times. But none of us never heard from Dania. After Teeter left to go into the service, Momma went back up to Cleveland. She told me she was gonna send for me in a week, but she didn't. She didn't come back for six months. I took over the apartment and I paid all the bills by myself. I stayed there 'cause I was hopin' Dania would've come back."

Aunt Amelia takes another swallow of her drink.

"When Momma came back home from Cleveland, she was so sick she couldn't hardly hold herself up. All that drinkin' and whatever else she was doin' got to her. She looked real bad. She took to her bed. She kept askin' for Dania before she died, but we didn't know how to find her. After momma died, I moved to a new apartment and that's when me, and them two ladies you met the other day took to the streets."

Aunt Amelia lowers her chin onto her chest and closes her eyes.

"I had no idea that my grandmother went through what she did," I finally say. "Now I can understand why she was the way she was."

"Aldania turned out like she did 'cause she was a unforgivin' person," she says, opening her eyes. "Dania ain't never forgive nobody. That's why her soul ain't never gonna rest."

I become defensive, listening to my great-aunt talk about my grandmother so harshly.

"But I can understand how she felt," I tell Aunt Amelia. "I would have been mad at all of you too, especially you and Uncle Ambrose. If I had risked so much to make sure you were taken care of and you turned your back on me to reconcile with a mother who left you the way she did, I might not have been so forgiving either."

I can tell by the way Aunt Amelia stares at me that she doesn't like what I had just said.

"What did you come down here for anyway?" she asks me, squinting, changing the subject.

"What did I come down here for?" I repeat after her.

"Yeah. Why did you come to see us?"

"Because I wanted to get to know you."

"What for? Why all of a sudden you so interested in knowing us? Your Gran'momma run off and ain't never spoke to none of us again in her life. You wouldnt've known about none of this if that white woman hadnt've told you about us. Dania didn't want y'all to know or else she would've told you."

"Well you said yourself she was mad, so I guess that's why she never told us about you."

"And how do I know she didn't tell y'all about us? Maybe she did. Maybe she told y'all long time ago and since she weren't speakin' to us, y'all decided not to either."

"Oh come on, Aunt Amelia. I don't play games. I don't take sides like that."

"Huhm," she says, rolling her eyes at me.

"What do you mean, 'huhm'?"

"I just wanna know why all a sudden you come outta the blue, lookin' for us."

"Well if I had known way back then, I would have been here sooner."

"It still don't explain why you came all the way down here to find us."

"You're my family and I wanted to see for myself who you were. You're the only relatives I know from Grandmother's side, so I came to you to find out about the family I never knew."

"Don't give me that, I wanna know about my family," she says mockingly. "You can take that shit on somewhere else, actin' like you all sweet and innocent. I ain't no fool. You up to somethin'."

"Why are you talking like this? I'm not up to anything."

"Yeah you are," Aunt Amelia says, rising from her chair. She picks up her empty glass and starts towards the dining room. "You is up to somethin'. And I know what it is."

I watch her disappear into the kitchen. I sit there insulted by the way she is acting towards me. She comes back into the living room with a full glass in her hand and sits back in her seat.

"What makes you think I'm up to something?" I ask her.

She drinks from her glass and puts it on the table.

"I know your kind," she says. "You just like Dania and she was uppity. As soon as she started workin' for that white woman, she changed. She turned her nose up to me and Teeter. She turned her nose up to Momma, too. And you just like her."

"What?!"

"You heard me. You just like her. You came down here to rub all this in my face. All these years, ain't nobody heard from that bitch or none of her chil'ren, and here you come lookin' to see who it was she left behind. You came to stir up all this confusion all over again. We was all at peace with Dania and what she did. We left all that in the past, and here you come bringin' it all back."

"What?! You're blaming me for what happened between you and my grandmother and the rest of your family?"

"You damn right!" she says, standing up from her chair, putting her hands on her hips.

I stand up with her.

"It's time for me to go," I say, picking up my purse from off the couch.

"Yeah it is!" she hollers. She rocks back and forth, trying to steady herself.

"You're right," I tell her. "I shouldn't have come here. I'm trying to bring our families together so that we can get to know one another, and here you are trying to keep us apart."

"Well you the only one from that side that was nosey enough to come down here. Them other ones must've cared less or they would've come too. They knew to leave well enough alone. They ain't wanna come see me and I don't wanna see them niggas either! I ain't got to see none of y'all ever again."

"Well, the feeling is mutual!" I tell her as I walk out the front door. I hear her footsteps coming behind me.

"Why you actin' like this?" she asks, changing the whole tone of our conversation.

I stop suddenly and turn to face her after I step onto the sidewalk in front of her house.

"Me?!" I say shocked. "That's you! You're the one getting nasty with me! It's time for me to go. I'm not staying in your house and let you talk to me like this!"

"Like what?" she asks as she sways back and forth standing near me.

I know she's drunk, but she has to be kidding.

"I don't know about you, but I don't let people talk indignant to me!" I tell her. "Maybe you and your family are used to treating each other like this, but I'm not having it."

"Aw shit, child. Everything that come outta folks' mouth ain't got to be nice all the time. You too sensitive. You need to grow up."

"I am a grown woman. Demanding respect from someone is not a sign of immaturity. That's why I'm not going to sit here and let you disrespect me with your tone of voice and these unfounded accusations. I don't hang in bars and get drunk and cuss people out and act like its okay."

"Looka here, gal. Don't go gettin' your feathers all ruffled. Ain't no need for you to get all upset."

"Why shouldn't I? You're accusing me of having some ulterior motive."

"A what?"

"Ulterior motive."

"Why you got to use big words on me? See, that's what I'm talkin' about. I don't know what that is. Talk to me so I know what the hell you mean!"

"I don't need to explain anything to you!" I yell at her. "I drove all the way down here to meet you and this is how you treat me? And you have the nerve to say the only reason I came is to rub my grandmother's memory in your face! You talk about my grandmother being an unforgiving, hateful person. You need to look in the mirror!"

I walk quickly towards my car.

"You go on and get outta here!" she yells at me.

"I will! And don't worry about me coming back."

She starts to cuss at me as I get into my car and drive away. I watch through my rearview mirror as Aunt Amelia goes inside her house.

I drive back to my hotel, wondering why she had turned on me the way she did. Maybe it was the booze. Maybe that's just how she is. Or maybe it was because after all these years she has been waiting to release the anger she had for Aldania, and I was the closest she could get to doing it. Whatever the reason for her outburst, it has caused a big rift in our newfound relationship.

I wake up the next morning to a ringing telephone. I look at the clock and see it is five minutes past eight. It rings three more times before I answer.

"Hello?" I say with the sound of sleep in my voice.

"You woke?" the voice on the other end asks.

"Kind of. Who is this?"

"It's me, your Aunt Amelia."

I can't believe she's on the line, calling me.

"I'm just getting up," I say.

"Well, what time you coming by today before you leave?"

Is she serious? I sit up onto the side of my bed.

"After last night, I didn't think I should come back," I tell her.

"Aw chile, don't be so sensitive."

"You think I'm being sensitive after the way you cussed me out?"

"That weren't no cussin' out."

"Aunt Amelia, you were very nasty. You put me out of your house."

"I ain't put you out. You left. You just get over what happened last night and make your way over here before you leave. Everybody wants to tell you bye. We'll see you in a little while."

Before I can respond, she hangs up.

She must be crazy!

I lie back down in my bed and pull the covers over me.

I doze off for another hour before I hear a knock at my door.

"Who is it?" I holler.

"It's Uncle Ambrose," he says.

"It's me, too," Rita says.

Damn!

"Just a minute," I yell to them through the door.

I get up and put on my robe. I crack the door and peek out.

"You still sleep?" he asks.

"I'm getting up," I say, opening the door. "Come on in. You have to excuse me while I wash up."

I walk across the room to the bathroom.

They close the door behind them.

"You all have a seat," I tell them as I close the bathroom door.

They sit in the chairs at the small table in my room.

My door is cracked just enough to still be able to talk to them as I wash my face and brush my teeth.

"I wanted to make sure you came to the house before you go." Uncle Ambrose shouts out.

"We heard about what happened last night," Rita says. "We didn't want you to leave up out of here with any hard feelings."

"Yeah, Aunt Amelia was truly out of order last night," I say. "At first she was fine, but after she had a few drinks she changed on me. She asked me why I came to see you all and accused me of being up to something."

"Like what?" Uncle Ambrose asks.

"I have no idea," I tell him. "She told me I was stuck up and made me out to be a snob."

I quickly finish and go back into the room to where they are.

"Girl, don't pay Grandma any attention," Rita says. "She acts like that to everybody. We've all learned to just let her say what she has to say."

"Well, if she does this to everybody, she needs to stop," I say as I sit on the bed.

"That's just how Amelia is," Uncle Ambrose says. "You have to look at the life your Aunt Amelia done had to live. I know she told you about the things that happened with us and our momma. She's come up through some hard times, and hard times make for hard folk."

"And I understand that," I say. "I was trying to tell her that was why Grandmother was the way she was and she told me no, it wasn't. She thinks it is okay for her to act that way, but not for anybody else to be like that. But that's still no reason for her to be so mean and nasty to everyone else. She can't go around with a chip on her shoulder all her life and take things out on people who had nothing to do with what happened to her. I felt like she was saying the things to me that she wanted to say to Grandmother."

"Maybe she was," he says.

"So you gonna stop by the house before you leave out?" Rita asks me.

"To be honest with you," I tell them, "I hadn't planned on going back over there. I was going to call you before I left and tell you good-bye, but that was it."

"You ain't got to stop at Amelia's," Uncle Ambrose says. "I got a house, too, you know."

I smile at his invitation.

"Your cousins want to see you before you leave," he says. "I can call everybody and tell them to come to my house instead."

"I really need to be getting back home."

"Now don't go giving us excuses," Rita says. "You're supposed to be staying until this evening, anyway."

"I know," I say. "But I got to thinking last night about all the things I need to do before I go to work tomorrow, and I didn't sleep well last night, so I really do need to leave earlier than I had planned."

"This might be the last time we get to see you," Rita says.

"You know me and Amelia is gettin' up in age," Uncle Ambrose says. "Ain't no tellin' when we might be leavin' this earth. Now you don't want it on your conscience that you didn't tell both of us good-bye the last time we seen you."

I study Uncle Ambrose's solemn look and sincere eyes.

"Alright," I say, giving in. "Let me get ready and I'll be over to her house."

Uncle Ambrose's face lights up as he gets ups from the chair, grinning at his victory of convincing me not to leave so soon.

"I'll see you all in a little while," I tell them as they leave.

You would have thought I was someone important, the way they were all sitting in the back yard and standing around, waiting for my arrival. There had to be about twenty of them. As I walked down the back porch steps, a few of them walk up to greet me with smiles and hugs. Some of them I saw the day before. Others I'm meeting for the first time. Most of them are relatives from the other sides of my cousins' families.

"'Bout time you got here," I hear one of them say.

"I thought you weren't coming," another one says.

"Me too, since I hurt your feelin's so bad," I hear Aunt Amelia say.

She's seated on one of the lawn chairs close to the patch of grass near the back of the house.

"Well, now you know," I say. "People in this family don't get run off easily. Takes more than one angry, old lady to keep me from my people."

I hear one person laugh and then the others chime in. I smile at Aunt Amelia, who doesn't think my comment is funny. She smirks and rolls her eyes at me. Uncle Ambrose is sitting next to Aunt Amelia. He laughs and nudges her with his elbow.

I find a seat next to Bernard. We all sit and talk for a few hours. Some go in and out of the house. They offer me something to drink and eat. A few more come to the house as a few of them leave. I try to remember names. They ask me to write down my phone number and they give me theirs. I look over from time to time and find Aunt Amelia staring at me. When the time comes for me to go, I'm hugged and invited back by them all. They tell me to have a safe drive home and to call someone and let them know I made it.

Aunt Amelia is the last one to say good-bye.

"Come on over here, gal," she says to me without moving from her seat.

I go over to her. She reaches out and takes my hand.

"You be sure and call me from time to time to see how I'm doin'," she tells me.

"I will," I tell her.

"And I'm sorry for them things I said about you. I didn't mean to hurt your feelins'. You a good woman and you stay that way. Don't let nobody tell you otherwise, you hear?"

"I'll remember that," I say. I bend down and hug her tightly.

As I straighten myself back up, I notice that many of them are silent and looking as if something amazing has just happened. Others raise their eyebrows while a few turn down the corners of their mouths.

Uncle Ambrose gets up to walk me to my car. I smile and say good-bye to everyone as we walk up the driveway.

"What was that about?" I ask Uncle Ambrose.

"We all was shocked," he says. "Amelia ain't never apologized to nobody for nothin'."

"Maybe that was meant for Grandmother, too."

"Maybe," he says.

Part IV

Francine

———◦◦———

I still don't like funerals, but I'm okay with being at this one. This one is different. My sadness is real. The loss is great for me. Some folks look sad as they pass the casket and greet one another and our family. Others remark lightheartedly about some of the wild and crazy going-ons of a fun-loving person who will be deeply missed.

The abundance of bouquets and planters surrounding the casket has filled the whole funeral parlor with their fragrance. A large, youthful portrait sits on an easel at the foot of the casket. There's no chaos, no shouting, no howling. It's just a gathering of folks from all walks of life, bidding farewell to a soul that touched so many lives in so many different ways. I've cried because my heart aches, and I've rejoiced because I got to know a woman who could cuss me out one minute and hug and kiss me the next. I'm glad I got to know a woman who was hard when she had to be and soft when I needed her to be. A woman who made me want to kick her ass one minute and take her out to dinner the next. And I want everyone here to watch me cry and smile for my Aunt Amelia.

Two and a half years ago, after my first meeting with Aunt Amelia and the rest of the family in Hamilton, I had made up my mind that I didn't want to keep in touch with her. I didn't care for her. I liked my cousins and Uncle Ambrose and everyone else, but I knew that if I maintained a relationship with them, I would have to deal with Aunt Amelia. Even after she apologized for hurting my feelings with her mean remarks, I wasn't keen on her.

I called Uncle Stanley and Aunt Josette as soon as I got home from meeting Aunt Amelia and her family the first time, and told them some of what I found out about my grandmother's family. Actually, I lied and told them that Grandmother's father died when they were young and their mother couldn't take care of them and that she took them to stay at the orphanage while she went to find work in another town, and when she came back they all had been placed with different people and lost touch. I explained that somehow Aunt Amelia and Uncle Ambrose were able to find one another, and it took them a few years to find their mother, sister and brother. I told them Grandmother must not have known how to find them, since they all were displaced in other cities and maybe that was the reason she never went back to find them. I also threw in the possibility that she may have gone back to her hometown once or twice, trying to find them without success.

Aunt Myrtle was the only one I told the truth about everything, when I had the chance to get her alone. After all those years of not liking her mother-in-law, she now took a different stance about how she felt about her. I didn't even bother telling Uncle Wendell. I hadn't told him I got in contact with them in the first place. He wouldn't have wanted to know they even existed, just as he still hadn't acknowledged that my mother was still alive.

I thought long and hard and wasn't going to call Aunt Amelia ever again, but a few weeks after my first visit to Hamilton, Aunt Amelia had Rita drive her, Simone, Bernard and Uncle Ambrose to Indianapolis to my house.

Aunt Amelia hadn't made plans to stay at a hotel and she didn't wait for me to invite her to spend the night with me. She just told me she was. I didn't want to be bothered with her, but I just couldn't tell her to go away. After all, she was family. Uncle Ambrose and the rest of them found a hotel not far from where I lived and they stayed there.

Aunt Amelia didn't hesitate to bear hug Lisa when I introduced them to one another. Lisa smiled gleefully like a little kid as she talked to Aunt Amelia and showed her around our house, pointing out the room that Aunt Amelia was going to sleep in.

That first night that Aunt Amelia spent with us, she and Lisa talked all night. Aunt Amelia told Lisa who was who in the family, giving her the child's version of the family history, leaving out the things I planned on telling Lisa when she becomes an adult. I thanked Aunt Amelia for that.

Aunt Amelia toned down the foul language a little but not completely when she was talking in front of Lisa. She told me she wanted to be a better example for me and Lisa since she felt she never had been for her own children and grandchildren.

The next morning, I took Aunt Amelia and the family to see my mother at the nursing home. I explained my mother's condition to everyone letting them know Momma didn't talk or respond to anything. That had no meaning to Aunt Amelia. She talked to my mother like she was talking to a small child, asking her if she was hungry or needed to use the bathroom. She even sat next to Momma and held her and rocked her in her arms.

Later that day, Aunt Amelia insisted we all pile into my and Rita's cars and head for Westfield. I tried to explain to her that we couldn't just drive up to see them without calling and letting them prepare for our visit, but she wasn't hearing it. She told me family didn't have to prepare for their kin, and to call them now and let them know we were on our way. Aunt Amelia was adamant. She wanted to see her sister's children.

When we got to Uncle Stanley and Aunt Myrtle's house, they welcomed us all with open arms. I took them to Grandmother's house to meet Aunt Josette, who was apprehensive at first, but she eventually came around and warmed up to them. Of course, Aunt Amelia opened her big mouth and told Uncle Stanley and Aunt Josette the truth about the family history. When they got me alone to chastise me for not telling them about Grandmother, I reminded them that they hadn't told me the truth about my parents until recently, so we were even.

The first time Aunt Josette heard the barrage of curse words come out of Aunt Amelia's mouth, I thought she was going to have a heart attack, and when

Aunt Amelia insisted on staying at Grandmother's house, Aunt Josette almost fainted. She pulled me aside and told me she couldn't let strangers stay in her house. Uncle Stanley already knew that Aunt Josette wouldn't take kindly to them staying at Grandmother's house, and he tried to get them to stay with him, but Aunt Amelia insisted she stay at her sister's house. She made Aunt Josette show her Grandmother's room, which had been kept the same since she died. As Aunt Amelia fumbled around in Grandmother's closet, feeling her clothes and sniffing sleeves, she broke down into tears. Aunt Josette felt so sorry for Aunt Amelia, she wept with her. She let Aunt Amelia pick out a few of Grandmother's things to keep as mementos, and that night Aunt Amelia slept in Grandmother's bed. When she woke up the next morning, she swore to us that sometime during the night, she felt Grandmother's hand patting her back.

Aunt Josette called Uncle Wendell and tried to convince him to come over and meet his aunt and uncle, but he refused. Of course, that didn't stop Aunt Amelia. She insisted we drive over to his house. He came to the door with that same scowl on his face that we all had become accustomed to, but he wouldn't invite any of us in. Uncle Ambrose reached out to shake Uncle Wendell's hand and he refused. When Aunt Amelia started cussing him out, he slammed the door in our faces. Before we left, Aunt Amelia spat at his doorstep.

Three months later when Uncle Wendell died, Aunt Amelia and the family all came back for his funeral and brought more relatives with them. Aunt Amelia cried and hollered like she had known him all her life.

Uncle Stanley, Aunt Myrtle, Aunt Josette and I visited Aunt Amelia numerous times and I even talked the doctors into letting my mother go with us once. Each time we had gone to Hamilton, Aunt Amelia introduced us to yet another one of her friends or some other supposed distant relative. She would beam proudly as she showed us off, saying how pretty we all were. She hugged and doted over my mother almost the whole time during our visit.

I took my brothers to see Aunt Amelia and the first time she met them, she decided she would have some fun with Lorenzo. She thought he was so handsome and she tried to embarrass Lorenzo by telling him if she were younger she would give him a run for his money. Being the son of L.C., he jokingly told her if she were younger, she would be running from him! All we could do was laugh.

Jennifer had been pestering me to go out with Guy's friend, Rodney, but I still wasn't ready to devote time to a romantic relationship. I had to work and see about Lisa and my mother. Jennifer told me I needed a break from all of that. She said I should take some time out for myself, but I just didn't see it happening.

Jennifer and Guy came down to Indianapolis to spend the weekend with me and to take me out to dinner. We just happened to run into Rodney at the restaurant. At least that's what they all wanted me to believe. I had a great time that night. I hadn't been out on the town with a man in so long that I had forgotten how nice it could be. We've been together ever since that night.

Lisa is trying to get used to me being with someone other than her father. I told Lisa that no one can take Gerald's place with her and that I never expect that anyone will. I just want her to understand that Rodney has taken Gerald's place with me. She's slowly accepting the concept.

My aunts and uncles like Rodney. Aunt Myrtle told me it was about time I got into a new relationship with a man. Aunt Amelia told me men like him don't come along often and for me to hold on to this one.

My mother caught pneumonia and died a month after Uncle Wendell. When the doctor called me that night to tell me I needed to get there, I called my family in Westfield and my family in Hamilton. They were all there within a few hours, waiting and praying with me. And although the time we all had with my mother wasn't of the best quality, I was so grateful that I found her before she died alone up there in that nursing home in Missouri. She didn't know any of us, but at least we were there by her side the way a family should be when one of their loved ones passes on.

My brothers and their families and Uncle Elias and Aunt Eunice, all came to my mother's funeral. Lorenzo and Guy never saw her while she was in the nursing home. Not because of the circumstances surrounding my mother and our father, but because they couldn't handle seeing her, knowing a beautiful, probably sane woman was placed in a mental hospital and was left there to become the broken women she was.

Two months after Momma died, Uncle Ambrose was diagnosed with liver cancer and died a short time later. He refused any treatment and said it was his time to go on home. We all came together as a family and stayed with him. Right before he died, he told Aunt Amelia he would see her on the other side. She told him she just hoped she made it to the same place as him.

One time when I made a trip to Hamilton to spend the weekend with Rita and Simone, Aunt Amelia had us take her to one of the nightclubs. She sat there, clowning around and making fun of folks. She didn't say anything malicious. She was just being silly and having fun. Aunt Amelia told me she loved having her family around. She laughed and joked and cussed and got mad at us. And later apologized and laughed and joked and cussed us out some more. And after many visits and a few years, she stopped some of the cussing and getting mad, and mostly laughed and enjoyed our times together.

Other times we all went to dinner and would come back to Aunt Amelia's house and play music, and she would get drunk and dance. She would talk about days gone by and some of her experiences with her customers, telling Rita, Simone and me things we didn't need to hear, but she would have us cracking up laughing so hard our stomachs would hurt.

Rita and Simone's mother, Nadine, calls me her "other daughter" but I haven't met Nellie's mother yet. It took Nellie a while to come around to me. I think at first she was jealous that I had a good relationship with her sisters. She felt like I was on their side. Aunt Amelia told me not to worry about it. She said Nellie had a small mind and that she didn't know any better. But after a long talk between us, and reassurance that she was a cousin just like they were and that I wasn't into favoritism, Nellie warmed up. She still isn't close to Simone, but they're much more civil than they were.

During one of my visits with Aunt Amelia, when we were alone, she told me, "I wish I would've listened to Dania when she tole me not to go stickin' back with Momma, but Momma was the only somebody I really had. Muriel Susan had her husband, Lemuel Rick had his daddy. Dania had that lady, and Teeter had Miss Maybell. I was the only one ain't have nobody but Momma, so I turned out like I did. I ain't never been a decent woman, but now you done come around, I'm learnin' how to be. God brought you here 'cause He needed somebody in my family to teach me."

Two weeks before Aunt Amelia died, I was cleaning out my bedroom closet when I came across the money and two stacks of envelopes I had taken from Grandmother's safety deposit. In the midst of searching for my mother and finding Aunt Amelia, I had put them there and forgotten about them.

Each stack had an envelope placed on top that had no writing on it. The first envelope felt lumpy and I could tell there was something other than paper inside. When I opened it, I was astounded by what I found. There was a beautiful, flawless, diamond wedding ring set and a pair of diamond earrings. I immediately called Aunt Myrtle on the telephone to tell her about my discovery. By my description, she knew these were the earrings and engagement ring my father had given to my mother. She said my mother had told her about it when Aunt Myrtle had gone to see her after I was born.

As I ripped open each of the other envelopes from that same stack, I told Aunt Myrtle what I saw. There were nine one hundred dollar bills, a twenty and a five stuck between the pages of my mother's savings account book. The last page of the book was stamped 'Closed June 7, 1956'.

There were four more envelopes in that stack and five in the other stack with my name written on each one, in Grandmother's handwriting. I found them full of twenty, fifty and hundred dollar bills, adding up to over five thousand dollars! I almost cried as I wondered where this money came from. I knew Grandmother hadn't saved it for me out of her own pocket. Aunt Myrtle told me she believed it was the money that my father faithfully gave to Grandmother for taking care of me. She said L.C. would go over to the house or have one of his boys put money in the mailbox, because Grandmother wouldn't take it from him when he came. Aunt Myrtle said not only did L.C. send that money to take care of my expenses but also to prove to Grandmother that he was who he said he was, a man who takes care of his children.

Grandmother must have put it away all those years, knowing eventually it would be found. I believe she left it for me to make my own decision as to whether or not I wanted to keep it.

The last envelope I opened had an old picture in it. It was the picture I sought when I first started my search. Uncle Ambrose is standing between Grandmother and Aunt Amelia near the back porch of a house. He has his arms around each one of their necks as he pulls their cheeks up to his. Despite all the problems they had gone through in their young lives, they looked happy, happy in the fact that they had each other.

When I gave the picture to Aunt Amelia a few days before she died, so she could add it to her collection of family photos, she cried.

After the funeral and burial, we all go to Aunt Amelia's house for the repast which is held in the backyard. There are a lot of people and a lot of food and a lot of noise. The music is upbeat and everything is cool. I'm surprised as I spot my prissy Aunt Josette flirting and giggling with some older gentleman. She winks at me as she catches my glance. Uncle Stanley and Aunt Myrtle are enjoying a chat with Mr. Chester and some other people. Both of my brothers are here with me. They actually treat me like I'm their little sister, like I need protection at all times. It feels so good for me to know I have that security, to not feel alone.

Rodney is here by my side too. It's so nice to be in love with a good man and I mean a really good man.

Mr. Roy comes over and sits down next to me in one of the lawn chairs.

"Hey there, young lady," he says with that toothless smile.

"How are you, Mr. Roy?" I ask, smiling back at him.

"I'm alright," he tells me. "You know, I'm gonna miss that ole gal. I ain't gonna have nobody to raise hell with me and cuss me out!"

His remark makes us both laugh. We sit quietly for a few minutes, watching everyone around us.

Mr. Roy turns his attention back to me.

"Hey, don't take this the wrong way," he says to me, "but you know the first time I met you, I picked up on a bad vibe comin' from you."

"Oh really?" I question with raised eyebrows.

"Yeah," he says. "You was uptight. It wasn't nothin' you said, but I could tell you was a sad person inside, like you was searchin' for somethin'. But since you been hangin' around your kinfolks, you done mellowed out."

I think about what Mr. Roy just said. I put my hand on top of the hand he has resting on the arm of his chair.

"You're right, Mr. Roy," I say, smiling softly. "You are absolutely right."

Dusk starts to appear. I break away from the thinning crowd in the back yard and walk to the front of the house. I sit by myself on the front stoop, feeling the warm, May breeze gently blowing around my body as I reflect on the magnificence of God and where He has brought me in my life thus far.

The emptiness I once felt about not having a loving relationship with my grandmother is gone, and now it has been replaced by the reality of accepting what we did have. Aunt Myrtle told me one day I would realize my grandmother loved me. She probably did. Maybe not the way I wanted, but the only way she knew how.

Now I understand how, from her trials and tribulations as a young girl, she turned out to be the woman she was. I think my grandmother was afraid to forgive and show love because the people she had the greatest bonds with all left her in one way or another. The man she loved with all her heart died accidently, her father was killed, her mother ran out on her, as did her older brother and sister, and her two younger siblings went against her when she felt she needed their backing the most.

I think that having to deal with all that heartache in her life, my grandmother actually believed she was doing what was best for my mother by physically separating her and me from my father. I think she felt that my mother's life would have been nothing but hurtful and that my mother would have been back and forth with my father. But I think that after a while she realized she had made a mistake. And although she would never admit it, I believe she left that ring for me to know that my father did love my mother enough to want to marry her, even though in Grandmother's eyes it wasn't right. Maybe she wanted me to know that the way things ended wasn't their fault, but hers.

Knowing what I do about my father, I see what Aunt Myrtle meant when she said he was a smart man. I believe he was going to tell me about his and my mother's relationship when I was old enough to understand. I also believe he knew that living the way he did, he might not get the chance to tell me himself what I needed to know. But he did know that a small gesture like buying his little girl some candy could make for an impressionable memory for her to hold onto. As minimal an act as some folks think it might have been, it's all I have, that one brief moment when we exchanged smiles and it's enough for me.

I truly believe that after my grandmother took on the task of raising me, she felt she needed to make me like her, hard hearted and defensive, not worried about who loved me or who stuck with me, but able to make it out here in the cruel world on my own.

But I don't think of the world as so cruel that I have to be bitter and angry to be in it. I know there's more love than there is bitterness and anger and cruelty. I look at the new relationships I made with my family and I see it. I touch my new man Rodney and I share it. I feel it from my brothers, and it shields me. I've had it from all my aunts and uncles and I know it. And most importantly, I've been told about the love from and of my parents, so for me there's no doubt about it.

Now I truly understand how life has a way of shaping folks, and life doesn't always shape folks the way we think it should. And I can't keep others from making their mistakes, mistakes that might hurt me, intentionally or unintentionally. I've learned that there's no way around making mistakes, hard, cruel, unjustifiable mistakes. That's what happens in life and it is with this wisdom that I'm able to forgive and let go.

I come from a family of women who have made foolish mistakes in love, and raising children, and living their dreams, and not dreaming enough. I now realize that grandmothers and mothers don't always love their children as expected. And children don't always love their mothers and grandmothers. But you can bet on one thing. Real love may not come from where you think it should, but it will come to you and only a starnader fool doesn't know the difference.

About the Author

From the time she was a child, Sylvia Waldon loved to read stories. As a teenager and adult, she was impressed with the writings of many talented authors whose works conveyed heartfelt stories of human interest. Some of her favorite novels are *A Raisin in the Sun, The Color Purple, To Kill a Mockingbird* and *Fences*, to name a few.

Sylvia received an Associate of Arts Degree in Social Sciences from Miami University, Ohio and a Bachelor of Arts Degree in Liberal Arts from Xavier University, Ohio. She currently works for Cincinnati Children's Hospital Medical Center where she has been employed for over 25 years. She still resides in Cincinnati with her husband, son and extended family.

A Starnader Fool is her debut novel.